PLAY THE GAME 2

TIM ROUTCH

CHAPTER ONE

February 1977

A nip is in the air as the shop owners along Saint Paul Street in Old Montréal sweep the flagstone sidewalks in front of their establishments. A milkman tips his hat and smiles at everyone he encounters as he makes his deliveries. Upstairs in a historic townhome the morning sunbeams slip through the gaps of the period shutters. A thick white comforter and down pillows lie in disarray across the king-sized bed. Anne Marie's every curve is flattened against Ryan's toned body as sounds of heavy breathing fill the room.

Their rhythmic movements slowly come to a stop, and Ryan rolls onto his back, releasing a deep and satisfying breath. Anne Marie snuggles close, her hand resting on his chest. He inhales the flowery scent from her silky hair as he lightly caresses her body. Feeling the firmness in her belly, he comments, "We should get married soon."

Anne Marie lifts her head, pushes her dark brown hair away

from her face, and looks at him with raised eyebrows. "That was not a very romantic way of asking me to marry you." Her words drip with a French accent. "You make it sound like an obligation."

"I mean, you *are* pregnant and . . . Okay." Ryan slides off the side of the bed and kneels on the carpet. Taking Anne Marie's hands in his, he looks deep into her dark brown eyes. "Will you marry me?"

She smiles, leans over, and softly touches his lips with hers. "I love you."

They stare into each other's eyes for a few seconds.

"No," she replies.

"Huh?" Ryan jerks his head back then climbs onto the bed beside her. "Whaddaya mean, no?"

"I do not believe you would have asked me to marry you if I were not pregnant."

"But you *are* pregnant, and I love you."

"You have loved other women. Would you have married them if they became pregnant?"

There's an awkward moment of silence as the question bounces around inside his head. Searching for an answer to a distorted version of the real issue confuses him. "Well, yeah, I suppose . . . if I loved them."

"Then there is no telling where you would be or who you would be married to if you had gotten someone else pregnant. You could be in Thunder Bay, Texas, or Virginia doing who knows what."

Caught off guard, Ryan's face is a mix of curiosity and disbelief. "But I'm not somewhere else. I'm here with you, and you're going to have my baby . . . Our baby."

"I love you, Ryan, and nothing is going to change between us. I just need some time." She gently touches the side of his face. "I have this four-season policy. I will not marry someone until I have known them for all the seasons."

Ryan blinks several times before staring at her, wide-eyed. "For a year?"

"*Oui.* I have known you barely seven months, and two of those months, you lived elsewhere. Also, your time in Montréal you spend playing sports and traveling."

"It'll be different now."

"I hope so. But you were a draft evader. You have been out of your country and away from your home and family for nearly five years. You have a lot to catch up on."

"Conscientious objector," he corrects impassively.

"*Peu importe*. You need to adjust to your new life."

They lie facing each other, their eyes conveying adoration. "You are my new life."

"I want to be with you," she replies. "But with amnesty, you can choose where you want to live. You are free to play American base-ball. Who knows where that will take you and for how long. You have many decisions to make."

"It'll never take me away from you. I love you." He clasps her hands.

"I love you, too. Do not worry; nothing changes." She kisses the tip of his nose. "We will be okay for now not being married. You must know I am very happy. I always wanted to have a baby, and you are the perfect man to get pregnant with."

The corners of Ryan's mouth turn up. "Were you just using me as a sperm donor?"

"A very good sperm donor," she quips, a gleam in her eye.

Ryan is content letting the marriage issue drop for the time being. *It's just a matter of time. I'll win her over*, he tells himself.

Later that morning, Ryan is at the LeClair Center in downtown Montréal. He and Clarence Foxe, the general manager of the Expos, sit on plush leather chairs. Across from them at a large mahogany desk is Matt LeClair, co-owner of the baseball franchise.

LeClair steeples his fingers as he studies Ryan. "We're aware you have offers from the Yankees and the Rangers."

Ryan shrugs nonchalantly. "I'm happy here, Mr. LeClair. This is Anne Marie's home, and you've been good to me."

Foxe leans back in his chair and crosses his legs. "This isn't a big market franchise. We don't have the money to spend on players like New York or Texas does."

Ryan glances at LeClair. He'd rather negotiate directly with him. However, LeClair shows no emotion. Ryan looks back at Foxe. "As long as the salary is competitive, I'll be happy."

Foxe grabs ahold of his knee. "We already have our Major League roster set. You'd probably start the season in Double-A. I doubt you'll spend much time between April and September in Montréal." Foxe is talking a lot of static, which discourages Ryan.

Ryan shifts his gaze to LeClair. He's busy scribbling notes, appearing not to be paying attention to the discussion.

"I guess I'll hire an agent and let them work out the details."

LeClair lays his pen down and looks up. "Do you think that's necessary?"

"It looks like you have your agent negotiating for you, sir."

LeClair nods. "Clarence, I'll speak with you later. I want to talk to Ryan alone."

"That's not customary, Matt." The color drains from Foxe's face. "I'm sure the other owners of the team would prefer that I be part of the negotiations."

LeClair nods toward the door. "We'll talk later."

Foxe closes the door as he leaves the room, allowing LeClair to give Ryan his full attention.

"You're one heck of a ballplayer, Ryan. You're also part of the family."

Ryan slides his chair close to LeClair's desk, ready to talk.

CHAPTER TWO

After negotiating with LeClair, Ryan heads home. As soon as he enters his apartment, he drops onto his easy chair and dials his brother's number.

"Hey, Trey. How's it going?"

"Probably way better than I deserve."

"Cute. So, when are you and Kelci expecting the baby?" Ryan asks, keeping with the small talk.

"Any day now. Okay, little brother, enough with the chitchat. Last time we spoke, you were looking at offers from two baseball teams."

Ryan grins with excitement. "I'm going to sign with the Expos!"

Trey bubbles with energy. "Fantastic! I'm proud of you."

"Thanks, Trey." Ryan beams with pride. He's worshipped his brother since he was a kid, and his praise is special. "Yeah, it's been a long journey, but I finally made it." He pauses for a moment. "They'll probably start me in Double-A."

"You got your foot in the door. That's important. You'll be in the big leagues in no time."

Ryan shoots to his feet. His adrenaline is flowing, and he's too excited to sit still. "I won't be satisfied until I get there."

"You won't be satisfied until you're an all-star. You've always expected a lot from yourself."

Ryan bounds about his apartment. "Not just an all-star, the World Series! That's my goal." He can hear Trey cackling on the other end of the phone.

"I love your exuberance," Trey rags. "You're carrying on the same way you did when Larry told us we were joining the youth league in Kerrville."

They both laugh at the silliness of the childhood memory.

"Hold on a sec. Kelci wants to talk to you."

The next thing Ryan hears is his sister-in-law's bubbly voice. "Congratulations, Ryan. Anne Marie's pregnant, a pardon, and now a baseball contract."

"Well, I haven't signed yet, but I'm feeling pretty fortunate."

"Speaking from a legal standpoint, there are a few things you should be aware of moving forward."

Ryan backs down from his high. "Such as?"

"If your baby is born in Canada, is he or she going to be a Canadian citizen? Also, you've been out of the U.S. a few years. If Canada is your primary residence, and if the Expos are held by a Canadian company, you're probably going to have to declare your citizenship."

"Guess I never thought about it." Ryan frowns. "Do you think it's going to be an issue?"

"It could be for the baby. When it comes to custody, citizenship is a big issue. There's a lot to consider, such as taxes, property ownership, healthcare. Did you have an attorney review your contract?"

"No, I trust Mr. LeClair to do the right thing."

Kelci sighs in disbelief. "I understand he's a nice guy, but there are many things to consider. You need to think about injury clauses, call-ups to the majors, trade clauses, and performance bonuses— just to name a few. Did you discuss *any* of that?"

Ryan shakes his head, deflated and a little confused by everything that's being thrown at him. "No. It's a typical two-year contract that they offer to rookies." He laughs softly into the phone. "How did you become an authority all of a sudden?"

"Let's just say Trey and I saw this day coming. He didn't want you to make the same mistakes he did. So, he asked me to put my law degree to work for you."

"Cool." He feels better knowing someone is interested in his welfare.

"Do you consider yourself a typical rookie? What if you get called up to the majors within the first two years?"

"I'll get the minimum Major League salary. I was told it's around twenty thousand per year."

"I read the average Major League salary last year was seventy grand. Don't you think you're worth that if your batting average is higher or you hit more home runs than half of your peers?" Kelci pauses for a beat, then continues. "What if you're injured? What are the guarantees?"

Ryan's head starts to spin. "I don't know if anything is guaranteed these days, other than death and taxes."

"Send me a copy of your contract. And don't sign anything until you have an attorney or agent represent you."

"Whew." Ryan laughs meekly.

"Are you okay?" she asks in a concerned voice.

"Talking with you and Anne Marie complicates my thinking."

"You're not a kid anymore, Ryan. You got a baby on the way, and you've got legal issues to deal with. This isn't pickup baseball anymore."

CHAPTER THREE

Ryan strolls through the front door of Anne Marie's antique shop a few minutes before closing. She smiles broadly as their eyes make contact. Ryan stands quietly off to the side amongst the armoires and dressing tables as Anne Marie finishes a sale with a customer. As soon as the woman leaves the store, carrying her Louis XIV tortoiseshell clock, Anne Marie waltzes over to Ryan and gives him a hug and a peck on the lips.

"We are leaving now," Anne Marie tells Renee, one of her employees. Renee is a thin woman with pale skin and rust colored hair. "Please lock up when you leave."

Ryan helps Anne Marie into her leather coat. He grabs her hand as soon as they're out the door. A brisk wind makes for a chilly February evening. They stroll down Rue Saint-Paul, past Notre-Dame Basilica and across Place d'Armes.

"The Maisonneuve Monument is so beautiful when lit up," Anne Marie comments.

"There are many beautiful things in Montréal," Ryan replies, gazing at her intently.

She nuzzles close, feeling serene.

Their walk leads them to Chez Queux. Once they're inside the restaurant, the maître d' greets them and promptly seats them at the table where they first met. Subdued lighting and soft music create a relaxing ambiance.

Anne Marie purrs. *"Très romantique."*

After dinner is ordered, Ryan fills Anne Marie in on his negotiations with LeClair and Kelci's willingness to assist him with a contract. She listens intently until he's finished speaking.

Although happy he chose to play for Montréal, she asks, "Would the future not be better for you in a large U.S. city?"

Ryan shrugs a shoulder. "Live for the moment, and the future will take care of itself."

"Who said that? Yogi Bear?" Anne Marie asks, her eyebrows raised.

Ryan rubs his eye and chuckles. "No, I'll take credit for that one. I want to be around when our baby is born." His face is aglow from the candle on the table.

She rests her hand on top of his, thinking how handsome he is with his strong jawline, high cheekbones, and clear, smooth skin. "You are such a sweet man. The baby will not be here until October. I do not think they play baseball in October."

"I want to be around if you need me." He slides his chair closer to her. "I can't be certain where the Expos will send me to start, but I think it will be to their Minor League team in Quebec City. We'll be close, and I can visit often."

"Is that the only place they send you to learn before you can come back to Montréal?"

"Quebec City is what they call a Double-A team. They have a Single-A team in Palm Beach, Florida. Their top Minor League team is in Denver." Ryan takes a sip of wine as their eyes lock. "Spring training starts next week in Florida."

"They will train you in Florida to play baseball?" she asks, an eyebrow curled up.

"It's not like training dolphins to do somersaults. It's conditioning. Getting your body in shape for the long season. It's only for a month."

"Your body is already in excellent shape."

The dimly lit room doesn't hide his blush. "The coaches in Florida will give me feedback on things to practice to help improve my game."

"Hopefully they will bring our food soon. I want to get you home early so I can enjoy you before you take off and leave me again."

CHAPTER FOUR

"Welcome to Daytona Beach." A bright neon sign inside the airport terminal greets arriving passengers.

Ryan stands at the baggage carousel, waiting for his suitcase, while surrounded by a mass of boisterous college kids in town for spring break.

"Where's the party?" Ryan asks a jiggly coed who bumps into him.

She looks at him with eyes full of contagious energy and enthusiasm. "We're staying at the Streamline Hotel." She gives him a smile and points to a gaggle of young women. "Those are my friends. You can join us if you like."

"That's a very hospitable offer." Ryan helps the young lady lift her bag off the luggage belt. "That's a small suitcase. Are you planning on staying long?"

"Don't need much clothing down here. I'll be in a bikini most of the time. I brought a few tank tops and shorts. Are you a NASCAR driver?" She looks at him with admiration.

"No, ma'am, I am not. Driving in circles tends to make me dizzy. Why do you ask?"

"You're too old to be a college student, and you're in great shape.

I figured you were an athlete. You do know the Daytona 500 is this weekend?"

Ryan chuckles softly. "You think sitting behind the wheel of a car makes you an athlete?"

"I think race car drivers are really sexy. My name's Debbie. What's yours?"

"Richard Petty." Ryan sticks his hand out to shake.

"You're funny. Come by the hotel for a visit." She winks, then scampers off to join her girlfriends.

Ryan grabs his bags and heads to the curb, looking for a cab. After twenty minutes competing with college kids for a ride, he finally hails one.

"Holiday Inn," he informs the cab driver as he drops his luggage in the trunk.

A voice comes from behind him. "Excuse me, sir."

Ryan turns to face a tall Black man with a thin layer of muscle over his slim frame.

"I'm going to the Holiday Inn, also. May I share the cab with you?"

"Sure." Ryan looks him over and guesses him to be about eighteen or nineteen years old. "In town for spring break?" he asks after they settle in the cab.

"No, sir. I'm a baseball player. I'm here for spring training with the Expos."

"Same here." Ryan extends his hand and introduces himself.

"Andy Dawkins," the young man replies. "This is my first spring training."

"This is my first workout with the Expos as well," Ryan replies.

"You look like you've been around for a while, sir. Have you been to spring training with other teams?"

"Wise guy," Ryan mumbles. "Are you trying out for the team or were you drafted?"

"I was the Expos' top selection in this year's draft," Andy says, his eyes gleaming and a proud smile on his face.

Ryan looks him over. Andy has a narrow face with big ears that stick out like radar dishes and a nose that looks like the beak on a hawk. "You must be a pretty good ballplayer."

"Yes, sir. Mr. Foxe come all the way down to Mississippi hisself to sign me. He told my mama that I have a rare blend of speed and power. Said I'll be the next Willie Mays."

Ryan can't contain his laughter. "That sounds like Foxe babble."

Once Andy and Ryan are inside the hotel, they notice a billboard in the lobby that directs the ballplayers to a conference room. An Expos representative sitting behind a table gives them their room assignments and an itinerary telling them where to go and when to be there.

"Are Cromartie, Foli, or any of the big-league players staying here?" Ryan asks.

"Nope." The representative chuckles. "Major Leaguers rent houses or stay in four-star hotels."

"Silly me," Ryan stammers.

The next morning, two school buses are parked under the canopy outside the entrance of the hotel. Their engines run as they wait for the players to board.

Ryan casually stands by the front door of the hotel, watching players file onto the first bus. "Most of these guys aren't old enough to buy alcohol," he says softly. After a few minutes of watching, he boards the second bus. Walking down the aisle, he notices an empty seat next to Andy and slides in.

"Sleep well?" Ryan asks as he gets comfortable.

"Yes, sir, I did," Andy replies. "How about you?"

Ryan purses his lips. "I stayed up all night trying to remember if I have amnesia or insomnia."

Andy gives Ryan a fishy look. "I'm sorry."

The bus backfires and jolts forward as it pulls out of the hotel parking lot. Fifteen minutes later, it pulls off the main drag and into a sports complex with multiple baseball fields and an exercise facility. Ryan notices "Jackie Robinson Ballpark" written across the outside wall of one of the stadiums.

Looking at Andy, he asks, "Was Robinson from Daytona?"

"No, sir. He was born in Georgia," Andy replies in his soft voice.

"Why'd they name this place after him?"

"I was told when Jackie was in the minor leagues, some Southern cities wouldn't let colored men play on their fields due to segregation laws. Daytona allowed him to play in their park, and it became a big deal in the Civil Rights Movement. Guess it's a historic tribute to Black folks."

The first couple of days of spring training focus on conditioning. Players are broken into groups of twenty to stretch, do some light throwing, and run wind sprints. Shortly after completing a series of wind sprints, Ryan strolls past Jerry Carter and Billy Daniels, two of the Expos' starters from the previous year. He hears one of them say, "Dog."

Ryan immediately stops and glares in their direction before approaching them. "Excuse me?" he says, looking at Carter.

"Dog," Carter repeats as he stands face-to-face with Ryan. "You're a hot dog. You act like you have to finish first in the wind sprints and every exercise we do. It's not a competition out there— it's just conditioning." He gives Ryan a friendly smile and wink.

Feeling like he was just put in his place, Ryan's hands hang at his side as he watches Carter and Daniels go about their business.

The first scrimmage of spring is a game between the minor and major league players. Ryan is sitting in the dugout with the minor league players when one of the coaches hollers out, "Hutson, play third base with the veterans."

"What?" Ryan gives the coach a surprised look, then proceeds to jog over to the major league dugout. He sits on the bench next to

Carter. "I'm not sure what I'm doing playing third base. Not my normal position."

"Most of the roster spots are taken. You want to make the team, you got to be flexible," Carter says as he straps on the catching gear. "I played left field my first year."

Carter leads off the bottom of the first inning and drives a hard line drive into the seats in left field. No telling how far it would have traveled if it had any loft to it. He promptly rounds the bases and sits down on the bench between Ryan and Billy.

"Not trying to show off, were you?" Ryan asks, mocking Carter.

"Nah. Just trying to teach that young pitcher a lesson. If the first pitch you throw is a strike, don't give me the same thing on the next pitch."

Two batters later, Ryan hits the first pitch thrown to him out of the ballpark.

Carter is laughing when Ryan gets back into the dugout. "Hey, Dog, a home run's a home run. It's not a competition to see who can hit the ball the farthest."

Ryan slaps hands with Billy. "Hey, if the fans come out to see us, the least I can do is give 'em a good show."

Ryan's first practice game is against the Phillies. The Expos' squad hops a train to Clearwater for the contest.

Pete Rose and Mike Schmidt sit in the Phillies' dugout with their feet propped up and their heads tilted back while they watch Ryan spray balls around the outfield during batting practice. An occasional offering from the pitching machine is blasted over the fence.

Rose looks over at Schmidt and comments, "The kid has a great body."

Schmidt, a muscular guy in his own right, sits quietly, ignoring Rose's comment.

"I'd trade my body for his any day," Rose continues. "Hell, I'd trade my wife's body for his and throw in a thousand dollars."

Schmidt's face contorts as he looks at Rose. "You're way too easy with your money."

"Bet you a hundred bucks he hits the next pitch over the fence," Rose says.

Once Ryan finishes batting, Rose lifts himself up from the bench and catches up with him before he reaches the dugout. In a gravelly voice, he says, "Nice hits, kid."

"Thanks, Pete. That's quite a compliment coming from someone who has four thousand hits. What's your secret?"

Pete looks at Ryan complacently. "You got a round ball, a round bat, and you hit it square."

***

The moving vans are packed and ready to head north after the final spring practice. Only two rookies, Andy and a pitcher, make the trek to Montréal with the big league team.

After showering and changing into his street clothes, Ryan heads out of the training facility to the waiting bus.

As he walks across the parking lot, a rental car pulls up next to him. Don Ellison, the manager of the Expos' Double-A team in Quebec City, rolls the window down and sticks his head out. "Want a ride to the hotel?"

"Sure, what the heck." Ryan throws his bag in the back seat, then hops into the car.

While weaving the car through Daytona traffic, Ellison peers over at Ryan and asks, "Are you upset about not being assigned to the Expos?"

"I'm a little disappointed," Ryan admits, looking out the window toward the beach. He's more than a little disappointed. Living in Montréal with Anne Marie was his goal, but he plays it cool with Ellison. "Foxe told me up front that I probably wasn't going to make the team out of camp."

"You did a good job and did everything asked of you," the coach says. "The final decision is you need to play every day. In Montréal, you won't be getting four or five bats a night. We can get you more at bats and look at doing more things with you in Quebec City."

They stop at a traffic light, and a swarm of college students in bathing suits crosses in front of them. Ryan takes a close look to see if the young lady from the airport is part of the group. "I'm fine with everything. I still have a lot to learn. Besides, Quebec City is close to home. I might be disturbed if I were assigned to Denver."

Ellison pulls the car to a stop in front of the entrance to the Holiday Inn. "Go home and rest up this weekend. We'll see you in Quebec on Monday."

CHAPTER FIVE

Ryan immediately spots Anne Marie, looking hot in her Gloria Vanderbilt jeans and brown leather jacket, as he steps off the jet bridge at the Montréal airport. The edges of his lips curl into a half smile as they make eye contact. He watches as she hurries toward him while dodging other disembarking passengers. Ryan wraps his arms tightly around her when she reaches him.

"I missed you so much," he whispers in her ear. He immediately pulls back a little on the hug, thinking he might be pressing too hard against her belly.

Anne Marie shakes her head at his silliness. At three months, her pregnancy is barely noticeable.

Within fifty minutes of getting off the plane, they're in their favorite place: naked in bed. Forty-five minutes later, she relaxes with her head resting on his shoulder.

"How do you look so beautiful all the time?" Ryan asks as he circles her taut nipple with his fingertip.

"French women understand that a good relationship and great sex are the secrets to true beauty." She raises her head and looks into his eyes. "Love is as vital to the way we look as it is to our happiness."

"Well, you look awesome." He kisses her softly on the lips. "I need to clear stuff out of my apartment today. Can I leave some of it here?"

"I think maybe I can make a little room for some of your things," she replies coyly.

"Great." Ryan leans on his elbow. "I have to head up to Quebec City this weekend to find a place to live."

"I will go with you." Anne Marie sits up, excitement shining in her eyes. "We can explore together. I will take the train back."

Early the next morning, Ryan is at his apartment, tossing everything he wants to leave at Anne Marie's and whatever he feels he will need in Quebec City into his Trans Am.

A couple hours later, Ryan's things are stowed in Anne Marie's home, and she's sitting next to him in his car.

"It will be close to a three-hour drive," she says as they pull away from the curb.

Ryan's eyebrows rise as he guides his car into Vieux-Québec, the walled colonial city in the heart of Quebec City. "The stone buildings and cobblestone streets are neat."

"This is the only city in the U.S. or Canada that still has a fortified wall surrounding it," Anne Marie says. "It is almost like going back in history."

"You seem to know a lot about Quebec City."

"I love it here." She beams. "It is a predominately French-speaking city and maintains a very European feel." She nudges him playfully. "You will need to pronounce it properly if you are to live here. It is pronounced 'key beck.' It is an Algonquin Indian word meaning the narrowing of the river."

Ryan nods. "Good information."

"It is," Anne Marie replies. "I do not want you to sound like a tourist."

They share a quick laugh.

"Okay, where to now, Mademoiselle Tour Guide?"

"Drive to that large building on the hill." Anne Marie points to a massive brick compound in the distance. "That is the Chateau Frontenac Hotel. It is a very *grande* hotel and a National Historic Site in Canada. We will stay there tonight to celebrate your new job as a baseball player. It is my treat."

"This place looks like a medieval castle," Ryan comments as they walk through the lobby of the century-old building. He admires the massive circular towers, marble staircases, and ornate gables. "Very cool."

The stone walls and wooden floors inside their suite are reminiscent of a time many years ago, as is the antique furniture. Ryan puts his arm around Anne Marie's shoulders as they stand on the balcony and gaze into the distance. "What a beautiful view of the St. Lawrence River with the cargo ships and sailboats."

She leans into him, feeling content. After a few minutes, she pulls away. "I am famished. We should go to the restaurant for a midday dinner."

When they walk into the dining room the rich, earthy aroma of beef bourguignon, today's special, causes Ryan's mouth to water. He breathes deep, savoring the scent. Anne Marie is unfazed. As a French woman, she expects her palate to be stimulated by French chefs. Freshly baked croissants made with homemade butter are placed on their table when they sit down, further stimulating Ryan's olfaction.

After their meal, they stroll leisurely through the century-old neighborhood. The setting sun casts shadows from the vintage cafés, restaurants, and shops onto the cobblestone streets.

As they meander across a stone courtyard, Ryan watches several young mothers taking their children for walks in their carriages.

"French mothers seem to be in excellent shape soon after having babies."

"You do not need to be looking at the bodies of other ladies." She pushes his shoulder.

Ryan turns his palms upward. "I was just looking at the children, and the mothers got in the way."

"Ah, *je vois*," Anne Marie says, not totally appreciative of his sarcasm. "If you must know, French women are given a state-funded course on post-birth physiotherapy. The class is designed to help women strengthen crucial muscles, which allows them to reclaim flat tummies." She grabs his arm. "Come now. We should walk back to the hotel before you stick your foot in your mouth again."

Back in their hotel room, Ryan sits down on the bed, then leans back. Anne Marie sits next to him. "Let's freshen up and grab a cold drink at the bar," she suggests.

"I like that idea."

"I am going to change out of my sweater." She grabs ahold of it and starts pulling it over her head.

Ryan leans over to help her. Then he moves on to her blouse. Not surprisingly, they find it easier to resist liquid refreshments than the temptations of the flesh. Their visit to the bar is delayed.

Most of the next day is spent in pursuit of a place to live. After visiting several apartments in various sections of town, Ryan finally finds something acceptable. His new home is a small furnished efficiency. It's near a park and close to the Saint-Charles River.

They sit solemnly on the couch, studying the apartment.

"Nice furniture and a beautiful view," Anne Marie comments hesitantly as she peers out the picture window.

"And close to the baseball stadium," Ryan replies.

They sit quietly for a minute before Anne Marie says, "It is very small."

"Yep." Ryan bounces his head as he looks around.

Anne Marie hops to her feet, an enthusiastic smile on her face. "It is a clean apartment and a nice building. Together, we will decorate it and make it a home."

The next morning, hotel room service delivers a medley of eggs, meats, potatoes, fruits, and pastries for them to enjoy in their room. After eating most of their food and playing with the rest, they clean up and then take a leisurely stroll along a paved path through the maple and oak trees of nearby Lake Saint Joseph. They sit on a wooden bench holding hands and watch as a small sailboat passes by.

Anne Marie kisses Ryan on the cheek. "It has been a beautiful few days, but I must get back to Montréal."

"I'll drive you."

Anne Marie shakes her head. "It is nonsense for you to think to do that. I look forward to sitting next to the window on the train and enjoying the beautiful countryside. I also need time to read several magazines from Paris that I brought with me."

Knowing he can't change her mind once she decides to do something, Ryan drives her to the Gare du Palais, a combination train and bus station.

People bustle about the facility like a herd of cats as Ryan guides her through the crowd to her train. They share a warm embrace and a deep kiss before she walks up the steps to the train.

Anne Marie stops on the top step and blows Ryan a kiss.

As soon as the door to the train closes behind her, he feels a mixture of sadness and emptiness. As he walks to his car he reminds himself to get his mind back on baseball.

CHAPTER SIX

Two hours before the start of the first game of the season, Ryan and his teammates start drifting into Stade Canac in downtown Quebec City. It's an older stadium, built in 1937, with minimal updating since. Chatter fills the musty-smelling locker room as the players change into their hand-me-down uniforms from the Expos. The lucky ones get uniforms that don't have tears or patches on them.

Ryan sits on a wooden bench in front of a locker covered in rust, unbuttoning his shirt.

Coach Ellison barges into the room in full uniform and stands before his players. The room goes quiet. Rats can be heard scurrying across the concrete floor.

The coach takes his ball cap off and scratches the top of his head. A few hairs from his retreating hairline fall to the floor. "Welcome to Quebec." He paces in front of his players, staring closely at each of them. "We're here to win games, but the goal is to prepare you for the big leagues. Things happen fast around here. You could be called up at a moment's notice. Play good baseball, and the people in Montréal will notice."

Coach Ellison offers another fifteen minutes of inspiration, after which the players file from the locker room to the dugout. Several players jog onto the field to stretch while others grab baseballs to toss. The Jersey Indians are already on the field, loosening up.

After a half hour of running and stretching, Ryan jogs back to the dugout and grabs a seat next to Terry Dye, a tanned, blond-haired twenty-year-old. They watch as fans slowly file into the stadium.

"Did you get settled in over the weekend?" Ryan asks.

"I'm sharing an apartment with a couple guys in the suburbs."

"That's cool. Did you play on the team last year?"

"I played Single-A in West Palm the last two years. I have family in the area, so I had a place to stay." Terry rolls his shoulders as he looks over at Ryan. "What about you?"

"I got a flat over by Duran Park."

"I noticed you pulled up in a new Trans Am. Most of us drive older cars."

"I bought it last year when I was working for a construction company in Montréal."

Terry gazes at Ryan with his head tilted. "You the same Hutson who played for the Alouettes?"

"Um-hmm," Ryan replies softly.

Before Terry can ask any more questions, Coach Ellison hollers for the starters to take the field. Ryan jogs to center field and Terry hustles to left.

The seating capacity of the stadium is 4,500. Today's announced attendance is 5,300. Celebration and loud music fill the stadium leading up to game time. The Quebec Metros were formerly known as the Carnavals because of the festive attitude of their fan base.

Ryan hits a deep fly to center field his first at bat as a professional. The ball is caught by the fielder, but the runner scores from third, so he is okay with it.

Tom Franklin, a strapping six-foot-four and 250-pound first baseman for the Metros, bats next. He knocks the ball into deep center field for a double. The rout is on. The Metros win 11 – 2. Ryan has two hits and scores a run during the slugfest.

. . .

After the game, Ryan wanders about the playing field, congratulating his teammates. "Nice hits, Tom," he says to Tom Franklin.

Franklin slaps him on the back with his massive hand. "My friends call me Frank."

The Metros win all three games in their series with Jersey City. Everyone on the team is in an upbeat mood in the locker room.

Ryan shouts out, "Hey, guys, let's go celebrate. We have tomorrow off."

The boisterous locker room goes quiet.

Davis Cole, one of the pitchers, breaks the silence. "I'm up for it. Let's meet at the L'Oncle Antoine on Rue Saint-Pierre in an hour."

"See you there," Ryan replies, a little curious why no one else says anything.

Davis is seated at the bar, talking to a couple of young ladies, when Ryan wanders in. A jazz band is playing Wes Montgomery's "A Day in the Life." Relaxed lighting, leaded glass windows, and wood beams are part of the character of the two-hundred-year-old pub.

"Yo, Davis," Ryan says as he walks up and puts his hand on his back.

Davis turns. "Hey, Ryan." He nods toward the two women next to him. "This is Christina and Penelope. They were at our game tonight."

"Cool," Ryan replies, studying them. "He's a pretty good pitcher, isn't he?"

They look at each other and shake their heads.

"You need to learn French if you want to score with the women."

"Oh, really? I can't score by being a famous baseball player like you?" Ryan says with a smirk.

"Never hurts to speak French in Quebec. You get treated much better by everybody at the stores and restaurants." Davis kisses a hand of each of the women, then says to them, *"Excusez-moi. Mon ami et moi devons parler."*

The ladies stroll from the bar with their shoulders thrown back and hips swaying.

"French women can be pretty sexy, but you have to keep them in their place," Davis says.

"Really?" Ryan replies in mock surprise. "I'll keep that in mind. Where you from, Davis?"

"Houston. I graduated from Rice University last December."

"I used to live in Texas."

"I heard you played in the Canadian Football League last year?"

Ryan tries to play it down. "I filled in when a few people got hurt. Baseball is my passion."

Davis' expression is relaxed. He doesn't really care what sport Ryan plays. "Let's get you a brew," he says when the bartender approaches. "This place has a good selection of ale."

"Whatever he's having is fine," Ryan tells the bartender. Ryan looks about the room. "Doesn't look like any of the other guys are gonna show up."

Davis takes a long draw from his mug before answering. "These guys don't make much money. Some less than six thousand dollars a year. A worker at McDonald's makes more than that. By the time they pay their rent and buy food, there's not much left to party with."

"Hard to imagine, considering some players in the majors make a hundred thousand a year. They could disperse the money a little better."

"I'm sure it's a grind for a reason," Davis replies. "Players might not work as hard to get to the top if the minors were comfortable."

"You seem to be doing okay. How do you get by?"

"Our family is in the oil business." Ryan senses a certain smugness in Davis' voice. "Mom and Dad will fund me for a couple years while I chase the dream."

"What if you don't make it?"

"I have a finance degree. They'll find a place for me in the family business." He tilts his head forward as he looks at Ryan. "What if you don't make it?"

"Not an option." He chugs the rest of his beer. "Next round is on me."

CHAPTER SEVEN

After two weeks of home games, it's time to hit the road. Two buses are parked outside of Stade Canac at 8 AM. The manager, coaches, trainers, and members of the media board the first bus while the players climb aboard the second. Once the equipment is loaded and everyone is accounted for, they start their journey to West Haven, home of the Yankees' Double-A team. After three games in West Haven, they'll venture on to Waterbury, Bristol, Reading, and Holyoke before returning home.

Ryan grabs a window seat toward the back of the bus. A few minutes later, Leon Dreyfuss, a young outfielder, slides in next to him. The driver grinds through the gears of the bus as it gathers momentum moving forward. Once it reaches cruising speed, the worn-out parts of the diesel engine produce a constant rattling noise.

Leon is a thin man with tousled hair. He maintains a constant grin, showing off his two crooked front teeth.

"Hey, Ryan," Leon chirps.

"Hey, Leon."

"This is going to be fun, all of us going on a trip together. How long of a drive you think it'll be?"

"I heard eight hours."

Leon has a concerned look on his face. "Ya think they'll stop along the way so we can pee and get something to eat?"

Ryan stares at him, lost for words. "Where you from, Leon?"

"Just outside Holly Springs, Mississippi."

"How long you been playing ball?"

"All my life. My pa put a baseball glove in my hand when I was five years old. Said he wanted me to be just like Guy Bush, the Mississippi Mudcat. He was from the next town over. Played fifteen years in the majors."

"You have any brothers or sisters?"

"I have two brothers. Well, actually three, but one has a hard time with numbers. He don't count."

Ryan yawns deeply. "I'm going to rest for a little bit, Leon." He lays his head back and closes his eyes.

After a minute of silence, Leon asks, "Hey, Ryan, why don't someone make mouse-flavored cat food?"

Ryan opens one eye and looks at Leon. "Probably because no one knows what a mouse tastes like."

Leon continues to be a constant annoyance, depriving Ryan of a nap.

After three hours on the road, the buses pull into a Jack in the Box so that everyone can have lunch and a restroom break.

Ryan gobbles down a couple burgers, then wanders across the street to a Rexall drugstore and buys sleeping pills and a bottle of Yoo-hoo. He puts five pills into the Yoo-hoo bottle, shakes it up, then gives it to Leon when they're back on the bus.

A half hour later, Leon is out cold—huffing and growling like a bear. A dribble of spit drips from the side of his mouth onto his shirt.

Terry leans over from the seat behind Ryan. "I hope you didn't damage his brain, giving him all them pills."

Ryan sighs. "I had to do something. He was driving me nuts with all that nonstop yapping."

Leon is quick to recover. A half hour before the start of their game, Ryan and Terry sit on the bench, watching in amazement as the young man loosens up in the outfield.

"Look at him running around out there like a spooked rabbit," Terry says, his mouth agape.

Ryan watches Leon closely. "The sleep must've done him good."

A voice comes over the public address system. *"Anyone interfering with balls in the field of play will be removed from the stadium."*

Leon stops in his tracks. He looks around, confusion written all over his face.

"Oh, shit." Terry howls with laughter. "Think someone should tell him that they're referring to the fans?"

The Metros are in their fourth city in ten days. The cheap hotel rooms begin to blur together in an endless stream. Ryan wakes up at the crack of dawn and wanders over to the window to see what town he's in.

"All these New England towns look the same," he mumbles. "Must be Holyoke. I think somebody mentioned it on the bus last night." Once he gets his wits about him, he remembers passing a Denny's the previous night. "I guess that'd be a good place for breakfast."

Ryan grabs a seat at the counter. A middle-aged waitress welcomes him. Her dark hair is covered in a net, and she wears a stained apron. "What's doing? Conna help ya?"

"Coffee and a menu."

She returns promptly with the coffee. "Like to auder now?"

"I'll have fried eggs and bacon."

"Would you like some b'daydas?"

"Fried potatoes would be nice."

Ryan is reading the local newspaper while waiting on his food. *Apple Computer Inc. releases Apple II, the first fully integrated personal computer.*

"Heah you go," the waitress says, disrupting Ryan's reading. She sets his food in front of him. "You need more nackins? Or your coffee wommed?"

"Nah, I'm fine."

Ryan finishes his breakfast and gives the waitress a five-dollar bill. "Keep the change." Looking at the clock on the wall, he figures he has a few hours to kill before the game.

As he walks out the door of the restaurant, he's immediately bathed in warm sunshine and fresh air. "What a beautiful day. I think I'll trek down to the river valley and check out the dinosaur footprints I heard about."

Ryan shows up at Mackenzie Stadium two hours before game time. He notices a sign above the door to the locker room that reads, "No Visitors Allowed."

About that time, Leon walks up behind him. Ryan looks at Leon and points above the door. "Don't pay any attention to that."

The game doesn't start off well for the Metros. The Holyoke Millers are pounding them 8 – 0 in the fifth inning. Davis Cole storms off the mound at the end of the inning and throws his glove against the dugout wall in disgust.

"The hell's the problem with you?" Frank asks in a perturbed tone.

"How do you expect a pitcher to win when you don't give him any runs?"

Frank kicks Davis' glove across the dugout. "You got a big ego."

"My girlfriend said that also. I thought she was talking about my dick."

The Metros lose the game 10 – 2.

The team files into the locker room. Several players are covered in sweat and dirt. Coach Ellison is the first to comment. "Damn, there's no air-conditioning. It's hotter than Hades in here."

"You can cool off in the shower," Davis grumps. "There's no hot water."

Terry looks over at Ryan. "You think they have hot water and AC in the home-team locker room?"

"You know it." Ryan wipes the sweat off his eyebrows with the back of his hand. The dirt on his arms and face is turning to mud from the sweat. "I'm just thankful the water doesn't smell like sweaty socks," he says, recalling his time in Mexico.

CHAPTER EIGHT

Ryan camps under a lazy fly ball to left field. He makes the catch for the final out of the game. Quebec drubs the Bristol Red Sox 8 – 2.

Ryan leans back, his ankles crossed as he sits on the bench, watching the fans file out of Stade Canac. Meanwhile, the grounds crew rushes onto the field with rakes and hoses to manicure the infield.

Coach Ellison trudges into the dugout and stops in front of Ryan, blocking his view. "Be in my office in five."

Ten minutes later, Ryan walks into a drab office in dire need of paint and ventilation. Several tarnished trophies rest on top of a banged-up metal bookshelf, and an autographed picture of Joe DiMaggio hangs on the wall. "What's up, Coach?"

Ellison points toward a chair opposite his desk. "Sit."

Ryan drops down on the chair, crosses his arms, and leans back.

"Dawkins was hit by a pitch on his hand and bruised a couple fingers."

"Aww, man," Ryan grumbles. "I hate to hear that. I genuinely like that guy."

"You're going to have to hit the road immediately," Ellison says.

Ryan nods. "Sure, Coach. I'm ready to move up."

"Good." Ellison stands up and pats Ryan's shoulder. "You need to get on the next bus to Denver."

"What? I thought Andy got hurt?"

"He did. An outfielder was brought up from Denver to replace him. We're sending you to take his place."

Ryan's brain has a hard time processing the information. "You want me to take a bus to Denver—now?" He spreads his arms wide and scrunches his nose as he glares at Ellison.

"Yep. Now go on. Get outta here."

Ryan sits in the back of a dark Greyhound bus, leaning his head against the window. A steady stream of headlights streak past the ambling bus. With no one else to speak with, Ryan has taken to talking to himself on the long trip. "Geez, I thought they were keeping me in Quebec so I'd be close to Montréal when they needed me. Now I'm going halfway across the world to Denver." His mind races, preventing him from getting the restful sleep he needs.

The bus stops in Chicago, where he gets off to catch another bus to Denver. He has an hour to kill.

He spies a phone booth in the crowded terminal. He steps inside and closes the door.

"Yuck." He pinches his nostrils. "It smells like puke and piss in here." He drops a dime in the slot and dials Anne Marie's number. The call goes to an answering machine. *She must be asleep. I wish she would keep a phone in her bedroom.* After the beep, he says, "Hey, babe. I'm on a bus to Denver. I'll give you a call when I get there. Everything's good. Don't worry about me. Love you."

He opens the door of the booth for a breath of fresh air and looks down at his watch. *It's late, but I bet Trey is still up. I'll give him a call.*

Trey picks up the phone after the third ring. "Yello."

"Hi, Trey, did I wake you?"

"Hey, Shorty. You didn't wake me. You might have woken the baby. But you'll have to deal with his momma on that one."

"Oops."

"You're going to find out soon enough that babies are bundles of joy. But they're also little terrorists. They realize as soon as they're born that they can use sleep deprivation to break you. What's up?"

"I'm in Chicago waiting on a bus. The Expos are shipping me off to Denver."

"Change is inevitable," Trey says.

"I know, except with vending machines," Ryan curtly replies. "I thought they were keeping me in Quebec so I would be close to Montréal. You know, for a quick call-up in case of emergency. The first time somebody gets hurt, they send me two thousand miles away." Ryan continues ranting, "Anne Marie is six months pregnant. It's going to be hard for me to be there if she needs me. They also got me riding around the countryside in a stinking bus and staying in cheap hotels."

Trey lets out a deep breath. "Okay, Ryan, get your bags off the bus and get a hotel room. I'll drive up tomorrow and pick you up."

"What?" Ryan is stunned by Trey's response.

"I'll bring you back to North Carolina with me. We can teach you how to operate a bulldozer. Working construction will be good for you. You'll learn how to do an honest day's work."

After a few seconds of silence, Ryan responds, "Nah, but thanks, anyway."

"Good. Now get your ass on that bus and show them they made a mistake sending you to Denver instead of Montréal."

"Hey, Trey?"

"Yeah?"

"Thanks, man."

Ryan clamors off the bus midmorning the next day. After gathering his belongings, he hails a cab. Sitting in the back seat of the yellow car, he says, "Good morning."

The driver doesn't respond. The inside of the cab smells like Oud, a woody fragrance popular in the Middle East. Ryan looks at the taxi license on the visor. *Hazid Mohammed.* Ryan hands him the address of the motel. Hazid drives the cab toward downtown on Broadway, then exits onto a narrow street in the seedy part of town, not too far from the ballpark. He stops the cab in front of Big Dick's Halfway Inn.

"Good grief," Ryan mutters. He can't believe his eyes.

He hands Hazid five dollars. Hazid keeps his hand held out, waiting for Ryan to give him a bigger tip. Feeling antagonistic, Ryan drops a nickel in his hand.

He stands on the curb, staring at the motel. If the building could speak, it would scream, "Run away." The neighborhood is replete with sex shops, strip clubs, and greasy diners. It's the kind of area that attracts people you'd cross the street to avoid.

Ryan strolls through the door of the motel. He comes face-to-face with a skinny kid in his early twenties, wearing a filthy white tank-top undershirt. The kid sits behind the counter, smoking a cigarette next to a no-smoking sign and staring at a worn-out issue of *Penthouse.* His arms, which aren't much thicker than a broomstick, have red dots along the inside of his elbow. Cheap, homemade tattoos cover his shoulders and forearms.

"You need something?" he asks, seeming a little put out by Ryan's presence.

"Could you have the bellhop grab my bags?"

"Fuck you. We ain't got no rooms for smart-asses."

"I have a reservation." Ryan's patience is dwindling with his lack of sleep.

"You must be the fucking baseball player." The guy reaches for a key and tosses it across the counter.

Ryan stares at the kid, shaking his head. "Your brain is way too small for you to have such a big mouth." He looks at the key lying on the counter and wishes he had some disinfectant.

Ryan enters his room from the parking lot. The room smells like an ashtray, the carpet is threadbare, and the surfaces in the bathroom are coated with dust. There are also a few stains that he chooses not to think about. A used condom is stuck to the bottom of the wastebasket. The bedsheets appear to have been washed, but several pubic hairs are still stuck in the threads.

Exasperated, Ryan stands in the middle of the hot and stale room, staring at a cockroach racing from under the bed into the bathroom. *All right*, he tells himself. *I need to get some sleep. I got a ball game to play.* He knocks the thermostat down ten degrees, then lies on the bed. Two minutes later, he jolts two feet in the air when the air conditioner kicks in. It sounds just like a kid banging on his mother's pots and pans.

Still a little delirious from the past twenty-four hours, Ryan arrives at the ballpark two hours before game time. The other players file in while he lies on a bench in the locker room, napping. Once the room gets crowded and he can't sleep any more, he rises slowly to his feet to socialize. Most of the team remembers him from spring training.

The manager, Ted Thompson, welcomes Ryan and informs him he won't be in the starting lineup. Ryan is fine with watching the action from the bench. He figures he might catch a few Z's during the game.

The Bears are soundly defeated by a team from Omaha. After the game, the players shower, washing off the dirt and shame of awful playing.

Don Schneider, one of the assistant coaches, walks in. "Hurry up, girls," he hollers. "The buses are waiting to take us to Indianapolis." The coach is a tall, slender man with a Fu Manchu moustache. He looks like the kind of guy who would play the villain in a spaghetti western.

Ryan approaches the coach and stares at him. "Are we *really* going to Indianapolis on a bus *right now?*"

They stand head-on, locked in a silent, intense stare-off.

"Yup," the coach says in a throaty voice.

"Incredible!" Ryan turns to Mason, the husky catcher who just happens to be standing next to him. "I get off a bus after traveling two thousand miles west to Denver, just to get on another bus going a thousand miles east. I feel like I'm on *Candid Camera*."

"We had to get you here today in case we needed you," Mason replies.

Ryan furrows his eyebrows as he looks at Mason. "The team is in the middle of a six-game losing streak and fifteen games out of first place. How bad did you really need me here today?"

CHAPTER NINE

Ryan is the first to board the bus. He grabs his usual window seat near the rear. The last two guys onto the bus plop themselves down next to him.

Ryan smiles politely. "Hey, Jed. Hi, Bruce."

"Hi, Ryan. How ya doing, partner?" Jed replies with enthusiasm.

"What's going on, buddy?" Bruce asks.

"Just looking to chill on the long ride," Ryan replies. "I've been zigzagging across different time zones the past couple days."

After a few moments of obligatory small talk, Ryan rests his head against the window and closes his eyes.

They're several miles out of town and cruising east on I-70 when Jed pulls a bottle of bourbon out of his gym bag. He nudges Ryan and holds the bottle out to him. "Try this. It may help you sleep."

"Bourbon may not be the answer, but it's worth a shot." Ryan takes a drink from the bottle, then leans his head back. He's asleep within minutes.

After drinking close to a quarter of the bottle, Jed pulls out a pack of Marlboros. He and Bruce each fire one up.

As soon as the smoke reaches Ryan's nose, he's startled awake. His first thought is the bus is on fire. Then he notices Jed and Bruce each with a smoke in their mouth. If looks could kill, there would be two fewer Denver Bears. "Seriously?" he asks.

Taken aback by Ryan's terse behavior, Jed replies, "You know, Ryan, you're not much fun to be around."

"Do you *really* need to smoke a butt now . . . on this crowded bus?"

"Sometimes smoking a cigarette can be the difference between pacifism and mass homicide," Bruce says.

"Can you sit somewhere else if you're going to smoke?"

"These were the last two seats together on the bus. Besides, having an occasional smoke is harmless," Bruce replies.

Ryan shakes his head in disbelief. "Cigarettes are like hamsters—they're harmless until you stick one in your mouth and light it."

After eight hours of listening to drunken banter and breathing blue smoke, Ryan is relieved when the bus pulls into the lot of a Motel 6.

"They should call it a Motel 8," Jed says. "I heard they raised their daily rate by two bucks."

"Truth in advertising is not guaranteed in the American constitution," Bruce prudently replies.

It takes a day for Ryan to get his biorhythms in line and two games for him to get a feel for Triple-A pitching. After ten games, he averages a hit every three at bats and a home run every twelve times at the plate. Despite his hitting, the team still stinks. He's like a beautiful flower flourishing in a pungent pile of crap.

After three weeks of playing baseball in fun and interesting places like Evansville, Springfield, and Des Moines, the team begins the journey back to Denver.

It only takes a few trips on the team bus for Ryan to appreciate the value of a front row seat—the driver doesn't tolerate any antics occurring near him.

Ryan is relaxing in his seat, reading *The Hitchhiker's Guide to the Galaxy*, when the team trainer squeezes into the seat next to him.

"Hey, Ryan."

Ryan sits up straight. "What's up, Johnny?"

"You got all your clothes and stuff with you?"

"Yeah, I wasn't about to leave anything at that dump I was staying in."

"Good news," he replies. "A family in Cherry Creek wants to put you up for the rest of the season."

"What do you mean, put me up?" A confused look crosses Ryan's face.

"They want you to live in their house with them. They'll sponsor you."

"I'm not comfortable living in a house with people I don't know. I like the freedom to come and go and do as I please."

"They're a wealthy family. He's the CEO of a sporting goods company, and she's an attorney. From what I hear, most of the houses in Cherry Creek are pretty luxurious. You'll probably be given the carriage or pool house to live in."

"The pool house!" Ryan's eyes light up. "And it's free?"

"Yep. Someone will be waiting for you when you get off the bus."

"Cool," Ryan replies. "Who do I thank for this?"

"Got me," Johnny says. He gets to his feet and then heads back to his seat.

Mrs. Tina Housem and her teenage kids, Robyn and Chris, and toddler, Matt, are waiting for Ryan when he gets off the bus. Tina and Robyn each give Ryan a hug and kiss on the cheek. Chris gives him a proper handshake and "How do you do, sir." Matt is only four and couldn't care less about Ryan.

Chris helps Ryan load his belongings into the back of the Land Rover.

After twenty minutes of weaving through downtown traffic,

Tina turns down a street lined with large maple, chestnut, and oak trees. Ryan looks out the window, admiring the houses, which resemble small castles. The Land Rover pulls onto a winding brick driveway and stops in front of a three-car garage. A stone house the size of a department store is attached to the garage.

Tina looks over at Chris. "Show Ryan to the guesthouse. I have things to tend to."

"I'll help," Robyn eagerly offers.

The kids lead Ryan along a meandering brownstone walkway toward the back of the house. The stone walkway segues into a stone patio that surrounds a huge swimming pool. On the other side of the pool is a miniature version of the main house.

"Sure beats Big Dick's Halfway Inn," Ryan murmurs.

Robyn's eyes are ablaze. "Are you getting fresh with me?"

"Huh?" Ryan gives her a surprised look. "No. That was the name of the last place I stayed."

"Oh. It's all right if you were getting fresh."

Ryan follows Robyn into the pool house. Chris quickly disappears. It's mostly one large room with sliding glass doors that face the pool. It possesses all the basic necessities of home: a bed, dresser, couch, dining room table, small refrigerator, and a stove. All with designer labels. The latest in entertainment equipment is mounted on the wall. An attached bathroom has a shower large enough to accommodate four or more people.

After he unpacks, Ryan calls Anne Marie. "The team has arranged for me to stay in the guesthouse of a wealthy family. It has all the modern conveniences, including a swimming pool."

"That is wonderful news. I was concerned about you living in a sleazy part of town and sleeping with the nasty little roaches."

Ryan smiles as he imagines her shuddering while thinking about cockroaches. "Don't worry, I'm safe now."

CHAPTER TEN

The next morning, Ryan, Tina, and the children sit at a large mahogany table, illuminated by an overhead crystal chandelier. An original Camille Pissarro hangs on the wall. Elena, the Bolivian housekeeper, dishes breakfast off a silver dining cart. Despite her quiet demeanor, Elena is a stunning woman with black hair, dark brown eyes, and a full figure.

"Do you have plans for today?" Tina looks at Ryan as she places a couple slices of avocado on a piece of toast.

Ryan has a mouthful of a hot breakfast burrito, so it takes a few seconds for him to answer. "Our game isn't until seven thirty. I thought I might go for a jog and relax around the pool for a bit."

"I have some errands to run," Tina says. "Make yourself at home."

Decked out in a pair of shorts and a T-shirt, Ryan jogs along Race Street. His run takes him through a tree-lined neighborhood and, eventually, to a shopping district. He casually jaunts past swanky cafés, galleries, and spas. Outside of trendy boutiques, ladies wearing Gucci sunglasses walk their Yorkies and King Charles Spaniels. Leaving the small shops behind, he jogs into the Denver

Country Club and is promptly chased off the property by security guards. After a little more than an hour of running in the full sun, he plods back toward the house, exhausted. The air is a little thinner than what he's used to.

Standing on the patio, chugging a large glass of water, Ryan watches the sun reflect off the water in the pool as he contemplates his next move. The pool is thirty yards long, so it's functional for exercise as well as cooling off.

After a quick change into a swimsuit, Ryan attempts a somersault off the diving board. It starts well but ends in a belly flop. As soon as the sting wears off, he swims several laps, alternating between backstrokes and breaststrokes. Fifteen minutes later, breathing heavily, he makes his way to a lounge chair to catch his breath.

Not long after he lies down, Robyn strolls out of the house in a bikini that barely covers her developing body. Being a gentleman, Ryan only looks at the parts that are covered. She slides her chair close enough for Ryan to get a good whiff of coconut oil.

"How was your run?" she asks, admiring his muscular arms and shoulders.

"Nice neighborhood." Ryan laces his fingers behind his head.

She gives him a little wink. "Maybe when you make it big in baseball, you can buy a house here."

"Wouldn't make sense. Montréal is home."

Making soft, lingering eye contact, Robyn places her hand on his thigh. "Who knows. You might find something here you like."

Ryan reaches over and tactfully removes her hand from his thigh.

She gives him a pouty look.

"The mountains look pretty awesome," he says, looking off into the distance. "I can almost make out Pikes Peak."

Not one to give up easily, Robyn asks, "You ever been with a sixteen-year-old?"

"A few times." Ryan watches her pout turn into a smile, then quickly disappear when he says, "When I was sixteen."

She leans back in her chair and crosses her arms. "You know, girls mature a lot quicker these days."

Ryan decides it's time to move on to another subject. "You and your brother look about the same age. Are you twins?"

"Yeah," she replies, rolling her eyes. "He claims we're identical twins."

"Really? How does he figure that?"

"He thinks he's a girl trapped in a boy's body. He keeps bugging Mom and Dad about getting a sex change."

"Oh, boy." Ryan doesn't want to go there either. "Geez, um . . . You know, I haven't seen your dad since I got here."

Robyn moves from her chair and sits on the lounge chair with Ryan. "He travels a lot and isn't home much. When he's home, he takes his pleasure with Elena, the housekeeper."

Ryan tosses his head back, grinning. "Come on, now. You're making that up."

"Nope." Her tone is unwavering. "Elena is a moaner. You can hear her throughout the whole house when they do it."

"Does your mom hear it?"

Robyn shrugs. "Probably. But she pretends she doesn't. She has her own caretakers."

Little Matt charges out the back door and runs up to Robyn and Ryan, chatting incoherently about metal balls. A minute later, Tina rushes out the same door, wearing a short silk robe tied at the waist. "Grab your brother and take him into the house," she tells Robyn.

"Aww, Mom, me and Ryan are talking."

Tina glares at her daughter. "Don't sass me."

Matt can sense his sister's displeasure and sticks his tongue out at her.

Ryan looks at Tina and Robyn, slack-jawed. "You know, when a four-year-old sticks their tongue out at you, it's the same as an adult giving you the finger."

"You're cute. I'm not done with you yet," Robyn says as she grabs her brother's hand and leads him away.

Tina sits in the chair next to Ryan and removes her robe, leaving her breasts unencumbered. Ryan is caught off guard by the move, but doesn't complain.

Turnabout is fair play. Tina gets a twinkle in her eyes as she studies Ryan's toned pecs. "You must exercise quite a bit to maintain such a beautiful body." She lightly caresses his abs. Her delicate touch continues down his stomach to his belly button. "Nice treasure trail," she says while playing with the line of hair above his swimsuit. "You'd be a big hit at our swingers' club."

Ryan puts both of his hands around hers and holds them—for his own protection. "I don't think I would be very good on a trapeze."

"But I'm sure you would be wonderful in a fantasy swing." She gives him an alluring stare.

Not intimidated, Ryan holds her gaze with steady, unwavering eyes until Tina abruptly breaks eye contact.

"I need to go. We can continue this discussion later." She bends over, pressing her teardrop-shaped breasts against his shoulder, and gives him a kiss on the cheek. "I'm planning a birthday party for the kids this weekend." She stands up and slips her robe back on. "I have no idea what to buy a sexually confused boy for a present."

Ryan turns his palms up. "How about a straight jacket?"

Ryan leaves the mansion at 4 PM for the game with the Oklahoma City 89ers. Half the team is in the clubhouse drinking beer, smoking cigars, and playing cards when he walks in.

After he changes into his uniform, he asks, "Anybody want to loosen up?"

"That's what beer is for," Bruce replies without looking up from the card game.

Ryan stands next to the card players and waves the cigar smoke away from his face. "A little practice before the game might improve your play." He tilts his head and forces a smile while his teammates study him with blank expressions. "I guess that was a stupid thing to say."

"Come on, Ryan. You're starting to sound like my old man with all this talk about practice," Jed says as he gives him a dismissive hand wave. "You get noticed for what you do on the field, not before the game."

Ryan shakes his head in amazement. "I thought *The Bad News Bears* was a movie about a bunch of twelve-year-old kids, not the Denver Bears." He strolls from the locker room, mumbling to himself.

The Bears lose to the 89ers 9 – 1. Ryan gets three hits in four at bats. The one time he doesn't get on base, Manny, a 300-pound Black man with dreadlocks, blasts a monster home run that leaves the stadium. Manny leads the league in home runs. He also leads the league in strikeouts.

After showering and changing into street clothes, Ryan heads for the exit while his teammates lounge around the locker room. "See you all tomorrow," he says flippantly. "It'll be a whole new opportunity to raise our incompetence to another level."

Before he's out the door, Ryan hears Bruce squawking to his teammates, "The guy's a heck of a ballplayer, but he needs to learn to chill out."

CHAPTER ELEVEN

Ryan sits on the bench, watching the fans file out of the Evansville stadium after the home team trounces the Bears 9 – 2. Coach Thompson wanders in from the locker room and sits next to him.

"Hey, Coach," Ryan says, looking into the seats behind first base.

"Hey, Ryan." The coach peers across the field to see what Ryan's looking at.

Ryan points into the stands. "Right above the home team dugout. See that Asian guy with the movie camera?"

The coach squints to get a better look. "Yeah."

"His name is Phil Ming."

Coach Thompson looks toward the heavens as he lets out a gasp of air. He returns his focus to Ryan. "You've been playing good ball since you've been here."

Ryan leans back, his ankles crossed in front of him. "Thanks. Is that what you came out here to tell me?"

"Nope. I came out here to listen to your stupid jokes. I'm going to miss them."

"Am I being sent back to Quebec?" he asks with great anticipation.

"Nope. Time for September call-ups to the majors."

Ryan uncrosses his legs and sits up straight. His heart beats faster. "And?"

A grin stretches across the coach's face. "You're leaving tomorrow to join the Expos."

Ryan jumps to his feet and thrusts his fist in the air. "Woohoo! I'm off to The Show." He reaches to hug Coach Thompson, but it's awkward because the coach is sitting, so he rambles excitedly back and forth in the dugout instead.

As soon as he gains control of his emotions, he heads to the shower then joins his teammates on the bus.

"You, dancing in the back of the bus, sit down!" the bus driver hollers.

Ryan ignores the command as he bounces up and down in the aisle next to Jed and Bruce. The three of them alternate taking swigs from a bottle of Old Grand-Dad.

Jed holds the bottle high. "To Ryan, the oldest young man I know. May all your ups and downs be under the covers." He proceeds to slug down a slow heavy mouthful of whiskey. "We are going to miss you...but probably not nearly as much as you'll miss us."

Ryan grabs the bottle and takes a long pull. "Playing ball with you guys is like a bad haircut. You can't fix it and just have to suffer through it."

The bus comes to a complete stop in front of the Knights Inn. Ryan wobbles off and heads directly to his hotel room. He's anxious to share the good news with Anne Marie.

The phone rings three times before he hears her voice. *"Bonjour."*

"Good news, babe. I'm coming home." He wanders about the cramped hotel room, bouncing on his toes as he talks. "I'm going to play the rest of the year with the Expos."

"*C'est magnifique!*" Her voice radiates with excitement. "When do you leave?"

"I'm catching a flight tomorrow."

"I will see you tomorrow night?"

"Well, no. Actually, I'm flying to Philadelphia."

"Then you will catch a flight to Montréal from Philadelphia?"

"Nope. I'll be in Philadelphia for four days."

"That is no problem. I can wait four days to see you."

There's a brief pause as Ryan clears his throat. "I'm going to New York for four days after that."

"I do not understand. You call me to tell me you are coming home, then you tell me you are going to Philadelphia and New York?"

"I'll be in Montréal in nine days," he says eagerly, hoping to reignite her excitement.

"Okay, we will celebrate you becoming a Major League Baseball player then."

"I haven't necessarily made the team full-time yet."

"*Excusez-moi?* Why do you go to Philadelphia if you are not on the team?"

"I am on the team, but . . ." He releases a deep breath and runs his fingers through his hair. "I love you and can't wait to see you."

Ryan, Manny, and a relief pitcher shuffle off to the airport, where they board a chartered flight to Philadelphia. Ryan and Manny sit next to each other in first class. Smoked salmon and champagne are served during the flight.

Leaning back in his padded leather seat, Ryan snickers as he reflects on his month in Denver. *I batted .319, hit ten home runs, drove in twenty-one runs, and visited the thriving metropolises of Wichita, Springfield, and Des Moines.*

Manny glares at a smirking Ryan, wondering if he has mental issues. "Are you okay?"

"Just thinking about my time in Denver." I shared a residence with a vixen, a transsexual, and an underage drama queen—while playing baseball alongside alcoholics and halfwits." He looks at Manny and smiles. "Thankfully, all good things come to an end."

A limousine meets the Bears players at the airport and delivers them to the Bellevue-Stratford Hotel. The bellhop grabs their bags from the trunk and leads them to the check-in counter.

As Ryan crosses the lobby, he notices Davis Cole sitting at the bar in the lounge.

After checking in, Ryan strolls into the lounge. It's pretty upscale as far as hotel bars go. A gentleman sits behind a baby grand piano, tickling the keys, while a chic woman bartender in a starched white shirt and black tie serves drinks.

"Where have I seen this pitcher before?" Ryan asks when he walks up behind Cole.

"Ryan, my man." Cole stands up to shake hands. "This is my new friend Darla," he says, pointing to the lady behind the bar. "Fix my friend a Glenlivet on the rocks."

"Are you a baseball star, also?" Darla asks as she sets the Scotch in front of Ryan.

Ryan nods toward Cole. "I'm as much a star as he is." He takes a sip of his drink, then asks Cole, "How long have you been here?"

"I flew in yesterday."

"Lucky you. Made it up to the bigs without having to go through Denver."

Cole shrugs. "They must like me better than you."

"Good grief." Ryan turns his face away. "You still got that big ego."

"Everyone has an ego, Ryan. Mine just happens to be bigger and better than everyone else's."

Ryan chews on an ice cube. "Anybody else get called up from Quebec?"

"Frank."

"Think we'll get much playing time?"

"Hard to say what they'll do with you guys. The team is below .500 and out of the pennant race. As for me, they always need a fresh arm in the bullpen."

"Typical Cole," Ryan says. "I'll leave you to bask in your self-admiration. I'm heading upstairs and calling room service."

Ryan enters a spacious, well-lit room with thick carpeting and a plush velvet sofa. The accommodations have the elegant details you expect in a five-star hotel, such as his and her bathrobes and a wall-mounted phone between the bathtub and toilet.

Ryan orders a lobster tail and petite filet. While waiting for delivery, he calls Anne Marie. She's happy to hear he made it safely to Philadelphia.

"I miss you terribly," she says. "My stomach gets bigger every day, and I have many cravings. You being the biggest one."

"Hold on a second." Ryan sets the phone down and opens the door to let room service wheel his dinner in. He picks the phone back up and says, "I miss you, too. It's been almost two months since I held you. Will you come to New York?"

"I am eight months pregnant. I prefer not to travel far from home or my doctor, unless necessary. I will see you in a week or so."

After finishing his meal and conversation with Anne Marie, Ryan punches his brother's number into the phone.

As soon as Trey picks up, Ryan spouts, "I'm on the Expos roster for the rest of the year!"

There's stunned silence on the other end of the line before Trey's excitement quickly radiates through his voice. "All right! You get to play with the big boys now," he quips. "I'm happy for you, Ryan."

"Thanks, Trey." Ryan's voice softens. "You've been my biggest cheerleader."

"Maybe I'll drive up to Philly and catch a game."

"I'd love to see you, but it's probably not worth it. No telling when I might get in."

"Well, I could at least take a picture of you sitting on the bench with some major league players."

CHAPTER TWELVE

Midmorning the next day, the Expos players pile into two buses parked outside the front entrance of the Bellevue-Stratford. Ryan ambles down the aisle of the already crowded bus, then hears a voice ring out.

"Hey, Dog!"

His eyes lock onto the smiling faces of Jerry Carter and Billy Daniels.

"Welcome to the major leagues," Carter says.

After a small burst of laughter, Ryan replies, "Glad to be here."

"Always remember the two words that will open up doors for you."

"What would they be?" Ryan responds, almost afraid to ask.

"Push and pull." Carter and Daniels giggle like a couple of schoolgirls.

Ryan shakes his head. "You guys suffer from insanity."

"*Au contraire*. We don't *suffer* from insanity," Daniels says. "We enjoy every minute of it."

Ryan spots an empty seat near the rear of the bus and settles in next to the window. A few minutes later, Ken Singletary, a fifteen-year Major League veteran, drops down on the seat next to him.

"Welcome to the big leagues," Singletary says, shifting in his seat to get comfortable.

"Feels good already," Ryan replies, a satisfied smile on his face. "I logged thousands of miles on noisy, rough-riding buses this summer. Each one had spotty air-conditioning and uncomfortable seats. Now I'm on a bus with reclining seats, individual air-control outlets, and extra leg room just to ride a few miles across town." His face lights up. "I can get used to this."

The Expos' caravan arrives at Veterans Stadium two hours before the game. Ryan and the rest of the team unload from the bus and then venture through a myriad of tunnels in the underside of the stadium before reaching the locker room. Unlike the concrete floors and rusted lockers in the minor league locker rooms, these floors are carpeted, and the lockers are polished ash. A padded chair sits in front of each locker. Mounted on the wall is a sound system and color television. Ryan has a content look on his face. *This is the way a locker room should be.*

Ryan heads out to the field for some stretching after changing into his uniform. Once his hamstrings, hips, and thighs are loose, he grabs a seat on the top step of the dugout and gazes at a sea of more than fifty thousand fans. Andy, who recently came off the injured list, sits next to him.

"They look like a bunch of ants scurrying around," Ryan says.

"The fans here are pretty excited. Their team is tied for first with fifteen games remaining."

Ryan slowly bobs his head. "That's what I heard."

"The Phillies are keenly focused on winning every game," Andy says, looking across the field at their players. "We're merely a nuisance to them at this time."

Ryan slaps Andy's thigh, then stands up. "Let's make life miserable for them."

. . .

The game enters the top of the ninth with the Phillies up 5 – 4. The stadium is all abuzz. Montréal has a runner on second with one out, and the pitcher's spot is up next.

Ryan sits at the end of the bench, focused on the action on the field, when the coach hollers, "Hutson, grab a bat."

Ryan jolts upright, and his heart skips a beat. "Whoa! I wasn't expecting that." He bounds to his feet, then scurries over to the bat rack.

"Go get 'em, Dog," Carter hollers.

An anxious grin crosses Ryan's face as he turns to look at Carter.

Standing in the on-deck circle, Ryan looks at the massive crowd as he rubs a rosin bag on the bat handle. The fans are stomping their feet, clapping their hands, and shouting, "Let's go, Phillies!" The significance of the moment is not lost on Ryan. Adrenaline flows through his veins, exciting every muscle and nerve ending in his body. He calms his breathing to let his heart rate settle. *My first at bat as a major leaguer,* he tells himself, feeling a sense of pride. *It's a dream, almost twenty years in the making.*

He steps to the plate, digs in, and then takes a few practice swings to ready himself.

The pitcher throws a wicked curveball, which breaks inside for a called strike. Ryan steps out of the box and nods at the pitcher. *He's got good stuff.*

The second pitch is a fastball that just misses the outside corner of the plate. Ball one.

Ryan takes a deep breath between pitches. His eyes are focused on the pitcher's hand as he releases the next pitch. Ryan swings at a slider and misses. Strike two. "Dang it," he mutters.

A curveball breaks inside on the next pitch. Ball two. *Phew.*

The next pitch is an outside fastball. Ryan makes contact, then watches as the ball flies into the stands behind first base. Two balls, two strikes.

The pitcher throws another slider. Ryan locks his elbows as he checks his swing. The ball hits the dirt in front of the plate. *Whew!* He steps out of the box to refocus.

As he prepares for the next pitch, Ryan reminds himself, *He's got three balls on me, and he has to be careful. But he also has first base open, so he can gamble a little.*

The pitcher throws an inside curve, which breaks across the plate. Ryan fouls it to the backstop. He's happy to make contact. The next pitch is a curveball. Ryan takes a big swing and nicks the ball, sending it crashing into the catcher's chest protector. The catcher snatches it as it bounces off his chest and holds on to it for an out.

Ryan slaps the top of his helmet as he sulks back to the dugout. "Dang it!" he snarls. *Not a fond memory for my first at bat as a major leaguer.* He plops down on the bench next to Singletary, upset with himself.

The veteran gives him a sympathetic look. "A man once told me to walk with the Lord. I told him I would rather walk with Steve Carlton on the mound and the game on the line." Singletary pats Ryan's thigh. "He'll be a first ballot Hall of Famer. A tough pitcher to break in on, kid."

"I've struck out before and I'll strike out again. But I'll never like it, no matter who's pitching," Ryan says.

The next batter hits a ground ball to shortstop for the final out of the game.

Ryan isn't in the starting lineup the next game. The Expos fall behind 7 – 1 after five innings. With nothing to lose and looking to get Ryan some experience, the Expos' manager subs him in the left field position. Ryan leads off the top of the sixth and crushes a line drive down the third base line. Unfortunately, the third baseman steps in front of it for an out.

At least I made solid contact, he consoles himself while walking back to the dugout.

In the bottom of the eighth, the Phillies batter hits a high pop-up down the left-field line. Ryan sprints over and makes a difficult catch look routine. His first defensive play in the big leagues.

He comes up to bat in the top of the ninth with the Phillies leading 9 – 1. Jack Eastwick enters the game as the Phillies' relief pitcher. Ryan promptly slams the first pitch offered to him into the gap between right and center field for a single. Carter and Daniels immediately jump to their feet and stand at attention on the top step of the dugout, saluting Ryan.

Ryan stands on first base, laughing. "What a bunch of clowns," he says to Richie Hebner, the Phillies' first baseman.

The next batter hits into a double play. Game over.

With the most recent defeat, the Expos are mathematically eliminated from the race. "Whew, the pressure's finally off," Daniels declares, providing a little comic relief.

Ryan and several other minor league call-ups start the next game. The Phillies, in the midst of the pennant race, stay with their starters. Jim Kaat, the crafty veteran pitcher, shuts down the Expos' hitters for six innings. Ryan hits the ball hard twice, but they're at 'em balls that don't fall in for a hit.

The Phillies are up 4 – 0 in the seventh when Jack Eastwick is brought in to pitch. There's a runner on second when Ryan steps to the plate. He patiently waits until he sees a pitch he likes, which is the fourth one. He sends it into deep center field for a stand-up double, scoring the runner from second. His first major league run batted in.

Carter and Daniels stand in front of the Expos' dugout, clapping. Ryan gives them a polite bow. *Now, if I could just get a hit off somebody other than Eastwick.*

With the score 4 – 2, the Phillies bring in Tug McGraw to pitch the ninth. He quickly shuts down the Expos' batters in order. Game over.

Carter nudges Ryan before he can head to the locker room. "Come out to the field. I'll introduce you to McGraw. He's a fellow droll."

McGraw stands near the pitcher's mound, watching a young boy run in circles.

Carter introduces Ryan to Tug then asks, "Who's the little guy?"

"It's my son, Tim. He wants to be a singer."

"Well, he should have good pitch," Carter replies. "When did you start bringing him to the ballfield?"

"He's usually at day care, but security at the school called today. They said he was resisting a rest."

Ryan laughs halfheartedly. "I saw a kidnapping outside my window once."

"Did you call the police?" Carter asks.

"Nah," Ryan replies. "I just went out and woke him up."

The Expos travel up the road to New York, where they drop three out of four games to the Mets. Ryan gets four hits in thirteen at bats during the series. Although it's a respectable .300, he's a little disappointed. He expects to do better. The good news is—the team will finish the season at home, which means no more traveling this year. The thought of being with Anne Marie generates a warm, tingling feeling inside him.

CHAPTER THIRTEEN

It's a good day when the sheets are pulled back before the suitcases are unpacked. Anne Marie anxiously anticipated Ryan's return home by researching sexual positions for pregnant women. As soon as he's through the door of her home, she has him on the bed, experimenting with the supernova, laptop, spider, reverse cowgirl, and clip positions. "I love them all," she says, her face flushed after their vigorous lovemaking. "We will have to try them again so I can decide which one I like best."

Ryan laughs. "Let me catch my breath. I exert more energy having sex with you than I do playing baseball."

"Just as well." Anne Marie looks at Ryan with hungry eyes. "I love you, and I have missed you tremendously, but now I am famished. I am eating for two."

A slowly flickering candle on the table provides just enough light to read the menu at Chez Queux. Ryan wears a dark suit, while Anne Marie is dressed in a black silk dress with spaghetti straps.

"You look fabulous," Ryan says, holding her hand. He has a difficult time maintaining his gaze on her eyes.

"Men are so easy to read." She slips a finger under Ryan's chin to lift his face upward. Her normally pert boobs are swollen to almost twice their usual size. "I read in a journal that everything I consume passes through the developing baby." Anne Marie takes a drink from a glass of water. "Therefore, I won't expose her to alcohol, caffeine, or acidic foods."

Ryan dismisses her comment with an upward roll of his eyes. "You can't believe all the bunk you read nowadays."

"Oh, I disagree. She and I listen to classical music every night to stimulate her developing mind."

Ryan reaches for her hand. Anne Marie grasps it, feeling the strength of his grip. "You will be a wonderful mother." He looks at her with adoring eyes, his pupils dilated and his gaze unwavering for the moment. "And the boy, a great athlete."

Ryan shows up early for his first home game. A couple players mill about as he sits in front of his locker, changing into his gear.

Daniels sits a couple lockers over from Ryan, changing into his uniform. "How's it going, Dog?"

Ryan opens his mouth in a wide smile, showing lots of teeth. "It feels incredible to wake up in a familiar bed and share breakfast with a loved one before heading to the ballpark." His voice is full of passion and enthusiasm.

"Don't you love us?"

"Even more than you love to ask stupid questions." Ryan bends over to tie his cleats. "Looks like we got the Dodgers for the next three games."

"Yep," Daniels replies. "They need two wins to clinch the West. Then we got the Pirates for the last four games of the year. They're a game out of first in our division."

The September call-ups start the first game against the Dodgers, much to the annoyance of the teams chasing the Dodgers.

The game is tied 2 – 2 in the eighth inning. Ryan has gotten one hit in three at-bats up to this point in the game. He relaxes in the dugout as Frank comes to the plate with a runner on second base.

A fuzzy orange creature in an Expos uniform runs from the stands onto the Dodgers' dugout and starts jumping up and down to rouse the crowd. His stomping creates a racket that drives the Dodgers' manager onto the field, screaming, "Get the fuck off my dugout!"

The creature looks at the manager with his hands turned up like, *What did I do?*

The confrontation brings the third-base umpire over to see what the ruckus is about, resulting in a delay in the game.

"That thing jumping up and down on the top of the dugout is irritating as hell," the Dodgers' manager complains loudly.

The umpire glares at the creature, points his finger toward him, then sternly says, "Stop it!"

The creature hangs his head momentarily. But as soon as the umpire turns his back, he stomps once on the dugout roof. The umpire stops in his tracks, turns, and hollers, "You're outta here!"

The creature falls to his knees with his hands folded in front of him, like he's pleading for mercy. The fans along the third base line boo the umpire.

Daniels looks over at Carter. They're both sitting on the bench next to Ryan, watching the antics unfold from the other side of the field. "What the heck is going on over there?"

"I'm not positive, Billy," Carter replies. "But I believe the umpire just tossed Youppi, our mascot, from of the game."

"The next thing you know, they'll be tossing fans from the game, and we'll be playing in front of empty seats," Billy laments.

Jerry and Billy's constant levity helps keep Ryan at ease.

After the excitement settles, Frank strikes out. The Dodgers get three runs in their half of the inning then hold on to win 5 – 2. The Dodgers' magic number to clinch the pennant is one.

. . .

Ryan heads straight home after the game, anxious to be with Anne Marie. When he opens the door to the townhouse, he finds her sitting on the couch next to a box of tissues. Her eyes are swollen and bloodshot, and tears stream down her face. His body immediately tenses.

CHAPTER FOURTEEN

Ryan stands behind Anne Marie and puts his hands on her shoulders. "What's the matter, sweet pea?" He gently strokes her hair.

"My sister, Jacqui." She struggles while trying to breathe, talk, and cry at the same time. "She was killed last night."

"Oh, geez." Ryan has to catch himself as his legs almost fall out from under him. He moves to the front of the couch and sits next to her. "What happened?"

"Kids were drinking and driving. They ran a stop sign." Tears flow freely down her cheeks as she clutches Ryan. "They hit her car broadside." Anne Marie labors to catch her breath. "None of the kids got a scratch on them." She buries her face in his chest—her shoulders heave as she sobs.

Ryan's throat burns and his chest tightens as he holds her close. He valiantly fights to contain his emotions to be strong for her.

"I am leaving tomorrow for Thunder Bay," she says between sniffles.

"I'll clear it with the Expos in the morning then join you."

Early the next morning, Ryan shows up at the Expos' offices. He spies Rick Williamson, the manager, walking down the hall and approaches him. "Something's come up that I need to talk with you about," Ryan says.

"Grab a seat in my office. I'll be with you in a minute."

Ryan practically wears a path in the carpet as he paces back and forth, waiting for the manager. Williamson returns in twenty minutes, steam rising from the cup of coffee in his hand. He grabs a seat at his desk and looks at Ryan. "Things are kind of busy around here. What can I do for you?"

"My girlfriend's sister died last night. I need a few days off."

"That's not how we do things around here," Williamson replies. He pulls a pint of bourbon out of a desk drawer and pours a shot into his coffee.

"How do we do things around here?" Ryan replies brusquely. He glares at Williamson with intense eyes and flared nostrils.

"First, you request time off, not tell someone you're taking time off. Second, we only offer time off for a death in the immediate family or the spouse's immediate family."

Ryan and Williamson lock eyes. Ryan ponders his next move.

Williamson breaks the silence. "Are you going to whine to LeClair?" He says it sarcastically, knowing Ryan and the owner are close.

Ryan grits his teeth. "You jerk!" he mumbles under his breath. In a louder voice, he asks, "Do these rules apply to *all* players?"

Williamson nods.

"Fine," he says in a strained voice. "I don't expect special treatment."

Ryan sits in front of his locker before the next game. His teammates are in various stages of dress and mill about the locker room.

Clarence Foxe, the Expos' general manager, wanders into the

locker room and stops at Ryan's locker. "Sorry to hear about your sister's girlfriend."

Ryan doesn't look up at him. "It's my girlfriend's sister," he replies, hoping he will go away.

Singletary is standing close by and partially overhears Foxe's comment. As soon as the GM walks away, he ventures over. "Someone in your family get hurt?"

Ryan nods. "A close friend died yesterday."

"I'm sorry," Singletary responds. "Talk to Williamson. He has the authority to release you for a couple days."

"I already tried. He wasn't very cooperative."

"He takes joy in being a control freak." Singletary gets a sour look on his face. "He doesn't want anyone to appear more important than him."

"He does tend to have a generally annoying demeanor at times."

Singletary puts his hand on Ryan's shoulder. "You're playing good ball. Might be best for you to stick around. You don't want to anger Williamson if you want to earn a spot on the team next year."

Ryan twists his face. "I suppose. It's going to be tough dealing with a personal loss while fighting to make the team."

The Expos drop the next two games to the Dodgers, who clinch the National League West title. Ryan does a good job keeping his mind focused while he's in the game. It's when he isn't playing that his grief overcomes him.

Ryan walks into Anne Marie's condo. He pours himself a large glass of milk, grabs a chicken leg and some pasta from the fridge, and then drops down onto the easy chair. Eating in the living room isn't allowed in Anne Marie's home. What she doesn't know never happened.

Ryan glances at a picture of Gerard and Jacqui with their kids on the fireplace mantle. He leans forward, his eyes focused on Jacqui. "Anne Marie loves you dearly." He grimaces, and his eyes burn from the moisture buildup. "So do I. You and Gerard were like family to me when I lived in Thunder Bay. It hurts to think of the pain Anne Marie, Gerard, and the kids are going through right now. I wish I could be there for support." A pain above his eyebrows accompanies his agonizing thoughts.

While the Expos are losing to the Dodgers, the Pirates and Phillies split their four-game series. Pittsburgh heads to Montréal for their last four games of the year, trailing the Phillies by one in the loss column.

Ryan sits at his locker, changing out of his street clothes before the game, one eye on the television. "The *New York Yankees beat the Cleveland Indians by ten runs to clinch the American League East title. Meanwhile, the U.S. Open tennis tournament is won by Guillermo Vilas and Chris Evert.*"

Singletary stops next to Ryan. "Hey, buddy, how you doing?"

"I'm hanging in there."

"Good." Singletary gives him a close look for good measure. "I heard the Pirates' pitchers threw a lot of innings against the Phillies. They're going to start one of their September call-ups tonight."

"Yeah, I heard they're starting Odell Jones. I batted against him in Double-A and Triple-A."

Watching Jones pitch to the first couple hitters, Ryan can tell he still throws the same pitches as he did in the minors. This helps to bolster his confidence. Once the first pitch of the game is thrown, Ryan's mind focuses on the game. But when he comes to bat, the anger and disappointment of losing Jacqui gives him added strength and determination. He slams a home run thirty rows deep into the bleachers his first at bat, then crushes a line drive into the gap for a double his next turn. The hits account for three runs in the Expos' 5 – 4 win.

The Phillies lose to the Mets. The Pirates remain one game back. The next game, Ryan goes two-for-four at the plate. He scores a run and knocks a run in. The rest of the team doesn't do much to help the cause. The Expos lose to the Pirates 7 – 3.

The Phillies lose their game, leaving them tied with the Pirates for first place, with two games left in the season.

Ryan starts the next game on the bench. The players seem to be going through the motions without any real effort. The score is 4 – 0 in favor of the Pirates in the fifth. Ryan sits next to Singletary on the bench.

"No one seems to be playing with much enthusiasm," Ryan says.

"This is our 160th game of the year, fifteen games out of first place. No reason to get excited," Singletary replies. "The game means nothing to us. Hell, the fans are only here because it's fifty-cent beer night." Singletary chuckles. "Most of them are probably from Pittsburgh, anyway."

"Is this what it's like to play on a losing team?"

"Yep . . . And if you have a multi-year, guaranteed contract, you don't really care."

In the bottom of the fifth inning, the coach subs Ryan and three other players in. Ryan bats second after Andy.

"Come on, partner. Let's have some fun," Ryan tells Andy while they stand near the on-deck circle.

"Yes, sir." Andy squeezes his bat handle as he walks to the plate. He ends up working the pitcher for a walk, then promptly steals second base. Ryan slaps the next pitch into the gap in right-center field. He hustles around first then slides headfirst into second base, beating the tag. Meanwhile, Andy safely crosses home plate. Two batters later, Carter comes to the plate, works the pitcher into a full count, then blasts a fastball into the upper deck in left field.

Ryan waits for Carter at home plate with a big smile on his face. "Not showing off, are you?"

"Your enthusiasm inspired me," Carter wisecracks as they jog to the dugout. "Besides, I didn't want them to think I was some bum they could take lightly."

The Pirates get a run in the top of the seventh and go up 5 – 3.

Ryan steps to the plate in the bottom of the seventh with two runners on. He hits the ball deep to center field. The outfielder backs up against the fence then times his jump, leaping as high as he can. His effort falls a bit short. The ball ricochets off the top of the fence and into the field of play. Two runners score. Ryan stops at second base. A broad smile stretches across his face as he peers into the dugout and watches Carter and Daniels do a little jig for his benefit.

Chuck Hanner, the manager of the Pirates, sits in the dugout and shakes his head in disgust. "We were having a good game until they put that kid into the lineup."

The game is locked at five in the bottom of the ninth. Andy leads off with a line drive double. Ryan bats next and hits the first pitch deep to right field. The fielder gets to it in time to make the catch. Andy tags and beats the throw to third base. Ryan would have liked a hit, but he's happy—he moved the winning run to third base.

With one out, Hanner intentionally walks Valentin and Carter to get to the light-hitting Gomez. The hope is the weaker batter will hit a ground ball to allow for a play at home or to turn a double play and send the game into extra innings.

The Expos' manager counters with his own move. He inserts the power-hitting Manny for Gomez.

The Pittsburgh outfielders scoot to a depth in the outfield where they can make a comfortable throw home on a fly ball.

Manny wildly swings at two pitches before he plunks the third pitch over the head of the center fielder. The fielder turns and makes a terrific running catch over his shoulder. He immediately stops, plants, and throws. The ball reaches the catcher one step after Andy crosses home plate with the winning run.

The Phillies lose their game, too. The Pirates and Phillies are tied for first place going into the final game of the year.

CHAPTER FIFTEEN

Anne Marie's flight is scheduled to arrive at 2:10 PM. Ryan drives her Peugeot to the airport and parks it in the short-term lot. When he arrives at the assigned gate, he's informed the plane is delayed.

"Good gawd! You can count on the airline being late more than you can on it being on time," he tells the gate agent, who does her best to ignore him. He pops a quarter in a vending machine, retrieves a ginger ale, and then plants himself on a seat in the arrival area. A few kids and an occasional adult scurrying down the concourse slow down to look at him. They're unsure where they've seen the face before.

Eventually, Anne Marie's plane arrives, and she gets off carrying a small box. She holds her head high despite the solemn look on her face. Ryan grabs her elbow and leads her away from the crowd. When they stop, he wraps her in a delicate hug and kisses her on the cheek. He looks into her eyes. She holds his gaze. It's a look he's not used to seeing and one that weighs heavily on his heart.

"Tough week, huh?"

She nods and smiles meekly.

They hold hands as they walk through the busy airport. After a stop at the baggage claim, they load Anne Marie's luggage into the trunk of her car. She holds the box on her lap while Ryan drives.

Ryan notices the name of a funeral home on the box and assumes that Jacqui was cremated. He touches Anne Marie's leg. "I'm so sorry. I know it's going to take some time to get through this."

"My thoughts will always be with her. She was my sister and my best friend." After a few moments of silence, she says, "I have been asked to take her remains to the family farm in France, where she can be laid to rest."

"Whatever you need to do, I'll be at your side." His eyelids are heavy. "Tomorrow is my last game of the year. After that, we can go away for as long as you want."

The baseball season is down to the final game for the Pirates, who need a win tonight against the Expos to force a playoff. The Phillies played their last game earlier in the day and won.

The Pirates' ace, Dan Robertson, is slated to pitch in the do-or-die contest, while the Expos counter with best pitcher, Steve Rogers. Ryan sits on the bench, keenly focused on every pitch. This is the most consequential game he has ever been part of.

Both pitchers are at their best, and hits are hard to come by. The game works its way to the bottom of the ninth inning with the Pirates up by one. There are two outs and nobody on base. The Expos coach hollers at Ryan to pinch-hit. Excited to get an at-bat in a critical game, Ryan springs to his feet, his senses heightened.

Chuck Hanner, the Pirates' manager, takes a slow walk to the mound to check on his ace. Robertson keeps the ball in his glove, unwilling to give it up. Ryan watches the exchange from home plate. The pitcher is adamant about finishing the game. Hanner nods, puts his hands in his back pockets, and walks back to the dugout.

Robertson gets two quick strikes on Ryan, relieving some of the anxiety from the Pirates' manager. Ryan watches two balls go by before he drives the next pitch over the wall in center field. After rounding the bases, he jumps on home plate for emphasis.

Feeling energized, he scutters to the dugout, where Carter promptly confronts him. "What the heck, Dog? Now we gotta keep playing."

Ryan sits in the dugout smiling as Hanner trots onto the field to take the ball from Robertson. The pitcher hangs his head as he walks off the field. A left-handed relief pitcher is waved in from the bullpen.

The relief pitcher faces one batter and gets him to ground out to end the inning.

Ryan stays in the game and plays left field. Neither team scores in the tenth. In the eleventh, the Pirates get two runs off Davis Cole, the Expos' reliever.

"Shit! The stinking ump wasn't giving me a damn thing," Davis bitches as he throws his glove in disgust. Manny walks over and spits tobacco juice on it.

The Pirates take the field in the bottom of the eleventh with a 3 – 1 lead and visions of a one-game playoff three outs away.

The Expos make two quick outs before Ryan comes to bat. The infielders pound their fists into their gloves and shout encouragement to their pitcher. Everyone hopes for a quick end to the game. Pirates fans are on their feet, cheering enthusiastically.

Ryan hits the first pitch thrown to him up the middle for a base hit. Valentin follows with another single. Carter works the pitch count to 3 and 2 before he slams the ball into a gap in the outfield for a double, scoring Ryan and sending Valentin to third. The first three pitches to Singletary are balls. He sends the fourth pitch to the wall in center field. The center fielder plays the ricochet perfectly. Valentin scores easily from third, tying the score. Carter boldly rounds third and races for home. The center fielder fires a bullet to home plate. The ball bounces in front of the catcher, who snags it on one hop and puts the tag on Carter as he slides headfirst, extending his arm and hand forward across the plate. The umpire sweeps both arms to the side and bellows,

"Safe!" The game's over, as is the season for both the Expos and the Pirates.

Ryan bounces around the locker room after the game, celebrating the victory.

"Chill out, Dog," Carter tells him in between laughs. "No need to celebrate another man's misfortune."

"This is the first time I delivered in a critical game in my career, and I'm going to enjoy it."

Singletary approaches Ryan and offers him his hand in congratulations. "Nice series. You greatly increased your chances of making the team next season."

Ryan's smile stretches to his ears. "You have *no* idea how bad I want to be in Montréal next year."

Manager Chuck Hanner; Pete Harding, the Pirates' general manager; and John Galbert, the seventy-year-old owner of the Pirates, meet in a plush conference room in the Pirates' downtown offices. The Three Rivers confluence is visible from the window.

Still mourning what could have been, Hanner pounds his fist on the table. "That kid stole the championship from us. The rest of the Expos were ready to roll over and play dead."

"You know, I was thinking the Hutson name sounded familiar," Harding comments. "I had one of my guys look it up for me. Turns out, his brother was our first-round draft pick ten years ago."

"Where the heck is his brother?" Hanner asks. "If he's as good as this kid, we could use him."

"He played a year in the minor leagues. He was projected to start at third base for us the next year, but he got injured in Nam."

"Stupid war," Hanner says, shaking his head in disgust.

"We could use that kid on our team," the general manager says.

Galbert looks over the top of his glasses and calmly says, "Go get him."

CHAPTER SIXTEEN

Ryan and Anne Marie board the morning train to New York City. They sit quietly and gaze out the window as the first hint of sunlight appears as a yellow globe on the horizon. It gradually becomes more saturated with reds and oranges as it climbs upward. Anne Marie cradles the box with Jacqui's ashes on her lap.

"The first time I was ever on a train, I was going from Thunder Bay to Montréal," Ryan says. "So many things have happened since then."

Anne Marie's eyes smile at his revelation. "Time is carving you. Let it shape you into your true nature."

Ryan grabs ahold of her hand and gently squeezes. "Sarah is looking forward to seeing us when we're in Paris."

"It will be nice to meet your sister. How long has she been in Paris?"

"She's been studying at the Sorbonne for almost three years."

They arrive at Grand Central Station. Ryan places his hand on the small of Anne Marie's back and guides her through the bustling crowd. Everyone is going in different directions, yet nobody seems to be getting in anyone's way. Carefully orchestrated chaos.

Anne Marie stops every so often to enjoy the beauty of the massive granite building. She tugs on Ryan's sleeve. "Look at the ceiling. The painting depicts all the constellations of the zodiac." She points at a grouping of stars. "That is Capricorn, the sea-goat, your sign."

Ryan stops and looks at it for a few seconds. "Cool," he replies, then nudges her forward.

As they continue their way down the main concourse, Ryan spots an elderly gentleman in a transit authority uniform standing near a large opal-faced clock. "Excuse me, sir. Could you tell us where to catch the subway to the airport?"

The gentleman looks at Anne Marie's belly. "Fug-geddd about it, buddy. Do yous self a favor and take a cab. Especially with your doll in that condition." He points to the exit. "Just step outside that door, hold up your arm, then yell, 'Taxi!'"

A taxi drops them off at John F. Kennedy International Airport, where they board a Concorde for a three-and-a-half-hour flight to Paris.

Anne Marie and Ryan move unobstructed through Charles de Gaulle Airport. She clutches the box in both hands while Ryan holds her elbow. They stop at a bank in the concourse and exchange dollars for francs, then proceed to the baggage claim.

"*Puis-je vous aider avec vos sacs?*" a porter inquires.

"*Oui, merci,*" Anne Marie responds.

The porter gives Ryan a haughty look. "An American is not worthy of such a beautiful French woman," he says out of Anne Marie's earshot.

After loading their bags onto his cart, the porter totes them to the curb. With a quick wave of his hand, a cab magically appears. Before he allows the luggage to be loaded into the trunk, he informs Ryan, "*Cent francs.*"

"Twenty bucks!" Ryan howls. "What a scoundrel."

"Arrogant American."

"Pompous ass," Ryan replies.

Anne Marie grabs his arm. "Ryan! Try to behave like an adult . . . Now get yourself in the cab."

"*Veuillez nous emmener à' l' Hotel Rive Gauche,*" Anne Marie informs the driver.

<hr>

"What a neat old hotel," Ryan says as they settle into their room. "I can see Notre Dame from the window. And there's the river we crossed in the cab."

"I stay in this hotel whenever I come to Paris. I adore it because it is small and charming. And everywhere is an easy walk."

"We'll meet my sister at Bouillon Chartier at seven o'clock."

"Sarah has good taste. It is a historic restaurant typical of old Paris. And it serves excellent food."

After unpacking and freshening up, Ryan and Anne Marie stroll along the Seine River, holding hands. Artists sit behind their easels, painting the Paris landscape. Families, lovers, and friends stroll along the old river where so much tragedy and jubilation occurred over the past four hundred years.

"A person would be in Seine if they jumped off the bridge here," Ryan says with an impish smile.

"*Oui,* that is the name of this river."

Ryan grunts, thinking his witticism is lost on her sometimes.

Their stroll takes them down a side street adorned with cafés, art studios, and various small businesses before they reach the restaurant. They pass through the front door of the Bouillon Chartier into a large Belle Époque dining room with mirrors, columns, and high ceilings.

Ryan spots Sarah sitting at the bar with a glass of wine and chatting with a well-dressed gentleman. Sarah stands when she notices them working their way through the bustling crowd. She gives Ryan a hug and a kiss on the cheek. "I'm so happy to see you. I wish it were under better circumstances."

Ryan stands back and takes a good look at her. She's five feet, nine inches tall and has thick honey-blond hair cropped at her shoulders. A pair of black jeans shows off her slim hips and long legs. "Look at you, all grown-up and ladylike."

Sarah scoffs at him before giving Anne Marie a light hug and a peck on the cheek. "I'm so sorry for your loss, Anne Marie."

"Thank you, Sarah. It is so nice to meet you." Her eyes move from Ryan to Sarah, noticing the similar facial features. "It must have been interesting growing up with two older brothers. It was just my sister and me," Anne Marie says.

"Older brothers pick on you for their own entertainment and beat up anyone else who tries," Sarah jokes. She loops her arms inside each of their elbows. "Come, let's go sit down. The table's ready for us."

"Is your friend going to join us?" Ryan asks, nodding toward the gentleman at the bar.

Sarah puckers her lips and shakes her head. "I don't know him."

The food arrives quickly and does not disappoint. They start with avocado and shrimp, followed with spaghetti Bolognese, duck confit with baby potatoes, and roasted chicken as the main courses. The aroma from the mother sauces arouses their sense of smell and taste buds.

"How are your studies at Sorbonne?" Anne Marie asks.

"I've completed my undergraduate degree," Sarah replies. "I'll start graduate studies at the *Institut pour l'Etude des Methodes de Direction de l'Entreprise* in Lausanne the first of the year. I'm going to stay in Paris with my friend Jeanne until then." Sarah looks at Ryan. "Have you spoken with Dad lately?"

Ryan shakes his head without saying anything.

"You should try to stay in touch. You know Billy died a couple months ago?"

"Trey told me." Ryan looks down, quietly contemplating. "I loved that dog. He was so incredible. I heard he went downhill pretty fast after Mom passed." The sadness in Ryan's eyes is evident.

"He had a good life," Sarah says. "He was almost nineteen."

The next morning, Sarah meets Ryan and Anne Marie for coffee at a small café on the Champs-Élysées. The coffee shop is a block from the Arc de Triomphe. They sit at a small table on the sidewalk, under a canopy, as the early morning traffic circles the Place de l'Étoile.

"I must meet with Frederic Bert this morning. He is my associate who arranges my purchases of French antiques and their shipment to Quebec," says Anne Marie.

"I'll take good care of Ryan," Sarah replies. "Take your time."

Ryan and Sarah stroll along the sidewalk next to the Seine River. "What made you decide to go to school in Switzerland?"

"The IMEDE has a fabulous program in international law. I'm interested in foreign investments and doing business on a global basis."

They casually meander across the Seine on the bridge Pont Alexandre III.

"Cool bridge," Ryan comments as he admires the detailed sculptures of lions, cherubs, and sea monsters that adorn the walkway.

"Many people consider this to be the most beautiful river crossing in the world. I like to think of it as Paris' premier open-air museum."

They get to the middle of the bridge and stop to take in the view. The Eiffel Tower is visible on the horizon.

Sarah grabs Ryan's hand as they dawdle across the bridge.

Ryan smiles at her. "A sister is one who reaches for your hand and touches your heart."

"Aw." She leans her head against his shoulder.

Once they reach the other side of the river, Sarah stops and points to a collection of old homes and art studios along the bank. "That stone building with flower boxes under the windows is where Jeanne and I live."

Ryan nods in appreciation of the old architecture. "How did you meet Jean?"

"We met while I was visiting her studio. She's a very talented artist."

"She? I was thinking Jean was a man, like Jean-Claude Killy."

Sarah shakes her head. "Jeanne is very much a woman. A warm and beautiful person."

Ryan can see adoration in Sarah's eyes. "Can we visit her?"

"Not today. We have too many things to see. Besides, I don't think you're ready to meet her," she says with a mischievous laugh.

"Next visit. We're leaving in the morning," Ryan says. He wraps his arm around her shoulder, pulling her close. "It's been great to see you. I wish we had more time, but we're on a mission."

CHAPTER SEVENTEEN

Ryan and Anne Marie clamber aboard a train early the next morning. The train chugs south from Paris through the historic providence of Beaujolais.

Ryan gazes out the window, admiring the magnificent vineyards that are separated by dense pine forests. "It's beautiful here."

"The farther we are from Paris, the more captivating the countryside becomes," Anne Marie tells him. "It is like traveling back in time. Some of these villages have been around for centuries. The buildings are made of thick stone walls and thatch roofs."

The train continues its trek in a southeasterly direction. It slowly gains altitude as it climbs into the rocky gray Alps, traveling back and forth in hairpin turns. After several kilometers of passing through peaks rising from the earth like jagged teeth, the train starts a slow descent into a valley.

"This is Annecy," Anne Marie says as the train comes to a stop at a small stone station. "We will get off here and lease a car."

Ryan carries their bags along the cobblestone streets of the old town. A block from the train station, they cross a bridge over a canal lined with several small cafés. On the other side of the bridge vendors sell fruits, vegetables, meats, bread, and flowers.

Anne Marie points to a stone building on the next block. "That is the car rental office."

They leave town on one of the lesser-traveled roads in a small Renault. Anne Marie sits quietly in the passenger seat with the box on her lap. It's a mostly sunny day and unseasonably warm for October. High-altitude clouds race across the sky, pushed into the mountains by winds blowing in from the Mediterranean Sea.

Cars become less frequent the farther they travel into the countryside. They mostly share the narrow two-lane road with occasional bicyclists, tractors, and produce-toting trucks.

As the Renault climbs a hill, Anne Marie asks Ryan to pull over when they reach the crest.

Ryan finds a safe place to stop, then helps Anne Marie out of the car. She leans against him as they sit on the hood. Ryan is mesmerized as they gaze into a village that's no more than a kilometer away. Hundreds of rows of grapevines thrive in a valley that lies between them and the town.

"These fields used to be full of olive trees," Anne Marie says softly. "A deep freeze killed most of the trees in 1956."

Ryan has a confused look. "Why didn't they grow more?"

"Olive trees grow to be more than a hundred years old. It takes many years for them to reach their prime and optimal production. Most of the growers, including our family, could not endure the financial hardships of waiting for new olive trees to mature, so the damaged trees were replaced with hardier and quicker-growing grapevines."

They sit silently, looking across the rows of grapevines and into the small town in the distance. "The village beyond the grapes is Lourmarin. This is where Jacqui and I grew up." She takes a deep breath. "Come. Let's go."

"Are we going into the town?"

Anne Marie shakes her head. "Maybe another day. The streets are very narrow, and no cars may enter the town. Horses were the only mode of transportation when the town was built."

Back in the Renault, they cruise down a narrow road lined with trees that were planted during Napoleon's era to provide shade for his marching troops. After seven kilometers, they turn through a weathered stone gateway. On the other side of the entryway is a dirt driveway that winds through a cluster of large trees and leads to a stone farmhouse.

Anne Marie gazes out the window as the car slowly rolls toward the main house. She gives a long look at a large oak tree set back from the driveway. The massive trunk is five feet across, and the lower branches are more than two feet thick. Her attention is quickly diverted to two young girls chasing a brood of squawking chickens while a mixed-breed puppy follows close behind, yapping. Under the oak tree, a small herd of black-and-tan goats chew on fallen acorns, paying no attention to the commotion.

Anne Marie points to the house ahead. "This was our home when Jacqui and I were children. The farm has been in our family for six generations."

Behind the house is a weather-beaten wood barn. The rear of the barn opens to a fenced pasture in which several plow horses and milk cows graze. Parked in front of the barn is an old tractor and an even older produce-hauling truck.

When the car comes to a complete stop in front of the house, an elderly woman and gentleman step onto the porch.

"That is my grandpapa and grandmama." She grabs Ryan's hand before they get out of the car. "You must wait here. I am not sure how they will respond to you."

Ryan furrows his brow but doesn't say anything. He helps Anne Marie from the car, then sits on the hood.

As soon as she steps onto the front porch, Anne Marie's grandmama smothers her in a hug. "Come inside and let me take care of you, my child," she says to Anne Marie in French. "A woman with child should be taking it easy." Grandmama makes no effort to look at or speak to Ryan.

Ryan wanders around the outside of the barn to check everything out before he returns to the car to grab their luggage. As he walks toward the house, Anne Marie comes out the door, her shoulders sagging. She startles Ryan by grabbing him by the arm and then pulling him back toward the car.

"What's going on?"

"We are not staying here!"

"What . . .? Why?"

Anne Marie stops and puts her hands on her hips, gazing blankly at Ryan. "I should have told you beforehand. It is a disgrace to the woman and her family if she is not married when she is pregnant." Anne Marie's eyes are red, and she's near tears. "Bastard children are not looked upon kindly in the old country." She squeezes her eyes shut. "I was hoping she would understand when I told her I love you."

Ryan turns his palms up. "I offered to marry you."

"I told her, but she thinks I am making excuses for you."

"Now what?"

"Give me a few moments." Anne Marie grabs the box from the car and trudges toward the large oak tree they drove past. Ryan follows closely behind. She stops at the base of the tree, then drops to her knees. Using a stick and her bare hands, she scrapes away a foot of dirt, creating a hole deep enough to reach a root. Turning the box upside down, she pours the contents in the hole, then gently pats dirt over it.

Looking down where the ashes are buried, she speaks in a hushed tone. "When the life-giving rain falls upon the ground, your ashes will be absorbed into the roots of this magnificent tree. This grand oak will be a living monument to you for hundreds of years to come." She remains on her knees for several minutes, quietly reminiscing.

Ryan kneels next to her, and she rests her head on his shoulder.

She looks up at him as a tear rolls down her cheek. "I am ready to go now."

Grandmama and Grandpapa watch from the porch as Anne Marie leans against Ryan while they walk back to the Renault. Before getting into the car, she looks to the porch and blows her grandparents a kiss. "*Je t'aime,*" she mouths.

They retrace their original journey in reverse and arrive back in Montréal two days later.

CHAPTER EIGHTEEN

Ryan calls the doctor's office and informs the nurse that Anne Marie's contractions are five minutes apart.

"Is this her first child?" the nurse asks.

"No, this is her husband," Ryan replies.

"Funny man," she chides. "Stay calm and gather up her belongings, then start heading our way."

A half hour later, Ryan stops in front of the hospital, and two orderlies help Anne Marie from the car and into a wheelchair.

"I'll be with you as soon as I park the car." Ryan kisses her forehead before she's quickly whisked away.

When he's made his way to the maternity ward of the hospital, Ryan is met by a rather stout nurse with a heavy French accent. "Your wife is being prepped."

Ryan bites his tongue. He's not about to tell a French woman they're not married.

"Will you be going into the birthing room with her?" she asks.

"Yes," Ryan replies, nodding.

"Have you ever been present at a childbirth before?"

"Just once."

"How did it go?"

"Well . . . it was dark for the longest time. Then, suddenly, it got light."

"Cute," the nurse replies with a playful snigger.

"When do you think the baby will move?" Ryan asks.

"Hopefully, after he finishes high school," she says with a straight face.

Ryan's eyes light up. "I like you!"

She pats him on the butt. "Come on, handsome. Let's get you dressed and ready for the childbirth."

Ryan tries to quietly slip into the delivery room.

Anne Marie spies him. "*Allez au diable* . . . You devil!" she cries out in between contractions.

Ryan sits on the hospital bed next to Anne Marie as she cradles their newborn boy. "For such a proper French woman, you screamed like a truck driver in the delivery room."

"Your son has a fat head," she replies. "And for your information, a woman endures a lot of pain during childbirth. Having a baby is as painful as a man getting hit in the testicles."

Ryan thinks on it. "Yeah, but no man wants to get kicked in the balls more than once. Women seem to like having babies."

"*Mon Dieu*. Okay, so we will talk about something else now. We both agree that we will name our son Jacque?"

"Yes, in memory of your sister," Ryan responds.

"After your father as well. Jacque is French for Jack. I hope he will help bring you two closer."

Months Later . . .

Anne Marie sits in the back room of her home, tending to paperwork for her business while Ryan lies on the floor of the den, making silly faces at Jacque. The little boy stares at him like a startled owl. To be connected to something so innocent and precious triggers a rush of emotion in Ryan.

The sounds of Ryan's blabbering prompt Anne Marie to take a break and join her loved ones. She sits on the floor with her back against the couch. A gleam is in her eye as she looks at Ryan. "You look like such a happy man."

Ryan reaches over and squeezes her hand. "I couldn't be happier. I have a beautiful son and an incredible woman in my life. On top of that, I'm being paid to play a game I love."

Jutting out her lower lip, Anne Marie softly replies, "Yes, but that game takes you away from us."

"Next season, I'll convince them I belong in Montréal. I can't tell you how incredible it feels to come home after a game and be with my family." He leans over and kisses her on the lips. "I'm excited about our future together."

"*Moi aussi.* I hope you play baseball in Montréal for a long time."

CHAPTER NINETEEN

Each December, representatives of all the major league baseball teams and their minor league affiliates convene to discuss existing issues and set the tone for the future of the game. This winter, the meeting is held in Honolulu.

Four gentlemen in flowered Hawaiian shirts sip cocktails on the patio of the Moana Hotel. Their bamboo table overlooks the turquoise waters of the bay, which is dotted with outrigger canoes. Diamond Head can be seen in the distance on this beautiful sunny day.

Matt LeClair, the Canadian real estate tycoon, has property that John Galbert, the construction magnate from Pittsburgh, wants. Each businessman is joined by the general manager of their baseball club: Clarence Foxe and Pete Harding.

"My guys like that Hutson kid," Galbert informs his counterpart. He taps his cigar on the edge of an ashtray.

"I'm sorry. He's not for sale," LeClair says, moving his head side to side.

"You have several young outfielders on your roster, and, quite frankly, your pitching isn't that good. I think we can work something out."

Foxe takes the umbrella out of his drink and tosses it aside. "He's an excellent young prospect. We think he's going to be a heck of a player."

"Cut the crap." Harding slaps the table. "He's older than every outfielder on your roster."

"Maybe so, but he has a lot of talent," LeClair responds, not showing any emotion.

"You like him better than Valentin, Raines, Dawkins, and Cromartie?" Harding asks. "All of whom are younger than him."

LeClair looks upon the bay. The sound of the small waves gently washing ashore is calming. "We're fond of the lad in Montréal. I don't believe we could ever trade him away."

"You're going to have to sign him to a Major League contract and put him on the big-league roster or lose him in the Rule 5 draft," Harding says as he studies LeClair. "Somebody will draft him."

LeClair calmly takes a swallow of his Rob Roy.

"If you're going to lose one of your young outfielders, you might as well get something in return. We'll give you a pitching prospect and cash," Harding offers.

"Excuse us. Clarence and I have things to tend to," LeClair politely informs the Pirates' representatives as he slides his chair back to stand up.

"Damn you," Harding says. "All right, final offer. We'll give you a starting pitcher and a pitching prospect."

LeClair looks over at Galbert. "How much cash are you willing to throw in?"

It's been nearly three months since Anne Marie and Ryan returned from France. Ryan relaxes in his favorite easy chair in front of a fire as he watches Renee, Anne Marie's employee and tonight's babysitter, play with Jacque. Anne Marie is in the bathroom, putting the finishing touches on her makeup before they head out to dinner. The ringing phone breaks the serenity of the moment.

Ryan picks up the phone. "Hello."

"Ryan. Matt LeClair."

"Good evening, Mr. LeClair."

"I felt obligated to make sure you hear it from me first." He pauses for a second. "The Expos have traded you to Pittsburgh."

"Huh?" Ryan's mouth opens in a silent scream. "I've been traded to *Pittsburgh?*"

"It was strictly a business decision. We ran out of options for you."

"I don't understand options, sir. This is my home. Anne Marie and my kid are here. I'll stay for less money if that's an issue." Anxiety kicks in, and he starts to get lightheaded.

"Money isn't the issue. You're a heck of a ballplayer, but we're loaded with players in the outfield. The Pirates gave up a lot of talent to get you. We need that talent more than we need you sitting on the bench or playing in the Minor Leagues."

"Couldn't you trade someone else?"

"The other outfielders are locked into major league contracts. You're not. By the way, you may want to get an agent before you talk to Pittsburgh."

"Aww, geez."

"Barclay and I watched you come to town from Thunder Bay as a wild-eyed kid. You've grown into a man with determination. We were asked to keep an eye on you. Now it's time for you to step up and take control of your destiny."

Ryan takes a deep breath, then slowly lets it out. "Anne Marie and I are heading out to dinner. We'll talk it over."

"I'm sorry, Ryan. There's nothing to talk over. You're a Pittsburgh Pirate now."

Anne Marie enters the room as Ryan hangs up. "Who was on the phone?"

Ryan's brain is numb as he grabs Anne Marie's coat and helps her put it on. "I'll tell you over dinner."

. . .

Their favorite table is waiting for them when they arrive at Chez Queux. Ryan pulls the chair out for Anne Marie. A flickering candle flashes shadows across the dimly lit table.

"*Excusez-moi*," the waiter says as he reaches in to pour each of them a glass of wine.

"Will you tell me what the telephone call was about? It seems to have upset you."

Ryan takes a deep breath through his nose then blows it out his mouth. He slides his chair closer to her and grabs her hand. He looks into her eyes, searching for the right words. His heart is pounding, his mind racing. "You have beautiful eyes."

"Ryan!" She gives him a stern look.

He looks down, knowing the disappointment the news will bring. He looks up with a heavy heart and says, "The Expos traded me to a team in Pittsburgh."

Anne Marie's eyelids droop as she releases a mournful sigh. "Just when things were going so well, and it looked like we would be spending more time together." Her voice trembles ever so slightly. "I won't see you often enough during the summer months."

"You and Jacque can move to Pittsburgh with me. Think how much fun that will be," Ryan says, trying to pick up her spirits.

"No. I have my shop in Montréal."

"We can sell the shop. You don't have to work. You can be a full-time mother."

"I love my shop. It is my career. Antique collecting is as much my life as baseball is yours."

"Then we'll buy you a shop in Pittsburgh. I'm sure they like antiques in Pennsylvania."

"French artwork and antiques are my specialty. My business has a connection between Paris and Quebec. It would be difficult to get my products into Pittsburgh. Besides, what if you transfer next year to St. Louis and then San Francisco? Am I supposed to sell my shop and move every time they want you to go to another city?" She fidgets with her earrings while talking. A tear glistens on her cheek in the candlelight. "I knew from the first moment I fell in love with you that you would always be away from home. When it looked like you might play sports in Montréal, my thoughts drifted toward marriage and our future together."

Ryan runs his fingers through his hair then holds his hand at the back of his neck. "I have to go to Pittsburgh if I want to be a baseball player," he says softly.

"You *are* a baseball player—you must go. Jacque and I will be fine here. I love you and will look forward to seeing you every opportunity possible. I survived when you were in Mexico, Quebec City, and Denver, and we will survive while you are in Pittsburgh." She smiles meekly to mask her disappointment. "Let's have more wine to celebrate your good fortune."

"I love you. I'm so lucky to have you," he says in a hushed tone.

The next morning, after reading about his trade in the *Montreal Gazette*, Ryan gives his brother a call.

"Hi, Trey. What's up?"

"Hey, Ryan. You remember Uncle Joe? We found out he was gay during a recent family outing."

"I guess he didn't know about the new contraceptive for men. You put it in your shoe, and it makes you limp," Ryan counters.

"Cute. So, how are things in the North Country?" Trey asks.

"Looks like I'm moving south. The Expos traded me to the Pirates."

"Some mistakes are too much fun to only make once. I guess they didn't learn anything when they signed me."

"Is Kelci around? I'd like to talk to her."

After a few minutes of silence, Kelci picks up the phone. "Hey, wander boy. How are you? How's the baby?" she asks in her usual spirited voice.

"Anne Marie and the baby are both doing great. I'm heading off to Pittsburgh."

"Seems like you're always on the go."

"I was traded by the Expos to the Pirates. I'm going to need some legal representation. I believe you offered your services?"

"Sure. I'd love to work with you. This stuff is kind of new to me. Give me time to do some research, then let's get together and talk."

"I'll talk to Anne Marie. Maybe we can come down for a visit. It'll be nice to get out of the cold weather for a while."

———

Ryan sits at the kitchen table, talking on the phone to a travel agent about flights to Asheville.

Anne Marie walks up behind him and puts her hands on his shoulders. "If you are looking at flights to North Carolina, you should know the change in cabin pressure triggers ear pain in babies."

Ryan hangs up the telephone. "Guess we'll drive or take a train." He presses his lips together and smiles. "Either way, it's going to take a day to get there."

CHAPTER TWENTY

The early morning train ride from Montréal to New York is uneventful. They share a cabin with an elderly couple who take turns holding Jacque and doting over him, a reprieve for Anne Marie and Ryan.

In New York, they transfer to a train headed to Washington, D.C. Things heat up in the cabin when a young lady with spiked blond hair and heavy makeup sits in the seat across from them. She removes her full-length wool coat, exposing a red vinyl miniskirt and a low-cut cashmere sweater.

Ryan leans into Anne Marie and whispers, "Do you think that's a flower above her left breast?"

He obviously didn't whisper it soft enough because the young lady replies, "No. It's the wing of a butterfly. Would you like to see it?"

"He does not need to," Anne Marie immediately responds.

"It's no big deal," the young lady says. "Nowadays, you can see boobs and sex on TV. By the way, my name is Chris."

"I am Anne Marie, and this is Ryan. And just to be clear, Chris, we do not have sex on the TV in our house."

Ryan nods in agreement. "You can hurt yourself if you fall off."

Anne Marie rubs her forehead. "He is always going to be my biggest child and the one that requires the most attention."

The comment brings a smile to Chris' face. "Your wife's pretty hip, Ryan."

"We are not married," Anne Marie responds. "Marriage is a fine institution, but I am not ready to be put into an institution. Although he drives me in that direction sometimes."

Chris clicks her nails nervously as she feels Ryan studying her closely. "Is something bothering you?"

"Have you ever lived in Denver?"

"I did for a little while," Chris replies. "Why do you ask?"

"I knew a boy named Chris that lived there."

Chris' eyes open wide, and she's clearly appalled. "Do I look like a boy to you?"

"Well, no. Not now."

Anne Marie knows what's going through Ryan's mind. Looking to save everybody from any more embarrassment, she politely asks, "Do you have any sisters or brothers, Chris?"

"I'm an only child. What's the deal with him?" she says while looking at Ryan, who's sitting grim-faced.

"He had a lightbulb moment," Anne Marie replies.

Chris gets a nervous look on her face. "I'm going to see if there's a bar on this train." She quickly gathers up her belongings and slinks out the door.

Ryan turns his palms up. "Sometimes my thoughts run free."

"Try to control them around other people."

They get off the train in D.C. and, after a brief layover, board a train to Asheville. Shortly after they've gotten comfortable in their compartment, three college kids burst in, apparently looking for a place to crash. As if on cue, Jacque starts screaming bloody murder. The piercing sound sends the kids scampering to find another place to chill.

"Good timing, son," Ryan says as he watches Jacque latch onto his mother's nipple.

The sound of the grinding wheels on the track lull Ryan to sleep. After what seems like minutes, the train screeches to a stop, awakening him.

He opens his eyes to see Jacque's smiling face and gives him a kiss on his nose.

"Welcome to North Carolina," Anne Marie says.

Trey stands on the platform, watching the passengers exit the train. He spots his brother shuffling down the steps and races over to take their suitcases from him. Ryan grabs ahold of Anne Marie and Jacque to help them off the train.

As soon as everyone is on solid ground, Trey grasps Anne Marie's hand, then kisses it. *"Bonjour, mademoiselle."*

Ryan gazes at his brother, rolling his eyes at his mock chivalry.

"Coucou, little *bébé*," Trey coos as he lightly touches Jacque's nose. Then he stands up straight, puts a hand on Ryan's back, and shakes his hand. "Welcome to North Carolina, Shorty. How was the trip?"

"It was kind of boring until this young lady . . ." Ryan pauses when he notices Anne Marie glaring at him.

"What about the young lady?" Trey asks.

The sound of the train pulling out of the station fills the air.

"Sorry. I lost my train of thought."

The sun dips toward the distant mountains, turning the bright blue sky into a sea of glowing pink clouds. Trey leads everyone along a walkway next to the brick train station to a small asphalt parking lot. He nods in the direction of a dual-color Ford Bronco. "Your chariot awaits." He tosses their suitcases in the back.

Ryan hops in front with his brother while Anne Marie settles in the back with the baby.

Trey guides his truck onto a two-lane road, then looks at Anne Marie in the mirror. "I'm sorry Kelci couldn't come with us. The pregnancy wears her down. Plus, C.J. was sleeping when we left."

"It is fine. I do not mind sitting back here and listening to you two talk nonsense."

"I love talking about nothing," Trey replies. "It's my best subject."

"You and your brother," Anne Marie sighs.

"How's your boy doing?" Ryan asks.

"C.J. will be a year-old next month. Our next baby's due in four months."

"Jacque's fourteen weeks," Ryan replies. "It's got to be a handful to have a little one running around with Kelci being pregnant."

"When you got a kid acting up, you take two aspirins and follow the directions on the bottle." Trey chuckles as he steers the truck onto a highway. "Especially the part that says, 'Keep away from children.'"

"C.J.'s a good nickname for Carl Jackson," Ryan comments.

"Yep," Trey replies. "Grandpa was Carl. Dad's Jack. And, of course, I'm Trey."

A few miles south of Asheville, they exit the highway, then migrate onto a side road lined with trees. Trey hits the high beams as he navigates down a narrow, curving road that's barely wide enough for two cars. After a couple of miles, he turns onto a one-lane gravel road that slowly climbs up the side of a hill. The gravel road eventually turns into a concrete driveway, which leads to a stone ranch.

Two large dogs circle Ryan, making low throaty noises as he gets out of the Bronco. "Shoo," Trey hollers, scattering them. Ryan takes the baby as Trey helps Anne Marie out of the car.

There is a crackling sound followed by flying sparks as embers in the fireplace collapse. A deer head mounted above the mantle keeps a watchful eye over the room. Kelci rocks Jacque in her arms as Trey sits close on the leather love seat. Anne Marie sips from a glass of wine while Ryan gets comfortable next to her on the matching sofa.

"Nice pad," Ryan comments. "It's a step up from the trailer that used to sit on this lot."

"I kind of liked that old trailer," Trey muses. "But you know how women are. They don't think a home should come with wheels."

Kelci glances at Trey in a loving way. "I prefer something a little more stable."

"It's gotta be neat living in the mountains, surrounded by rivers and forests," Ryan comments.

"It's beautiful." Kelci pats Trey on the thigh. "We're very happy here. This part of the country is growing fast, and Trey has enough work to keep three crews busy."

Trey and Kelci's cheerful demeanor is comforting to Anne Marie. It makes her feel like family. "Are you a full-time mother?" she asks.

"I do odd jobs at home," Kelci replies. "My office is in the back of the house. I manage Trey's business while he's out on projects. I also review legal documents for a couple companies. It keeps me challenged, plus I can stay at home with C.J."

CHAPTER TWENTY-ONE

Shortly after breakfast, Ryan and Kelci meet in her office. An antique oak desk, a bookshelf that occupies the better part of one wall, and an oval conference table take up most of the room. A large picture window overlooks an expansive, grassy backyard that blends into a wooded hillside.

Ryan grabs a seat at the conference table. "Nice workspace."

"It's functional." Kelci grabs a manila folder off her desk then joins him at the table. "I talked with Mr. Harding, the general manager of the Pirates. When I mentioned that I was married to Trey, he asked me to invite him to spring training as his guest."

"That was nice of him," Ryan says.

"Not really." Kelci shakes her head. "Just a negotiating ploy to soften us up."

"Oh, okay." Ryan sets his hands on the table and intertwines his fingers while Kelci leafs through the folder. "Where are we at in terms of a contract?"

"You're entering the second year of a two-year contract. According to the original agreement, you're to be paid the Major League minimum of $21,000 if you make it to the big leagues." Kelci looks up from the documents she's perusing. Ryan gives her a blank look. "The Pirates realize that's unreasonable, so they're offering you a three-year contract for $75,000 per year."

Ryan half shrugs. "Sounds reasonable."

"It's not," Kelci says in a direct voice. "The average Major League salary is expected to be $91,000 a year next season. Do you think you're an average player? Trey doesn't think you are." Kelci grins as Ryan's face flushes with pride. "Mike Schmidt of the Phillies is the highest-paid player in baseball. He earns $560,000 a year. Do you think you're as good as Schmidt?"

"No, but I could be."

"Exactly my point. Do you want to be stuck at $75,000 two years from now if you're one of the better players in the league?"

Ryan shakes his head. "Not really."

They look at each other in silence for a few seconds before Kelci responds. "I cancelled negotiations with the Pirates. I told them you were willing to play out your contract at the $21,000 minimum salary."

Ryan's eyes bug out. "You're kidding!"

"Nope. They countered with $92,000 a year for four years."

"Good girl," Ryan responds enthusiastically.

"I rejected that offer, also."

Ryan freezes. "Huh?"

"I've talked with some people, and they believe team owners are colluding to keep salaries down. There's been a tremendous increase in cash flow from television and other advertising outlets." Kelci leans back and crosses her arms. "Players aren't being paid in proportion to this growth in revenue. A rumor's bouncing around that something could be breaking soon in terms of salaries. Let's not lock into anything just yet."

Ryan lets out a weak laugh. "I don't know what to think."

"Let me do the thinking." Kelci gives him a playful look. "We stick at the current $21,000 salary. If you're concerned about money, I'll pay you the difference between $92,000 and $21,000."

"I couldn't ask you to do that."

"Don't think I'm doing this for free. As your representative, I get ten percent of all your future earnings. I'm pretty sure I'll get that $71,000 back tenfold."

She slides a piece of paper across the table and hands him a pen. "This is a representation agreement. Sign and date it for me, partner."

Ryan smiles at her. "Should I have my lawyer look at it?"

"You already have."

"Wow. I never would've figured all this stuff out myself."

"You just focus on playing baseball, and I'll take care of every-thing else."

CHAPTER TWENTY-TWO

Ryan and several of his Pirates teammates jog along the outfield fence in their shorts and T-shirts. Today is the first day that position players report for spring training. Most of the minor league players, including Ryan, arrived several days earlier.

The Pirates' spring training facility in Bradenton, Florida, has players' dorms, coaches' suites, offices for the staff, and four full-sized practice fields. All minor leaguers are required to stay in the dormitories, two per room. The Major League players prefer accommodations more fitting their stature.

Ryan slows his jog to a walk. His shirt is covered in perspiration. Jerry Harris, his dorm mate, ambles alongside him, huffing and puffing. The air feels like a wet blanket, suffocating and clinging to their bodies. Several major leaguers make their way onto the practice field as Ryan and Jerry catch their breath.

Jerry nudges Ryan in the ribs and points toward the entrance to the field. "There's Dave Parker."

"I heard he had a pretty good season last year."

"Have you heard the latest on him?"

"Not yet."

"He signed a five-year, five-million-dollar contract. First million-dollar-a-year professional athlete."

"All right!" Ryan pumps his fist. "That's good for all of us."

Ryan and Jerry continue walking across the outfield when Olivares, one of the young Latinos invited to camp, jogs up to them.

"Hey, *amigo*," he says to Ryan. "Some man is looking for you."

"Oh yeah? Who would that be, Ollie?"

Olivares turns and points to a small group of players chatting. Right in the middle is someone wearing an Asheville Tourists baseball shirt who has everyone in stitches.

"Oh, geez." Ryan breaks into a hearty laugh. He looks over at Jerry. "Excuse me. I need to go talk to my brother."

When Ryan gets close enough to the congregation, Trey announces to everyone, "Hey, everybody, here's my baby brother."

Ryan's face takes on a rosy hue as he glances around. "If you're trying to embarrass me, Trey, it's working."

"I want to introduce you to some of my friends, Shorty." Trey rests his arm on Ryan's shoulder. "This is Willie Stargell and Doc Ellis. They played for the Pirates when I was on the team."

Stargell looks at Ryan with the big smile that typically adorns his face. "My friend Jerry Carter says you're a hot dog."

Ryan snorts. "That comes from a man who thinks cow tipping involves leaving a gratuity."

"That'd be Jerry," Stargell responds with a belly laugh. "I beat your brother in a home run–hitting contest when we first met." He looks Ryan up and down. "I challenge you."

"Age before beauty, Pops." Ryan points toward the plate.

Stargell grabs a bat and lumbers toward the batter's box. "Í got you beat in both categories."

A large gathering of players and sportswriters gather to watch the power-hitting contest.

Stargell blasts the first four pitches well over the fence in right field. On the fifth pitch, he reaches back and slams the ball with all he's got. It leaves the practice field while still ascending.

"Definitely foul," Dale Berra, one of the young players watching the competition, declares.

Stargell purses his lips and glares at Berra. He turns to Ryan. "Your turn, Hot Dog. Let's see if you can beat four in a row."

Ryan steps up to the plate. He sends the first pitch a few feet over the fence in left. The next pitch, he connects for a high fly that clears the fence in right by several yards. The next two hits are line drives over the fence in straight-away center. On the fifth pitch, he slams another line drive, which lands at the base of the fence in right field.

"Okay, we keep going," Stargell announces.

"No, I'm humbled just to tie you, Willie. Let's leave it at that," Ryan says, resting his bat on his shoulder. "And please, don't get accustomed to calling me Hot Dog."

Stargell slaps his big hand into Ryan's. "Okay, Ryan."

Trey playfully bumps shoulders with Ryan as they walk away from the crowd. "That was a class act, bro."

"Thanks. I was afraid that last one might clear the fence when I hit it. Definitely didn't want to show up the Captain the first day at practice." They take several steps in silence before Ryan says, "Did you hear about Parker's salary?"

Trey rubs his index finger and thumb together. "*Mucho dinero.*"

Ryan nods. "Kelci's pretty sharp. She saw a salary spike coming."

"She's usually right on about most things," Trey replies. "But if not, like a good wife, she forgives her husband when she's wrong."

Stargell, Berra, and a couple other Pirates wander over to Ryan and Trey.

"You two seem pretty tight," Stargell comments.

"We're family," Trey responds.

Stargell smiles and nods. "Family, I like that."

Berra extends his right hand to Ryan. "Hi, Dale Berra."

Ryan gives him a wondering look as he shakes his hand. "Ryan Hutson. You related to Yogi?"

"He's my dad."

Ryan laughs. "Your dad, Plato, and Winnie the Pooh are my favorite philosophers."

Dale grins at the bizarre comment. "Bertrand Russell once said, 'Whoever wishes to become a philosopher must learn not to be frightened by absurdities.' That's how Dad thinks."

The comment gets a chuckle out of Ryan. "Do you play catcher?"

"Nah, I play third base."

"Really? What does your dad think of that?"

"He says third ain't so bad, so long as nothing's hit at you."

"That's funny." Ryan grins. "What's the craziest thing he ever said to you?"

Dale ponders for a moment. "Probably when we were sitting with Whitey Ford at Yankee Stadium watching an Old-Timers' game. The scoreboard flashed the names of deceased Yankee greats. Dad turns to Whitey and says, 'I hope I never live long enough to see my name up there.'"

Trey grabs a ball and tosses it with Willie. After a few throws, Willie informs him, "You don't throw the ball as hard as you used to."

"Willie, I still throw the ball just as hard as I ever did. It just doesn't get there as fast nowadays." Trey takes off his glove and sticks it under his arm. "I have too beautiful a mind to be wasting it on you guys. I'm going to go hang out with the coaches."

After a long day of workouts, the coaches send the players on a quick jog before stopping practice for the day.

"You going to join us for a run?" Ryan yells up to Trey, who's standing in an observation tower with a couple of the coaches.

"I don't jog anymore, little brother," he hollers back. "The ice cubes keep falling out of my glass of bourbon when I run." Trey looks over at the coach standing next to him. "You don't realize how easy this game is until you're up here criticizing the players."

"Brings back a lot of memories, doesn't it?" the coach asks.

"Yeah, I had some good times," Trey replies.

"Are you upset how things turned out for you?"

"Nah. Doesn't pay to be upset. Besides, I got to play for a month in the big leagues and bat against some of the best pitchers in baseball. Every kid's dream. Now I have a house in the mountains, a beautiful wife and kid, and another kid on the way. Even got a hunting dog to boot."

"Yeah, I suppose we all find happiness in different ways. I love staying busy with baseball. I met the woman of my dreams. But as soon as we got married, she put on fifty pounds."

"She's growing on you," Trey teases.

"I tell her I love her just the way she is, but she never listens. She just keeps putting on more weight."

The Pirates break camp with Ryan penciled in as the starting left fielder.

A light dusting of snow is on the ground as Ryan rushes from the airport terminal to Anne Marie's Peugeot. A brisk wind makes it feel like it's twenty degrees colder than it is. He gets in the car and quickly slides his hands under her heavy sweater, warming them on her ribs.

"Eeeiii, *mon Dieu*," Anne Marie shrieks. "Do not touch me."

"But I miss you, honey, and I can't keep my hands off you." He moves his hands to her belly. "You used to not be able to resist me when I came back from long trips."

She pushes away from him. "Yes, but not when your hands are ice-cold and we have our son in the car."

Ryan looks into the back seat. Jacque's strapped into his car seat, giggling. Ryan leans back and gives his son a kiss on the cheek. "I've only been away two months, and he looks like he doubled in size."

CHAPTER TWENTY-THREE

Ryan starts his first full season of major league Baseball in a respectable manner. The first month and a half, he bats .289 with nine homers. The Pirates play a little less respectably. They trail Montréal by six games for first place in the National League East.

Ryan maintains a steady pace as he jogs through Schenley Park. His run takes him along the streets of the Oakland neighborhood of Pittsburgh, which are lined with buildings of exquisite architecture that include homes, eateries, and lively pubs. Sweat rolls down his back as he slows his pace to a steady walk. When he gets to his new home, he sits on the front steps and takes a drink from a water bottle, then dumps the rest on his head. He rents the second floor of a vintage house from an elderly couple. From his perch on the steps he looks into the Monongahela Valley and the smog rising from the steel mills. *I wonder how much of that crap I'm breathing in.*

When he gets his second wind, he heads up to his apartment. The landlords keep the living quarters in pristine condition: eighty-year-old hardwood floors that look brand-new, leaded glass windows with wood frames in perfect condition, and restored antique fixtures in the bathroom and kitchen. He grabs a ginger ale out of the refrigerator, then plops down on the couch with the phone in hand. He punches #1 on the speed dial.

"*Bonjour.*"

"*Bonjour, mon amour,*" Ryan replies.

"Ryan, how are you?" The excitement in Anne Marie's voice is contagious.

"I'm well, baby. I miss you."

"I miss you, also. So does Jacque. He was scooting across the living room on his bottom today. He is so cute. Yesterday, I heard him say, 'Mama.'"

"He's growing up fast," Ryan says, feeling a little dejected about missing these precious moments.

"When are you coming home?"

"We don't travel to Montréal until next month."

"Jacque may be walking by then," Anne Marie says, in jest.

"It's hard being away from you guys." Ryan grimaces. "Will you visit me in Pittsburgh?"

"*C'est possible.* Maybe next weekend?"

"Argh. We're flying out to the West Coast for two weeks on Monday."

"Oh, my goodness." Anne Marie laughs. "Jacque just fell over sideways while he was trying to crawl."

"Is he okay?"

"Yes. He is giggling his little head off." She picks him up and puts the phone next to his head. "Say hello to Papa."

A garbling sound reaches Ryan's ear as Jacque tries to stick the phone in his mouth.

"We should record him speaking now so when he learns to talk, he can tell us what he was trying to say."

"I am sure he was saying he loves his daddy . . . It is beautiful outside. We were getting ready to go for a walk when you called."

"Go ahead. I'll talk with you later. Love you."

"We love you, also. Good day, dear."

Ryan holds onto the phone, wishing he was going on the walk with them, then puts it in the cradle.

Ryan can't get a hit to drop the next three games. The Pirates lose two of the three games, each by one run. *Don't let it get into your head,* he tells himself. But it may be too late.

Monday morning, Ryan tosses his personal belongings in the overhead bin, then grabs a seat next to the window. Stargell lumbers down the aisle of the TWA 747 and eases his large body onto the seat next to Ryan.

"Hey, Willie."

"What's up, Ryan?"

"Nothing."

Willie glares at him. "I mean, what's going on with you? You're not your jovial self, and it shows in your batting. We need you to start hitting the ball so we stop losing ground to Montréal."

"All I hear lately is Montréal, Montréal," Ryan grumbles. "You know I got a family there, Willie. My kid's nearly eight months old, and he's starting to recognize things and trying to talk." Ryan's eyelids droop. "He doesn't know who his dad is." He pauses for a beat. "You got a home, Willie? You got kids?"

"Yeah, I got five kids. And Pittsburgh is my home. It's not a fancy city, but it's real. It's a working town, and money doesn't come easy. People expect an honest day's effort, and I've given it to them for a long time. They're looking for the same from you."

"Sometimes, it's hard to give it your all, especially when you've got other things on your mind."

"You need to get back to having fun. This shouldn't be work. Don't overthink it."

Ryan takes a deep breath and sighs.

Willie looks at him intently. "Having a family to think about makes you a man. That's what separates you from the young kids on the team who've got nothing to worry about but themselves and where their next beer is coming from."

Willie stands up and strolls down the aisle of the plane. The cabin is quiet. Most of the players are reading or listening to music. "Listen, everyone," he bellows. "We need to start having some fun. Henceforth, I'm going to give out Stargell Stars. Everyone will get a gold star for making an exceptional play."

Laughter fills the airplane.

"You the man, Willie," Parker hollers.

"I haven't gotten a gold star since my elementary school teacher passed them out for spelling," Berra spouts.

Fans slowly trickle into Dodger Stadium on a sunshiny Southern California afternoon. With a bat in hand, Ryan heads toward home plate to take a few swings before the game. Bill "Mad Dog" Madlock, a hefty Black man with a full beard and a mass of wild hair falling from beneath his hat, walks away from the plate. He has an attitude about as gruff as his looks.

"Yo, Mad Dog," Ryan says as he approaches his teammate. "You been swinging a hot bat lately. Any tips you can give to get me back on track?"

"There ain't no right or wrong way to bat, Hutson. People always trying to make up new ways. There ain't no new ways. The game's not changed in two hundred years, and it's going to be the same for the next two hundred. Just go up there with determination and hit the damn ball."

Ryan stands at the plate, looking to regain his confidence. He hits shots to the different fields and jacks an occasional one over the fence. Eventually he feels better about his hitting and heads to the dugout.

Stargell is sitting on the top step of the dugout and slaps him on the backside as he walks by.

"Things are good, Pops. Thanks for the pep talk the other day."

"I knew you'd come around," Willie says.

"I just lost my focus for a bit. I'm used to having my mind one hundred percent on the game when the first pitch is thrown."

Willie grins. "It's all right. You're allowed to be human."

Ryan sits on the bench between Berra and Harris.

"You know the Pirates used to be called the Alleghenies," Harris says.

"I didn't know that," Berra replies.

"Yep. They kept stealing players off other teams, so the other teams started calling them the Pirates. Eventually, the nickname stuck."

"I'll be darned. You learn all kinds of things playing baseball," Berra remarks.

Ryan steps up his game in California. Knowing he has Anne Marie's full support in everything he does helps him to keep a clear mind. He loves his family, and thinking of them makes him feel good inside instead of bothered. He gets sixteen hits, including three home runs, during their West Coast swing. The Pirates take eight of twelve games from the Dodgers, Padres, and Giants. They close the gap to six games behind the Expos before they head to Montréal for four games.

CHAPTER TWENTY-FOUR

Anne Marie leans against her Peugeot, wearing a stretchy miniskirt and stylish V-neck blouse as she waits outside the airport. It's a hot day, and it's only going to get hotter. Several young men stop to introduce themselves. She's flattered, but they aren't what she's looking for.

Ryan strolls out of the sliding doors of Montréal-Mirabel Airport, wearing a pair of jeans and a T-shirt.

"*Tres* sexy," Anne Marie murmurs, looking at her man. She waves her hands over her head to get his attention.

Ryan smiles at her as he picks up his pace. As soon as they are next to each other he wraps his arms around her and lifts her off her feet. After a long, passionate kiss, he sets her down.

"I have missed you," she purrs into his ear while kissing his neck.

His hands slide down the small of her back onto her hips, then across her small, firm tushy. "Um, you have nothing underneath."

She pushes him away. "You drive," she says, handing him the keys.

"Am I going to be safe behind the wheel?"

She looks at him and tilts her head. "Jacque is at Renee's for another three hours. Do you want to talk about it or drive?"

. . .

While Anne Marie is in the process of unlocking her front door, Ryan pulls her close and slides his hand up her miniskirt.

She slaps his hand. "Stop that!"

Ryan whispers into her ear, "Sexual stimulation in unexpected places releases hormones that increase passion."

"My passion does not need to be increased. What if somebody is watching us?"

"Then they will see what a beautiful ass you have."

Twenty-five minutes later, the washing machine finishes its final cycle. Ryan steps back and pulls up his pants, and Anne Marie hops off the machine.

As they sit on the couch in the living room, Anne Marie hands Jacque to his dad. Ryan hasn't seen his son in three months. The boy immediately starts screaming and reaches for his mother. Despondent, Ryan hands his son back to her, instantly silencing his shrieks. "You'd think I was poking him with a needle."

Anne Marie scoots closer to Ryan while holding Jacque. "It is okay. This is Papa."

A big tear runs down Jacque's cheek. He sticks his finger in his mouth as he keeps a watchful eye on Ryan from the safety of his mother's arms.

"Hi, Jacque." Ryan leans toward the boy while softly talking to him. He appears to be winning him over until he reaches out for him. All hell breaks loose again.

"He will be okay. He is not used to being around men—most of his time is spent with me and the girls at work. Give him time. He will come around to you."

. . .

By the second day, Jacque is getting used to having his dad around. The two of them sit at the kitchen table, Jacque in his highchair. He looks at Ryan with curiosity and hesitantly allows him to stick a spoonful of strained carrots in his mouth. Everything seems to be going okay until Anne Marie walks by. Then Jacque sticks his arms out and says, "Mama."

Ryan gets an exasperated look on his face. "I guess you need a pair of boobs to keep his attention?"

"Just like his father," Anne Marie replies.

"Yeah, but I don't look at them as lunch."

By the third day, Jacque is sitting on his dad's lap. Ryan feels a mix of warmth and joy as he bounces the smiling boy on his knee. "Can you say 'Papa'?"

The Pirates' first game against the Expos is on an overcast Saturday afternoon. Ryan receives a polite round of applause when he comes to bat in the bottom of the second. The Pirates have a runner on second base. Jerry Carter is crouched behind home plate in his catcher's gear.

"I was thinking about you today, Hutson . . . I was at the zoo looking at the baboons."

"You know, I used to like you, Carter. Until you talked me out of it."

Ryan swings at the third pitch and sends the ball crashing into the tenth row behind the left field fence for a two-run home run. He looks into the stands as he rounds the bases. The fans are mostly quiet, except for a few clusters of people standing and cheering. "Geez, I used to be popular in this town," he murmurs.

"Hot Dog," Carter rags from his catcher position as Ryan crosses home plate.

Ryan gains a greater appreciation for the hit when Coach Hanner informs him the homer was off the pitcher the Expos traded him for.

A back-and-forth ball game works its way into the fifth inning.

The Pirates cling to a one-run lead. Ryan comes to bat with a runner on second and promptly drills a line drive in the gap, driving in another run. Ryan smiles, looking at a clearly unamused Carter standing behind home plate with a deadpan look on his face.

The Pirates are still up by two in the bottom of the seventh. Andy Dawkins leads off with a shot down the left-field line. Ryan rushes over, fields the ball after two bounces, plants his back foot, and guns Andy down as he slides headfirst into second base. Andy gets to his feet covered in dust, then touches the bill of his cap and nods at Ryan. The Expos fans politely applaud Ryan's throw. They know how fast Andy is.

The game ends 5 – 3 in the Pirates' favor.

Ryan is sitting in the chair in front of his locker after the game when Willie ambles up. In his booming voice, he announces, "Three Stargell Stars for Ryan's outstanding plays today."

Ryan laughs off the perfunctory award. "All the plays in the game were important," he tells his high-spirited teammate. "Let's carry the momentum over to tomorrow."

Nights spent with Anne Marie and Jacque and their ample leisure time together allow Ryan to unwind and decompress, fostering a tranquil state of mind. He plays some of the best baseball of his life while in Montreal. He fantasizes about this moment never ending.

The Pirates end up taking three of the four games against the Expos, and their deficit in the standings is cut to four games.

On Ryan's sixth and final day in Montréal, Jacque calls him "Papa" for the first time. He also doesn't squirm and try to get out of his dad's arms when his mother walks by. Ryan feels a sense of connection and gives the boy a kiss on the cheek. "Hopefully, you'll remember me when you see me again in a month."

CHAPTER TWENTY-FIVE

The season reaches the halfway point with the Pirates three games behind the Expos in the standings. The team has been playing good ball, but hasn't been able to string enough wins together to catch the Expos.

Ryan is batting .309, with twelve home runs. Mad Dog is leading the league in batting average, and Parker is in the top five in batting, home runs, and runs batted in. They're loaded with individual talent but aren't playing with unity. As captain of the team, that bothers Willie. He calls everyone together for a players-only meeting before everyone disperses for the All-Star break.

Willie stomps about the room as everyone sits in front of their lockers.

"What's up, Willie?" Mad Dog shouts out. "We got places to go."

"I know, and that's the problem," Willie says. "Everyone has somewhere to go, and nobody has time for each other."

"Come on, Willie. Cut through the crap," someone barks out.

"All right, I will," Willie says, bouncing his head. "We're getting excellent pitching and hitting the ball well. We're winning enough games to stay in the pennant race, but we don't have what it takes to be champions."

There's grumbling and snickering in the locker room.

"We're playing like a bunch of individuals, not a team." Willie pauses as he thinks back to spring training when Trey had his arm around Ryan's shoulders and said, *we're family.* "We need to come together as a team," Willie says. "Rally around each other. Act like a family. And that includes everybody: the players, fans, concession stand workers, and even the front office." Willie looks around the locker room. "Go on, get out of here. But come back from the break with a new attitude."

Ryan has three entire days to spend with his family in Montréal during the All-Star break. The happy couple dote on their son, pushing him through Old Montréal in his carriage and playing with him in the grass at Parc Angrignon. The little guy shrieks with delight when they visit a petting zoo and a baby llama licks his fingers.

Ryan and Anne Marie share a deep intimacy during his time off. They constantly kiss, hug, and touch each other, even in public. Their profound affection for each other and for their baby fills their days with laughter and joy. After three days of beautiful union, the heartache of parting settles in again as Ryan prepares to leave.

He gazes into her big brown eyes. "It never gets easy, does it?"

She smiles, masking her sorrow. Instead of sharing her disappointment, she projects positive energy to keep his spirits up so he'll stay focused on baseball. "Go out there and show them what a great player you are."

He looks at her with tender eyes. "You're my biggest cheerleader."

Ryan leaves Montréal to join the Pirates in New York for the second half of the season.

The Pirates are in the locker room, preparing to take the field, when Stargell strolls to the center of the room with a boom box. He punches the play button, and the sound of Sister Sledge bounces off the walls. *"We are family. Get up, everybody, and sing."*

Stargell starts swinging his big hips and snapping his fingers. He grabs Olivares and Berra in each of his huge hands and pulls them into the middle of the locker room. "Dance!" he commands.

Mad Dog immediately jumps to his feet and shows more moves than a bucket of worms. Halfway into the song, everybody on the team is doing their best disco dancing.

Full of adrenaline, the Pirates hit the field and proceed to pound the Mets 9 – 0.

Following the same pregame ritual, the Pirates win fifteen of twenty games and pull within one game of the Expos. High fives, back slapping, and playful jostling is the norm in the locker room during the winning streak.

Late August, the Expos pay a visit to Three Rivers Stadium. The Pirates can take over first place during the three-game home stand.

Things aren't going as well as the home team would like during the first game. They trail the Expos by two in the ninth. As the Pirates come off the field to bat, Stargell looks up to the press box and nods.

"We Are Family" blasts through the stadium speakers, and the fans jump to their feet and start singing and bouncing. The song continues until the first pitch is thrown. Sadly, the first batter strikes out, and groans of disappointment fill the stands.

The music and singing start up again as Berra approaches the plate. He hits a deep fly to left—the crowd jumps to their feet. The left fielder backs up to the warning track, reaches above his head, and snags the ball.

Ryan's up next. The fans are back on their feet as Sister Sledge blares through the speakers. He responds to the fans' gaiety by hitting a hard grounder in the gap between first and second for a single. The fans clap in unison as Mad Dog comes to the plate. He watches two balls go by before he smashes a line drive into right-center field. Ryan races to third, and Mad Dog stops at first. Sister Sledge is cranked up to a near deafening loudness, maintaining the enthusiasm of the crowd and players.

Parker, the million-dollar man, is up next. He swings at the first two pitches, fouling both off, then watches two balls go by. He cranks the fifth pitch into the upper deck in right field. The Pirates win 3 – 2. Each of the three hitters is awarded a Stargell Star.

With "We Are Family" as their anthem, the never-say-die Pirates are on a roll. They sweep three games from the Expos and take over sole possession of first place.

The players are in the locker room hooting and hollering when Coach Hanner ventures into the middle of the room. "Great playing, team. First place!" he shouts, projecting his voice to be heard over the celebration. "Now let's build on that lead!"

The room fills with cheers.

Hanner points toward the locker room door, which immediately opens, and two assistant coaches cart in several tubs of beer on ice.

Everyone is quick to grab a bottle and toast each other. The cheering and locker room antics heat up until a toast between Rick Rosen, a starting pitcher, and Bart Howell, a utility infielder, is a little too exuberant. The bottles smash when they make contact. The room erupts in laughter until players notice blood gushing from Rosen's hand.

A jagged piece of glass creates a deep slice in Rosen's palm that ends up requiring eleven stitches. The doctor anticipates the starting pitcher will miss at least five starts.

Owner John Galbert and general manager Pete Harding meet in

Galbert's downtown office. Harding paces about the room as the owner sits behind his desk.

Galbert releases a menacing growl, then raises his voice. "It's been six years since we won a championship. The entire city is rallying behind the Pirates. Even the mayor is pulling for us—he says it's great for the local economy."

Harding shakes his head. "The Expos are a game behind us. It's going to be a gamble to go into the homestretch minus one of our top pitchers."

"Then make a trade." Galbert leans back in his chair. "I don't want to let this city down. We've come too far not to finish the job."

"It's going to cost us," Harding says, pulling on his ear.

The Pirates have just beaten the Braves 6 – 4. Ryan sits across from Harding in the general manager's office at the stadium. He's still in his uniform, covered in dried sweat and dirt. The cologne the GM is wearing overwhelms the room.

"Holy socks," Ryan sputters. "You traded me to the California Angels?"

Harding sits quietly, a cold stare in his eyes.

"I'll be thousands of miles away from my family." A wave of dread washes over Ryan. *Take a moment to breathe and stay calm,* he tells himself. It's easy to think that but harder to do.

"Sorry, son," Harding says. "Baseball is a business."

"And I'm just a pawn," Ryan says, gritting his teeth.

"You can go now." Harding points to the door. "I have things to tend to."

"Good to know." Ryan stands. He glares at Harding as a variety of names he'd like to call him come to mind. He decides he's a better man, and leaves quietly.

Ryan returns to an empty clubhouse and sits in front of his locker, struggling with his thoughts and the knots in his stomach. *Three thousand miles from Anne Marie and Jacque. I don't know when I'll see them again. They're the most important part of my life.* The revelation jolts his senses. *The most important part of my life is what I always said about baseball.*

Before he can ponder the subject any further, Stargell ambles into the room and positions his large body next to him. "The coach told me the news. Hate to see you go, Ryan. You're a heck of a ballplayer."

"Obviously, not everybody feels that way," Ryan replies. His eyes are narrowed, and he has a slightly raised upper lip.

"When the Angels heard we were looking for a pitcher, they zeroed in on you." Stargell puts a hand on Ryan's shoulder. "They want you pretty bad. They gave up a good veteran pitcher, which we need, and a second-round draft pick."

Ryan starts to change out of his uniform. "Wonderful."

"You sorta forced the issue," Stargell says with a raised eyebrow.

Ryan throws his shoulders back and gazes intently at Willie. "Really?"

"Really. You're playing under a minor league contract, which expires at the end of the season. You could walk away, and the Pirates may not get anything."

There's a silent pause as Ryan recalls his salary conversation with Kelci.

Willie's voice brings him back to reality. "The Angels are in first place in their division, a couple games ahead of the Royals. You're jumping into a competitive situation. They're going to need you to bring your best."

"So I could play against the Pirates in the World Series?"

Willie shakes his head. "No. You and the pitcher we get aren't eligible for the postseason because of the timing of the trade. The good thing for us is by then Rosen will be off injured reserve and able to pitch in the playoffs."

When Ryan gets back to his apartment, he grabs an Iron City lager from the fridge and sprawls across the couch. The shock still lingers. He picks up the phone to call Kelci.

She answers after five rings.

He fills her in on his conversations with Harding and Willie, then groans. "I love Anne Marie and Jacque. I don't want to move farther away from them."

"I don't see that you have any options if you want to play out the rest of the year." Kelci's voice is thick with unspoken sorrow.

"Can I sit out the rest of the year and sign a contract with a new team?"

"First off, you aren't going to be a totally unrestricted free agent at the end of the season. The holder of your contract—in this case, the Angels—owns your rights. And, even if we could find a way to get you out of your contract, it's not likely the Expos would take you back. They traded you because they didn't need you."

Ryan heaves a deep sigh.

"Go home for a couple days, Ryan. I'll clear things with the Angels." There's a moment of silence on the line before she says, "Take it easy and talk it over with Anne Marie."

CHAPTER TWENTY-SIX

Not wanting to be interrupted, Anne Marie and Ryan hold off discussing their future until Jacque is asleep. They sit across from each other at the grand Victorian dining table in Anne Marie's condo.

"I've been traded to a baseball team in California."

They stare at each other in silence.

Anne Marie's lower lip trembles. "Are there no options?"

Ryan looks down at the table, shaking his head. "Not really." He chews on his bottom lip for a few seconds. "Will you marry me?"

She quickly jolts her head back. "That does not solve the situation. You confuse me talking like this."

"I love you and Jacque. I don't want to be so far away. I'll quit baseball and find a job in Montréal."

Anne Marie's body tightens at his response. "Baseball is your dream, and you are just now starting to live that dream." There's fire in her eyes. "Do not give up. You would not be happy without baseball."

"I'm not happy at the thought of living across the country from you and Jacque."

"I will always support you in your dream." She grasps his hand and looks deeply into his eyes. "Maybe one day you will settle with a team, and we can get married and live together year-round. For now, we can be happy living apart for five months and visiting each other when we can in the summer."

"What do you mean, when I settle with a team?"

"You have been playing major league baseball for only a year, but already you will have been on three different teams."

"And?"

"I cannot marry you, sell my business, and follow you around the country with a child my entire life."

"What are you saying?"

"I have read that some baseball players stay with one team their entire career." She looks at Ryan with a tight-lipped smile. "You find a place where you can stay permanently, and then Jacque and I will come live with you."

Ryan looks at her, his eyes squinted. "Are you okay with me going to California?"

"I am not happy, but it is what you must do for now."

Ryan has a devilish grin on his face. He gets up, walks over to her side of the table, and then helps her to her feet. "I love you for more than your beautiful looks." Putting his arm around her waist, he guides her to the bedroom.

Standing next to the bed, they slowly undress each other. Ryan kisses her neck as he lowers her onto the bed, then gently lies against her. Heat radiates outward from Anne Marie's body with the touch of Ryan's lips on her skin.

Anne Marie stops her car at the curb in front of the Air Canada departures. "Do well, Ryan. This is a wonderful opportunity for you."

He kisses her deeply then backs off. "One day, I'll control my destiny, and we won't have to keep saying goodbye."

She blinks back a tear. "I look forward to that day."

Jacque is in his car seat. He wiggles his fingers after Ryan kisses him goodbye.

Ryan catches a flight to Minneapolis, then grabs a cab to Metropolitan Stadium. He arrives midafternoon, three hours before the game.

Wandering beneath the stadium seating, he encounters a security guard, who points him in the direction of the visitors' locker room. Ryan enters a large room with cubicles made of light-colored wood. Most of the floor is covered in gray carpeting, and several black leather easy chairs and matching couches are situated in the middle of the room. Behind the dressing area are individual shower stalls, treatment rooms, and the coaches' offices.

Ryan wanders around, checking everything out until he locates a cubicle with his name on it. His new uniform and equipment are stored within. He sits in a padded chair in front of his cubicle and starts changing into his uniform.

Fifteen minutes later, a stream of players begin entering the room. Ryan takes a minute to chat with each of them. Most knew he would be showing up today.

"Hi, Ryan. I'm Joe Rudi," a pleasant sort of guy says in passing.

"Welcome to the Angels." A large Black man sticks his hand out. "I'm Don Baylor."

A tall man with a quiet demeanor walks by and nods at Ryan.

"Hey, Ryan. I'm Bobby Gregory. The talkative guy that just walked by is Nolan Ryan."

"I recognized his face."

"That's his game face. He's intense on days he's pitching. Especially today. We've dropped our last six games, and our lead over the Royals has dropped to one game."

"No shame in losing, as long as you don't give up fighting," Ryan says.

"Maybe you can give us a needed shot of adrenaline."

Laughing softly, Ryan shakes his head. "I'm here to play ball, not be a cheerleader." He finishes buttoning his jersey. "I'm going to head out to the field and loosen up. I haven't played in a few days. I'll catch up with you later, Bobby."

Nolan Ryan is matched against Jerry Koosman, his ex-teammate on the Mets. Both pitchers are on the top of their game today. Nolan gives up three hits and one run while striking out nine through eight innings. Koosman, on the other hand, hasn't given up a run.

In the top of the ninth, Joe Rudi leads off with a walk. Playing it cautious, the Twins' manager brings in a relief pitcher to close out the Angels. Two batters and two outs later, Ryan steps to the plate. Rudi is still on first.

Ryan watches the first two pitches. The first one is a ball inside. The second pitch is a strike on the outside corner. The third is a fastball down the middle, which he blasts over the wall in right-center field for a two-run homer and the lead. Ryan jogs around the bases, feeling a lightness in his body. He's happy to come through in the clutch in his first game with his new team. As soon as he touches home plate, his teammates mob him.

Nolan walks onto the field next to Ryan in the bottom of the ninth. Looking at Ryan, he says, "I just needed a little run support. I'll take it from here."

Nolan shuts down the Twins in the bottom of the ninth with greater velocity on his pitches than he started the game with.

The players mingle on the field after the game. A middle-aged man dressed in khakis and an Oxford shirt makes his way over to Ryan. He looks like an ex-jock with his athletic build. Streaks of gray hair highlight his mustache and sideburns. "Hi, Ryan. Dean Goetz, *L.A. Times*. How'd it feel to get that hit?"

It strikes Ryan as a silly question, but still pumped from getting the game-winning hit, he responds anyway. "It felt awesome. I hit it solid. I knew even if it didn't clear the fence, Rudi would score. Once it cleared the fence, I was pretty happy."

Goetz walks away to interview another player. Baylor, the veteran on the team, comes over to Ryan and puts his arm around his shoulders. "A word of advice. L.A. is a big media center. The sportswriters can make you or break you."

"Thanks. I'll keep that in mind."

The Angels and Twins square off again the next night. Ryan nails another two-run home run and a run-scoring double. He accounts for four of the runs in the Angels' 5 – 2 victory.

Goetz approaches Ryan after the game. "Nice hitting today, Ryan. The Royals keep winning, also. You think you guys can hold them off?"

"I don't think about the Royals. I'm only concerned with the Angels," he tells Goetz before he turns to walk away. Under his breath, he says, "You ask stupid questions."

Goetz stops in his tracks and looks at Ryan. "Excuse me?"

Ryan looks at Goetz and shakes his head. "We just need to focus on our game and not worry about what anyone else is doing."

The Angels close out their series with the Twins the next night. They fire on all cylinders. The Angels collect fifteen hits, three of which are home runs, and cruise to a 10 – 2 victory. Ryan has three hits and a home run.

Goetz searches out Ryan after the game. "Three home runs in three games. You seem to have inspired the offense since joining the team. Do you think your teammates look to you for leadership?"

Ryan has a far-off look in his eyes, like he would prefer to be talking to a wall, but he remembers what Baylor said about the press. "Baylor and Rudi are the leaders," Ryan says. "I just happened to get some key hits that helped the team."

The White Sox are next on the schedule. The Angels continue to play lights out and win three of the four games in Chicago. Ryan has seven hits, two home runs, and nine runs batted in during the series.

After two weeks on the road, the Angels head back to California.

CHAPTER TWENTY-SEVEN

Carl Langston, a twenty-year-old rookie, sits next to Ryan on the flight to Los Angeles. He seems like a nice guy to Ryan, maybe a little brash. Word is he's busting with talent.

"You're a popular guy in L.A. right now," Carl says.

Ryan shrugs nonchalantly.

"Goetz has been submitting articles about you to the *L.A. Times* on a daily basis. According to him, you saved the season for the Angels."

Ryan leans forward, his eyes opened wide. "You're kidding me! He really said that?"

"Yep. The local sports anchors have been singing your praise. You're all the rage in L.A."

"How do you know this stuff?"

"My wife. She keeps me up-to-date on what the L.A. media is saying about us when we're on the road. By the way, she thinks you're kinda cute and wants to know if you're single. Her sister is a knockout."

"How does she know that I'm an incredibly handsome and charming man?"

"Um, she said kinda cute. You do know they televise our games back home, and the newspapers have published pictures of you?"

"I wasn't aware they were televising our games. And how'd they get pictures of me? Can they use my picture without me knowing?"

"I thought spotting the TV camera is one of the first things you learn when you reach 'The Show,'" Carl says.

"I must have slept through that class."

Goetz wanders over to where Carl and Ryan are sitting. "Excuse me, Carl. I'd like to speak with Ryan. Could you swap seats with me for a few minutes?"

"Don't do it. Don't do it," Ryan mutters softly so only Carl can hear him.

"Absolutely, buddy," Carl replies.

"Aww, geez," Ryan mumbles.

Goetz slides onto the seat next to Ryan with his notepad in hand. "You've put up some impressive stats since becoming an Angel. Five homers and eighteen RBIs in seven games. You're going to get a hero's welcome in L.A."

"I hope not. I don't like being the center of attention."

"L.A. is a sports-crazed town. The Angels were riding their longest losing streak of the season when you showed up. Their lead was reduced from six games to one. To put it mildly, there was a little anxiety amongst the fans." He taps a pen on his notepad while talking. "As soon as you arrive, the team wins six of seven games and builds their lead to three games. You're a savior. The fans have fallen in love with you."

"They don't even know me."

"I've written some favorable articles about you."

"Aww, man. It's a team game—it's not all about me. And I can't believe you're using pictures that I don't know about. Is that legal?"

"The pictures are property of Major League Baseball. You signed a release with the Pirates, which is where I got the pictures. L.A. fans love you and are clamoring for information about the new guy. Everyone loves a good personal success story. You know, rags to riches. From what I hear, you've had a very colorful past. Want to talk about it? Maybe give me an exclusive?"

"No!"

———

The Angels deplane at the Orange County Airport. Kelci and a tall, slim gentleman with slicked-back gray hair greet Ryan in the waiting area. He gives Kelci a quick hug and kiss on the cheek.

The Angels players passing by acknowledge the man standing next to Kelci.

"Hey, Buzz."

"Hi, Buzz."

Goetz wanders by. "Hi, Kelci."

Ryan looks at Goetz, then frowns at Kelci.

The gentleman with Kelci steps forward. "Hi, Ryan. Welcome to Los Angeles. I'm Bill Buzzi, general manager of the Angels."

Ryan shakes his hand. "Pleased to meet you, sir."

"I've arranged a room for you at the Hyatt Regency. Your belongings will be sent over."

Ryan looks at Kelci, who smiles at him. "I was sleeping with fleas a year ago," he says.

"A car and driver are waiting outside to take us to the hotel," Buzzi says. "We'll use a conference room there to go over a few things."

Ryan sits next to Kelci in the limousine. Buzzi sits across from them.

"You started your career with the Angels with quite a bang. Mr. Arturo, the owner, is impressed," Buzzi says.

Kelci winks at Ryan and replies, "It also gave your agent a little leverage in negotiations."

"Mr. Arturo has no problem paying players that produce," Buzzi says.

. . .

Kelci and Ryan sit across the table from Buzzi in the hotel conference room. Ryan peruses a stack of papers. "You've read through all these and agree to the terms?" he asks, looking at Kelci.

Kelci nods. "That contract is the result of several days of negotiations."

Ryan looks at her and raises his eyebrows. "Three years for $975,000?"

She nods, a content look on her face.

"Only three other people on the team make more than $300,000 a year," Buzzi says, a proud look on his face. "Two of them are future Hall of Famers."

"Also, you're in Los Angeles, the entertainment capital of the world," Kelci says. "Several companies have inquired about your availability for endorsements. There's even some guy from the *L.A. Times* that wants to write a story on you."

Instead of showing excitement, Ryan has a solemn look. "I'd like to talk this over with Kelci in private, Mr. Buzzi."

Buzzi immediately springs to his feet. "Sure, son. Y'all know how to get ahold of me."

Alone in the conference room, Kelci asks, "What's on your mind? This is a very good contract."

Ryan shrugs. "Anne Marie and I talked. We're not sure we want to commit to living in California."

Kelci grabs his arm to make sure she has his full attention. "You've been playing on an outdated contract. You need a major league contract. First, this one is good money *and* has excellent terms. It doesn't mean you're going to spend the rest of your life in L.A. We can always renegotiate. You need control over things like trades, free agency, and other issues that may arise. Just consider this offer a placeholder."

"I don't understand all this contract stuff. I just know I don't like being so far from my family."

"Trust me. A couple good years and you can write your own ticket. We need to do this for now."

"Okay." A wave of relaxation washes over Ryan. He releases a deep breath and gives Kelci's hand a squeeze. "My first major league contract. I couldn't be more thrilled. Thanks, Kelci."

She tilts her head toward the door. "Let's grab something to eat and celebrate."

———

Three weeks are left in the regular season, and the Angels are home for the next two. The California sunshine feels like vitamins penetrating Ryan's skin. The aches in his joints feel much better, and other than daydreams about Anne Marie and Jacque, he maintains a clear mind. When possible, he talks with them on the phone every day. Anne Marie has the *L.A. Times* delivered to her office so she can keep tabs on how he's doing.

The Angels win ten of the next twelve games, increasing their lead over the Royals to five. Ryan stays hot, swatting four home runs and eleven RBIs. In the short time he's been on the team, he's won the adoration of the fans and has become a popular man around town. He takes his success in stride, greeting it with a friendly smile and a modest attitude.

On the last game of the home stand, the Angels are down by one in the eighth. Two runners are on base when Ryan comes to bat.

The announcer calls the at-bat. "*Hutson swings at the pitch. It's a shot down the line. Fair ball! It's a long run for Hufner, the left fielder. The ball ricochets around the left field corner. One run scores; Rudi is waved home. The throw to home is cut off. No throw to the plate. Everyone's safe. A two-out, two-run double by Hutson gives the Angels the lead.*"

The Angels win the game by one.

Lisa Bower, a reporter with a local television station, approaches Ryan in the festive locker room after the game. Standing 5 feet ten inches, she has a slender build and wears her long blonde hair in a ponytail. In her prior life she was a softball player at Pepperdine

University. She stands close to Ryan, one arm around his waist and a microphone in the other hand.

"Awesome hit, Ryan. You seem to rise to the occasion."

He laughs softly. "Every hit was big today, Lisa. Mine just happened to occur at a critical time."

"You seem to be able to go deep when you need to."

"You gotta nail it when you get the chance." He winks at her playfully. "Without the guys on base in front of me, my hit wouldn't have meant anything."

The Angels hit the road for the final seven games of the season. Their first stop is Oakland; then they close out the season with three games in Seattle.

They clinch first place after winning their second game against Oakland. After the game, the team rushes to the locker room where several cases of champagne await their arrival. It isn't long before everyone is doused in sparkling wine and hooting at the top of their lungs.

Lisa stands next to a shirtless Ryan in the locker room, her hair and blouse drenched. She holds a microphone near his face. "You've brought a lot of life to this team since you arrived."

"You brought a lot of life to this locker room when you arrived." Ryan chortles.

"You're always in the middle of the action. Seems appropriate you scored the run that clinched first place."

He shrugs the comment off. "I was just lucky to be in the right place at the right time." He gives her a shoulder hug. "Yeehaw!" he hollers while holding up a bottle of champagne.

Goetz works his way through the crowded locker room and separates Ryan and Lisa. "Way to come through in the clutch, partner. Now unclutch her."

"Hey, Goetz, success is making the best of opportunities that present themselves." Ryan douses him with champagne.

CHAPTER TWENTY-EIGHT

The Angels board a plane to Baltimore the day after the regular season ends. They'll face the Orioles in a five-game series for the American League playoffs.

Ryan is not eligible for the playoffs, but management hopes having him around will maintain the enthusiasm he's brought to the team.

No such luck. The Angels are eliminated on their home field, three games to one.

When Earl Weaver, manager of the Orioles, is asked what winning the pennant means to him, he replies, "Now days, you try to accomplish in five games what used to take 162."

Most of the Angels lounge in the locker room, acting apathetic after losing the final game.

Ryan sits next to Baylor in front of his locker. "I've been studying sign language," he tells him. "It's pretty handy."

"Read this." Baylor flips him the bird.

Goetz wanders over and joins the conversation. "Any thoughts on the game?"

"You know your team sucks when the highlights on television include a squirrel racing across the top of the dugout," Baylor says.

Goetz sighs. "It was a tough series."

"We're better than this. We just can't prove it," Baylor says, then slips away.

Goetz grabs Ryan's arm before he can escape. "What do you feel your absence meant to the team?"

"You media guys make a bigger deal of it than you need to," Ryan says. "The Orioles are an outstanding team. They had a great season."

"You know, the fans will have higher expectations next year with you on the team for an entire season."

Ryan is a little tired of Goetz's constant questions. "Good to know, Goetz." After taking a deep breath to compose himself, he says, "I play to win and do the best I can. Don't be filling the fans with any kind of expectations that I'll be a savior."

"You had a breakout year, Ryan. You batted .317 with twenty-six home runs and twenty-eight stolen bases. Had you played the entire year in one league, you might have won Rookie of the Year. I see great things for you."

"Statistics are like bikinis," Ryan replies. "They show a lot but not everything. Speaking of which, here comes Lisa. Excuse me."

Ryan strolls up to the young reporter. "Hey, Lisa, I was just thinking about you."

"Do you believe in coincidences?" Lisa asks.

"Are you kidding me?" Ryan says with a grin. "I was just going to ask you the same question."

Ryan has a message to call Kelci when he gets back to the hotel.

"Hey, Kelce. What's up?"

"I'm in town. Let's have dinner and talk."

"Sure. I have no plans. I don't catch a plane to Montréal until tomorrow."

"Uh, that's what I want to talk about. Let's eat at the hotel. I'll meet you in the lounge in half an hour."

Ryan has an uncomfortable feeling when he hangs up the phone.

The hostess at the hotel restaurant is a high school girl, smartly attired in a peasant dress trimmed in lace. She leads Ryan and Kelci to a quiet table in the rear. It's a nice restaurant, as far as hotel eateries go. It has clean tablecloths and subdued lighting. Ryan wears a pair of jeans and a golf shirt. Kelci, whose trim figure returned quickly after having her second child, is dressed in black slacks and a white silk blouse.

Kelci sets down her menu. "I understand you want to get home to Anne Marie and Jacque." She pats his hand. "But your popularity has jumped exponentially. We might want to take advantage of it while we can."

"That's why you're my business manager."

Kelci pushes her hair behind her ear. "First of all, you should show your face around town for a few weeks before you head back to Montréal. I've looked into a few charity events and a couple social outings."

Ryan slumps as he looks at Kelci. "There's going to be a disappointed lady in Montréal if I don't get on that plane tomorrow."

"We can fly Anne Marie and Jacque out here if you like."

"I've already asked her to join me. She doesn't want to fly with Jacque until he's older. He turned one recently."

Kelci presses her lips together. "It's your call. I'm just letting you know that several companies are willing to put up good money to get your face associated with their products."

"Are you talking TV commercials?"

She fidgets with her earrings as he speaks. "TV commercials, magazine ads, radio spots, billboards."

"I guess I'm cool with doing some promotions and earning extra cash. But I won't represent anything I don't believe in."

Kelci picks her handbag off the floor and removes some papers. "I wouldn't expect that of you. Here's a list of companies that reached out."

Ryan takes the list from her and gives it a close look. He frowns at a couple companies.

"How about the Chevrolet dealer?" Kelci asks. "He's offering good money. You do a TV spot and show up at his dealership for a couple hours one day to sign autographs."

"I don't know anything about them."

"They'll sell you a car at cost and give you a service package for free. That way you're a satisfied customer. You're going to need a car in L.A. anyway, and it looks good if you buy local."

"Okay, I'll check it out."

Kelci slides her chair next to Ryan. "I also like this men's clothing manufacturer." She points to it on the list. "You'll get a quality wardrobe for free. Plus, you'll get paid handsomely."

"Sounds like you got me covered."

They work their way through the list. Ryan nixes most of the inquiries. "No attorneys, chiropractors, or tobacco products," he says.

"All right, let's move on to other things. *Sports Illustrated* wants to meet with you, a local talk show has approached us about an appearance on their show, and Goetz wants to do a story on you."

"Goetz is a pest."

"He controls your public image. Be nice to him."

"I don't need him telling all these bleeding-heart liberals that I was a conscientious objector."

"Come on, Ryan. You're talking about California. These people are like granola bars—they're mostly fruits, flakes, and nuts. They would probably applaud your stand against the war."

"I'll think on it."

"Fair enough. One last thing. Tax protection. I have a house in Malibu I want to show you tomorrow."

"Seriously?"

"You can't stay in this hotel all the time. You need the tax break. Plus, it's going to be an outstanding investment." Her noses crinkles as she says, "Besides, I need a place to stay when I visit. Speaking of investments, I opened an account with a brokerage firm and bought a few stocks to get you started."

The first thing Ryan does when he gets back to his room is call Anne Marie.

She picks up after one ring. *"Bonjour,* Ryan. Jacque and I are so excited to see you tomorrow." The enthusiasm in her voice resonates through three thousand miles of telephone wire.

His heart sinks in his chest, and his voice warbles as he speaks. "Um . . . I need to stay in L.A. for a bit. There are business matters I need to tend to." He quickly raises the tone and speed of his speech. "But after that, we have the rest of the summer to do as we please."

There's a moment of silence on the line. Ryan can't see the sad look in her eyes, and she hides the disappointment in her voice. "Of course," she replies. "You must do what you think is best."

"Arrgh!" Ryan slams the phone down when they're through talking. He feels like kicking himself for agreeing to do the promotional work.

CHAPTER TWENTY-NINE

At 10 AM the next morning, Ryan is behind the wheel of a 1967 Corvette Stingray with an endorsement contract in hand. Kelci sits beside him in the passenger's seat. The top is off, and the wind blows through their hair as they race toward Beverly Hills.

"You could have gotten a new Vette," Kelci says.

"Yeah, but this baby is a classic. Look at it. It's in perfect condition. I love the removable hardtop."

Their next stop is the office of Bobbie Jones Clothiers on Wilshire Boulevard.

As soon as they walk through the front door, they encounter a well-built man in his mid-twenties sitting behind a glass desk and wearing a tailored three-piece suit.

"Good day. How may I help you?" he asks, taking a break from whatever it is he's doing.

"We have an appointment with Roberta. I'm Kelci Hutson."

"Ah, yes. She's expecting you. I'm Eduardo." He gets up from his desk while appearing to look down his long tanned nose at Ryan's attire. "Please follow me to the conference room."

They walk down a hallway lined with pictures of movie stars, athletes, and politicians wearing ensembles ranging from casual to formal. Eduardo opens the door to a glass-walled conference room. "You may wait here for Ms. Jones. Would you like a glass of wine?"

Kelci politely declines, but Ryan is quick to interject, "Would you fetch me a beer, Eddie?"

"We don't serve beer." He turns abruptly and walks away.

An oval cherry conference table surrounded by ten matching chairs fills the center of the room. Kelci grabs a seat at the table and opens the folder she brought with her. A TV with a built-in VCR and a large white marker board are positioned against the front wall.

Ryan walks over to the outside wall, which is a floor-to-ceiling window. He watches people stroll along Rodeo Drive for a minute, then suddenly lets out a snort. "Oh, my gawd! That lady dyed her poodle pink."

After a wait of nearly twenty minutes, a tall, statuesque woman enters the room. A form-fitting business suit adorns her shapely body. She quickly extends her hand in greeting. "Good day, Kelci. Hello, Ryan, I'm Roberta. It's a pleasure to meet you."

Ryan stands in front of her, looking directly into her eyes as they shake hands.

"Yes, I'm a tall woman who likes to wear high heels," she says brusquely.

In a moment of lightheartedness, Ryan quips, "Your heels elevate you to a whole new height."

"I wear high heels because I got tired of being kissed on the forehead." She picks up the phone and engages in a brief discussion with Eduardo.

Meanwhile, Ryan turns to Kelci and, in a hushed voice, says, "Her hair is pulled back so tight it makes her eyes look slanted."

"I think she might have had a face lift," Kelci whispers back.

"Do you think she had her boobs done?"

"Try to keep your mind on business."

"That's a lovely suit. Professional yet elegant," Kelci says after Roberta hangs up the phone.

"Thank you." She looks at Ryan, who's studying her outfit. "Women dress for women and undress for men."

"If women dressed for men, stores wouldn't sell much more than an occasional sun visor," Kelci replies.

Roberta slides a chair out from the head of the table and sits down, prompting Ryan to join the women at the table.

Roberta gives Ryan's arms and chest a piercing gaze. "If you come on board with us, you'll be required to wear our clothes when you're out and about. We'll provide a full wardrobe, custom-fitted, and it will be updated continuously. Fashion is something that goes out of style as soon as someone buys a piece of clothing."

Ryan looks at Roberta and grins. "In one year and out the other."

Roberta appears immune to Ryan's frivolities. "We will provide you with beachwear, jeans, T-shirts, casual slacks, shirts, suits, and tuxedos that will look good on you and reflect positively on Bobbie Jones Clothiers. As long as you remain a popular person in California, we will pay you monthly to wear our clothing."

Ryan has an inquisitive look. "T-shirts and beachwear will be custom-fitted?"

"Of course," Roberta replies with a flip of her wrist. "If any piece of clothing says one-size-fits-all, it doesn't fit anyone." Roberta continues to study Ryan's body intently. "We'll also furnish you with footwear. It's impossible to be well-dressed in a cheap pair of shoes. What size do you wear?"

"Eleven."

Roberta nods her approval. "Large feet as well as big hands on a man bode well."

There's a light knock on the door. A short man with round spectacles and gray hair enters, carrying a small pedestal.

"This is Giuseppe, your tailor."

Giuseppe asks Ryan to step onto the pedestal. He pulls a measuring tape out of his pocket and starts determining his inseam. He's moved on to measuring Ryan's shoulders when Eduardo enters the room with several typed forms.

"Would you like to come down from your pedestal and review these contracts?" Roberta asks.

Giuseppe looks up at Ryan and says, "It's all right, I got your back."

Ryan grabs a seat at the table and leafs through the contract. He looks at Kelci. "You've read these already?"

She nods. "I wrote the terms."

Roberta hands him a pen.

Ryan signs the contract and hands the pen back to her. She grasps his hand. "It will be a pleasure doing business with you. Giuseppe will finish taking your measurements, and we'll start making your clothes."

"Suits me," Ryan replies.

"Once the clothes are made, we'll meet with the photographers. You can expect to start seeing yourself in magazines, in newspapers, and on billboards immediately. Don't lose that cute smile. And please don't put on any weight."

"You don't have to worry about his weight. He's being paid to exercise at Atlas Gym. He'll work out," Kelci says.

"Where would you like us to send his wardrobe?"

Kelci scribbles down an address and hands it to Roberta. "Here's his home address."

Ryan gasps. "I own a house!"

Kelci nods.

"But I haven't even seen it."

She scrunches her nose and smiles. "You'll love it."

<h1 style="text-align:center">CHAPTER THIRTY</h1>

Ryan and Kelci cruise along Route 10 to Santa Monica and then proceed onto the Pacific Coast Highway. The elevated road curves sharply as it hugs the shoreline. "New Kid in Town" plays softly in the background.

"Beautiful ride," Ryan says, looking at water on one side of the road and the mountains on the other.

"Very nice. Keep your eyes on the road!" Kelci shrieks. She braces herself with her hands against the dashboard as opposing traffic zips by.

Ryan looks at her out of the corner of his eye. "Relax."

"You're going to take a left a quarter mile up the road," Kelci says with wide eyes. "There's a brick entryway with a gate . . . Slow down, dammit!"

Ryan beams with pleasure. "Nice." He walks around the spacious great room, which includes a custom bar and a kitchen island with Corian countertops. The floor is covered in white porcelain tile. Glass sliders line the entire back of the house and open onto a large deck.

Kelci leans against a kitchen counter, looking content. "Take a look out back."

Ryan opens a slider. The ocean breeze and smell of salt hit him in the face.

They walk onto the deck and take in the view and the sounds of the waves crashing on the beach.

"Sixty feet of beach frontage." Kelci waves her hand in front of her as though she were a game show host. "Even has an outdoor shower and custom-built stone grill."

"Cool. I love the easy access to the beach." Ryan walks over to the far side of the deck and stands next to a glass door with shutters. "What's in here?"

"That's my room," Kelci teases as she opens the door.

They walk into a guest suite, which includes a small living room, kitchenette, loft-style bedroom, and bathroom with a tub and shower.

"Looks like you'll be comfortable when you visit." He cocks his head back toward the house. "Let's have a look at the master bedroom."

Kelci leads him through the back door and up a curved flight of steps. "Your bedroom covers the entire second floor."

The first thing Ryan notices, other than the enormity of the room, is the entire back wall is glass sliders, which open onto a small deck. He flips a random wall switch, and a slight humming sound is emitted as a screen slowly covers the massive skylight in the cathedral ceiling.

"This will do fine," Ryan says as he steps lively about the room. He ventures into the bathroom, which is about the size of a boxing ring, and opens a cedar door. "Cool, a steam room." Back in the bedroom, he stands with his hands on his hips, looking around. "When do I move in?"

"You close in two weeks."

The next morning, Kelci and Ryan sit at a table in the dining room of the hotel, drinking coffee, as the busboy clears the breakfast dishes off the table.

"You're on your own," she informs him. "I'm heading home. Time to get back to my family."

"You don't have to rub it in," Ryan says. A pained look covers his face.

"Here's a list of everything you need to tend to." She slides a piece of paper over to him. "Call me if you need anything."

Ryan heads back to his room, takes a deep breath, and then calls Anne Marie.

Anne Marie's voice bubbles with enthusiasm. "Are you coming home today?"

Ryan groans softly. "I wish. I have a couple of things I have to take care of before I can leave."

"How much longer will you be?" Her voice is soft. "We miss you terribly."

"I miss you more. I'll leave as soon as I can. I need to put everything in place so we can enjoy the rest of the offseason without interruption." His voice elevates with energy. "I bought a home on the beach. I can't wait to show you."

"I am so happy for you." As always, she maintains an upbeat attitude when talking about Ryan's career. "We love you and look forward to being with you."

"I love you, too. Give Jacque a hug for me."

Three weeks have passed since the baseball season ended. Ryan has completed all his obligations and closed on his Malibu Beach home. He sits in the back seat of a cab, completely at ease, as it cuts through traffic to get him to the airport on time. "Finally, I can go home and be with my family."

CHAPTER THIRTY-ONE

B*eeeeeep, beeeeep!* The light has changed from red to green.

"Okay, okay, hold your horses," Ryan fusses as he removes his hand from under Anne Marie's blouse and his lips from her earlobe. "Some people have no patience." He takes his foot off the brake and accelerates through the intersection. With one hand on the wheel, his other hand lightly rubs the front of her silk blouse. The delicate motion causes tingling and the buildup of pleasure within her.

When the car comes to rest in her parking space, they are both so worked up they can hardly think straight.

As they scamper toward the steps of Anne Marie's townhome, Mrs. Bizby, her neighbor, steps from her house. "Excuse me, Miss Peltier. Have you noticed how early in the morning the garbage trucks arrive? I find the noise very irritating while trying to sleep."

"Um, um." Horny as hell, Anne Marie struggles for the proper response. "I am sorry, Mrs. Busy Butt, I have an urgent need to take care of in the house. I will discuss it with you later." She grabs Ryan by the arm. "Come with me. I need you to help me."

Ryan barely has time to close the door before Anne Marie

smothers him in a passionate kiss. They drop onto the couch but end up falling on the floor while quickly trying to remove each other's clothing. After a half hour of rolling across the living room and knocking over an end table, they come to rest in an open spot in front of the fireplace. Afterward, they drift into the shower with carpet burns on their butt cheeks and knees. Warm, pulsating water and soapy hands start the rambunctious behavior all over again.

Lying in bed, totally spent, Anne Marie leans across Ryan and gives him a kiss. "Welcome home."

"What a fabulous welcome." He lies back, relaxed, his arm behind his head.

"You looked very handsome getting off the plane in your new clothes."

"Thank you."

"Several wardrobe boxes came special delivery yesterday."

"She wants me wearing her clothes year-round."

"Who is she?"

"Bobbie Jones, the clothier I was telling you about. She pays me to wear her clothes."

"She dresses her men very nicely."

"Probably undresses them just as nice." Ryan snickers.

Anne Marie gets a curious look on her face. "Why would you say that?"

"I'm just teasing. I was thinking of her personality."

"Should I be concerned?"

"*What*? About her? Nah, don't be silly."

"You stayed in Los Angeles for several weeks after you finished playing baseball. We missed you. Jacque will be happy to see you when the babysitter brings him home."

"Sorry for the delay. I thought about you constantly. Everything needed to get put in place before I left so we could enjoy my time off."

"I do not understand. You never had this business before."

"Los Angeles is a big city. People admire me because I play good baseball. Companies look for popular people to be their spokesperson." He rolls over and gives her a big hug. "We're in the big leagues now."

"I am so happy for your success."

"Come to L.A. and see our new home. It's a beautiful house with a back door that opens onto the beach. It was seventy-five degrees there yesterday. What's it here? About forty?"

Anne Marie shrugs. "Temperatures should not matter that much to a person."

"Jacque can go outside and play in the sand and ocean. We can go to Disneyland and Marine World."

"Sounds like a nice place to visit."

Renee drops Jacque off at home later that afternoon. Ryan sits on the living room floor, his back against the suede couch. Jacque grabs Ryan's finger to help himself stand up, toddles a few steps, and then falls on his butt.

"Good thing you have thick diapers to dampen the blow," Ryan says.

Jacque bends over and picks up a plastic toy phone and starts babbling into the mouthpiece.

"*Bonjour*, Jacque," Anne Marie says as she walks into the room.

"These are for you." She hands Ryan a stack of envelopes. "Some of them are a month old. I was not sure if I should hold on to them or forward them to you."

Ryan sorts through the envelopes while Anne Marie sits on the floor, playing with Jacque.

"Here's one from my dad." He tears it open then reads quietly for a few seconds. He chuckles softly. "He's getting married."

"*C'est tres bien*," Anne Marie replies. "It is nice to have company when you get older. When is the big day?"

Ryan silently reads for a few seconds and then looks at the date on his watch. "A couple of days ago." He picks up the envelope, checks the postmark, and then continues reading the letter. "Sounds like he wanted a private ceremony with just the two of them. But we're all invited to visit and meet his new bride."

"You should give him a call."

"In a bit," Ryan says as he snags another envelope.

Anne Marie scoots next to Ryan, her back against the couch, legs crossed in front of her.

Ryan crumples up the letter he was reading and tosses it aside.

"Are you okay?"

"Things have been kind of hectic. It was a request for me to do some promotional work in L.A."

"You are home now. Just relax and take it easy."

Ryan sucks in a deep breath, lets it out slowly, then puts his arm around Anne Marie and pulls her close. "I will." She nestles her head against his chest.

"You seem a little different," she tells him.

"Life is a little different. We're so far apart and we can't see each other as often as I'd like. It can be unsettling."

"We have been apart before. You spent three months in Mexico. Maybe the endorsements and promotional appearances weigh on you?"

"Maybe, but they'll bring in a lot of money for us."

"We do not need more money, Ryan. We have plenty to live on comfortably."

Ryan tilts his head slightly. "I like staying active, getting involved in things." He turns to face her full-on. "I wish you and Jacque were in California with me."

"I have been to L.A. before, Ryan. It is not for me. It is crowded, there is smog, and the people are different there. I love you, but I prefer Montréal. It is quaint and personable. Is it possible that maybe Montréal is not right for you?"

"We've talked about it before. I can't play baseball in Montréal. Besides, there are other opportunities for me in L.A."

"Is this about baseball or making money?" She gives him a pondering look. "I always stood beside you while you pursued your dream of playing baseball. Now you are talking about spending time away from us to make more money."

"You know I love you guys."

Anne Marie kisses his forehead, then stands up. "You should give your father a call before you forget."

Ryan sprawls across the easy chair as he punches his dad's number into the telephone.

After six rings, a woman with an Asian accent answers the phone.

"Good afternoon. This is Ryan. May I speak with my dad?"

"Hello, Ryan, this is Oshi. Your father is in the barn. Hold on a few minutes—I will go get him."

"Thanks."

Anne Marie walks by Ryan with Jacque in her arms on her way to the kitchen.

"Dad must have hired a housekeeper," Ryan comments.

"Why do you think that?"

"An Asian woman answered the telephone."

"Maybe it is his wife."

"Not likely." Ryan smirks. "My dad is an Archie Bunker clone."

After several minutes, Jack picks up the phone. "Ryan, how are you doing, son?"

"I'm doing well. I just read your letter. Congratulations on getting married."

"Thank you. Did Oshi introduce herself to you?"

"The lady that answered the telephone? Yeah."

"She's my wife."

Ryan slaps his palm to his forehead. "She sounds like a nice lady."

"She's a remarkable woman. She's hardworking, caring, and intelligent."

"Cool. How did you meet her?"

"I met her at the university. I was taking some agriculture

classes. She does research and is teaching a class on herbal medication."

"You mean, like if you eat your spinach, you'll grow up big and strong?"

"No, Ryan. We're beyond Popeye cartoons. Oshi is considered a master pharmacognosist in Japan. She came to New Mexico to study with the local Native Americans on their use of plants for medicinal purposes."

"Oh, okay." Ryan feels a tad silly.

"She's a wonderful companion and takes good care of me. We do yoga together, and she fixes me nutritional foods. She's not a replacement for your mother, nor does she want to be."

"I would never think that."

"Sounds like you had a great end of the season with the Angels. I'm proud of you."

"Never heard you say you were proud of me before," he murmurs, his mouth a safe distance from the phone. "Thanks. How are things on the ranch?"

"Things are going well. You remember Joe, our ranch foreman? His wife just had a baby. We hired a few more workers to help keep up with the increased workload. There're a lot of horses passing through here these days. How's my grandson doing?"

"Growing like a weed and smart as can be."

"When are you going to marry his mother?"

Ryan hesitates for a moment. "I don't really want to get into that right now."

"We don't need a bastard kid in the family."

"Come on. It's the 1970s. We aren't living in the Dark Ages. Universities are studying artificial insemination and in vitro fertilization. With sperm and egg donors, you might not know either parent. At least Jacque knows who his parents are and that we love him."

"You're a grown man. You make your own decisions. I'd like to meet the boy someday."

"I'd like him to meet you and spend some time in the country."

CHAPTER THIRTY-TWO

Ryan spends the entire day with Jacque when Anne Marie is at work. Being one who doesn't like to be stuck inside, he's always up for doing outdoor stuff. Anne Marie knows this and is a little concerned. January in Canada can sometimes feel like being on a polar ice cap, especially when the wind blows. She makes sure before they venture out into the frigid air that Ryan bundles the youngster in multiple layers of clothing—a sweater, snowsuit, scarfs, mittens, and a wool cap. The boy's face is barely visible, and his arms and legs are so encased in all the clothing that he almost looks like a snowman.

Being a manly kind of guy, Ryan enjoys doing things with his son that his mother would never consider. She might take him for a walk in his carriage, whereas Ryan will push the carriage across a frozen pond while he ice-skates. He also takes his son cross-country skiing with him by securing Jacque comfortably in his backpack before they make tracks. The boy coos and kicks his feet in happiness when they zip through the wooded knolls. According to Ryan, though, his son's favorite thing to do is sled in the park. Jacque shrieks with delight while he sits in his dad's lap and they slide down the snowy hill. His excitement and screams almost match those of Ryan.

One sunny afternoon after trekking in the wilderness for a couple hours, the Hutson men stop at a quiet little pub down the street from home. It's a small place built of stone with worn wood floors and dim lighting. Ryan orders a hot toddy and a Montréal smoked meat sandwich for himself and a glass of warm milk for Jacque. He would never admit to Anne Marie he took their son into a tavern lest he lose his parenting privileges.

Jacque sits on Ryan's lap sipping his milk from a glass when three young ladies wearing mukluks and tight jeans come over to shower the boy with affection.

"Oh, he is so cute," one woman says.

"He is such a handsome little guy," another one says.

"He gets his good looks from his dad," Ryan replies, although he might as well be talking to himself.

One of the young ladies leans close to Jacque and the boy pinches her breast. The women think that is so cute.

"He does that to calm himself," Ryan says. "He doesn't think milk should be drunk from a cup."

A couple of young bucks notice the ladies loving on Jacque. Envious of the child, they venture over to the table hoping to add some sparkle to their evening.

"Good day, sir. Could we borrow your son for a bit?"

Ryan shakes his head. "Sorry, guys. I don't think his mother would approve of me passing him around the bar for salacious purposes." Ryan gazes at them sympathetically. "If you need help meeting girls, maybe you should get yourselves a puppy."

Ryan and Jacque's day together ends with Ryan carrying his son to bed—the young boy's arms wrap around his father's neck and his head rests on his shoulder. "Love you, Papa," Jacque garbles when Ryan lays him down. A warm feeling fills Ryan.

After work and on weekends, Anne Marie and Ryan spend precious time together with Jacque. Anne Marie believes in exposing Jacque to culture at an early age. Whenever she hears of a symphony or music recital, she'll dress Jacque and Ryan up and haul them to the performance.

Their current outing is to see the McGill University Symphony Orchestra. The ensemble is halfway through Barber's "Adagio for Strings," and both son and father are sound asleep.

While driving home from the show, Anne Marie informs Ryan that Jacque had a peaceful sleep during the recital—absorbing the balance and homophonic textures of the music. "On the other hand, the music did not soothe the savage beast in you, as you occasionally snorted like a boar."

"Well," Ryan replies, "the chairs were uncomfortable, and I was sleeping upright. Besides, I don't have the emotional connection with classical music that I do with rock."

Ryan and Anne Marie cherish their time alone. They might enjoy an occasional moonlight cruise on the St. Lawrence River, snuggling close and gazing at the stars, or a romantic candlelit dinner at a nice restaurant or at home.

Sometimes Jacque will spend the night at the babysitters, and Anne Marie and Ryan will spend half the next day in bed. "I didn't think it could be possible to love you more each day," Ryan tells Anne Marie as he holds her in his arms.

Her body is aglow like the early morning sun. "I love every moment I spend with you," she replies. "Your love touches my heart." They embrace and kiss deeply.

Late February arrives and Ryan must return to California. Four months of euphoria turns to heartache.

They sit in the car outside the airport entrance. "It's more painful to leave each time we're together," Ryan says. "Feeling your body next to mine every night in bed fills me with contentment." He turns and lightly touches the side of Jacque's head. The boy is asleep in his car seat. "There are no words to describe how I feel about him."

A single tear flows down Anne Marie's cheek. "We love you, Ryan," she whispers. "I know you are doing what you think is best for us." He brushes the tear off her face with his fingertip. "I hope we can spend more time together this baseball season."

"The thought of giving up baseball to be with you full-time crosses my mind occasionally."

"Never give up. We will find a way to make it work."

Honnnnk!

"Watch out, you nut case!" a driver screams at Roberta as she swerves her Mercedes sport coupe between cars while working her way down the Santa Monica Freeway. In spite of the smog, it's a beautiful day to be cruising with the top down.

Roberta reaches over with her right hand and rubs along Ryan's left thigh. "I can't tell you how much more handsome you look since you started wearing our line of clothes."

Ryan smiles at her, gently picks her hand off his thigh, and puts it on the steering wheel. "I'd feel much safer if you kept both hands on the wheel."

Roberta pouts as Ryan fiddles with the radio knob. He stops scanning when he hears Van Halen singing "Runnin' with the Devil."

"So, where exactly are we going?" he asks.

"We're on our way to Del Mar Beach. The resort has a lovely pool area and access to a beautiful stretch of shore. Perfect for doing a shoot for our new men's line of swimwear."

Roberta guides her 450SL up to the front entrance of the Caribbean-style hotel. The concierge rushes to open her door. She hands him the keys and walks away without a word.

Ryan and Roberta march side by side through the hotel. Mosaic tile covers the floor of the open-air lobby. Large tropical plants are scattered throughout. They whisk past the front desk, through the lobby, and around a tiki bar, which is situated next to an oval-shaped pool. All of which is located on a terrace overlooking the ocean.

Two young ladies in skimpy bikinis sit along the side of the pool with their feet in the water.

A photographer and several production assistants are busy preparing the area for the shoot when Roberta makes her entrance.

A trim young blonde with a clipboard in hand rushes over to greet Roberta. She's wearing a white polo shirt, beige slacks, and white tennis shoes.

"Ryan, this is Vicki. She'll be working with you during the shoot."

Ryan smiles at her and gently shakes her hand. "Hi."

"Right now, she's going to show you to the workout room. Let's get those muscles pumped up before we begin the shoot."

Ryan looks down at his torso and shrugs. "I think they look fine."

"Come now. Shoo." Roberta motions him away with her hands. "Chest and arm muscles look extra toned after a good workout."

A half hour later, Ryan returns to the pool area wearing a pair of shorts, sandals, and a Hawaiian-print shirt unbuttoned in the front. Vicki leads him over to Roberta, who's waving her arms and barking orders to everyone.

Roberta stops bossing everyone around long enough to look at Ryan. "Very nice." She looks over at Vicki. "His skin would look better with a little shine."

Vicki scampers off and quickly returns with a bottle of coconut oil.

Roberta pours a small amount on her hand and rubs it on Ryan's chest. "Yes, very nice. Vicki, please continue."

Vicki grabs the bottle and, in a businesslike manner, rubs Ryan's exposed skin with oil. Roberta exits the pool area.

After four hours of Ryan posing in and around the pool, on the beach, and in the ocean while wearing different clothes and accompanied by a bikini-clad woman with her arms around him, the photographer finally calls it a wrap.

Roberta grabs Ryan by the arm after he gets back into his regular clothes, then leads him to her car.

"We took several hundred photographs today. Let's meet at your place tomorrow for a glass of wine and look them over?"

"Sorry, I don't have time, Roberta. I've got to do a spot for a radio station, and then I have to drive down to Palm Springs for spring training. I trust your judgment on the pictures."

"Of course you do, my dear." She hastens to her car with Ryan in close pursuit. "The pictures will be published in *GQ*, *Playboy*, and possibly a few other national magazines."

Ryan is in the bedroom of his Malibu home packing his clothes when the phone rings. He picks it up and hears, "Yo, Ryan, it's Gregory. What's up, man?"

Caught off guard, Ryan thinks for a moment before he realizes it's Bobby Gregory, one of his teammates. "I'm getting ready to drive down to Palm Springs for spring training. What's up with you?"

"I'm already here. Some of us got rooms at the Palm Springs Resort. Want to join us?"

"I thought the veterans were staying at the Hotel California?"

"This place is better. It's a full-service resort on a couple hundred acres with a golf course, tennis courts, steam room, and lotsa other cool shit."

Three hours after hanging up the phone, Ryan pulls his Vette to a stop in front of the reception area of the Palm Springs Resort. Despite the fact the hotel's in the midst of the desert, the welcome area is surrounded with lush vegetation and thick green grass. The concierge opens the car door as soon as Ryan cuts off the engine.

"Good day, sir. You may proceed to check-in. I will park your car and have your bags transferred to your room."

"Give her a wash and wax and top off the tank," Ryan wisecracks before heading into the reception area. He stands at the check-in counter, face-to-face with a young woman in a tropical-print silk blouse.

"Good day, sir. How may I help you?"

Ryan looks at the name tag above her pocket. "Hi, Alicia. I'm Ryan Hutson."

She fumbles through a couple of sheets of paper. "Yes. I see you're with the California Angels. You'll receive the special rate of two thousand dollars per week."

Ryan is soon joined by Candy, another young woman in a tropical blouse, who escorts him to his room. As they walk through the lobby, Candy points out the activity desk. "You can book a massage, reserve a racquetball court, schedule a tee time, or arrange a local excursion there."

They head out the back door of the lobby and walk past a swimming pool surrounded by palm trees and large ferns. The entire complex is like a desert oasis with Mediterranean architecture. The buildings have tiled roofs, decorative arches, and a stucco finish.

Candy leads him to his room, a nine-hundred-square-foot suite with separate living, sleeping, and kitchen areas. Candy slides open the door to the balcony. "Straight ahead you have a view of the San Bernardino Mountains. Off to the right, you can see the first green and the tee box for the second hole."

CHAPTER THIRTY-THREE

Ryan sits on the grass near the dugout of the practice field on the first day of spring training. His legs are extended out in front of him. Bobby Gregory lies next to him, stretching his thighs, while several other players mull around the infield. A short, stocky player charges up the steps of the dugout, trips on the top step, and falls on his face.

A few of the guys in the infield break out in laughter.

"Grand entrance, Red," a sarcastic voice rings out.

"Ouch, I hope he didn't hurt himself," Ryan says.

"That's Red Dawson. He bounces good," Bobby says with a grin.

After waiting a few seconds to ensure Red makes it to his feet, Ryan gets up and heads toward the batting cage. "Catch up with you later," he tells Bobby. He stops after a few steps when he notices a slim Black man exit the dugout, toting an equipment bag. Ryan tilts his head in that direction. "Who's that?"

Bobby cranes his neck to have a good look. "Rod Carew."

"He's been an all-star more than fifteen times," Ryan mumbles softly. He jogs over to the superstar and extends his hand. "Hey, Rod, Ryan Hutson."

"Good morning," Carew responds in a heavy Panamanian accent. He studies Ryan for a second, then says, "I remember you. You were getting big hits for the Angels down the homestretch last season."

Ryan smiles shyly. "I had a good run to end the year," he says. "But I've never had my picture on the cover of *Time* magazine with the headline 'Baseball's Best Hitter,' like you."

Carew accepts the compliment in stride. "It comes from a lot of hard work and study."

"I'm impressed with the way you slap the ball around for base hits," Ryan says. "I read last year you were getting on base almost half the time before you hurt your hand and sat out the rest of the season."

"That is my style. From what I hear, you are good at base hits and home runs. I am a slap hitter. The year I batted .388, I only hit one home run."

"I'd like to be more consistent at getting hits with runners on."

Carew nods toward the empty batting cage. "Come. I will show you a few things."

Standing outside the batting cage, Carew holds a bat to demonstrate his technique. "Once you are set up in the batter's box, your eyes never leave the pitcher's hand. Always turn your head to bring your dominant eye into play as much as possible." Carew grips his bat and turns his head to demonstrate. "Watch for the pitcher's release point and the spin on the ball. As the pitcher comes out of his motion, your hands should start to churn."

"Churn?" Ryan furrows his eyebrows.

"Release your tension and start to get your body into a rhythm. This is your trigger point, the beginning of a hitting motion that includes every part of your body. It's a pendulum effect."

"Okay." Anxious to give it a try, Ryan grabs a bat and enters the batting cage. John Anderson, a recently signed relief pitcher with the Angels, tosses balls to Ryan under the watchful eye of Carew.

When Ryan's through batting, Anderson comes up to him and, while looking at Carew, says, "I've been pitching against that guy for ten years. The hardest out I ever had. He punches the ball to right field. He lobs it to left. He does about anything he wants with the ball. I've never seen him not in control of the pitcher."

Ryan nods, more to himself than Anderson. "I want to be like that."

CHAPTER THIRTY-FOUR

The Angels open the new season on a festive afternoon in Anaheim. The grounds crew hoist the West Division championship flag as Captain & Tennille sing "Do That to Me One More Time." Afterward, the Blue Angels soar overhead in formation just as Toni Tennille hits the final note of the national anthem. The fans break out in a loud and energetic cheer. They look forward to another banner season.

In spite of the festivities and beautiful weather, the game does not go well for the home team. Ryan plays left field and goes two for four at the plate, but the Blue Jays beat the Angels 9 – 2.

The players traipse into the locker room after the beat down. Lisa Bower catches up with Ryan at his locker as he pulls his jersey over his head. She leans against him, her left hand pressed against the small of his back, her right hand holding a microphone in front of his face. Ryan has his right arm around her waist as the television camera rolls.

"You had some nice hits tonight."

Ryan gives a half shrug. "It doesn't mean much if we don't win."

"You'll get over it," she says with a smile on her face.

"Already have."

"You know how to poke it in the hole," she says, tilting her head and looking up at him.

"I'll put it in the gap if I get what I like."

"They threw you a lot of outside pitches. Do you think pitchers are afraid to come inside?"

He gives a noncommittal jerk of his shoulders. "Safer to come outside."

"Very true."

Late that same afternoon, Ryan lies on a chaise lounge on the deck of his beach house. The sun hangs low in the sky; its orange glow creates a vivid line where the air meets water. A glass of Glenlivet and ice is in one hand and a cordless phone is in the other.

"*Bonsoir, mon coeur,*" he purrs into the phone.

"Ryan, my dear, how are you?" Anne Marie replies.

"I'm well. We played our first game of the year today."

"Yes, I know. It was broadcast across North America."

"Did you watch it?"

"I saw the end of the game and the interview with the young lady in the locker room afterward. You are quite the player."

There's a moment of silence as Ryan thinks about the possible double entendre. "We were having a little fun."

"She must be fun. It was evident you could not keep your hands off her."

"Just a little harmless joking around."

"Hmm, I see. Just like the joking around with the young ladies in the *GQ* ad?"

Ryan's jaw drops. "Yikes!" he says, barely audible. Fear of the unknown quickly overcomes him. He doesn't know which pictures Roberta used in the *GQ* ad. There was some pretty hot action going on around the pool. Ryan squirms in his seat. "I'm paid to sell leisurewear."

"Having a practically naked young lady leaning against you with your lips almost touching sells swimsuits?"

"According to Roberta, sex appeal sells. Wearing her clothes is supposed to make ordinary guys think they can score with hot women."

"Is Roberta promoting sex with hot women or selling clothes?" Anne Marie asks, her voice quivering. "Oh, Ryan, I wish you were here. I miss you so much."

"I'll be in Toronto next month. We have a day off after the last game. I'll come over, and we can have dinner. Then I have three days off at the All-Star break. We'll do something special."

The Angels continue to struggle in the new season. Their offense is driving in runs, but the pitching is not keeping the opposing teams' offense in check. After thirty-five games, they are six games below .500 and ten games behind the Athletics in the standings.

The Angels amble about the locker room after losing 7 – 6 to the Royals. It's their third loss in a row during a ten-game road trip. Ryan had eleven hits in thirty-eight bats during the ten games.

Goetz of the *L.A. Times* approaches Ryan as he gets ready to hit the showers. "Tough loss, partner."

Ryan stands with a towel around his waist, glaring at him. *Do you really need to talk to me at this moment?* he says to himself. Out loud, he replies, "There've been a few tough losses lately. We have a lot of young arms in the rotation. They'll come around, and we'll be all right."

"On the positive side, you've been hitting the ball well. Can you attribute your success to anything specific that you're doing?"

"I'm seeing the ball well." He pauses for a second. "Also, being around Carew is like having my own personal batting coach. It helps to have an experienced guy to talk hitting with."

. . .

The Angels begin a home stand against the last-place Mariners, hoping to get a winning streak going. The first game is tied in the top of the ninth 2 – 2. Seattle has two outs and a runner on second. Their next batter hits a hard shot to right-center field; it looks like it's going to drop in for extra bases. Red Dawson charges from right field and dives headfirst, his body fully extended. He hits the ground, bounces a few times, and then holds his glove high for all to see that the ball is caught. Ryan rushes over from left field and reaches down to help Red to his feet.

"Heck of a catch, man. You ran that down like a gazelle. A drunken gazelle, mind you, but still a great effort." Ryan takes a close look at Red. He can see a bruise forming on his cheek where his head hit the ground.

Red comes up to bat in the bottom of the ninth, the game is still tied. There are two outs, and Carew is on third. After making a game-saving catch, Red has the opportunity to be the hero with a hit. The fans are on their feet, screaming encouragement. He watches the first pitch for a ball. The pitcher offers up a big sweeping curveball—Red takes a big swing and fouls the ball off his head. He crumbles to the ground like dirty laundry.

Ryan is sitting on the bench between Bobby and Langston.

"Looks like he's down for the count," Bobby comments.

"Aww, man. He's going to have a big goose egg on his forehead," Ryan bemoans.

After several minutes, Red is assisted off the field by the trainers. Marv Reitman, a left-handed hitter, comes in to finish off Red's at bat. The Mariners counter with a left-handed relief pitcher, Dane Rawlins. Rawlins is known for his slow windup and big leg kick.

"Play ball!" the umpire hollers.

Carew takes a modest lead off third. The third baseman isn't holding him close. Carew looks back and forth between the pitcher and third base while slowly inching toward home. As soon as Rawlins starts into his windup, Carew takes off for home plate. The pitcher can see Carew out of the corner of his eyes and quickly modifies his windup, resulting in an off-balance throw to the catcher. Carew slides safely below the catcher's tag. The Angels win 3 – 2.

"Hoowee!" Ryan shouts as he races to home plate to congratulate Carew. "That was one of the most incredible plays I've ever seen."

Ryan sits next to Carew on the bench the next game while the Angels are at bat. "Stealing home last night was so cool."

Carew appreciates his enthusiasm. "I am sure you could do it. You are quick and smart."

The corners of Ryan's eyes crinkle as he smiles. "Tell me how."

"You start by taking a slow walking lead instead of coming to a stop. How far you go off the base depends on how far the third baseman is playing off the bag and whether the pitcher takes a stretch or a windup." Carew pats Ryan on the thigh. "A walking lead is essential because you are creating momentum toward home plate. You need to time it to the split second. When a pitcher winds up, instead of pitching from a stretch, I count the number of seconds between when he begins his windup and his release. Then I know how much time I have to make it home safely. The batter can help by getting in the catcher's way as much as possible without being called for interference."

"So," Ryan says, pursing his lips while in thought. "You need to be on the same page with the batter?"

"You give the hitter a sign, and he should flash it back to you." Carew tugs at his earlobe.

The Angels are sixty games into the season, and Ryan is hitting at a torrid pace. Sitting on the bench next to Carew and picking the superstar's brain has bolstered his batting. Ryan is the first player since Carew to bat over .400 this deep into the season. His mentor is his biggest fan and continually offers advice. His incredible hitting streak has drawn the attention of journalists from both coasts and in-between.

CHAPTER THIRTY-FIVE

The Angels are in Kansas City and trail the Royals by six runs in the top of the ninth. Ryan is on third base with one out. Rob Nielson is pitching for Kansas City; his nickname is "the Spider" because of his long, dangly arms.

Ryan takes a walking lead off third base on the first two pitches; Nielson and the third baseman pay no attention to him. Red Dawson is at the plate. Ryan gives him the steal signal then nods to him. Red nods back. On the next pitch, the Spider goes into a big, slow windup, and Ryan takes off running for home. It's going to be close—it looks like the ball and Ryan will arrive at the same time. Ryan drives headfirst toward home plate. Instead of getting out of the way, Red squares up and bunts the ball. Ryan crashes into Red, who falls on top of him, blocking him from reaching home plate. Ryan struggles to untangle himself from Red as the catcher retrieves the bunted ball and tags out both players. Players on both teams break out in hysterics as Red and Ryan sit in the dirt, looking at each other. Game over.

"My first attempt to steal home in the major leagues, and I'm the laughingstock of the fans and players. I can't wait to try it again," Ryan sarcastically tells the catcher as he helps Red to his feet.

Red weaves his way off the field as blood trickles from his lower lip. "I thought you gave me the bunt sign."

The team hits the showers after the game, then boards a bus to the airport. Two hours after boarding a plane, they disembark at Toronto Pearson Airport and hop on another bus to the hotel.

Ryan walks into a one-room suite with a king-sized bed and a seating area, which includes a couch, desk, and mini-fridge. A red light is flashing on the telephone next to the couch. He drops his carry-on bag on the bed. The concierge will have his other bags brought up to the room. He loosens his tie and unbuttons the top button to his shirt before sitting on the bed to retrieve his message.

"Ryan, it's Kelci. Call me when you get this message."

He grabs a Molson from the fridge, kicks off his shoes, and then dials Kelci's number.

"Hey, Kelce. How's it going?"

"Fabulous. Your popularity is skyrocketing during this hitting streak. The phone is ringing off the hook with endorsement offers."

"Anything good?"

"Chevrolet is looking for a spokesman for their line of trucks."

"I don't drive a truck, and I don't endorse products I don't use."

"It's a national contract and worth quite a bit of money. Maybe we could get you in a K5 Blazer and see if you like it."

"Do they make Land Rovers?"

"Made in an entirely different country."

He takes a gulp of beer. "Okay, we can at least talk to them."

"That's the spirit. By the way, you're escorting Roberta to a fashion show on Sunday."

"No way!"

"Way. You agreed three months ago to attend two shows of her choosing. She wants to cash in while you're hot."

"I've got plans. Get me out of it!" His voice is stern.

"You're under contract. And I'm almost positive she's the kind of person who would file a lawsuit against us if you don't follow through."

"Grrr." He stands up and walks around the room, stretching the cord to the limit. The phone ends up falling off the table and crashing to the floor. "You still there? What's the show?"

"I'm here, and it's a sportswear fashion show that just happens to be in Toronto."

"Why couldn't it be in Montréal?"

"Because it's in Toronto. I'm sure she'll have someone come over to dress you properly for the event."

Ryan hangs up the phone and looks at it for a few minutes, steaming inside. He lets out a deep breath then punches in Anne Marie's number.

"*Allo.*"

"*Bon soir, mon amour,*" Ryan replies.

"*Salut, comment allez-vous, cherie?*"

His heart smiles momentarily. "I'm doing wonderful. It's great to hear your voice."

"We are looking forward to seeing you in a couple days. I told Jacque his daddy is coming home, and he is so excited."

"Is his mother excited?"

"In ways that only you would know and can satisfy."

Ryan lets out a soft groan.

"You sound upset."

"Something came up, and I can't make it Sunday."

"Is it something to do with baseball?"

"Actually, it's business related. I forgot about a commitment I made a couple months ago."

There are several seconds of silence.

"I'm sorry, sweetheart," he says softly. "I feel awful. There's no way I can get out of it."

"You have to do what is important for you."

He senses the disappointment in her voice. "Thank you for understanding."

"You are playing good baseball right now. I do not want to say or do anything to upset your mind."

They finish talking, and Ryan hangs up the phone. "Damn!" He slaps the nightstand. He looks at the floor for a few moments, disgusted with himself, then puts his shoes on and heads to the lounge.

The lights are subdued. Most of the tables are occupied by ballplayers, businessmen, and young groupies looking to score.

The DJ is spinning "Stayin' Alive" when Ryan wanders into the room. He notices an empty seat next to Red at the bar and slides in.

Langston and Bobby are on the dance floor, each holding a young lady close as their bodies sway in rhythm to the music.

The bartender wipes the bar in front of Ryan. "What can I get for you?"

"Glenlivet on the rocks . . . Double."

Red points toward Langston and Bobby. "Some guys are lucky. Athletic and good-looking."

Ryan shrugs. "Don't compare yourself to other people. They're more screwed up than you think."

Within minutes, a young vixen with flowing blond hair and sporting a tight miniskirt approaches Ryan. "Buy a girl a drink, handsome?"

Ryan takes a close look, then nods in appreciation. He puts both hands on her butt and pulls her close, his mouth touching her ear. "I'll buy you a bottle and give you a hundred bucks to take my friend upstairs and not let him up until he begs for mercy."

She takes a close look at Red, who's staring at her. She politely smiles at him. "I'd rather be with you," she whispers in Ryan's ear.

"It wouldn't be fair to my other suitors," Ryan replies.

She thinks about it for a few seconds, then holds her hand out, palm up. Ryan pulls out his wallet and counts out five twenties.

The music transitions from the Bee Gees to Earth, Wind & Fire.

At the change in song, Langston and Bobby make their way back to the bar.

"Was that Red walking out of here with a hot chick and a bottle of champagne?" Bobby asks, a smirk on his face.

"Your eyes are not deceiving you," Ryan replies. "The man is off to fulfill his libidinous desires."

CHAPTER THIRTY-SIX

Renee quickly closes the magazine she's reading when Anne Marie walks into her shop Monday morning.

"*Bonjour*, Miss Peltier," Renee says while standing behind the checkout counter.

"Good morning, Renee." Anne Marie walks around the counter. "What are you reading?"

"The latest issue of *Maclean's*," she dolefully replies.

Maclean's magazine is a weekly periodical that provides news from a uniquely Canadian perspective. Most of Anne Marie's friends and clients subscribe to it.

Anne Marie picks up the magazine and is immediately taken aback. Plastered across the cover is a picture of Ryan looking incredibly handsome in a perfectly fitted tuxedo. The disturbing thing is, Bobbie Jones is draped all over him, wearing a silk gown, her breasts half exposed. The headline stamped across the top of the picture reads, "Baseball's Latest Superstar Escorts the Elegant Roberta Jones to Canada's Premier Fashion Show."

"Oh, Ryan," she painfully murmurs to herself.

The Angels caravan rolls into Boston for a weekend series with the Red Sox. Anne Marie takes the morning train from Montréal, which arrives in time for her to catch an evening game at Fenway Park.

Full of adrenaline knowing that his *grand amour* is in the stands, Ryan blasts two home runs.

It's nearly 11 PM by the time the Angels blow a three-run lead and fall to the Sox 6 – 5. They have become quite talented in finding creative ways to lose close games.

Anne Marie waits patiently for Ryan near the Fenway Park ticket office on Yawkey Way. Several inebriated Red Sox fans try to make her acquaintance.

"Buy you a victory drink?" a staggering, potbellied man in a Red Sox shirt asks.

Anne Marie shakes her head and slowly walks in the opposite direction.

"Must be from California," he responds brusquely.

"*Je suis Canadienne,*" Anne Marie replies.

The drunk fan gives Anne Marie a confused look for a few seconds before commenting to his partner, "She's from some foreign country. Probably don't know much about our ways."

Ryan bounds out of the front gate of the park and immediately spots Anne Marie. He sidesteps his way through the remnants of the crowd lingering outside the stadium. They lock eyes and rush toward each other, joining in a smothering embrace.

"Let's get a cab, go to the hotel, and put out some fires," Ryan says as he presses his body close to hers.

Sunlight slips into the room from the space between the curtains. Anne Marie pushes Ryan's shoulder as they lie in bed. "Wake up," she says. "It is a beautiful morning. I want to visit the Freedom Trail."

Ryan rolls over, pulls her close, and gives her a kiss. He takes a deep breath and gathers his senses. "Sure. That should be fun. A journey though American history."

They hold hands as they stroll down Tremont Street on a slightly overcast New England day. A brush of warm, moist air hits them in the face. "Why do you not tell me beforehand about you and beautiful women in magazines, in newspapers, and on television?"

Ryan stops walking and grabs both of her hands. "It's my job to promote baseball and my sponsors' products. There's nothing going on with the ladies. I don't say anything because I don't want you to worry."

Anne Marie gives Ryan a piercing look. "Maybe you should let me decide what worries me."

Ryan sighs and looks upward at a plane flying overhead. "Every time I do a shoot with a woman, I feel uncomfortable inside."

"Then why do you do it?" She has a pleading look in her eyes.

"Because I'm under contract." He presses his lips together for a few seconds. "I also thought we could use the extra money."

"Aiee! I do not understand you." Anne Marie pulls on his hand. "Come, we should continue walking. I do not wish to upset you."

The first point of interest they come across is the Boston Common.

"This is America's oldest park," Anne Marie tells Ryan. "Hundreds of years ago, the colonists doled out public humiliation at this site."

Ryan chuckles. "Now they do it on television and in newspapers."

As they continue their jaunt through history, their next stop is the corner of State and Congress Streets. "This is the site of the Boston Massacre," Anne Marie reads from a plaque.

Ryan tenses up.

"What bothers you, *mon chèrie*?"

"A bad memory. Redcoats opened fire on colonists protesting unfair British legislation. Five were killed. Two hundred years later, national guardsmen killed four college students during a peaceful protest."

"*Si triste*. We should learn from history."

"Respect one another without resorting to violence," Ryan says as he pulls her close.

She kisses him, then pulls away. Looking at the map, she says, "It looks like Bunker Hill is our next stop. This was the site of one of the earliest battles of the Revolutionary War."

From Bunker Hill, they continue their leisurely stroll until they encounter a small gathering of people.

"What's the attraction here?" Ryan asks.

Anne Marie looks at the text below the picture on her map. "This is the oldest public school in the United States. Established in 1635. Ben Franklin and five signers of the Declaration of Independence attended school here."

"'We were all born ignorant, but we must work hard to remain stupid,'" Ryan says.

Anne Marie's eyes widen in confusion at the comment. "*Excusez-moi!*"

"It's a Ben Franklin quote. I like to use it around the knuckleheads I deal with."

An endearing smile crosses Anne Marie's face. "'Money has never made anyone happy. The more man has of it, the more he wants,' is also a Ben Franklin quote. I like to use it around knuckleheads that I adore." She clasps Ryan's hand and leads him down the trail.

Their meander through history leads them to the Union Oyster House, a popular restaurant located on the bottom floor of a two-hundred-year-old brick building.

"I'm getting a little hungry. Why don't we grab a bite?" Ryan suggests.

Soon after they're seated, Anne Marie orders a glass of Chardonnay, and Ryan orders a Glenlivet on the rocks. "Make it a double," he informs the waiter. He notices Anne Marie sigh and lower her head. "What's the matter?"

She looks at him emotionlessly, without replying.

"If something's bothering you, please tell me."

"Okay." She closes her eyes briefly, thinking about how to word her next comment. "Remember you told me how unhappy it made you to see your father drink so much?"

Ryan quickly cuts her off, shaking his head. "That's different."

Her shoulders sag as he changes the subject.

"The team is traveling to Detroit from here for four games with the Tigers. I'll be meeting with execs from General Motors while we're in town. I'm going to talk with them about promoting their new line of trucks."

"You are stretching yourself pretty thin. Maybe you should take a break from promotions."

"I need to take advantage of the opportunities while they're available."

"Opportunities will always be available."

He pats her hand as he drains his glass of Scotch.

Anne Marie's eyes brighten as she thinks ahead a few weeks. "Well, at least we have the All-Star break coming up." She squeezes his hand and smiles. "We will have three full days to relax and spend time together as a family."

"Um, I was meaning to talk to you about that."

Anne Marie's face goes slack. "Ryan, please do not tell me something has come up."

"Baby, I *have* to play in the All-Star Game. I'm the top vote getter in the fan balloting. I'm kind of the poster boy for the league right now."

"You are also the poster boy for Roberta Jones, Chevrolet, and others. You are pushing yourself hard with all these endorsements, plus the pressure and attention of batting .400. Your mind and body need a break. Players have surely skipped the game in the past to rest injuries."

"It's an honor to play in this game, and I'm going to play. I don't want to discuss it further."

Anne Marie is not used to being spoken to so curtly. She slides her chair back. "Excuse me. I must use the ladies' room."

Ryan motions toward the waiter. "I'd like another Scotch on the rocks." He rolls his shoulders to release the tension he's feeling.

Anne Marie returns from the ladies' room with fresh makeup below her eyes and on her cheeks. They smile and touch each other often while enjoying a mostly quiet dinner.

Their walk back to the hotel takes them past the lit-up Massachusetts State House and the Old City Hall. Ryan talks about the many promotional opportunities he has. Anne Marie listens quietly. His peace of mind is important to her.

CHAPTER THIRTY-SEVEN

The wheels of the Delta 737 bounce when they touch ground, and the plane rapidly decelerates. Red, sound asleep next to Ryan, jolts forward, bumping his head on the seat in front of him. He rubs his forehead to see if there's any blood. "Where are we?"

"Detroit." Ryan looks closely at him. "You gonna be okay?"

"I've got a thick skull."

"Thank goodness."

Ryan walks down the airport concourse toward the exit joking with several of his teammates. He stops when he notices a tall man with a shaved head who's wearing a blue silk suit and holding a General Motors placard. "Are you looking for Ryan Hutson?" he asks.

"Yes, sir. I'm Ruppert. If you're Mr. Hutson, I'll be driving you to the Renaissance Center for your meeting. Do you need help with your bags?"

Ryan shakes his head. "Nah. They'll be delivered to the hotel."

Ruppert leads Ryan to a black Cadillac limousine parked next to the curb outside the baggage claim. He opens the rear door for Ryan.

Ryan thinks for a second about getting into the front seat, takes a close look at Ruppert, and slides into the back. Once he's situated, he opens the door to the liquor cabinet and studies the contents before he grabs a bottle of Highland Park Scotch whiskey. He pours a couple shots over a glass of ice, then flips on the stereo and relaxes to the sounds of "Morning Dance" by Spyro Gyra.

The Cadillac stealthily glides through the dismal concrete jungle of downtown Detroit before it reaches the Renaissance Center, home to Chevrolet headquarters. The shiny new complex stands out like the castle in *The Wizard of Oz.*

Ruppert parks the vehicle in the underground garage and leads Ryan to an elevator, which passes the floors containing a hotel, upscale restaurants, and pricey boutique shops before stopping at the corporate offices of Chevrolet.

As they ride up the elevator, Ruppert stands tight-lipped and looking forward like a guard at Windsor Castle. Ryan's ears pop as the elevator ascends rapidly. It decelerates almost as quickly. When the door opens, Ruppert motions Ryan out; the man hasn't said more than five words to Ryan since he met him at the airport.

The two men enter a large room with a marble floor and light panels covering the entire ceiling. What looks like a large glass bowl is actually a circular desk. A middle-aged woman sits in the middle of it, wearing a headset. A panel of telephone extensions flash in front of her. Ruppert leads Ryan over to the desk and stands at attention as he patiently waits for her to get off the phone. At the first available moment, he interjects, "The gentleman is here to see Mr. Rosal."

"Thank you, Ruppert. I'll take care of him from here."

"Good day, Mr. Hutson," Ruppert says as he turns to walk away.

"Hey, Ruppert," Ryan calls out. "Life is too short to be serious all the time. If you can't laugh at yourself, call me . . . I'll laugh at you."

After a few minutes of standing in the reception area with his hands in his pockets, a slim woman approaches Ryan. She's wearing a neon jacket and loud makeup, and her hair is permed and teased to perfection. She pleasantly smiles as she extends her hand. "I'm Denise. I'll take you to see Mr. Rosal."

Denise leads Ryan down an adjoining hallway and into a conference room where three important-looking men in suits sit around an oval glass table. A large picture window on the outside wall provides a stunning view of the Detroit River. Across the river is Windsor, Ontario.

Everyone promptly stands when Ryan enters the room. The first to approach him is a middle-aged man with a potbelly and male-pattern baldness. He appears ready to get down to business; his suit jacket is off, his tie is loosened, and his shirt sleeves are rolled up. A big smile crosses his face as he extends his hand. "Hello, Ryan. I'm Ian Rosal, head of marketing for Chevrolet."

The second man to approach Ryan is tall and slim. He's wearing a perfectly tailored pin-striped suit. The silver on his sideburns and along his temples accentuates his dark hair. "Good morning, Ryan. Mitchell Byars." He hands Ryan a business card. "Byars, Sellers, and Moore Advertising" is printed across the top. "President" is typed beneath his name.

The third person in the trio is a younger man, possibly in his early thirties. He has an athletic build and slicked-back hair. "Hi, Ryan. I'm Richard Starr, account executive for Chevy trucks at BS and Moore Advertising. Just so you know, it was my idea to bring you on board."

"I'm not a huge baseball fan," Rosal says, "but Richard informs me you're drawing national attention with your play."

Ryan starts to say something but is cut off by Starr. "We want a rugged, outdoors type of guy that men can relate to. We noticed you've done an outstanding job promoting a local Chevrolet dealer in California."

"Thank you for the compliments. I drive a Vette, so I'm comfortable promoting Chevy cars. I don't drive a truck, and I make it a point not to promote products I don't use."

"Your agent told us that," Byars says as he fidgets with a pen. "She's a tough negotiator. Is she your wife?"

"Sister-in-law."

"Depending on the number of commercials filmed and residuals, this deal could be worth a couple hundred thousand dollars to you. Would you reconsider driving a Chevy truck? We could provide you with a nicely outfitted El Camino."

"You know, Mitch—may I call you Mitch?"

"I prefer Mitchell."

"Okay. Well, I've been giving this some thought, and an idea came to mind. My dad has a ranch in New Mexico, and my brother owns a construction company in North Carolina. Give them each a new pickup truck, and then you can show Chevy trucks actually doing some work. I'll be your spokesman for your trucks, and we can tell everyone my family uses Chevy trucks in their businesses. That might mean more than some city slicker driving around town in a pickup."

The three men talk quietly amongst themselves while Ryan looks out the window. "I heard you have to go south from here to get into Canada?"

No one pays attention to him.

Byars clears his throat, getting Ryan's attention. "It's an interesting concept, Mr. Hutson. I'm sure we can make it work."

"That's some creative thinking on your behalf," Rosal tells Ryan. "Ever thought about going into advertising?"

"I have a lot of hidden talents," Ryan replies, then chuckles. "I just wish I could remember where I hid them." He looks around the table at blank stares. "The only issue I see is getting everyone together to film the commercials."

"That's not an issue," Starr says. "We'll use actors to film the ranch and construction scenes. After we finish filming, we'll mix in your parts."

CHAPTER THIRTY-EIGHT

The words and music to "It Never Rains in Southern California" fill Dodger Stadium. Ryan sits on the bench of the visitors' dugout with a couple other all-stars, watching as rain pelts the tarp covering the infield. Thoughts of not being with Anne Marie and Jacque in Montréal weigh on him.

Fred Lynn of the Red Sox sits next to him. "The weather got you down, big fella?"

"My mind is three thousand miles away, and my body wishes it were there with it."

Hundreds of multicolored umbrellas are scattered through the stands. The fans without protection from the elements squeeze under the overhang of the upper deck of the stadium or crowd around the beer stand in the concourse.

Most of the players hang out in the locker room. Some play cards, some nap, and others run around like little kids.

As Ryan and Fred sit chatting and watching the rain, two young men and a young lady strip down to their birthday suits, climb over the railing, and run onto the field. Soon, they're sliding headfirst on the rain-drenched tarp. The naked slide quickly becomes a Keystone Cops routine as security guards rush onto the field to put a halt to the gaiety. Fans scream encouragement to the wet and slippery streakers as they dodge and weave to evade the security guards. Ultimately, the cheers turn to boos as they are captured and escorted off the field.

"That girl slides very nicely," Reggie Jackson comments as he takes a seat between Lynn and Ryan. Looking at Ryan, he says, "The Angels signed you last year to replace me. However, there is no replacement for me."

"That's why they boo you in half the cities you play in," Lynn replies with a hearty laugh.

Unperturbed, Reggie replies, "The fans don't boo nobodies."

Lynn slaps Ryan on the shoulder. "I'm heading back to the locker room." He grabs Reggie by the arm. "And I'm taking this clown with me."

Shortly after they leave the dugout, in bounces Lisa Bower wearing an Angels T-shirt that hugs her upper torso like a latex glove. Her cutoff jeans are just a little shy of covering the entirety of her perfectly rounded cheeks. She nestles next to Ryan. "Looks like the rain may stick around a while."

"Everybody talks about the weather, but no one wants to do anything about it," Ryan says, staring straight ahead.

"I suppose." Lisa looks at Ryan. "I think storms are sensual. Sometimes, a girl enjoys getting wet."

A faint quirk of Ryan's lips hints at inward amusement. Looking at the fans sitting in the rain, he comments, "A lot of people have raincoats. A man should wear protection at every *conceivable* moment."

Lisa gives him a spirited shoulder bump. They sit quietly next to each other with their feet propped up as they listen to the raindrops fall. "The best thing one can do when it is raining is to let it rain," Lisa casually comments. Ryan glares at her, his head slightly tilted. "Wadsworth," she says.

"Good to know."

The midsummer classic, intended to be played on a sunny afternoon, ends up being played on a damp evening.

J.R. Richard, the starting pitcher for the National League, overpowers the first five American League hitters. Ryan, the sixth hitter, receives a standing ovation when he comes to bat in the second inning. He looks around at the exuberant crowd, then tips his hat before settling in the batter's box.

"Don't be such a Dog," Carter, the National League catcher, tells him.

Ryan smiles as he looks down at him. "Shame you don't know what it's like to have fans that adore you."

"It's not a popularity contest, it's a game," Carter says.

After looking at the first two pitches, Ryan lines a shot to right-center field for a base hit.

Steve Garvey, the National League first baseman, stands next to Ryan on first base. "You know, Steve, I think he eased up so I could get a hit."

"Well, *it* is your hometown and you've got a lot of fans here," Garvey replies. "Plus you're the poster boy for baseball right now."

The hit is inconsequential, as Richard strikes out the next batter.

Ryan is the only base runner in the first four innings. He heads toward the bat rack in the fifth and is cut off by his coach. "We're going to let you sit the rest of the game out."

Ryan looks at him with wide eyes. "Really?"

"It's a cold, damp night. No need to risk an injury."

Having a competitive nature, Ryan is disappointed. He grabs a seat on the bench next to Carew. "I'd like to have been the one to bust this game open."

"A meaningless accolade," Carew responds.

The honor of breaking the scoreless tie goes to Fred Lynn, who slams a two-run homer for the American League. Ryan is the first one off the bench to congratulate him.

The lead is short-lived as Ken Griffey Sr. starts the onslaught for the National League a couple innings later by blasting a home run.

His towering shot leads the National League to a 4 – 2 victory and earns him the MVP.

Ryan is in the process of changing into his street clothes after the game when Carter meanders into the American League locker room looking for him. "Hey, Dog," he says as soon as he spots Ryan. "Several of us are heading over to Club Dalliance. Want to give me a ride?"

A half hour later, Ryan tosses the keys to his Vette to the valet when they pull up in front of the West Hollywood bar. "Give 'er a wash and blow-dry."

"Nice wheels, man. I bet you get a lot of chicks with this car," the valet remarks.

"The day I need a car to get a date is the day I give up women," Ryan replies.

Ryan looks at Carter and shakes his head. "Kids."

"The good thing about valet parking is you never forget where you parked your car," Carter cracks.

"Do you ever forget where you are?" Ryan asks.

"Not intentionally."

They bypass the waiting line and fifty-dollar cover charge, and head directly into the smoky bar. The large room is dimly lit by blue lights and beams of white light that reflect off a mirrored ball hanging from the ceiling. Revolving speakers blasting "Heartbreaker" hang from the ceiling on both sides of the glistening ball.

Ryan and Carter work their way through the crowd on the dance floor and around surrounding tables with their sights set on the bar. Ryan notices the starting power forward for the Lakers on the dance floor, a head above everyone. He also notices Carl Strong, the leading man in several recent romantic movies, dancing rather closely with a young man half his age.

When they make it to the bar, Carter hollers at the bartender, "Two drafts."

"Make mine a Scotch. Glenlivet," Ryan says.

Carter nods in the direction of the men's restroom. Bo Willis, a tall, lanky baseball player, walks out with his nose surrounded in white powder.

Bo spies his contemporaries and wanders over to them, stopping every so often to kiss or hug a young woman. A line of ladies trail behind him. When he reaches the bar, he gives Ryan and Carter each a hand slap.

Carter chuckles. "Bo, you're the only person I know who spends five hundred bucks to powder his nose."

Willis rubs his nose and looks at the white powder on his finger. One of his female admirers sticks his finger in her mouth.

"Cocaine dealers seem to always stick their business in other people's noses," Ryan comments disparagingly. He looks at the women hanging all over Willis. "How do you spend all night womanizing and still play ball the next day?"

Willis puts his hand on Ryan's shoulder. "Being with a woman all night never hurt anyone. It's staying up all night looking for one that'll do you in."

"On that note, I think I'll wander around a bit," Ryan says.

"You might as well stay here," Carter replies. "You're only as cool as the people you hang with."

Ryan looks at the ceiling and shakes his head. "I'm so lucky to be standing next to you."

A slim man in his early twenties with long blond hair squeezes in next to Ryan. He looks at him as he waves to get the bartender's attention. "Ryan Hutson?"

Ryan sticks out his hand. "With whom do I have the pleasure of speaking?"

"John Paul," the young man responds. "My friends call me J.P." He looks at Ryan's empty glass. "What are you drinking, my friend?"

"Scotch, but I'm a little particular about the brand."

J.P. shows two fingers to the bartender. "Robert, a shot of Macallan single malt for me and my friend."

Robert sets two glasses in front of the men. Ryan takes a sip from his and raises his eyebrows. "Very smooth."

"It should be at eighty bucks a shot."

Ryan takes another sip from his glass, acting like he drinks from a thousand-dollar bottle of Scotch every day. "Are you in the movie business, J.P.?"

"No. Exploration and production of petroleum."

"Do you own oil fields?"

"No, just the mineral rights. The meek shall inherit the earth, but the rich will own the mineral rights. Nice to meet you, Ryan. I need to keep moving."

"Same," Ryan responds.

Ryan finishes his Macallan, orders another, then decides to hit the road. He grabs Carter by the shoulder to let him know he's leaving.

"It sure gets late early out here," Carter says.

"The time you enjoy wasting is not wasted time," Ryan replies. "I've got a lot of things to do tomorrow. Plus, I got an hour's drive home."

"Tomorrow's an off day. Just chill, Dog."

"It's not an off day for me. I got a photo shoot. Then I have to show up for a filming of *The Tonight Show*."

"*The Tonight Show*? I heard they're cheapskates, only pay a couple hundred dollars to appear on the show."

"Maybe so, but my sponsors pay me big bucks to mention their products on TV."

CHAPTER THIRTY-NINE

Ryan sits backstage at the Burbank studios of *The Tonight Show*, getting his nose powdered, but not in the same manner as Willis.

A young man in blue jeans with a headset covering his ears sticks his head in the room. "You're on in thirty seconds."

"Let's give a warm welcome to Ryan Hutson of the California Angels," Johnny says as the curtain parts.

Ryan strolls on stage, smartly dressed in a lightweight beige suit and a white dress shirt unbuttoned at the top. Everyone in the audience immediately stands. Applause, whistles, and chants fill the room. Ryan stands center stage and waves to the crowd.

After a brief pause to allow the audience to settle, Ryan walks over to Johnny, shakes his hand, then takes a seat in the guest chair.

"That was a rousing entrance," Johnny says.

"The Angels have great fans," Ryan replies, which starts another round of cheers.

Johnny looks at the crowd with a stupefied expression. When they finally quiet down he tells Ryan, "Nice suit."

"You like it?" Ryan adjusts the lapels on his suit coat. "It's part of the Bobbie Jones collection of silk blends. They tend to breathe well in this climate, unlike the bird cloth some people wear." Ryan playfully looks at Johnny's suit out of the corner of his eye.

Johnny tilts his head. "I'm not familiar with bird cloth."

"It's a fabric that screams, *'cheap, cheap.'*"

Johnny laughs. "Okay, let's move on. You are probably the most popular athlete in America at this moment. You're currently batting over .400, gathering the attention of sportswriters and baseball fans across the country. You're also on television and in newspapers and magazines promoting four major products."

Ryan smiles. "Actually, it's six, Johnny."

Johnny looks at the camera with his mouth agape. "Excuse me. I understand you have a new line of cologne?"

Ryan nods. "It's called 7, which is my uniform number. I've never really been big on wearing cologne, but I like this one. It's very light and has a fresh fragrance about it."

"Now that we've got the promotional material out of the way, let's talk baseball. Your current batting average is .406. No one has batted over .400 in almost forty years."

"That's right, Johnny. Ted Williams did it in 1941. He was only twenty-two years old. Ty Cobb actually accomplished the feat three times in his career."

"How hard is it to bat .400?"

Ryan shrugs, turning his palms up. "You bat five times a game, you get two hits."

"If it were that easy, everyone would be doing it," Johnny cracks. "Do you ever get down on yourself if you aren't hitting?"

"I never blame myself," Ryan replies. "I blame the bat. If it keeps up, I change bats."

"Last year, the Angels were contenders. This year, you're in the middle of the pack. What's the difference?"

"For one thing, our pitching is off this year. We didn't expect to lose Nolan Ryan to free agency."

"Is Nolan Ryan that good of a pitcher?"

"Well, let's just say blind people come to the park just to hear him pitch."

Johnny is looking down at notes on an index card. "It says here the Angels are hitting fewer home runs than in previous years."

"It's partly because Reggie moved on. He's a great home run hitter. Also, fans tend to fight over home run balls, and they end up getting hurt. So the Angels decided not to hit as many home runs, purely for safety reasons."

Johnny politely laughs. "Well, okay. On that note, we're going to a commercial break. When we come back, we'll be joined by TV and movie actress Suzanne Traylor." He looks over at Ryan. "Will you be leaving us?"

"I'll stick around for a bit. I had a crush on Suzanne when I was a kid. I loved that TV show where she was a young girl on a farm with a pet dog."

The show returns from commercial, and Ryan scoots from the interview chair to the couch.

Johnny stands up. "Let's give a big hand for Suzanne Traylor."

Suzanne saunters onto the stage wearing a full-length, form-fitting dress that shows off every curve of her body. She blows kisses and waves to the applauding crowd. After briefly pausing to shake Johnny's hand, she bypasses the guest chair and snuggles next to Ryan on the couch.

"Maybe we can rekindle that crush you had as a kid." She loops her arm through his and leans into him.

Johnny feels left out. "Suzanne, typically, our featured guest sits in the chair next to me."

"Don't interrupt, Johnny. I'm trying to make some time." Looking intently at Ryan, she says, "I bet you have to beat the women off with a stick."

"Actually, I—"

She cuts him off before he can say anything about having a girl-friend. "I just love a modest man. You probably score more around town than you do on the ballfield." She nestles her face in the nape of his neck. "I love the smell of 7."

Ryan wiggles sideways to put a little distance between them, pretty sure Anne Marie is watching. "You sure have changed since playing the farm girl on TV," he says while laughing softly.

"The trick is growing up without growing old." Suzanne repositions herself so she's leaning against Ryan again.

Back in Montréal, Anne Marie turns off *The Tonight Show*. It's late, and she has a busy day tomorrow.

Ryan maintains his torrid hitting pace into September. As his batting average continues to hover above .400, his popularity continues to skyrocket. He's on everybody's "A-list" for social activities.

On the tenth floor of a high-rise on Wilshire Boulevard, Suzanne Traylor sits opposite Julius Handler, her agent. It's a nicely appointed office with a large picture window that overlooks Beverly Hills. A large aquarium sits on a stand next to the window. Inside the enclosure, a six-foot python lifts its head to have a look around the office.

"Let's be honest, Suzanne. You haven't had a TV show or hit movie in years. You're falling out of the public eye."

"It's your job to promote me. Do something," she replies haughtily.

Handler groans under his breath then slides a copy of *People* magazine across his desk. Suzanne picks it up and looks at the picture of Ryan on the cover.

"The popularity of this Hutson guy you were with on *The Tonight Show* is soaring. The whole town seems to be smitten with him.

Spend some time with him. Get some pictures of the two of you together. It will help with your popularity."

Suzanne puts her hands on her hips. "How do you suggest I do that?"

Handler opens his desk drawer, pulls out two tickets, and hands them to Suzanne. "We'll start with these."

The 31st Primetime Emmy Awards ceremony is held the next time the Angels are in town.

Ryan is at Bobbie Jones' boutique; Vicki, Roberta's assistant, primps him to ensure his tailored tuxedo is a perfect fit. He's looking in the full-length mirror, admiring himself, when the chauffeur enters the room.

"Miss Traylor is in the limousine waiting for you."

Ryan slides in the back seat next to Suzanne. "Thanks for the invite. I've always wanted to attend a big Hollywood gala." He grins. "My sponsors like to see me at these events, also."

Suzanne grabs ahold of his arm. "So, it has nothing to do with being with me?" She has a pouty look on her face.

"I have a special lady and a baby boy back home. I don't want this to look like a date." He tilts his head and squints an eye as he looks at her, hoping she understands. "Let's keep it casual."

"Just relax and go with the flow. Everything will be fine."

Ryan puffs out his cheeks. "Only dead fish go with the flow."

Ryan and Suzanne sit in the back of the limousine, patiently waiting their turn at the red carpet entrance of the Pasadena Civic Auditorium.

As soon as they're out of the limo, flashbulbs go off and TV cameras zoom in. Suzanne's full figure looks stunning in her sleeveless red Valentino gown that sweeps the floor as she walks. She wraps both arms around Ryan, holding him close as they stroll together down the walkway.

Joan Rivers sticks a microphone in their faces. "Inquiring minds want to know. Is there a romance blooming here?"

Ryan shakes his head vigorously and emphatically says, "No."

Suzanne smiles for the camera. "Ryan likes to keep his personal life private. I love that about him." She plants a kiss on his cheek, leaving a red lipstick imprint.

"Aww, geez." Ryan's stomach tightens. *I'm sure that'll be on TV in Montréal.*

Anne Marie turns off the television. She squeezes her eyes shut as a tear rolls down her cheek. She misses watching *Roots* win the award for Best Mini-Series.

CHAPTER FORTY

As the end of the season approaches, the Angels are one of the hottest teams in baseball. With five games to go, they trail the first-place Athletics by two games. Both teams keep an eye on the scoreboard every day to keep track of each other.

Oakland loses two consecutive games to the Texas Rangers, while the Angels take two from the Twins. The two teams pull even with three games to play. The Angels drop their third game to the Twins, then beat the Mariners the final two games of the season. Unfortunately for the Angels the Athletics sweep their three games with the Mariners. After 162 games, the Angels come up one game short.

Ryan sits on the bench in the dugout after the final out of the last game, a faraway look in his eyes.

Gregory sits next to him. "Don't be too hard on yourself. We played our butts off and kept it exciting until the final pitch."

"I'm not upset. Just a little disappointed. Going to the World Series is my dream." Ryan bites his lower lip and looks at Gregory. "Guess I'll have to wait another year."

"You'd almost rather finish ten games out than one," Gregory says. "It's less frustrating. You tend to analyze every little thing that could have made a difference."

Ryan looks at him expressionless. He doesn't know what to say, so he says nothing. With a sharp exhale, he pushes to his feet and stalks off to the locker room.

While Ryan is in the midst of changing out of his uniform, Bill Buzzi, the general manager, enters the room. He sits next to Ryan and pats him on the thigh. "Our statisticians informed me you finished the season with a .399 batting average. One hit shy of .400."

"Three-ninety-nine is a good number. I wasn't getting a lot of good pitches to look at late in the year."

"I'll have my people go over film with someone from the commissioner's office. We'll see if we can find an error or bad call that can be reversed to get you that extra hit."

"Let it go, Buzz," Ryan says in a relaxed manner. "They could also find a hit where I didn't deserve one. It's just a number. It's not that important to me."

"But it's good for baseball, Ryan."

"It's only good if it ended up at .400 after the season without any meddling. Going back through old films . . . well, it just seems so . . . I don't know what the word is, but I don't like it. Batting .400 and winning the pennant will give me something to shoot for next year."

———

Decked out in a pair of surfer shorts, Ryan stretches out on the lounge chair on his back patio. The sun beats down on his bare chest as he watches a young couple frolic with their kids in the waves. He sets down his glass of Scotch and punches #1 on his cordless phone.

Anne Marie picks it up after the fifth ring. *"Allo."*

"Bonjour, mon amour, comment ca va?"

"Hello, Ryan."

"Hi, babe. I just wanted to let you know I have a few things to wrap up here, and then I should be home in about a week."

"We will not be here, Ryan. I am taking Jacque and going to France for an extended stay. I will be buying antiques and visiting with my family."

"Wait a couple days, and I'll go with you."

"You are not welcome with us. And I do not want you to come to my home in Montréal."

Ryan jumps to his feet. "Whoa! Back up a minute. What are you talking about?"

"I do not want to see you, Ryan," she asserts, masking her sorrow.

"What do you mean? I love you and Jacque. What's wrong?"

"You have changed. You are not the man I fell in love with. You no longer have that boyish charm I came to love. It seems money has become more important to you than family."

"We need money to have a good life and give Jacque the things he wants."

"We do not need a million dollars. We need each other. Jacque needs to spend more time with his father. You never had lots of money before, and you were happy. You once said you loved playing baseball so much you would play for free." She chokes up for a moment. After a few seconds, she continues in a soft voice, "I think of the cute little boy who spent days clearing a field so he would have somewhere to play baseball."

Ryan paces back and forth across the patio. "Come on, Anne Marie. We're older now. I worked hard to get to where I am. I'm living the dream."

"Thank goodness for your dream. My dream is to have a father around for my son and to fall asleep at night with my arms around my man. I would rather you play baseball in Montréal for a thousand dollars than a million dollars in Los Angeles. Please do not make this more difficult than it has to be." She pauses for a second as she wipes a tear from her eye. "Please just let me be."

Ryan is speechless. Several moments of silence pass as they listen to each other breathe.

Anne Marie breaks the silence first. "I am sorry, Ryan. When I get back from France, we can make arrangements for you to spend time with your son."

"Okay," Ryan murmurs. "I'll send you some money for the boy."

"We don't want your money. It is your desire for money that is the problem. I have my antique shop that keeps me busy and provides enough money for us to live on. I do not require or desire opulence. You have already given me the most precious gift in the world—a beautiful and healthy boy. Thank you so much for Jacque. He brings me great joy . . . Goodbye, Ryan."

Ryan holds the phone until the dial tone snaps him out of his trance. His jaw clenches as he stares at the waves crashing on the beach. A sense of emptiness sets in.

For the next several days, Ryan lingers alone at his seaside home, drinking alcohol, not bathing, hardly sleeping, and barely eating. He even refuses to answer the phone. His broken spirit slowly enables a darker side to develop. During his period of mourning, Roberta leaves several unpleasant messages on his answering machine.

Realizing the knot in his stomach is not going to go away on its own, he finally decides to man up after five days. Clean-shaven, showered, and dressed in fresh clothes, he heads out into the world to fulfill his obligations.

In a sullen mood, he spends the better part of the day on a photo shoot for Bobbie Jones; then he appears as a guest on a sports radio talk show, though he is far from his usual affable self. Once he's back home, he ignores the flashing red light on the answering machine and heads directly to the liquor cabinet. After pouring three fingers of Scotch over ice cubes, he reaches into the pantry for a pack of Fig Newtons. The phone starts ringing as he dips a cookie into the Scotch. He ignores it until he hears Trey's voice on the answering machine.

"Ryan, it's Trey. If you're there, answer the phone. I need to talk to you."

Ryan picks up the cordless phone. "Hey, Trey."

"Hi, Ryan. Are you doing okay? I've been trying to get ahold of you for a couple of days."

"Yeah, I'm good. What's up?"

"It's Dad. He had a heart attack."

Ryan's muscles tense. "More great news," he murmurs. Already feeling anguished, this is just another heavy rock added to his backpack. "Is he okay?"

"Yeah, Oshi got him through it until the paramedics arrived. He was in the hospital for a couple of days. They ran some tests. He has some clogging in his arteries."

"That can't be good." Ryan opens the back door and walks onto the porch.

"He needs to take medication and change his lifestyle."

"Did the doctors tell him to lay off the cigarettes and martinis?"

"He quit smoking and drinking when he got married." There's a moment of silence. "You okay? You don't sound like yourself."

"Don't worry about me."

"Okay. I'm going to put Kelci on the phone."

Kelci takes the phone from Trey. "Hi, Ryan. I'm sorry about your father."

"He'll be fine. He's got grit."

"Yeah, let's hope so. Anyway, I wanted to let you know, I think it's a good time to renegotiate your contract. How about I meet you in Montréal next week to go over some things?"

"Not a good idea. Anne Marie pulled the plug on our relationship. I'm not welcome there anymore."

"I'm so sorry. Are you doing okay?"

"I'll be all right."

"I hate to ask this, but I have to. Did she get a lawyer? Is she filing a petition for child support against you?"

"No, she would never do that. She said she's happy with what she has. She doesn't want anything from me."

"She could file suit against your estate in the future. I'll arrange to send her twenty thousand dollars a month just to be safe."

Ryan's expression turns solemn, a quiet nod confirms his thought. "Sure." He murmurs a faint, wry laugh. "It wasn't that long ago I wasn't making much more than twenty thousand a year."

"Giving her twenty thousand a month will be insignificant after we negotiate a long-term contract. While I'm at it, I'm also going to jack up your endorsement fees. You're a hot commodity, and we're getting a lot of inquiries."

"Whatever. I'm in no hurry to move out of L.A. now." Ryan downs his glass of Scotch. "I hear Trey in the background. What's he yammering about?"

"He just commented that you seem angry and he hopes the money will buy you happiness."

Ryan simmers in silence, his gaze fixed on a pair of seagulls gliding overhead. Money is the root of his despair.

"I'll start the paperwork for a new contract and send it off to the Angels' management. Stay positive and call us if you need anything."

"Later." Ryan pushes the disconnect button.

Ryan knocks down his third Scotch while lying in the chaise lounge looking out on the ocean's expanse. The sun appears as a blazing, molten ball, slowly sinking, often looking distorted as it nears the horizon.

"I need to get out and do something," he says in a loud and abrupt voice. He thinks for a few seconds, then punches a number into the telephone.

She picks the phone up after two rings.

"Hi. Want some company?"

CHAPTER FORTY-ONE

L isa lives in a quaint one-bedroom flat a couple of blocks from the ocean in Long Beach.

She sits across from Ryan at her small teak dining-room table, wearing a white V-neck T- shirt. After draining a shot of tequila and taking a bite of lime, she asks, "You talk to Suzanne lately?"

Ryan shakes his head. "I can't think of anything good to say to her or about her."

"If you don't have anything nice to say, say it anyway. The bitch needs to hear the truth. She fucking used you."

"You're a potty mouth when you drink."

"Psh." She brushes off his comment. "You know, I always wondered—when a baseball player grabs his crotch, does that make him want to spit?"

Ryan grabs the front of his pants, waits a couple of seconds, and then shakes his head no.

Lisa bounces a ping-pong ball off the table and into a shot glass sitting in front of Ryan.

"You're so lucky." Ryan laughs as he grabs the bottle of tequila and fills the shot glass. He downs the shot while admiring her cleavage, which is on display every time she leans forward.

"Ha. I can't believe you say *I'm* lucky. Getting the ball in the glass is all about focus and coordination. We both know who the better athlete is here."

"I think you get better the more I drink."

She smiles at Ryan. "I'll get another lime out of the fridge."

Ryan stares at the long, slender legs protruding from her shorts as she saunters to the refrigerator.

She gives her butt a little shake, knowing full well he's staring at it.

Ryan stands up and latches on to her before she gets back to the table. With his arms wrapped around her hips, he pulls her close to him and plants his lips on her mouth. Lisa accepts his exploring tongue. After a minute of slow, sensual tongue dancing, she puts her hands on his chest and pushes away.

"Whew!" She blinks while trying to gather her composure.

"What's the matter?"

"Never let a fool kiss you or a kiss fool you."

Ryan reaches for her, but she backs off.

"Do you think I'm a fool?" he asks, grinning.

"No, but you're a good friend. You're fun and a hoot to joke around with, and I don't want to lose that with you. You came over to talk with me because you were upset tonight. If I really thought we were right for each other or this could go somewhere, I'd be all over you because you're so fucking hot. But it's not going to go anywhere, and I'm not going to give you a mercy fuck because you're drunk and upset over losing your girlfriend."

"I can give you inside stories in baseball," Ryan playfully offers in compromise.

She laughs. "You already do."

He plops down on the couch. She sits on the armrest next to him and puts her hand on his shoulder. "We've been talking and drinking for hours. Why don't we call it a night? I'll fix the couch for you to sleep on."

"Nah, I'm going home. I'll put the top down and get some fresh air. Just wish I didn't live so far away. I need to get a place downtown."

As soon as he hits the Pacific Coast Highway, Ryan stomps on the pedal. The speedometer needle whips past eighty without hesitation. Christopher Cross plays on the radio. "Ride Like the Wind."

The next morning, Ryan is on the Palos Verdes Peninsula, decked out in a pair of shorts and a Hawaiian-print shirt. He's making an appearance at a Save the Whales fundraiser. Even though he thinks the whales are doing just fine, he's required to attend a specified number of charitable events.

He endures a long line of autograph seekers and answers a bunch of questions from the journalists assigned to cover the event. As soon as his obligation is met, he breaks from the crowd and speed-walks to his car. Before he reaches the parking lot, he's intercepted by a ditzy blonde in a tank top and cutoff jeans.

"Hi. You know, you're like, a totally hot dude."

Ryan puts his hands above his eyebrows to keep the sun from his eyes. "Yeah, I hear that a lot."

"You know what would look really great on you . . .? Me," she says giddily.

Ryan studies her for a few seconds as he sits on the hood of his Vette, then looks at his watch. "I don't have time for you today. I have to be somewhere in two minutes."

"Kay." She gives him a dumb look.

"K is the chemical symbol for potassium," he comments dryly.

"Oh my God, are you a noid?"

"Not even," he replies.

He doesn't bother with the door. The top is down and he simply hops over the side of the car into the driver's seat and takes off without even a wave.

. . .

The smell of burning rubber fills the air as Ryan's Vette makes a quick turn into the parking lot of the Artesian Beverage Company, Ryan's second appointment of the day. He coaxes the car into a vacant visitor slot near the front door and he makes his entrance.

A large clock with an image of a flowing stream on its face hangs on the wall behind the reception desk. "A quarter past three. I guess forty-five minutes late is socially acceptable."

A middle-aged receptionist trying her best to look the part of a younger woman smiles at Ryan. "May I help you?"

"I'm here to see Mr. Boozer."

She picks up a planner and takes a quick look. "I'm sorry, Mr. Boozer is in a meeting at the moment."

"I should be in that meeting with him. Tell him Ryan Hutson is here."

She picks up the phone and cups her hand over the mouthpiece so Ryan can't hear her. She promptly hangs up the phone and leads Ryan to a large corner office.

Emile Boozer, vice president of marketing for Artesian Beverage, and John Ball, account executive at Makum Bye Advertising Agency, are seated at a conference table chatting, when Ryan walks in.

After a quick exchange of pleasantries, the trio gets down to business.

"You're one of the most prominent athletes on the planet right now," Ball says.

"Some people seem to think so," Ryan replies curtly.

"Trust me on that one," Boozer says. "We think you're the perfect spokesman for Kinetic, our new sports drink. Your agent provided us with terms for an endorsement contract, should you agree to promote our product."

Ryan looks at a couple aluminum cans of Kinetic sitting on the conference table. "I'd like to have a taste."

Ball slides a can over to him. "I'm not sure if it's still cold. We expected you earlier."

Ryan pops open a can and takes a chug. "Bleah!" He swallows hard. "This tastes terrible! What the heck is in this stuff?"

Both executives go bug-eyed at Ryan's crude reaction.

"The ingredients are proprietary," Boozer says.

"At least tell me what the energy portion is."

The marketing execs look at each other and shrug. "I guess it wouldn't hurt," Boozer replies. "It's mostly caffeine, high-glucose syrup, and potassium."

"K," Ryan says.

Ball and Boozer look at each other, confused.

"Is that an okay? Are you going to join our team?" Ball asks.

"K is for potassium. Nah, I can't join your team. I could never drink this stuff and couldn't ask anyone else to."

Feeling a little riled, Boozer guilelessly informs Ryan, "Kinetic is the culmination of extensive research and testing to develop the ideal solution to replenish a stressed body."

"Meaningless if no one likes the taste," Ryan is quick to respond. "I dread the day that the development of technology supersedes human interaction. The world is going to be left with a generation of idiots." Ryan looks at the two men sitting across from him. "Thanks for your time, but I've got to go. I need to get a drink to get this awful taste out of my mouth."

Boozer opens the door for Ryan. "I'm sure you can find your way out." He looks over at Ball once they're alone. "What a jerk."

After spending fifty-eight minutes getting across town, averaging seventeen miles an hour, Ryan pulls into the parking lot of Musso & Frank Grill. He enters through the front door into a dimly lit room with tables in the middle and red vinyl booths along the walls. Ryan spies Xavier Arturo, the owner of the Angels, and Bill Buzzi, general manager, sitting across from each other at a table covered with a white tablecloth. Each of them is sipping on a martini. Ryan eases onto the seat between them.

A snappily dressed waiter, full of pep, prances over to the table, softly singing, *"Hum dum de dum. I'm so rumbly in my tumbly."* He stops next to Ryan, no longer singing. "Good day, sir. What may I get for you?" he says in a chirpy voice.

"Whatever they're having."

"Very good, sir. That will be one dry martini and prime rib, rare."

The waiter walks away singing, *"Oh, I wouldn't climb this tree if a Pooh flew like a bee. But I wouldn't be a bear, so I guess I wouldn't care."* He promptly returns with a martini for Ryan.

"We received a contract proposal from your agent yesterday," Buzzi says. "Naturally, we decided it would be a good idea to meet with you in person to discuss it."

Ryan takes a gulp of his martini. "I don't get involved in contract negotiations. Someone is bound to get their feelings hurt. Kelci takes care of that stuff."

"We don't think that's totally appropriate, Ryan. It takes the personal element out of an agreement. This is between friends," Arturo tells him.

"We'd like to extend your contract, but it needs to be for less money than she's asking," Buzzi interjects.

The owner and general manager take turns attacking him from both sides.

Ryan downs the rest of his martini and waves at the waiter for another. "I'm confident she's done her research and has determined what my value is."

Arturo and Buzzi look at each other, slightly exasperated.

Buzzi reminds Ryan, "You're still under contract to the Angels."

"I know, and I fully intend to honor my contract and continue to play to the best of my abilities. But understand there are no contract negotiations during the playing season. If we don't reach an agreement before spring training, the door is closed until next October. The price could be higher then, or I could go to another team."

Arturo acts dumbfounded. "Ryan, you're like a son. The Angels are your family. Your well-being is of utmost importance to us."

Ryan looks at Arturo then Buzzi. "Then cut a deal with my agent."

"Let's not make this a money issue, Ryan. Let's keep it personal," Buzzi insists in about as sincere a voice as he can fake.

"I'm sorry, guys. Kelci doesn't tell me how to hit a curveball, and I don't tell her how to handle money."

"Let's at least discuss options," Arturo suggests.

Ryan releases a deep breath. The talk of money ruffles him. "With all due respect . . . sir, I've got something weighing heavily on my mind right now. I don't think I can focus on numbers." With one large gulp he finishes his martini. "I'm going to pass on dinner with you guys."

"We're here for you if you need anything," Arturo tells Ryan as he gets to his feet.

CHAPTER FORTY-TWO

The midmorning sun beats down on Ryan's shoulders as he walks across the beach after a swim in the ocean. He pulls his wet bathing suit off while standing under the shower on the patio, then walks naked up the stairs to his bedroom.

After shoving some clothes and toiletries into a suitcase and stowing it in the trunk of the Vette, he slides behind the wheel. The rear tires screech on the asphalt as he takes off for the Santa Monica Pier and Route 66.

After crossing town, Ryan pulls into a McDonald's on the outskirts of San Bernardino to grab a cold soda. As he walks back to his car, drink in hand, he's approached by a young man with long blond hair pulled back into a ponytail. A similarly colored, unmanicured beard extends past his Adam's apple.

"Hey, brother, can I catch a ride with you to Kingman?"

"What makes you think I'm going that way?"

"Just a guess."

Ryan looks him over. "Yeah, I suppose."

"Thanks, I'm Mason," he says, extending his hand.

Ryan shakes his hand then tosses Mason's backpack into the trunk. "I'd hate to see you walk across the Mojave Desert."

"Wasn't going to happen," he replies with a smile as he folds his tall, lanky body into the low-riding sports car. "Did you know this is the very first McDonald's?"

"No way!" Ryan says, acting like he gives a hoot.

"Yep, still has the original sign. It was built to capitalize on the large westward movement of the population along Route 66."

"For real?" Ryan punches the gas pedal, and the Vette fishtails onto the two-lane highway.

"Where you headed?" Mason asks.

Ryan thinks it's none of his business but replies anyway. "New Mexico. What's going on with you in Kingman?"

"Just a place to take a break. I'm actually headed to Chicago. I want to travel the length of Route 66."

"Why?"

"It used to be called the 'Main Street of America' because it wound through small towns lined with cafés, motels, gas stations, and tourist attractions. As soon as I-40 is completed, all the little mom-and-pop stores and points of interest will disappear. This may be my last chance to experience a little bit of nostalgia."

"We used to travel this route when I was a kid, going from Texas to California."

"Exactly, that's the way it used to be," Mason replies excitedly. "On their way to Disneyland, vacationers passed through the Painted Desert and Petrified Forest—and they would also be near the Grand Canyon."

"Been there, done all that," Ryan replies as fond memories occupy his mind.

"It's like a living photograph of American history," Mason says, gushing with enthusiasm. "The colorful billboards, teepee-shaped hotels, frozen custard stands, and reptile farms."

"The end of a legend," Ryan replies with a heavy sigh.

"You got it, brother. See that Route 66 logo painted on the road? The highway department had to put it there because people keep stealing the signs."

Ryan gives him a curious look. "Are you some kind of historian?"

"Not hardly. I teach astrophysics at Cal Tech."

"You study the universe and stuff like that?"

"Pretty much."

"You know, I was up all night wondering where the sun went . . . then it dawned on me."

Mason responds with a polite laugh. "Good to see you smile, man. You seem uptight."

Ryan arches an eyebrow. "Mind if I turn up the radio?"

With a flip of the wrist, Pure Prairie League's "Two Lane Highway" fills the car.

A little more than four hours later, Ryan steers the Vette onto the main drag of Kingman. "Where to, my man?"

"You can drop me off at the Route 66 Museum." Mason points toward a 1928 locomotive.

Ryan's next stop is Winslow. He pulls into an Art-Deco gas station clad in white porcelain tile and equipped with ten-foot red cylinder gas pumps that have clock faces on top to measure the gallons pumped.

An attendant dressed in a clean, crisp company uniform rushes out to pump the gas, check the oil and water levels, and wash the windows. After his tank is filled and his bladder drained, Ryan grabs a cold soda from the door of a vintage coke machine and wanders down Kinsley Avenue to stretch his legs. When he reaches the corner, he stops and waves at a girl in a flatbed Ford who slowed down to take a look at him.

Eastern Arizona is a long, boring stretch of flat, mostly sandy soil with prairie grass, sagebrush, and a few cacti. Cruising ninety miles an hour, Ryan zips past a deserted gas station that was beaten to death by intense sun and windblown sand. A rusty old truck and corroded pumps sit out front.

When he reaches Albuquerque, he exits Route 66 and cruises onto I-25, heading toward the mountains and the family ranch.

CHAPTER FORTY-THREE

Ryan's Vette hugs the pavement like a slot car as it speeds along the steep and winding mountain road. He eases off the pedal when he spots a scenic overlook on one of the sweeping curves. He pulls over, cuts the engine, and gets out of the car, stretching his arms and back. A cool, fresh mountain breeze hits him in the face. Leaning against a wooden guardrail, he peers down the mountainside. Five hundred feet below, the Jemez River carves a channel through a valley of aspens and evergreens.

Ryan takes a deep breath, then releases it slowly. "Just relax," he says to himself. "It seems like I've been on the go forever. It was a long baseball season. With all the public appearances and numerous photo shoots, it doesn't feel like I had much free time." Thoughts of Anne Marie and his dad's health further tax his mind and body. Watching an eagle casually drift in the current overhead momentarily fills him with a peaceful, easy feeling.

On his second day out of Los Angeles, Ryan steers his car down the gravel road leading to the family ranch. A light dusting of snow covers the ground. Next to the road, on the other side of a wooden fence, several horses casually graze on hay that has been set out for them. A couple of foals kick up their heels and race after each other.

Seems pretty quiet around here, Ryan thinks as he pulls the Vette to a stop in front of the house. He reminisces about his mother coming to the door to meet him when she heard the car pulling up and how Billy would come racing from behind the barn to welcome him home. Today, nothing. Not even the hired hands can be seen.

Ryan gets out of the car and trudges a little more than a hundred paces to a grassy area beneath a burr oak. He stands looking down at a white cross, his mind full of memories. Speaking softly, he says, "You were an incredible dog, Billy. You were the only one that understood me when I was a kid. I'll never forget your bright eyes and your endless enthusiasm. I love you, buddy." Ryan squeezes his eyes shut.

"Hello," Ryan softly calls as he walks through the living room and into the kitchen. "Where is everybody?"

A soft, steady buzz comes from the back of the house. Ryan follows the sound into what used to be his dad's office. There's no furniture in the room now, only pads on the floor.

"Whoa!" Ryan's eyes nearly pop out of his head when he sees his dad and Oshi sitting on the floor with bare feet and their legs crossed. Steady hums emanate from deep within their chests. He watches them for a few seconds before deciding they probably don't want to be disturbed.

He leaves them to their droning and returns to the kitchen, where he opens the refrigerator door and looks inside for something to drink. There's no beer or soda pop, only some type of thick green liquid. Inspection of the cupboards is next. Nothing but jars of roots, berries, and seeds with names like ginseng, echinacea, and lemon balm printed on the labels.

"Doesn't look like I'm going to find any booze or snacks in the house," he mumbles.

Jack and Oshi enter the room as Ryan, with a deep sigh of dejection, closes the door of a kitchen cabinet. Jack reaches out and pulls him into a hug. Ryan is a little taken aback. He doesn't recall ever receiving any physical display of emotion from his dad before.

"Welcome home, son."

"Good to see you, Dad." Ryan takes a step back. "Are you doing okay? I heard you had some issues with blood sticking to the sides of your vessels."

"That's not technically correct, but I'll be all right. I'm trying to overcome many years of bad habits by taking better care of myself." He looks at Oshi. "This is my wife, Oshi."

"It's a pleasure to finally meet you, Ryan," Oshi says. "Your father has told me so many wonderful things about you." Oshi is a short, slim woman with soft, healthy skin. Her long black hair is pulled into a bun behind her head.

"Thank you. Nice to meet you also."

"Please, sit down." Oshi pulls out a chair. "Let me fix you something to eat."

Ryan sits, skeptical of the food she might serve him.

Jack sets a glass filled with amber liquid in front of him. "Oshi just brewed a fresh batch of green tea."

Ryan takes a drink. "Nice."

Oshi places a plate with sliced apple, goat cheese, and homemade bread in front of Ryan.

"Looks delicious, thanks," he says, trying to sound sincere. "I guess you heard I was chasing a .400 batting average this year?"

"We certainly did. Very impressive, son."

"We were rooting for you, and of course, the Angels," Oshi says. "We saw your commercials and your spot on *The Tonight Show*. You looked so handsome."

"Thanks. Um, speaking of *The Tonight Show*, I'm not seeing Anne Marie any longer."

Jack has a pained look. "We're sorry to hear that. Oshi and I hope to still meet Jacque."

"I'm sure his mom will let him meet his grandfather," Ryan says while rubbing his shoulder.

Oshi puts her hands on Ryan's upper arm. "Do you feel pain in your joint?"

Ryan bobs his head slowly. "A little. A hundred and sixty-two games in six months can do that to you."

"I can make a compress with a couple of herbs that will speed up the healing process and help soothe the inflamed tissue."

"Thanks, but it'll be okay with a little rest." Ryan looks over at his dad and jokingly comments, "Pretty convenient to have office space to turn into a meditation room."

Wearing a calculated expression, Jack replies, "We set the room up to do yoga, but it turned out to also be a good place to meditate. The afternoon sun coming in the windows in the room is invigorating."

Ryan chuckles. "Have you given up martinis and cigarettes for yoga and vegetable juice?"

Oshi and Jack look at each other in silence.

"That's a strange comment to make," Jack says. "Especially since you're an athlete. It just makes sense to take care of your body." Jack looks at Ryan pensively. "Oshi and I believe in a healthy mind and body. Our lifestyle commitment ranges from the food we eat to the books we read to even the way we breathe. We normally go to bed shortly after sunset and get up before sunrise."

"Excuse me." Ryan's cheeks burn.

Oshi and Jack go to bed early, which allows Ryan to slip out the door and drive into town to grab a martini and pizza and watch some football.

The next morning, Ryan is going through some drawers in the kitchen, looking for a pen and paper. While shuffling some items around, he comes across several needles in a leather case.

Jack enters the room. "Can I help you find something?"

Ryan has a smirk on his face. "What are these? Voodoo needles?"

Jack takes a deep breath and sighs. He's been patient while politely ignoring Ryan's ridicule of their lifestyle. "No, son. Those are acupuncture needles. Oshi is knowledgeable of the central nervous system and how to treat pain and injuries with the placement of needles."

Ryan senses his father's decreasing tolerance of his smart mouth. *I don't need to upset anyone because I'm feeling unsettled. Probably a good idea to leave before I really say something rude.*

After taking a walk through the tall evergreens along the river and visiting with the horses in the barn, Ryan gorges himself on fresh fruits and a salad for lunch.

"I'll be moving on this afternoon," Ryan tells Oshi and his dad while they sit at the kitchen table. "There are some things I need to tend to."

"It was good to see you, son. We're sorry to see you go."

Oshi grabs both his hands. "This is your home. You are welcome here at any time."

"Thank you."

Jack gives Ryan a hug. "I love you, son."

Ryan's mind is a jumbled jigsaw puzzle. He misses the emotional and physical connection with Anne Marie. Now his father, who he always had a strained relationship with, suddenly acts all sentimental with him.

"Take care of yourself, Dad. I'm glad you're doing okay."

A few miles down the road, Ryan pulls into the parking lot of a small brick church his mother attended. He gets out of the car and strolls past the chapel, then continues along a grassy hillside, kicking up powdered snow along the way. Behind the church, he comes to a gathering of headstones surrounded by a white picket fence. His mom's headstone is nestled under a pair of ponderosa pines overlooking a beautiful river valley. A small concrete bench sits next to her grave. Ryan looks down at the poem etched into the polished surface of the bench.

Do not stand
By my grave, and weep.
I am not there,
I do not sleep—
I am the thousand winds that blow
I am the diamond glints in snow
I am the sunlight on ripened grain,
I am the gentle, autumn rain.
As you awake with morning's hush,
I am the swift, up-flinging rush
Of quiet birds in circling flight,
I am the day transcending night.
Do not stand
By my grave, and cry—
I am not there,
I did not die.
Clare Harner

Ryan sits on the bench and pulls a photograph out of his wallet. It's a picture of his entire family, including Billy, that was taken before he dropped out of college. It was the last time he saw his mother healthy. "I miss you and wish you could see me playing professional baseball," he whispers. "I have a beautiful boy. You would love him." After a few moments of silence, he continues, "Then again, you probably know what's going on. I felt you looking out for me on several occasions." He gazes at her headstone and smiles. "When I was traveling the Great Lakes, a Chippewa told me, 'If you hold loved ones that are deceased in your thoughts, they will come alive in spirit. The spirits go back to sleep when they are not in someone's thoughts.' I'll always keep your spirit alive."

He brushes the side of his face with his fingers, thinking the soft mountain breeze blew something against his cheek.

"Go Your Own Way" by Fleetwood Mac plays on the radio as Ryan sits in his car, pondering his next move. *What the heck? Go east, young man.*

He cranks the engine, punches the gas pedal, and directs the car to I-25 South.

CHAPTER FORTY-FOUR

After close to nine hours driving, not including an overnight stay in Midland, Ryan leaves the flat land and desert scrub behind and enters the Hill Country of Texas. When he zips past the exit for Junction, he knows Comfort isn't far away. His earliest memories were formed in this town. He remembers how he and Billy would play in the woods all day, and how his mom prepared the best breakfasts on the weekends. He laughs a little when he thinks about her constantly telling him he was going to go blind sitting so close to the TV. "My worst memory," he recalls, "I was terrible at baseball, and nobody wanted me on their team."

When he reaches Exit 523, he eases the car off I-10 and onto Route 87. He slowly cruises through Comfort, thinking the old town hasn't changed in fifteen years. He pauses at a four-way stop sign at the intersection where the bank and library sit on opposite corners. A calico cat is asleep on the bench in front of the library. There's still no need for a traffic light in the small town.

He drives to the house where he lived as a kid and stops his car out front. He sits for a few minutes, with the engine idling. The old place still looks the same, the trees are bigger and a couple new houses have been built close by. He pulls away from the front of the house and turns onto the road he and Trey walked down to get to their ballfield.

When he reaches the ballfield, he turns the Vette into the gravel lot and parks behind the third base line. Ryan gets out of his car and sits on the bottom row of the bleachers. It's a typical autumn day in Texas—sunny and in the mid-seventies. A few clouds lazily waltz across the sky.

"Ouch!" He shoots to his feet and pulls a splinter from his backside.

The old field hasn't aged gracefully. The chain-link backstop is covered in rust and is curled up at the bottom. Weeds populate a large portion of the outfield, and runners of grass invade the infield.

Lost in thought, Ryan pays no mind to a car that pulls into the lot. He's thinking back on the days the community came together to build the park when he gets a tap on his shoulder.

"What're you up to, boy?"

"Just enjoying the sunshine," Ryan replies without turning around.

"Would you mind showing me your driver's license?"

Ryan turns around and looks at a heavyset man in a sheriff's uniform. He notices the name badge above the right breast pocket. "It's in my car."

"I would be obliged if you would get it for me."

"I'm pretty comfortable sitting here for the time being."

"Listen up, wise guy. When a stranger pulls into my town and drives through slowly, stopping every now and then to check things out, I find it very suspicious. I also find it a matter of concern that someone with California plates on their car would be sitting at our ballfield in the middle of the day."

Ryan smiles. "Maybe it does look a little strange." He looks about the field. "For your information, I lived in this town many years ago. I used to play ball here when it was nothing more than a field."

The sheriff moves directly in front of Ryan, bends over, and puts his face as close to Ryan's as he can—without looking like he's going to ask him for a date. He stares at him a few seconds before asking, "You Trey Hutson's baby brother?"

"Yeah, Humble, you fat ass, I'm Trey's brother." Ryan stands up to face him. He's almost four inches taller than the sheriff.

"You best watch who you're calling a fat ass."

"Pfft," Ryan scoffs. "I'll never forget the first time I met you . . . but I keep trying." Ryan looks him up and down. "Why don't you get yourself in shape? You're a disgrace to law enforcement."

"Obesity runs in my family."

"Hell, nobody runs in your family."

Ryan notices Humble's face turning red and decides to back off. He reaches out to shake his hand. "How the heck are you doing, Dan? You married? Got kids? Anyone still around that we knew when we were younger?"

Turns out Humble can be a personable sort when given the opportunity. "I married Jolene, my high school sweetheart, and we got two girls in elementary school. My parents moved to Florida. We live in the house I grew up in. Hmm . . . let's see, who else is around?" Humble ponders for a few moments. "Joe Buckley still lives in the area. He's the mayor and owns a couple car dealerships north of San Antonio. He was valedictorian of our class. Oh yeah, and Larry, our baseball coach, lives in a large house in Uvalde. Owns an exploration company and a few drill rigs. I hear he's a millionaire." Humble gets a sad look on his face. "Tyler, Trey's best friend, was killed in Nam. Most everyone else has moved on."

"Why didn't you ever get away from here?"

"No reason. We're happy here. Every now and then, we take the kids to Six Flags or down to the Gulf to swim in the ocean." Humble stands in front of Ryan, his hands on his hips. "What's going on with Trey?"

"He owns a construction company in North Carolina. Married and has a couple kids. He seems happy about everything." Ryan squints, the sun in his face. "Is there somewhere we can go and grab a drink?"

"Not while I have the uniform on." Humble hesitates for a few seconds, then nods toward his cruiser. "I do have a pint of bourbon in the car. I keep it handy for my cough. I can grab it if you'd like to have a snort."

"That'd be neighborly of you."

Humble goes to his patrol car and returns with the bourbon. He gets a quizzical look on his face. "Are you *the* Ryan Hutson?"

Ryan takes a swallow of whiskey. "How many Ryan Hutsons are you aware of?"

Humble coughs a few times then grabs the pint from Ryan. "Don't be such a wise-ass. I'll shoot your balls off if you don't quit jerking me around."

A smile crosses Ryan's face. "If you're talking about the baseball player for the California Angels, yeah, that'd be me."

"Folks around here were wondering if you were the one who used to play ball here as a kid. They been talking about putting a plaque up with your name on it."

Ryan scans the run-down ballpark, thinking, *I wouldn't want my name on this dump.* "Anybody around town got any interest in sports or recreational activities?"

"There is interest. But typically, the wealthy families take their kids to the San Antonio suburbs to play sports. The facilities are better there. Nowadays, kids mostly come to this park to smoke pot or get frisky with their dates."

"I'll tell you what, Dan. You get a hold of Mayor Joe Buckley and tell him to build a sports complex here. I want a nice baseball field, a basketball court, and a facility with indoor plumbing that has rooms for art classes, reading, and exercise. Somewhere nice the kids can come after school that will hopefully keep them off drugs. Put the Hutson name on a plaque that goes on the building. Make sure it's something nice if it has our name on it."

"Going to be a lot of moolah, my friend."

Ryan whips Kelci's business card out of his wallet like it's an American Express. "Send the bill to my agent. Tell her the park is going to be named after her husband."

CHAPTER FORTY-FIVE

Having no other business to tend to in Comfort, Ryan jumps back onto I-10 and heads in the direction of Mobile. From there, he treks northeast across Alabama into Georgia and up to Atlanta. Three hours after leaving Atlanta, he leisurely cruises along the mountaintops of North Carolina. Breathtaking panoramas of wooded river valleys, rocky outcrops and cascading waterfalls flank both sides of the Blue Ridge Parkway.

When he reaches the Asheville exit, he pulls off the Parkway and guides the Vette down a winding mountainside road until he reaches Loblolly Pine Lane, the entryway to Trey and Kelci's home. He chuckles when he thinks *the developers cut the trees down, then named the roads and developments after them.*

At the end of the lane and nestled amongst wild azaleas, pines, and hemlocks is Trey and Kelci's sprawling brick ranch.

The same two large dogs that greeted Ryan the last time he was here immediately rush up to the Vette, barking. They prance in circles around Ryan, showing their fangs when he gets out of the car.

Trey rambles out the front door and walks toward the car to greet Ryan. He claps his hands and hollers, "Git!"

Both dogs back off while looking over their shoulders at Ryan.

Trey reaches out to shake Ryan's hand, then pulls him into a shoulder hug. "Vaya, look who has cometh."

"Ahoy hoy," Ryan replies. Looking at the dogs, he says, "They're a good deterrent to anyone coming here uninvited."

"They can be a pain in the butt sometimes. Just the other day, the sheriff stopped by and said the dogs were chasing people on bicycles. I looked at the sheriff kinda funny and said, 'That's gotta be someone else's dogs, Sheriff. Ours don't own bikes.'"

"Cute," Ryan replies. "Are they house dogs?"

Trey gets a broad smile. He appreciates a good straight man. "We made an attempt to housebreak them when they were younger. The bigger dog actually went on the paper three times one night. Twice while I was reading it. They've since been relegated to the outdoors."

"At least they provide you with a source of levity."

Kelci bounces out of the house, glowing, an infant in one arm and a toddler at her side. Ryan reaches out to squeeze her free hand when she reaches the driveway. She leans forward and kisses his cheek.

Shifting her weight between her feet, she nods to the bigger of the two boys. "C.J.'s almost three now, and his little brother, Sam, is going to be one soon."

Ryan twists his lips. "Jacque's nearly two."

Kelci disrupts Ryan's solemn reverie. "So, let's take a look at you." Her voice is vibrant and full of energy. "You look divine. I'm so glad you could make it." She tugs on his hand, leading him toward the house. "I have several things we need to go over."

Ryan looks around the property as he follows Kelci into the house. "Looks like you've made some changes around the homestead." He eyes the swimming pool and a three-bay garage in the backyard. "Construction business must be good."

"Booming," Trey replies. "Of course, Kelci keeps pretty busy, also."

"Really?"

Trey gives his brother a look of bewilderment. "Hello, Ryan, are you just visiting planet Earth? Kelci helps manage our construction company, but mostly, it's all about you, little brother. Do you have any idea how much time she spends on you?"

Ryan shrugs, his eyebrows raised. "I know she handles my baseball and endorsement contracts."

"She oversees *all* your legal matters and finances. Taking care of you is like running a small business." Trey looks over at Kelci, who gives him a stern look. He smiles at her. "Behind every successful man is a woman rolling her eyes."

Ryan looks at Kelci. "Thanks. I had no idea."

"You're welcome, Ryan. I'm glad to help you. Besides, you pay me well," she says, a glitter in her eye. "Come on. Let's go inside the house and relax for a bit."

"Great. I could use a dry martini."

"Sorry, Ryan, we don't keep liquor in the house," Trey says.

Ryan stops in his tracks and looks at his brother. "Dang, Trey. Some of Dad's new lifestyle rubbing off on you?"

Trey puts his hand on Ryan's back, gently pushing him toward the house. "Maybe some of his old lifestyle is rubbing off on you?"

"It doesn't hurt to have a drink to take the edge off every now and then," Ryan says.

"Ha! What have you got to be uptight about? You're a grown man who makes a million dollars playing a kid's game."

Ryan looks at his feet as he recalls his last conversation with Anne Marie.

"What's going on inside your head?" Trey asks, noticing the distant look in his brother's eyes.

"Right now, I'm having amnesia and déjà vu at the same time. I think I've forgotten this discussion before."

Trey holds the front door open as Ryan passes through.

After an hour sitting in the living room and talking baseball and life in L.A., Trey excuses himself to tend to the kids, allowing Ryan and Kelci to discuss business.

They head to her home office and grab seats at the conference table. Kelci opens a folder and pulls out several documents. "First of all, we need to go over your contract with the Angels." She slides the agreement over to Ryan. "After you visited with them, they contacted me and said they're willing to renegotiate. They want to increase the number of years they have you under contract."

"I guess more years in L.A. is fine since it doesn't look like I'm welcome in Montréal."

Kelci peers at him quietly for a few seconds before she returns to the matter at hand. "They presented two different options. One option is five years, four million, fully guaranteed. The other is four years, four million, and fewer guarantees."

"And the downside of fewer guarantees is?"

"You're assuming more risks. If they cut you, they don't have to pay you."

Ryan scratches his head. "Why would they cut me if I'm playing well?"

"Maybe because of injury or someone better coming along. Or maybe just because they're tired of paying you lots of money."

"So with the guaranteed contract, I would be making eight hundred thousand a year versus one million per year with the unguaranteed contract?"

Kelci pulls out a piece of paper and shows it to Ryan. "The unguaranteed contract is more like $750,000, $950,000, $1.1 million, and then $1.2 million in the final year. I'll negotiate some performance clauses in so we can get another $600,000 or so over the life of the contract."

"Okay, let's go with the unguaranteed." Ryan slaps the table.

"Are you sure? You're taking a big gamble."

"The Angels told me I'm like family to them. I'm sure they'll take care of me if anything happens."

"They'll tell you anything to save themselves money. All right, let's talk endorsements." She opens another folder. "As of today, you're under contract with four firms. Two other contracts have expired, and I don't recommend renewing. Last year, you grossed more than half a million in non-baseball income. Currently, there's a high demand for your services. We can't accept them all, so we're going to up your rate 25%. We're also raising your public appearance fees by 35%."

Ryan tilts his head as he looks at Kelci. "Aren't you afraid of losing clients?"

"We'll make up for what we lose in the number of clients with the increase in rates for the clients we keep." She winks at him. "Less work, more money."

"I like that."

"Just be sure to stay productive so you stay in the public eye." She picks up some other documents, humming as she skims them. "This is a list of your investments. I have power of attorney to buy and sell stocks, bonds, mutual funds, and real properties on your behalf. Would you like to review your investments?"

"Should I?"

"Not really. I make all decisions for you. You're doing pretty well. You got a 36% return on your investments last year. I'm continuously buying and reinvesting, so you're income averaging and getting compound interest."

"Sounds confusing, but hey, I'm sure you know what you are doing."

Kelci moves her head up and down in a positive manner. "Going forward, we need to take into consideration different tax breaks and shelters."

"Are you going to take care of it?"

"Of course. From your perspective, ignorance is bliss," she says with a smile on her face. "On another note, what would you like for dinner? I'm going to make a run to the grocery store."

"How about I take everyone out to dinner? I'd like to go somewhere I can get a drink."

"We can go to Pack Square Park. They're doing some wonderful things downtown."

With a kid in a highchair on each side of Trey and Kelci, the Hutson clan sits around the restaurant table, waiting for their food to be served. Ryan's on his second martini. Several people in the restaurant peer at him, recognizing his face from TV. A starry-eyed boy, probably around twelve, comes up to the table holding a pen. "Can I have your autograph, Ryan? You're my favorite player."

"Not when I'm out with my family," Ryan abruptly replies, leaving the boy speechless.

Trey gives Ryan a troubled look. "I can't believe you just did that. Did you forget what it was like to be a kid and admire a professional ballplayer?"

"I got other things on my mind, Trey." He downs the rest of his martini. "By the way, speaking of kids, you have a sports complex in Comfort named after you. The kids will love it. They'll have somewhere nice to go after school."

"Wonderful gesture," Trey says. "But just a thought. Maybe the kids will enjoy it more if you visit the park occasionally."

Sensing a bit of sarcasm in his voice, Ryan asks, "You're not getting pissed off, are you, Trey?"

"Better to be pissed off than pissed on. But never at you, little brother."

Looking to change the subject, Kelci asks Ryan, "What are your thoughts on Ronald Reagan as the next president?"

Ryan looks for the waiter to order another drink. "Hopefully, he'll stand up to Iran and get the hostages out. Carter's kinda wimpy at times."

"Politicians are like diapers," Trey responds. "They need to be changed regularly for the same reasons."

C.J., who has been sitting quietly while the adults talk, grabs a spoon and flings it to the floor. The boy is not fond of being ignored. Trey squints an eye and glares at his son. C.J. sticks his bottom lip out and looks at his dad with sad eyes.

"Don't the kids aggravate you sometimes?" Ryan asks while looking at the pouting boy. "It's got to be tough, especially with both of you working."

Trey shakes his head, perplexed by his brother's comment. "No, Ryan, these are our children. We love them."

Kelci notices Ryan cringe when Sam lets loose a piercing scream. "Do you miss Jacque?"

Ryan presses his lips together then lets out a deep breath. "I miss him and his mother."

"Any chance you and Anne Marie will get back together?" Kelci asks, seeing the pain in his eyes.

"I doubt it. I don't think she's cut out to be married to a baseball player. Of course, the media didn't help our relationship. They show up in the clubhouse or pester you in public and dig for rumors. Then they print the rumors as facts. Some journalists are nothing more than scamps."

Kelci gives him a sympathetic look. "It's the price of being a celebrity."

Ryan waves at the waiter and points at his empty martini glass.

"Why don't you slow down on the alcohol?" Trey says. "There are families and kids in here that recognize you. And if you're not aware, they look up to you."

"So what? Should I put on a happy face and visit all the tables?"

"A year ago, you would have. Now you're acting strange. Quite frankly, your personality seems kind of drab."

Ryan stares daggers at his brother. "Maybe I need to get away from everybody for a while and work out some of this drabness."

It's been two weeks since anyone has heard anything from Ryan. Kelci is in her office tending to paperwork when the phone rings. She sets her pen down and takes off her reading glasses.

"Hello . . . Hey, Ryan, how are you? . . . You're in the British Virgin Islands? . . . *You did what?* . . . Good grief. What are you doing buying a bar on a Caribbean island? . . . Oh, okay, it's more like a rum shack, a little shanty on a beach instead of a bar, even better . . . Well, that's good. You're just a partner, not the primary owner?" Kelci sighs with exasperation. "I never should have let you go to the islands unchaperoned . . . Um, hmm." Kelci nods. "Colin is an Australian, so he gets tax benefits in the British Virgin Islands . . . I'm sure he's a wonderful man."

CHAPTER FORTY-SIX

October 1983

Ryan is voted to the All-Star team each of the next three seasons. Even though his ball playing is impressive, he maintains an apathetic attitude off the field. Other people's feelings aren't of great importance to him.

The season after batting .399, Ryan hits .351 and swats twelve more home runs than the previous year. The following year, he slugs fifty-two home runs, the most anyone has hit since Roger Maris hit sixty-one in 1961. Last season, he won the Triple Crown with a .344 batting average, forty-six home runs, and 117 RBIs. Despite his stellar play, the Angels never make it to the World Series.

Ryan relaxes on a chaise lounge on the deck of his Malibu home. He feels the heat of the sun beating on his face. The World Series is on the radio in the background. He tilts his sunglasses up, dabs sunscreen on his face, and then rubs it in. A gentle breeze blows salt air in off the ocean. Kids are in school, and most people are at work, which leaves the beach mostly deserted.

The cordless phone starts ringing as Ryan dips a Fig Newton into a glass of Scotch. He picks it up after five rings. "Hello . . . Hey, Kelci . . . My contract has been extended four years for seven million?" He jolts to his feet, spilling his drink on his bare chest. "Are you serious? . . . Oh, okay." His breathing returns to normal, and he sits back down. "One point seven million or so per year." Pause. "No, are you kidding? I didn't really think they were going to pay me seven million a year . . . We're down to three endorsement contracts. Okay. Together they're worth over a million per year? . . . That's cool. I'm tired of being on the run all the time."

With the increase in disposable income, Ryan purchases a second home —the penthouse suite on the forty-third floor of The Ritz-Carlton. It's a premier downtown Los Angeles location that has style and elegance written all over it. Glass walls provide stunning views of the city below, and the inside was constructed using the finest materials and home technology. Gas fireplaces in the master bedroom and family room add warmth to the home with the flip of a switch. Remote control lighting and motorized shades throughout add convenience. The hotel spa and fitness center, dedicated concierge, valet parking, and a complimentary daily breakfast are included in the price of his new home.

Three weeks have passed since Ryan settled into his new digs. Kelci stands at the glass window, observing the scurrying headlights of the traffic six hundred feet below. Flames flicker in the fireplace as she sips on a glass of Pinot Noir.

Ryan stands at the bar, pouring Scotch over a glass of ice. "Awesome view, isn't it?"

"Absolutely. I love it. Downtown property is a great investment."

"Want a Fig Newton?"

Kelci shakes her head. "Nah, I'm good."

They sit down on opposite ends of a suede couch. Kelci comments, "I'm surprised you gave up on that Chevy gig. That was easy money."

Ryan dips a Fig Newton in his glass of Scotch. "It wasn't me."

She looks at him with raised eyebrows. "Really? So, what exactly is you?"

"What do you mean?"

She turns her body and faces him full-on. "I don't understand all this drinking and womanizing."

"I drink because it makes people more interesting. And the girls . . . well, you know."

"Yeah, I think I do." Kelci leans back and crosses her feet at the ankles. "You haven't been yourself since Anne Marie left you. Dare I say you've maintained a dispassionate attitude about everything not baseball?"

"Let's talk about something else."

"Do you talk with Anne Marie?"

Ryan quickly shakes his head. "No, she prefers to keep her distance. But I do enjoy spending time with Jacque." Ryan's enthusiasm picks up as he talks about his son. "He started kindergarten this year."

"Is he going to be a sports junkie like his dad?"

"I doubt it. I take him to the park sometimes during my visitation and try to toss the ball with him. As much as I try coaching him, he can't get the hang of catching and throwing a baseball."

"Be patient. Trey says you were pretty clumsy when you were younger."

Ryan allows a momentary grin to stretch across his face. "Yeah, I suppose so. I'll tell you one thing, he loves to play the piano. His mom started him on lessons early."

Kelci smiles as she notices the excitement in Ryan's voice. "You're still a good person, Ryan, even though you've been ornery lately." She gives him a hug. "I love you, brother."

A shabbily dressed man sits on the sidewalk, his legs stretched out in front of him. His slumped body leans against the granite wall of The Ritz-Carlton, just outside the bright lights of the covered entrance. Long hair hangs over the collar of his tattered shirt, and he looks like he hasn't shaved in a month.

He jumps to his feet when a black Maserati stops at the front door to The Ritz. The bright lights from the overhead canopy reflect off the shiny car. The doorman, dressed in a black tux, comes forward and opens the passenger door. A tall blonde in a strapless top and silk leggings slides out.

"Good evening, Roger," Ryan says as he gets out from behind the wheel. "Have my car parked. I'm in for the night."

"Yes, sir, Mr. Hutson."

The stranger steps from the darkness of the night and into the bright lights. "Yo, Ryan, hold up a second."

Ryan looks at him then scoffs. He takes a hold of the lady's hand and quickly leads her through the front door, looking to avoid any confrontation with the bum.

The next morning, after finishing breakfast with his guest in the main dining room of the hotel, Ryan says, "I'll have the concierge call a cab for you, Nancy."

"It's Nanette," she replies with a polite smile.

"Oh, okay. I'm going to hit the spa for a bit before I head to the ballpark. You take care of yourself."

"Sure, Ryan. It was fun. Maybe we'll do it again sometime?"

"Sure. I'll call you." He holds the back of her arm and leads her to the front door of the hotel, then gives her a kiss on the cheek.

The Angels play the Red Sox in an afternoon game.

Ryan comes to bat in the bottom of the third in a scoreless contest.

"How's it going, Rick?" he says to the Sox's catcher as he steps into the batter's box.

"It's Rich," the catcher replies.

Ryan takes the first pitch for a called strike then watches two consecutive balls. The fourth pitch he lines deep into the left-field bleachers, a couple feet on the meaningless side of the foul pole. The next pitch is a slow, arching knuckleball. It looks to be several inches outside of the plate.

"Sttrrike three!" the umpire bellows as he turns his body and pumps his fist.

Ryan drops his bat and looks at the umpire. "You got to be kidding me!"

The ump stares at him without saying a word.

"What's the matter? Did you lose the ball in the lights? Nope, can't be that, it's daylight. The sun must have gotten in your eyes."

The umpire removes his face mask and takes a step toward Ryan. "Are you done whining?"

Ryan steps closer to the ump, their noses almost touching. "Not yet. I know you're blind because I've seen how ugly your wife is."

The umpire jerks his thumb up in the air. "You're out of here. Anything else to say, wise guy?"

"Yeah, not only are you blind and stupid, but you're fat and you smell."

Ryan tromps back to the bench and plops down next to Trevor, a youngster on a recent call-up from their minor league team in Edmonton. "Never let them get the last word in, kid."

Ryan stops at the Frolic Room for a couple of martinis on his way home from the ballpark. It's a little after eight and the sun has dropped behind the downtown buildings when he pulls his Maserati up to the entrance of The Ritz. As soon as he's out of the car, the vagrant who approached him the night before reappears and walks toward him. "Yo, Ryan, got a minute for an old buddy?"

Ryan stops in his tracks and clenches his teeth. When he relaxes his jaw, he sounds off. "I'm not your buddy. Now get lost!"

The bum stands still, his arms limp at his sides. "Good to know."

There's an eerie familiarity to the voice. Ryan drifts over for a closer look.

The man's body is so feeble it would probably get blown over in a strong wind.

After a few seconds of looking into eyes that are sucked in from malnourishment, Ryan softly asks, "Josh?"

CHAPTER FORTY-SEVEN

Josh crosses his arms tightly across his chest and nods slowly.

"Aww, geez. What happened?"

"Things didn't go the way I hoped."

Roger, the concierge, quickly shuffles over. "Should I dispose of him, Mr. Hutson?"

"No." Ryan shakes his head. "This is my best friend from high school."

Ryan puts his arm around Josh's shoulders. "Come on. Let's go upstairs."

Once they're inside Ryan's condo, Josh's eyes sweep over the interior. "Nice pad."

"Let's get you cleaned up and into some decent clothes." Looking at Josh's skinny body, Ryan guesses, "About a thirty waist?"

"Probably more like twenty-eight."

"What size shoes?"

"Nine and a half."

Ryan points toward the hallway. "The guest bathroom is the second door on the right. You need to take a shower. There are extra razor blades and toothbrushes in there. Please, use them."

Ryan follows him to the bathroom then shuts the door behind him. He walks away grimacing. "What a mess."

Grabbing the phone off the kitchen wall, Ryan calls guest services. Cynthia, the shift manager, picks up. "Cindy, call Macy's for me and have them send over some clothes." He gives her the sizes. "Put them in a cab, Pony Express, or whatever, but get them here as soon as possible. After that, get ahold of the kitchen and have them send up a couple of steaks with all the fixings."

Josh wanders out of the bathroom, wearing a Ritz-Carlton bathrobe, about the same time the steaks arrive. They sit at the dining room table; Ryan casually eats his food as he watches Josh scarf his down.

Ryan looks at his friend's skinny arms and notices track marks. He grabs Josh's wrist and twists it to get a closer look at the crook of his elbow. "What's going on here?"

Josh dips his head. In a sullen voice he responds, "Nam. I got drafted eight months after graduation. I didn't have the guts to go to Canada. Besides, the Army said the war would be over in a few months." Josh is close to tears. "Shit. It went on for another three years."

Ryan releases a deep breath, feeling his pain. "Messed with your head pretty good, eh?"

"The Army brainwashes you into thinking communism is bad. It must be eradicated for the sake of a safe and free world." Josh's voice is unsteady and soft. "They teach you how to kill people. Damn, Ryan, I never held a gun in my life before the Army."

"I can't imagine you hurting a fly, buddy."

Tears run down Josh's face as he relives memories of Vietnam. "It was awful. The jungles are hot and humid. Snakes, bugs, and creepy things everywhere. You never knew if a gook was going to jump from behind a tree or from under a rock and shoot you. There was a lot of tension. We smoked pot to take the edge off."

Ryan clasps his hands in front of his face. "I'm sorry you had to go through that."

When they finish eating, Ryan heads to the bar to fix himself a Scotch.

Josh grabs a seat on a barstool. "I could use one."

"Sure, buddy. It has to be tough talking about this." He hands Josh a drink, then sits on a barstool next to him.

Josh continues reminiscing. "We were tromping through the jungle, and this guy, Ken, grabs my arm and about jerks it out of the socket. I turn and look at him, thinking, *What the hell?* He grabs a dead tree limb and throws it on a trip wire. Four sharpened bamboo sticks fly down from the trees with enough force to stick a foot into the ground. My mind went numb."

Josh downs half his Scotch in one gulp. "Ken and I hung out together after that. He was a good guy. He was raised on a farm in Ohio. He was good with a rifle and surviving in the woods."

Josh finishes his Scotch. "I could use another drink."

"You want some orange juice or milk?"

"I was thinking another Scotch."

Ryan looks at him and hesitates before pouring another shot. "So, how did things turn out between you and Ken?"

"One day, on patrol, we entered a VC village. There didn't appear to be anyone around. We scattered to search the huts and came across this crying baby. The mother was sitting in the distance, wailing. Ken went over to pick up the baby. The sergeant screamed, 'Freeze!' Ken must not have heard him because he picked up the baby, and it exploded. Jesus, Ken's body ripped open, his organs spewed out. His lungs were lying on the ground, charred and smoke coming off them. I fell on my knees and started puking until there was nothing left inside of me. Then I continued with the dry heaves." Josh pounds the top of the bar with his fist, fighting back the tears. "I don't think I'll ever get that vision out of my mind."

Ryan slides the glass of Scotch in front of Josh and puts his hand on his shoulder.

A tear runs down Josh's face. "Those fuckers strapped a bomb to a baby."

"Okay, man. You don't need to talk about it anymore."

Josh wipes the tear off his face. "One of the guys went over to the mother and pointed his rifle in her face like he was going to shoot her. Another guy came up and stopped him. Instead, they . . . I can't talk about it."

A soft, dulcet chime interrupts Josh's story. Ryan goes to the door and retrieves a package of clothes, which he hands off to Josh. "These are yours."

When Josh stands up, unbeknownst to him, a small package of white powder falls out of the bathrobe pocket and lands on the floor. Josh grabs the clothes and heads to the bathroom to change. Ryan bends over and picks up the packet.

Fifteen minutes later, Josh comes back into the room, dressed in khakis and a cotton sports shirt, both slightly too large for him.

"You've got some room to grow," Ryan says. He tosses the packet of white powder on the table. "You dropped this."

Josh's eyes lock onto Ryan's. After a moment of mutual gaze, he responds, "I got shot in the back in Nam. The field doctors were afraid to pull it out because it was close to my spine. I had that damn bullet in my back for two weeks before I saw a real surgeon. They kept me on morphine to deaden the pain. I started using heroine when they quit giving me morphine. The Army got me hooked, man."

CHAPTER FORTY-EIGHT

Ryan and Josh exit the elevator on the seventh floor of the hospital. "Drug Rehabilitation Center" is scrolled across a sign attached to the wall. Ryan passes his friend off to the nurse behind the admissions counter.

A muscular Black orderly soon joins them. The young man immediately recognizes Ryan. "Ryan Hutson, my man. What's up, brother?"

Ryan and the orderly bro-shake. "What's your name?"

"Eddie."

Ryan stuffs a hundred-dollar bill into the breast pocket of Eddie's scrubs. "Keep an eye on my friend and help him get cleaned up. He's a vet. Make sure he gets everything he needs. Whatever the government doesn't pay for, send me the bill."

"You can count on it, bro."

Ryan pulls Josh aside. He holds on to his arm and looks him in the eyes. "Let these people help you. It won't be easy, but hang in there."

Josh lowers his head. "Sure, Ryan."

Ryan stands in the hall and watches the orderly whisk Josh away in a wheelchair.

. . .

Ryan shakes his head as he rides alone in the elevator back to the main floor. He's bummed by Josh's condition, yet hopeful he'll be able to get back on his feet. The elevator abruptly stops at the fourth floor, jarring him from his thoughts. A little boy, probably no more than six, enters the elevator holding hands with a young lady. Ryan stares at him for a few moments, thinking about Jacque. "What's up, little man?"

"My brother has a problem with his heart and may not live."

"Hush, Ryan," His mother immediately scolds him. "Don't be telling strangers our problems."

"Hey, Ryan, that's my name, too." He gives the youngster a fist bump. "What's your brother's name?"

"Adam," the boy says.

"Well, Ryan, I'm sure the doctors will take good care of Adam."

The boy looks up at Ryan. "We don't have enough money to help my brother get better."

Embarrassed, his mother quickly jerks at his arm to quiet him. "I'm sorry," she says. "Sometimes you regret the day they learn to talk."

She hustles the little boy away as soon as the elevator doors open on the main floor.

That night, Ryan tosses in bed, in the plush bedroom of his penthouse that looks down on the world. Josh's condition weighs heavy on his heart. The innocence of little Ryan and the grief in the eyes of his mother compounds his melancholy.

Memories of his mom looking out for him when he was little occupy his mind. "You always knew what to do or say," he tells the image of her. He visualizes her warm smile and caring eyes looking at him. "I've been so obsessed with my own needs and feelings that I lost the ability to care about others." He remembers her telling him, during a fit of stubbornness, "Be thankful for what you have and those that care about you, and be understanding of those less fortunate." He recalls memories of leaving Texas State College and the many people who helped him along his journey.

The Angels have a night game the next day. Ryan gets out of bed soon after the sun rises and heads to the hospital to check on Josh.

He boards the elevator he rode the previous day and hits the button for the seventh floor. Before he gets to his destination, he pushes the button for the fourth floor.

Ryan steps off the elevator in the pediatric ward. He notices a nurses' station twenty yards down the main hallway and heads in that direction.

Across from the nurses' station is a room which has a large window that allows the nurse to look in on the patients. The door to the room is open. Ryan stands at the window, looking at children in various stages of repair. Everyone appears to have a bandage somewhere on their body or a cast of some sort—or they're sitting in a wheelchair. The atmosphere in the room is quiet and subdued.

The nurse at the desk looks up from her paperwork and asks, "Do you have a child in the room?"

Ryan shakes his head. "No."

"I'm sorry, sir. You'll have to leave the ward."

Ryan gives her a steely gaze. His attention returns to the room when he hears a minor commotion break out.

"Hey, everybody, look—it's Ryan Hutson!" a boy shouts.

Several kids call out to Ryan, begging him to come in.

As he heads for the door, he's cut off by the nurse. She stands in front of the door and sticks her head into the room. "Sit down, children, before you hurt yourselves."

Ryan watches the kids' reactions to the nurse's command. *These guys are sitting still because the nurse makes them, not because they're grieving over their injuries. These kids possess the enthusiasm of a brood of little puppies.*

Ryan sidesteps the nurse and makes his way through the door. He gets down on one knee and interacts with each kid, signing autographs on casts, books, or whatever is put in front of him. "You guys are awesome," he says. "Y'all sit here without complaining in spite of your injuries."

An hour after entering the room, the nurse informs everyone that Ryan has to go so they can take their naps.

The room is immediately filled with, "Aww. Please let him stay."

"Will you come back and see us tomorrow?" a little girl asks.

Ryan looks at the badge on the nurse's uniform: Jan Henley. She's an average-looking woman in her early forties. She's slightly overweight and has a paper hat pinned to her hair.

"I'll come back as soon as I can, but only if you listen to Nurse Henley and take your naps."

That seems to satisfy everyone. They march off to their rooms, babbling about meeting Ryan Hutson.

"You must be some type of celebrity, Mr. Hutson. Are you a television star?"

"No, ma'am, I'm a baseball player with the California Angels."

She doesn't appear overly impressed with this fact. "What brings you to the pediatric ward, Mr. Hutson?"

"I'm looking for a young boy named Adam."

Nurse Henley returns to the nurses' station. She picks up a chart and peers at it for several seconds. "It appears the only child we have named Adam is a two-week-old infant in our infirmary."

"What can you tell me about him?"

"I'm sorry, any information about the child is confidential."

Some women feel Ryan's eyes show the depths of his soul and are mesmerizing. Ryan stands close to Nurse Henley. She can smell the light scent of #7 cologne emanating from his body. He looks into her eyes with a piercing glare. "Jan, I want to help that child. It'll be nearly impossible for me to do so unless you tell me what's going on with him."

She takes a step back and gathers herself. "Speaking totally off the record, the child has a congenital heart defect. The doctors would like to operate, but the mother's insurance doesn't cover all the costs."

"So the hospital isn't going to do anything?" Ryan's pulse quickens.

Nurse Henley struggles to maintain a professional tone in her voice. "This hospital is a business, Mr. Hutson. We don't take on charity cases."

Ryan bites his lip.

"We'll provide whatever treatment the mother can afford. It's possible medication may alleviate some of the problem. After a period of time, we'll transfer him to County General, where they may be of further service."

Ryan looks upward in disbelief before he returns his glare to Nurse Henley. "What are the chances the boy will live a normal life without the operation?"

"I'm not a doctor. I can't make that judgment."

"Just your personal opinion, then."

Her lips quiver for a second as she tries to keep her emotions out of the conversation. "It's not likely."

Ryan pulls Kelci's business card out of his wallet and hands it to Nurse Henley. "See that Adam gets the best possible medical attention while he's at this hospital. Contact my attorney. She'll pay for everything that insurance doesn't cover."

Nurse Henley has a look of adulation on her face. "That's very generous of you, Mr. Hutson."

"Everyone deserves the best possible medical treatment, Jan."

A feeling of contentment fills Ryan's body. He leaves the hospital without visiting Josh.

CHAPTER FORTY-NINE

The next morning, Ryan returns to the hospital. The detox ward is his first stop.

Josh comes to the visitors' lounge dressed in blue scrubs and a terry cloth robe. His hair is cropped close. He looks more like the guy Ryan used to pal around with in high school, except for the dark circles around his eyes and his skeletal frame.

"Hey, buddy, how's it going?" Ryan asks.

"I'm trying to say no to drugs, but they won't listen."

They grab a seat across from each other at a table in the lounge.

"You don't need to be injecting heroin," Ryan says. "The only dope worth shooting is the ayatollah."

Josh squints. Ryan thinks it's the sun coming in from the window.

"Want to change seats?"

Josh waves him off. "I get anxiety twitches sometimes. I'm not addicted to heroin, you know. I just like the way the stuff smells."

Ryan's eyes light up. "Now you're starting to sound like the guy I know. Stick with it, buddy. You can kick this."

"Glad you think so." His voice is slightly strained. "I don't usually like people who take drugs. Especially customs agents and police officers."

Josh's doctor walks into the visitors' lounge and notices her patient wincing. She stops at the table, puts her hand on Ryan's shoulder, and whispers in his ear, "I think he's had enough for one day. Please, come back another time."

Josh and Ryan stand up at the same time. Ryan walks over to Josh and puts his arm around his shoulders. "I'm going to take off, dude. Get better."

"Don't get all mushy with me," Josh replies.

Ryan and the doctor walk shoulder to shoulder down the hall.

"He seems to be a little better," Ryan comments.

The doctor has a satisfied look on her face. "Josh is an extremely intelligent and emotionally strong person. He really wants to get better. But he has aches and pains and can get very upset when the period between treatments is too long."

Ryan stops at the elevator as the doctor continues down the hall.

From the detox ward, Ryan makes his way to the pediatric wing. He approaches Nurse Henley as she stands alone at the nurses' station. As soon as the kids across the hall notice Ryan, several try to rush to greet him. Nurse Henley proves to be a formidable barrier and stops them before they can leave the room.

Ryan looks at the kids with proud eyes. "Their enthusiasm is overwhelming," he tells Nurse Henley. He strolls into the room and heads toward a small chair at a children's table, hitting his chin on his knee when he sits down. The kids clamor around him, bombarding him with questions.

After several minutes of kidspeak, Ryan notices a young boy, about eleven, sitting in a wheelchair in the back of the room. Both arms and the side of his face are heavily bandaged. He isn't moving around like the rest of the children.

"Excuse me a minute," Ryan says to the kids.

He strolls over to the heavily bandaged boy and ruffles his hair. "Hi, I'm Ryan."

Ryan can see a smile on the half of his face that isn't covered.

"Yeah, I know," he replies in a meek voice. "Ow! It hurts to smile."

"Well, then I'll try not to say anything funny."

Ryan gives Nurse Henley a questioning look.

She stands next to Ryan and softly says, "He got transferred down this morning. He and some friends were playing with matches in his parents' garage, and there was a chemical explosion. He's been isolated for weeks because the burns were so bad the doctors were concerned about possible infection."

Ryan cringes. Snakes and burning flesh are two things that give him the willies.

Ryan kneels to get eye level with the boy. "What's your name, partner?"

"Travis."

"Are you an Angels fan, Travis?"

"I'm a Dodgers fan. But I know who you are. Everybody does."

"Who's your favorite player?"

"I play catcher, so Yeager is my favorite."

Ryan turns his palms up. "Why aren't you an Angels fan?"

"Ever since you guys let Nolan Ryan go, you haven't had any pitching. The Dodgers win with great pitching."

Ryan laughs. "Maybe you should talk to our general manager."

After spending an hour on the pediatric ward with the children, Ryan tells the kids goodbye and promises to come back. He walks over to the nurses' station and stands before Nurse Henley. "Can you take me to see Adam?"

They walk down an adjacent hallway together. Ryan turns to Nurse Henley. "What's the outlook for Travis?"

She goes into detail describing oils, massages, and medications that are common for that type of burn. "Ultimately, a skin graft is the final treatment."

Ryan is absorbed in thought for a few seconds before his focus returns to his surroundings. "When I was living in Canada, I read about some type of circulating gel bath that's supposed to be a good stimulus for burnt tissue."

Nurse Henley nods. "I heard about that also. I think it's still new in the U.S. Only the major burn centers have that type of equipment, and the list to get into those facilities can be lengthy."

Ryan and Nurse Henley round the corner in the hallway and see little Ryan and his mother with their foreheads pressed against a glass wall. They're peering into a nursery containing several cribs with infants in them.

"They know nothing of your offer," Nurse Henley whispers to Ryan. "The hospital is still reviewing details with your attorney."

Ryan looks at her and smiles. "They don't need to know where the money came from. If you'll excuse me, I'd like to visit with them alone."

Nurse Henley turns and walks away.

"Jan," Ryan calls after Nurse Henley after she takes a few steps. "Can you look to see what it would take to get a gel bath here?"

"Sure, Ryan. I would be glad to." Nurse Henley has a grateful look. "Your presence here helps the kids immeasurably. Positive emotions go a long way toward healing."

"Yes, they do." Ryan's body tingles from a helper's high.

Little Ryan sees big Ryan approaching, and his eyes light up. He waves. "Hi, Ryan."

"Hi, Ryan. How's your brother doing?"

"He's sleeping right now."

Ryan pats his shoulder and looks over at his mom. "Good morning, ma'am."

She gives Ryan a quick look, mumbles, "Hello," then returns her focus to Adam.

Ryan can tell exactly who they are looking at even before little Ryan points him out. He's a tiny little thing, not more than a foot long. A little knit cap is nestled on his head, and an oxygen tube is in his nose. Ryan wants to console the mother but doesn't know what to say. The three of them stand in silence for several minutes looking at Adam.

Ryan breaks the quiet contemplation. "Take care, buddy," he says to little Ryan. "Goodbye, ma'am." He looks her in the eye and, in a reassuring voice, says, "Your little boy is going to be all right."

CHAPTER FIFTY

The weeks roll by. Ryan's teammates notice he smiles more often and is quick to show off his sense of humor. The Angels string a small winning streak together and pull within five games of the first-place Royals. The clubhouse is filled with positive vibes.

Players mill about the locker room after soundly defeating the Mariners. Having just gotten out of the shower, Ryan stands in front of his locker with a towel wrapped around him.

"You going out with us tonight?" Red asks.

Ryan shakes his head. "I generally try to avoid temptation unless I can't resist it."

Red laughs in his goofy way, which is mostly through his nose. "It appears you've cut back on drinking and chasing women. Did you find religion?"

"Nah, I found something better." A content look occupies his face.

. . .

Each time Ryan sees Josh and the progress he's making, he feels uplifted. His visits with the kids in the pediatric ward provide him with lessons in resiliency. Seeing firsthand the outcome of his interactions with them and his contributions inspires him to do more.

A three-quarter moon hangs over Camden Yards. Lights from the buildings reflect off the water in the Inner Harbor. Kelci and Ryan sit at an outside table at Phillips Seafood House, waiting for their crabs. Kelci has been trying to catch up with Ryan for a week and finally corrals him after an afternoon game in Baltimore.

Kelci leans forward, her forearms on the table. "You need to stop buying baseball diamonds and medical equipment for everybody you meet."

"It's not like I don't have the money." Ryan's face is aglow. "Your husband said money can't buy happiness." Their eyes meet. "He was wrong. Helping others makes me feel good." He taps his hand over his heart.

"I love your inspiration, but you're driving the accountant crazy with your random acts of kindness," she says in an exasperated tone.

With a slightly humorous edge, he asks, "Whaddaya want me to do?"

Her mind quickly shifts into business mode. "Well, since you asked, we can set up a charitable organization from which you can withdraw funds to pay for your benevolent activities. If we plan and organize your contributions, we can do a better job of managing your taxes." She looks at Ryan, happy to see him excited about something. "Once there's a proper system in place, we can accept donations from corporations and individuals. With the extra money, you can help a lot more kids."

A huge grin covers Ryan's face. "I like that. We could call it the 7 Foundation."

The Angels play their final three games of the season against the Kansas City Royals, who coincidently are three games ahead of them in the standings.

The Angels arrive at the Kansas City airport the morning before a night game. Ryan spends a few minutes with autograph seekers and newspeople then takes the quickest route to the front door and the cabstand.

"Take me to Children's Mercy Hospital," he tells the cabbie as he gets comfortable in the back seat.

Ryan and Todd Kenney, the quarterback for the Chiefs, stand next to the bed of Robert, a twelve-year-old boy suffering from acute lymphoblastic leukemia. He isn't expected to live another year. A bald head and dark circles around his eyes make him appear down-trodden. But that is not the case. The youngster has a lively spirit about him.

"It's neat to have my two favorite athletes visiting me," he says, grinning proudly.

"Come on," Todd jokes. "You live in Kansas City. You should be a Royals fan."

"Heck yeah, the Royals are my team, but Ryan is the best."

Ryan feels his heart skip a beat. "No, Robert, you're the best. You're a fighter, and I admire that about you. I wish there was something I could do for you."

"Hit a home run tonight. I'll be watching the game on television."

After a few seconds of thought, Ryan shakes his head. "No."

Todd and Robert look at each other in disbelief, then back toward Ryan.

"No, you're not going to watch the game on television," Ryan says. "You're going to the game to watch me hit a home run in person."

. . .

Bud White, the Royals' ace, is on the mound for tonight's game. He's widely considered the best pitcher in the American League and the likely winner of the Cy Young Award.

Ryan's first at bat comes in the second inning. The score is knotted at zero. He walks up to the batter's box and looks up to the walkway above the bottom ring of seats where Robert is sitting in a wheelchair next to his mom and dad. Ryan tips his hat, and Robert responds with a thumbs-up.

Ryan connects on the second pitch from White and sends it deep into left-center field. It hits the top of the fence and ricochets up ten rows of seats. Ryan pumps his fist in jubilation as he rounds the bases. He jumps onto home plate with both feet and points toward Robert, who's bouncing in his wheelchair and waving his arms.

Ryan grabs a seat on the bench next to Red. "That felt good."

"Not as good as you think." Red points toward the field.

The umpires are huddled around home plate with an animated Royals manager. After a few moments, the umpires summon Ryan back onto the field. Once he's inside their compact circle, the umps order him to second base. "Ground rule double," the home plate umpire announces.

"Are you serious?" Ryan asks. "You could see that from behind home plate?"

"The call has been made. You got a problem with my decision?"

"I would never question your integrity, Gary, just your eyesight."

The next two batters are unable to get a hit. The game remains scoreless.

Ryan doesn't come to bat again until the fifth inning. He and White battle each other for nine pitches. Ryan hits four foul balls. The count is full. On the tenth pitch, instead of taking a walk, Ryan steps into an outside fastball and sends it screaming down the right-field line. *If it stays fair it should be a home run*, he tells himself as he scampers toward first base.

The right fielder sees it from a different perspective. He hauls ass as fast as he can toward the fence and at the last second he leaps high into the air, his arm stretched as far as possible without coming out of the socket. His glove is a foot above the fence when the ball drops into it.

"Rats." Clearly disappointed, Ryan looks up into the stands at Robert and shrugs.

The game works its way into the eighth inning with the Royals leading 3 – 0. White has pitched an overpowering game but is beginning to tire. After allowing a base hit, he walks the next batter. The Royals' manager motions for a relief pitcher. The closer is a veteran left-hander who saved twenty-nine games during the season with only three blown saves. He's pitched over a hundred innings of baseball during the season and only given up two home runs.

After two quick strikes, the first Angels batter he faces takes a big swing at the third pitch and hits a slow, trickling grounder down the third base line. The third baseman charges the ball, bare-hands it, and then fires it to first base. Not in time. Everyone is safe.

The table is set. Two outs, bases loaded, and the go-ahead run coming to bat. It's a must-win game for the Angels to stay in the hunt for the pennant.

Ryan strides to the plate, full of confidence; energy surges inside his body. These are the moments you play the game for. He's hit the ball hard his previous at bats, barely missing a home run each time. He's currently the hottest hitter in baseball, batting over .400 the past month with ten home runs. With one swing of the bat, the Angels are up 4 – 3.

The pitcher holds the ball as he stares at the catcher. Ryan glares at the pitcher. The catcher stands up from his squat and steps to the outside of the plate. The Royals intentionally walk Ryan with the bases loaded!

"Aww, geez!" The air rushes out of Ryan's lungs as if they were overinflated balloons. He was keenly focused on the challenge at hand, then poof, the confrontation disappeared.

The intentional walk makes the score 3 – 1. The next Angels batter steps up to the plate and drills a hard grounder up the middle. The second baseman makes a diving catch. By the time he can get the ball out of his glove and toss it to second base, Ryan has safely slid into the base, and the runner on third scores. The score is 3 – 2.

The next batter comes to the plate with the opportunity to give the Angels the lead and keep their playoff hopes alive. He hits a shot into the gap between left and center field on the first pitch thrown to him. The runners are off on contact. Two runs should score. The left fielder races full speed, then slides head first. His glove slips under the ball an inch before it hits the ground. He holds on for the third out. A loud cheer erupts as the home team races from the field up by one in the bottom of the eighth.

As often is the case with the Angels this season, their pitching staff is not up to the task. Willie Wilson, Hal McRae, and George Brett trigger an onslaught that results in three runs, making the score 6 – 2 in the top of the ninth. It turns out the four-run deficit is too much for the Angels to overcome in the ninth. The Royals clinch a spot in the playoffs against the red-hot Detroit Tigers.

After the game, the Royals invite Robert down to the field to meet the players. Ryan sits on the top step of the dugout, watching as the boy is pushed across the infield in his wheelchair. After a few minutes, Ryan gets to his feet and jogs over to Robert. Getting down on one knee, he looks the boy in the eye and says, "Sorry I couldn't deliver on my promise."

Robert's eyes gleam, and a big toothy grin fills his face. "Heck, Ryan, you're the coolest. You stared them down. They took one look at you and walked you with the bases loaded!" The boy couldn't be prouder of Ryan even if he hit three home runs that day.

The final two games of the year are meaningless to both the Royals and the Angels. The Royals elect to sit their starters.

Ryan thinks long and hard about playing. A few minutes before game time, he approaches the manager. "Stick me in the lineup. I'd like to get a few more swings in before the end of the season."

The Royals start a call-up pitcher from their minor league team in Omaha. Ryan is the fourth batter he faces in his major league career. Ryan crushes the first pitch offered to him high into the air. The ball is lost in the darkness of the night as it soars above the stadium lights. It comes back to Earth and hits the roof of the upper deck with a thud that echoes throughout the stadium.

Ryan's next at-bat is in the third inning. As he gets up off the bench, the coach steps in front of him. "Why don't you sit out the rest of the game?"

"One more at bat, then that's it."

Ryan settles in at the plate and patiently waits through three pitches that are outside the strike zone. On the fourth pitch, he crushes a line drive up the middle. The center fielder comes up with the ball on one hop, holding him to a single.

The next batter drives the ball to right field. Ryan rounds second base full speed and makes a charge for third. The outfielder comes up with the ball cleanly and makes a hard throw to pick Ryan off. It looks like the ball and Ryan are going to get to third at the same time. Ryan dives headfirst for the base, his arm reaching out. The throw is high, and the third baseman leaps to catch the ball. When he comes down, his foot lands on Ryan's lower arm. Metal cleats tear into the muscles and tendons of his forearm and hit a bone in his elbow.

CHAPTER FIFTY-ONE

Blood flows from Ryan's arm. He grabs his elbow and grimaces. He rolls over and, with the use of his good arm, he pushes himself to his feet. "That was bush-league!" His nose is six inches from the third baseman's face. "You could have avoided landing on my arm."

Thinking there might be a fight, the shortstop immediately rushes to restrain Ryan. All hell breaks loose once he has Ryan in his grip. Both benches empty, and the playing field is covered with players shoving and throwing wild and futile punches at each other.

After a few minutes, with no haymakers of consequence having landed, the melee is broken up. Players stand in the infield, jawing and pointing fingers at each other.

Red pulls himself up from the dirt and walks over to Ryan. The sight of blood on the front of Ryan's jersey infuriates him. He runs behind the third baseman and jumps on his back, clutching his neck. The free-for-all starts all over again.

The umpires and managers quickly respond to the mayhem and restore order again. After everyone has separated and gone their own way, Ryan, Red, and two Royals are ejected from the game.

Ryan is met in the dugout by a trainer, who applies pressure to his arm to slow the bleeding. He takes a look at Ryan's injury and shudders when he sees bone through the gash. After cleaning and wrapping the wound, the trainer leads Ryan through the locker room, out the back door, and into a waiting ambulance. The paramedics are about to close the back doors to the vehicle when someone shouts, "Hold on!"

The Angels' batboy loads Red into the ambulance. The doors slam shut and the siren blares as the ambulance pulls onto the main road and makes haste to the hospital.

Ryan scratches his head with his good arm as he looks at Red. "What're you doing here?"

"Well, during the first skirmish, I charged onto the field as fast as I could. I remember grabbing someone by the foot. Then when things settled down, I saw how bad your arm was bleeding, so I jumped on the asshole's back that cleated you. I started pounding the crap out of him."

"An eye for an eye only leads to a world full of blindness," Ryan responds. "So, how did you get that big gash on your forehead?"

"I don't recall. One of the Royals must have snuck up behind me and hit me in the head with a bat."

A paramedic who's cleaning Ryan's wound scoffs at Red's version of the ruckus. "We were parked in the tunnel that leads to the field. We saw the whole fracas. As I recall, you ran onto the field when the fighting started and tripped over first base. In the ensuing melee, you got kicked in the head while you were lying on the ground."

The shock of the injury starts to wear off, and Ryan begins to feel intense pain. When the ambulance pulls up to the hospital, the paramedics assist Red and Ryan into wheelchairs and push them into the waiting room. Once they're at the admittance counter, the paramedics get a call to go to the scene of a multi-car accident. Ryan and Red are left alone at the counter, sitting in wheelchairs, with bloodstains on their uniforms. No one is there to admit them. Ryan keeps his arm up to control the bleeding, and Red presses several pieces of gauze above his eyebrow.

After five minutes of sitting in front of the admittance counter with no one assisting them, Red wheels over to a pair of swinging doors, pushes one open, and hollers into the back room, "Hello? Anyone back there? We have injuries out here!" He looks over at Ryan. "Damn, they need some waiters in this waiting room."

A nurse comes out and tells Red to calm down. You can almost see the blood boiling as it flows from the cut above his eyebrow.

"Never in the history of calming down has anyone ever calmed down after being told to calm down," Red informs her, his arms waving. "In case you haven't noticed, we need medical attention. Preferably now!"

The nurse is as skinny as a rail, has a big forehead, and wears very little makeup. Her hat is tilted to the side. She looks down her nose at Red with scorn. "Okay, who wants to go first?"

Red points at Ryan. "My friend's arm is about to fall off, and he's going to die from blood loss." Red's voice is filled with contempt.

The nurse casually peeks at Ryan's arm and continues with her paperwork. Ryan is slumped in his wheelchair. He's sick to his stomach and is starting to get lightheaded. The nurse asks, "Do you have insurance?"

"Holy batshit, Robin!" Red hollers out. "Get him a doctor." He jumps out of his wheelchair, rushes over to the swing doors again, and hollers, "Helllooo, can we get a doctor out here?"

Two orderlies, who look like Kansas City Chiefs linebackers in scrubs, charge into the waiting area. The nurse nods in Red's direction. "Inject him . . . fifteen milligrams ketamine."

"Oh, no you don't," Red hollers.

The last Ryan sees of Red, he's running down a hallway like a scared rat with two orderlies in pursuit.

Eventually, a heavyset woman orderly in her mid-forties comes out of the mystical back room and wheels Ryan into an examination room. She helps Ryan onto an exam table without saying much. A few minutes later, an intern wanders into the room with a clipboard in hand.

"Let's see what we have here," he says as he picks up Ryan's injured arm and looks at it. "You must be a baseball player."

Ryan looks down at his dirty and bloody uniform and sarcastically replies, "I'll be darned. Good to know, Doc."

The intern twists and turns the injured arm while Ryan winces in pain. "We're going to need some X-rays."

Ryan is left alone for fifteen minutes. An hour later, after his arm is X-rayed, the wound is cleaned and bandaged, and he is given pain medication, the intern returns. "You have a tear in your tendon and a fracture in the bone below the elbow. The fracture is in a very precarious area. Surgery will be necessary."

The overweight woman orderly wheels Ryan down the hallway. They pass Red, who is strapped onto a gurney, unconscious. A piece of gauze is taped to his forehead. His tongue hangs out as drool runs down his cheek.

"What's with him?" Ryan asks.

"We had to sedate him. It took quite a bit to calm him down."

CHAPTER FIFTY-TWO

Kelci charters a medical flight to transfer Ryan from Kansas City to LAX. The assistant trainer of the Angels, a twenty-two-year-old medical student at UCLA, is waiting for Ryan at the airport. She drives him over to the UCLA Medical Center and helps him check in. After he's admitted, Ryan is visited by the team physician, Dr. Maroney. The next morning, surgery is performed on his arm.

Ryan wakes from the anesthesia confused. His right arm is encased in a hard cast from below his shoulder to the first set of knuckles and is raised in a sling above his head. He squints as he tries to focus on a dark-haired woman sitting in a chair across the room.

Noticing his movements, she walks over to him. "Did you have a good sleep?"

Ryan blinks slowly a couple times as he watches Kelci sit on the bed next to him. "I don't think we aren't in Kansas anymore, Toto."

"No, you're in La-La Land."

"I guess wherever you go, there you are," Ryan garbles, still delirious from the sedation.

Kelci smiles, leans over, rubs the side of his face, and then kisses his forehead.

"What's the prognosis?" he asks in a raspy voice.

She pours him a glass of water and watches him dribble most of it down the side of his face. "Hopefully, a complete recovery."

"How long will that take?"

She grabs a Kleenex and dabs the water off his cheeks. "You just got out of surgery. Chill. We'll meet with the doctors and see what they have to say. For the time being, just rest and let the healing process begin."

Ryan remains in the hospital on pain medication for two days. Several teammates and acquaintances stop by to wish him well. On the third day, the doctors back off his medication and remove the sling that holds his arm above his head. He's now free to move around the room and hallways.

Kelci is on the phone with Trey while Ryan lies on the hospital bed reading Mad magazine. There's a gentle knock on the door and Dr. Maroney enters the room with Dr. Duntsch, the attending physician.

Maroney walks up to Ryan. "I met with Dr. Butcher, the surgeon who operated on your arm. Everything appears to have gone well."

Kelci walks over to the bed. Ryan reaches out and squeezes her hand, releasing some of the tension he's holding.

Dr. Duntsch picks up the chart at the foot of Ryan's bed and studies it closely. "The cleats lacerated the extensor digitorum and triceps brachii tendons in your forearm. The extensor digitorum is what allows movement of the middle digits of your hand, and the triceps brachii extends the elbow." The doctor wiggles his middle fingers and extends and flexes his elbow to demonstrate. "A minor fracture of the radius also occurred. That's the bone responsible for proper movement of your wrist and elbow." He looks at Ryan. "Understand?"

"I can't wiggle my fingers or bend my elbow properly."

"Well, yes," Dr. Maroney replies. "The injury could impact your ability to grip a baseball and throw. Dr. Butcher surgically repaired the tendons and checked for secure attachment to the bone. The fracture near the elbow was properly aligned and secured with a screw. Your arm will be stabilized until healing completes." Maroney stands at the side of the bed, his hands in his pockets, looking down at Ryan. "Hopefully, there's minimal damage to the posterior interosseous nerve in your forearm. That could cause tingling or numbness in your hand."

Ryan tires of the medical gibberish. "So, everything should be back to normal soon?" he asks, a gleam of hope in his eyes.

"There are no clear-cut answers or guarantees. A period of rest is required for the wounds to heal. Afterward, a rigorous regime of physical therapy will be necessary." Maroney forms a fist and rolls his wrist. "The goal is to restore the proper mechanics of the elbow, wrist, and fingers. All three body parts working in unison ensure proper function of your arm."

Ryan glares at Maroney. "You just said the surgery was successful. Will my arm be healed by spring training?"

Maroney walks away from the bed. He stops, looks at Kelci, and then turns his gaze back to Ryan. "There's no guarantee your arm will return to the performance level you're accustomed to."

Breathing suddenly becomes difficult for Ryan. He sits up on the bed, staring forward as his heart races. *I'm not ready for my baseball career to be over.*

CHAPTER FIFTY-THREE

A Week After Surgery

Ryan stretches out in the passenger seat as Kelci guides the rented Buick Riviera along Route 1 toward Ryan's beach house. "I hate this drive at sunset," Kelci says. "You're totally blinded every time you round a curve."

Ryan tightens his seat belt. "Thanks for staying in town to help out."

Kelci smiles broadly. "Part of my job," she replies.

"So, strictly a professional responsibility?"

"I suppose being a sister-in-law does invoke the sympathy clause." She tilts her sunglasses down to wink at him. "I've made some calls and gotten everything under control, so I can get back home. As usual, the cleaning lady and landscaper will come by once a week."

"I bought a new vacuum cleaner," Ryan says. "But so far, all it's doing is gathering dust."

"Well, hopefully the housekeeper will put it to good use." Kelci flips the sun visor down. "She'll also take care of your laundry. I've hired someone to do your grocery shopping and cook for you."

"Thanks, but I'm not totally helpless."

"God knows if I didn't take care of things, you would probably just lie around and wither away. Then I'd be out my best client." She scrunches her nose and fakes a smile. "The doctors say you need to rest your arm for another couple of weeks before you start rehab."

<hr>

The next fifteen days are mostly a relaxing experience for Ryan. He gets a bit frustrated only having one working arm, especially when he wants to open a jar of olives. Thankfully, people pop in occasionally to keep him company and help out with opening beer bottles.

The best part of the R & R is when Jacque visits him for a week. The boy loves hanging out at the beach, especially now that he doesn't have to deal with his dad wanting to play catch with him.

Ryan and Jacque sit on the beach close to where the waves roll onto the sand. A young man in surfer shorts stands ankle-deep in the ocean tossing a Frisbee to his Border Collie.

"Great Balls of Fire," Jacque hollers as he watches the dog jump five feet in the air to catch the disk. That's his new go-to phrase since they attended a Jerry Lee Lewis concert.

One thing about only seeing his son part-time—Ryan splurges excessively on him, often to his mother's chagrin. One of the spoils is a Hammond B-3 organ. "Just like the one Emerson, Lake & Palmer use," he told Jacque when he gave it to him.

Anne Marie approves of the organ. Even though the gift is extravagant, she agrees Jacque should have an instrument to practice on when he visits his father. Although she is a little concerned some of the ZZ Top's and Mötley Crüe's music he plays at his dad's house might be a bit much for a nearly seven-year-old boy. At home, as far as she knows, he only practices Horowitz, Bernstein, and other classical pianists.

. . .

A light breeze blows in off the ocean, and the sun beats down on Ryan's bare chest as he relaxes on a chaise lounge on his deck. Jacque is back in Montréal with his mother. Fifty feet from Ryan, Roberta lies on the beach, sunbathing her store-bought breasts. A small bead of perspiration rolls down her toned belly and lodges in her navel. She hears the clicking sound from a camera and opens an eye to peer at a couple of boys. She calmly gets to her feet, shooing them away. "Come back when you're of legal age." Strolling up to the deck, wearing only a bright-red thong, she sits next to Ryan on his chaise. She grabs the glass from his hand, and takes a drink. "What, no alcohol?"

"I'm cutting down on pain medication."

"Are you cutting down on your work obligations also?"

Ryan leans his head back and rolls his eyes. "I just had surgery. Give me a break."

"I have a line of clothing to sell," she replies in a sharp and direct voice. "It affects sales when you're out of the public eye."

Ryan rubs his injured elbow. "If my arm doesn't heal properly, and I can't return to the game, nobody will care!"

"Good point." Her eyebrows are lowered and drawn together. "Get back in shape, or your contract will be terminated."

"Good to know, Roberta."

CHAPTER FIFTY-FOUR

Ryan is lying on the deck eating Fig Newtons and reading *Gray's Anatomy* when a call comes in from Kelci. "I've contracted a full-time physical therapist through an exclusive agency," she tells him. "She'll be there in two days."

Chandra arrives in a chauffeured limousine on a windy and overcast afternoon. Ryan stands at the door of his house, his eyes fixated on her as she gets out of the vehicle. Mocha skin stretches across the lean muscles of her six-foot frame. She gazes at Ryan with emerald-green eyes as they formally introduce themselves. Chandra is from the island of Martinique. She has a doctorate in kinesiology and has been in the business of helping celebrities rehabilitate for more than ten years.

"Is it always this hazy?" Her gaze shifts to the hills across the highway.

"Wildfires. I hate it when the wind blows in this direction."

Ryan directs the chauffeur to the guest suite to drop off Chandra's personal belongings. Afterward, he leads them to his workout room to unload her training equipment. Chandra unfolds a massage table in the room, then empties a footlocker full of exercise equipment, lotions, and oils.

"What are those?" Ryan points to two apparatuses Chandra set on a table.

"One electrically stimulates muscles, and the other provides deep heating to tendons, muscles, and ligaments."

"Cool."

After everything is put in its place, Chandra tells Ryan, "If you'll excuse me, I'd like to go the guest suite and freshen up."

Ryan heads to the deck and stretches out on a lounge chair. He watches a golden glow reflect off the bouncing tides as the sun drops toward the horizon. Chandra joins him, wearing a black nylon warm-up suit. She slides onto a lounge chair next to his.

"That was quick."

"It was just a baby shower," she replies. "It's beautiful here."

"It's peaceful yet only an hour away from total chaos."

After breakfast the next morning, Ryan joins Chandra in his workout room, her lean body covered in spandex shorts and a tank top. He wears a pair of cut-off sweats and a T-shirt.

"Today is the first day in the slow, methodical recovery process. We're going to stay away from the heavy stuff for a while," she says, looking at Ryan's free weights and Nautilus equipment. "Our focus will be on range of motion exercises. Later, we'll build some strength exercises into it."

"Lead the way."

She grabs his hand and bends his arm at the elbow, then pulls it outward. "The most

common problem after elbow surgery is stiffness. We're going to get this elbow moving. We'll be stretching all the muscles around the injury. How's your ability to pour a cup of coffee and drink from a glass?"

"It's fine . . . as long as I use my left arm."

"Okay, wise guy. We're going to get you used to using your right arm again. The ability to turn your wrist over so your hand faces up is called supination. Alternatively, forearm pronation is your ability to turn your hand over so your palm faces the floor. That's the motion that allows you to play the organ."

"I don't play the organ."

"You just own one for decoration?"

"I keep it around for my alter ego."

Chandra casually strolls from the ocean in a one-piece spandex swimsuit toward Ryan's deck. Small water droplets roll down the skin of her taut body like diamonds in the brilliant sunshine. She can feel the eyes of at least ten men on her.

"I declare," Chandra's Caribbean accent is very pronounced. "You'd think American men have never seen a woman's body before."

"Yours is not a normal body," Ryan replies as he scans the morning paper.

She ignores his comment and pours herself a glass of juice from a pitcher on the table. "I'm going to throw on some scrubs, then we can work on stretches."

Three hours later, Ryan is back on his lounge chair with ice packs surrounding his elbow and wrist. Chandra sits next to him. Relaxing with glasses of malbec in their hands, they gaze at the ocean, watching a cargo ship head out to sea.

She reaches over and rubs his shoulder. "How's it feel?"

"The massage feels great, but my elbow burns a little."

The phone starts chirping. "I'll get it for you." Chandra grabs the portable phone off the patio table. "Good afternoon. Hutson residence. . . Certainly. Hold one second, please."

"It's Kelci." She hands Ryan the phone.

"Hey, Kelce, how you doing? . . . Yeah, everything's good . . . I wondered what they were up to . . . Sure, that'd be fine . . . Okay, see you then."

"Everything good?" Chandra asks after he hangs up the phone.

"I guess. She's coming here next week for a few days. The Angels want to meet."

CHAPTER FIFTY-FIVE

Chandra leaves L.A. the same day Kelci arrives. The cleaning lady refreshes the guest room for the next visitor.

Shortly after Kelci settles in, the cook serves them filets with vegetables and potatoes grilled on the Jenn-Air.

"I don't think I've ever seen you eat in the dining room." Kelci laughs lightly. "Actually, I don't think I've seen you sit anywhere inside the house for more than a few minutes. Seems like you live on that patio."

"I come in to get out of the rain and to sleep." He refills her glass of wine, then stabs a roasted zucchini with his fork. "I haven't heard from the Angels in a while. Why the sudden interest?"

"Just a subtle reminder that your contract can be voided for medical reasons. But it has to be done prior to the start of spring training. Which is a couple weeks away."

He raises an eyebrow. "You think they would actually void my contract?"

"I've no idea." Kelci pushes her long dark hair behind her shoulders. "We'll be meeting with an orthopedic specialist of their choosing tomorrow."

"Can we get our own doctor for a second opinion?"

"We can do whatever you want." Her eyes narrow in a concerned look. "Are you nervous?"

"Not really. But we're giving them a lot of flexibility."

"When we signed the contract, we opted for a higher salary with fewer guarantees."

"Who knew?" He washes a piece of steak down with a sip of wine.

"By the way, Roberta is talking about cancelling your contract if you don't go back to work soon." Kelci pats her lips with a napkin. "She says she has an Italian race car driver who would be the perfect spokesman for her line of clothing."

"Pfft. Let her have him. I'm tired of her nonsense."

"I'm sure she's just bluffing."

"Who cares? I don't really need the money. I'd rather have the free time . . . Whoa!"

Kelci looks at him with big eyes. "Are you okay?"

"Yeah. I just had a deja vu moment. I actually surprised myself, saying that."

A medical assistant escorts Ryan and Kelci from the waiting area into the office of Dr. Beverly Grove, an orthopedist at Cedars-Sinai Medical Center. Dr. Maroney and Willis Schooler, an assistant to the assistant general manager of the Angels, are already in the office.

Ryan looks at Schooler, a young skinny Black kid. "They're really bringing in the heavyweights from Angels management for this meeting," he whispers to Kelci.

Dr. Grove offers her hand to introduce herself. "Good day, Ryan, Mrs. Hutson."

Maroney and Schooler nod at Ryan and Kelci. Maroney tells Ryan, "Angels management would like muscle strength testing performed on your right forearm, followed by a detailed report."

"We're willing to cooperate fully," Kelci replies in a businesslike manner. Ryan remains mum.

Dr. Grove leads the group down the hall into a testing laboratory equipped with a variety of free weights and mechanical test equipment.

"We'll be performing static triceps brachii force measurements in different elbow positions and dynamic isokinetic testing," Dr. Grove informs Ryan.

"Will I need to bring a dictionary for the tests?" Ryan jokes.

"No, you just need to follow instructions," Maroney replies with a fake smile.

"The guy's got a burr up his ass," Ryan says to Kelci.

Kelci puts her finger to her lips. "Shh."

Dr. Grove looks at Ryan. "Before we start, we need to record vital statistics. Your age?"

"Thirty."

"Sex?"

What a stupid question. "I used to be a man trapped in a female body, but then I was born."

"I will assume you are a male. Weight?"

"Two-twenty."

"Height?"

"Six-two."

"We will perform tests on both arms. The muscle strength in your good arm will be recorded as a reference."

After a litany of tests, using equipment Ryan would have to look up in a reference manual, the invasive prodding finally comes to an end.

"When can we expect to hear back from you?" Kelci asks, looking at Dr. Grove, then Dr. Maroney.

"As soon as we get the results," Willis says.

Ryan gives the kid a withering glance. "That quick, huh?"

Dr. Grove politely smiles at Ryan. "The tests performed today will provide early recognition of muscle weakness, which may lead to physical disability of the wrist and subsequent loss of hand functions."

"Are you confident these tests will accurately predict future muscle performance?" Kelci asks.

Dr. Maroney steps forward. "The overall reliability coefficient of the testing methods will demonstrate an acceptable level of consistency."

Ryan frowns as he looks at Maroney. "Can you talk in plain English?"

Maroney folds his reading glasses and sticks them in the inside pocket of his sports coat. "We'll be in touch."

Kelci and Ryan look at each other in disbelief. She's equally miffed by Maroney's disdain but, as always, she maintains a professional demeanor while on the job.

"I'll stick around town until we hear from them," she tells Ryan as they walk to the car.

———

Ryan and Josh sit on a bench in front of the halfway house where Josh has been living since he left the hospital. It's an older stone apartment building surrounded by other stone apartment buildings, in a neighborhood where cars are frequently parked in the front yard. The bottom floor of the halfway house was modified to provide offices and a reception area. Six small apartments are upstairs. The Veterans Administration pays Josh's rent; they want him somewhere they can keep an eye on him until they feel comfortable turning him loose on society.

"They got me a job landscaping," Josh says.

"That's cool. A little fresh air and sunshine will do you good."

"Gets me away from the crazy people inside." He tilts his head in the direction of the building. "Nowadays, when someone asks me if I'm seeing anyone, I automatically assume they're talking about a psychiatrist." He watches as a squirrel picks a nut up in both hands.

"It can't be that bad."

"No one has a job besides me. I was going to tell you a joke about unemployed people, but none of them work."

Ryan looks at the road as a car with its windows rolled down and music turned up full blast cruises by. *All we are is dust in the wind.* "Hang in there. You'll be out of here soon."

A social worker with a peach fuzz mustache, big butt, and narrow shoulders plods out the front door of the halfway house, munching on a Hershey's chocolate bar. "You have a phone call, Mr. Hutson."

Ryan stands next to the reception desk, clutching the phone. He listens intently as Kelci informs him the Angels intend to void his contract. It takes a moment to settle in. "What did they cite as the reason?"

"The strength test?" he questions. "Okay. And according to Dr. Maroney, there's no time frame for complete recovery nor any guarantee I will recover completely?" Ryan shakes his head like an angry horse. "So, now what?" His eyes widen when he hears her say, "They offered a hundred thousand dollars for this year?" Ryan paces as far as the cord of the phone will allow. "And I have to start the season in the minor leagues?" Ryan looks over at the social worker who is slouched in a chair at his desk and aggressively chomping on a mouthful of bubble gum. The young man seems engrossed in the conversation. "Don't you have something to do?" Ryan snaps. The popping of gum and smacking of lips aggravates his already frayed nerves.

"Nope." He leans back and puts his feet up on his desk.

Ryan runs his hand through his hair when he hears Kelci say, "I don't think they have much faith you'll recover fully from this injury. Otherwise, they would put more money on the table."

"Geez." Ryan looks down at his feet. He feels betrayed. "How many times during negotiations did they tell me I was like family? How many times did I hear, 'We'll always be here for you.'"

He holds the phone away from his mouth as he exhales, but he can still hear her. "They *are* giving you a chance to stay in the game and make a comeback."

"I need to think this over." He looks out the window and watches as Josh stands up and walks away from the bench. "Seriously? I have to decide by tomorrow?"

Ryan hangs up the phone and trudges outside. His head is bowed and his eyes are fixed on the sidewalk when he catches up to Josh.

"What's up, man? You don't look so happy."

"Just a little confused, I guess." Ryan opens his mouth, then closes it before reciting his conversation with Kelci.

Josh fights to keep a straight face when Ryan finishes his story.

"What are you smirking at?"

"I was thinking back to high school when you got kicked off the baseball team for not getting a haircut."

"Yeah. That was a tense moment."

"You didn't get a haircut. Just like you didn't go to Nam. You took off for Canada, not knowing what the future held for you."

Ryan grabs Josh's arm, stopping him in his tracks. "Are you trying to make a point?"

"You always did what was right for you. I love that about you, man. You don't need anyone dictating to you and forcing you to accept their terms. Just be yourself."

A state of calm returns to Ryan's body. The wheels silently turn in his head. "Things always turn out for the best when you make the best of the way things turn out," he murmurs.

"There you go, buddy." Josh puts his hand on Ryan's shoulder. "If this is the end, then go out on your terms, not theirs."

"No, Josh, this isn't the end. It's not even the beginning of the end." They turn and start walking back to the halfway house. "But it may be the end of the beginning. Let's get a sandwich. I'm hungry."

As they walk next to each other down the sidewalk, Josh asks, "Did you know you're twice as likely to die from a vending machine falling on your head than you are from a shark bite?"

The following afternoon, Ryan and Kelci stretch out on lounge chairs on the deck of the beach house. They relax in silent contemplation, each with a glass of wine in their hand. The sound of waves crashing on the beach and joyful screams of children fill the air.

Kelci interrupts the tranquility. "I'm heading back to North Carolina tomorrow. We need to give the Angels an answer."

Ryan moves his eyes from the ocean to meet Kelci's pondering look. "No, we don't. And if they call, don't answer."

She gazes at him steadily as a smile slowly spreads across her face. "Gotcha." She reaches out and they clink wine glasses.

CHAPTER FIFTY-SIX

Ryan continues the daily exercise regime Chandra established. The treatment plan includes swimming in the ocean every day. Playing Frisbee is also an acceptable therapy to help strengthen his wrist.

Ryan wanders up to the back deck of his neighbor's house and bangs on the door. A pair of surfer shorts is all he wears on this warm and sunny morning. "Morning, Bud. Can the dog come out and play?"

"Sorry, Ryan, he's taking a nap right now. Maybe later."

"Shoot." Ryan tries to hide his disappointment. "I guess I could get my friend Josh to play Frisbee with me."

Running through the breaking surf, Josh chases after the Frisbee with the grace of a newborn foal. With the ocean up to his knees, he lunges for the gliding disk. The Frisbee smacks him in the middle of the forehead, opening a small wound above his eyebrow. He thrashes about the water like a fish caught on a hook.

"Whew, at least he's conscious," Ryan sighs as he rushes toward him. He kneels next to his friend. "What happened, buddy?"

"Something in the water grabbed my foot and caused me to lose my balance."

"Like an octopus or starfish?" Ryan presses his thumb against the cut to stop the flow of blood.

"Coulda been a sea snake," Josh responds.

The terrifying thought encourages them to make a quick exit from the water.

On land, they slowly trudge toward the beach house. Ryan steadies Josh as they walk.

"Dang, Josh. Now we're going to have to post signs on the beach warning everybody of sea snakes." Ryan looks at him, grinning. "Why didn't you catch the Frisbee? The dog would have."

"You know, I was looking at it and wondering—Why is it getting bigger and bigger? Then it hit me."

"Yeah, right between the eyes." Ryan looks at him, a smile plastered across his face. "Want me to call for a pizza?"

Josh gives him a strange look. "Why? What I need is a medic."

"Around here you get a quicker response ordering a pizza than you do calling 911."

"What if the pizza driver has no medical training?"

"Then we just eat the pizza and hope the wound heals on its own."

They step onto Ryan's deck. Ryan takes another look at the cut. "Want some alcohol?"

"Is it going to burn?"

Ryan shrugs. "Not if you mix it with soda or fruit juice."

"I thought you meant rubbing alcohol."

Ryan turns his palms up and shrugs. "I suppose I could rub some Jack Daniels on your forehead if you want."

"Good to know."

"Let's go to the bathroom. I'll clean you up. We don't want any of that intellect leaking out of the hole in your head."

"The problem with being intelligent is some people aren't smart enough to appreciate it," Josh says.

Fifteen minutes later, they're stretched out on lounge chairs, watching kids play in the surf. Josh has a Band-Aid on his forehead. Ryan removes a cigar from his mouth and slowly exhales a cloud of smoke. "Sure you don't want a cigar? I had these Dominicans infused with Rémy Martin."

Josh shakes his head. "Smoking and consuming alcohol should be two separate actions." He takes a sip of cognac and lies back with his arm behind his head. "Do you know that Russia is larger than the planet Pluto?"

"I would think that would be hard to measure without rolling Russia into a ball," Ryan replies.

In the Blue Ridge Mountains of North Carolina, Andrew Mythoma, the Angels' attorney, sits across the desk from Kelci in her home office. He's a fit forty-year-old man, with a square face and cleft chin. "Mr. Hutson is under contract to the Angels," Mythoma says.

Kelci purses her lips as she shakes her head. "As I recall, the Angels were going to void his contract when he didn't pass their physical."

"Only the guaranteed compensation is voided. He's still under contract to the Angels at the new salary."

Kelci picks up a hint of hostility from the man. His eyes are cold and sharp as he speaks.

"No salary has been agreed to," Kelci cordially replies.

"You've not responded to our attempts to contact you. We sent you a revised compensation package." He lets out a deep breath, clearly frustrated. "Do we proceed with legal action, Mrs. Hutson?"

Kelci sits with her legs crossed and her hands folded in her lap. "Please, counselor." The pitch of her voice raises slightly. "We are not easily intimidated. The offer was unacceptable."

Mythoma reaches into his briefcase and pulls several sheets of paper out of a folder. "This is our final offer. Three hundred thousand a year with incentive clauses. But he needs to sign the agreement and report to spring training immediately."

Kelci tires of playing the game. "First of all, I disagree with your interpretation of the existing contract, but we can fight that battle another time." Her voice is strong and direct. "Currently, Ryan's injury prohibits him from attending spring training. His rehabilitation has been overseen by a private company at his own expense. We'll contact you when he is healthy enough to work out with the Angels."

Mythoma starts to object but bites his lip when Kelci stands. "If you will excuse me, counselor, we have nothing further to discuss." She holds the door open and politely smiles at the attorney.

"When can we expect to hear from you?"

"As your Dr. Maroney so eloquently stated, 'We'll be in touch.'"

Ryan grabs a Heineken from the refrigerator and heads to the deck. As soon as he sits down, the telephone rings. He reaches over and punches the speaker button on his new AT&T Merlin speakerphone. "Hello."

"It's Kelci, Ryan."

"Hey, what's up?"

He gulps down a mouthful of beer while Kelci rehashes her conversation with Mythoma. "He's like Loophole Larry," she says, laughing. "Always looking for an angle. So, what do you think? You want to negotiate up their offer?"

"I dunno. Something doesn't feel right." Ryan watches his neighbor toss the Frisbee to his dog. *Dang. I wish they'd have asked me to play.*

"Are you still concerned about your arm?"

Ryan can sense the apprehension in her voice. He rubs his right elbow. "I'm a little nervous about throwing as hard as I can. I'd hate to throw my arm out before it's healed completely."

"I understand. You want me to hire another therapist to work with you?"

There's a moment of silence as Ryan contemplates the state of affairs. "Nah. I have another idea."

CHAPTER FIFTY-SEVEN

Ryan cranks up the volume on the car stereo as Willie Nelson sings "On the Road Again." The Maserati blows past an eighteen-wheeler like it was sitting still. At ninety miles per hour, the engine purrs like a kitten as it cruises across the Arizona desert.

Jack and Oshi are sitting on the front porch in rocking chairs, sipping lemonade, when Ryan pulls up.

Two large dogs circle Ryan and yap at him when he gets out of the car. Ryan looks at his dad, his palms turned up.

Jack lets out a shrill whistle. The dogs amble away, softly growling. "They'd left you alone as soon as they knew you meant them no harm."

He and Oshi stand to greet him and take turns giving him a hug.

"I got the same treatment at Trey's with his dogs. What's with you guys and your dogs?"

"Dogs and cats are part of our community. The cats keep the small varmints away, and the dogs protect the livestock from fox, big cats, and bears. Everybody earns their keep around here."

"Perfect example of functionalism," Ryan wisecracks.

"Please sit down." Oshi offers him a chair. "Let me get you a glass of lemonade."

"Thank you."

Ryan leans back in the chair and lets out a deep breath—happy to be out from behind the wheel.

Jack says, "We heard from Trey and Kelci that you hurt your arm."

"I'm sorry. I should have contacted you myself."

"Not a problem. That's what you big shots have agents for," Jack replies with a smile that turns his thick mustache up. He's looking a lot like Sam Elliott these days, wearing his hair longer and sporting a straw cowboy hat whenever he's outside. "You mentioned on the phone you had something you wanted to talk about."

"Actually, there is something I want to ask Oshi."

Oshi returns with a large glass of lemonade for Ryan and refreshes her and Jack's glasses from a pitcher.

"This is delicious," Ryan says after taking a sip.

"We make it ourselves," Jack replies. "All natural ingredients. Lemon, honey, and ginseng. But I don't suppose you drove all this way to talk about lemonade."

"Well actually, in a way, I did." Ryan squirms in his seat.

Ryan recounts his injury, surgery, and physical therapy up to this point. "I don't have one hundred percent use of my arm right now. The recovery is taking longer than I hoped."

"I'm sorry to hear that, son. What can we do for you?"

Ryan stares at his feet for a few seconds before he looks up at Oshi. "I was hoping maybe you could help me?"

Jack grins at Ryan. "We thought you considered what Oshi does voodoo medicine."

Oshi puts her hand on Jack's arm and shakes her head.

She looks into Ryan's eyes as though she were trying to read his soul. "What I teach is a state of mind. It draws upon your internal positive energy. Do you have the belief and commitment to be cured?"

Ryan nods and softly replies, "Yes."

Oshi walks over to Ryan and pulls two cognac-infused Monte-cristo cigars from his shirt pocket. "Break them in half!"

Ryan pauses for a moment, then takes a long look at Oshi. "These are special cigars. I brought them to share with Dad."

"There will be no smoking or consumption of alcohol while you are my patient."

Ryan looks at his dad. Jack shrugs. "These are my last two," he quietly bemoans before breaking them in half.

Jack rouses Ryan out of a deep sleep at sunrise the next morning. "Meet us in the back room and wear loose clothing."

Ryan wanders into their workout room in a pair of gym shorts and a T-shirt. "Good morning. What's up?"

"We start each day off with stretches," Jack says as he turns his torso at the hips.

"Good. My arm feels a little tight."

Oshi, who is sitting on the floor, says, "We will be stretching everything from our toes to our scalp."

"You're going to stretch my head out?" Ryan chuckles.

Jack looks at Ryan with a cheeky grin. "No. Your head has already been stretched to its limit."

"The point," Oshi says, interrupting their antics, "is to stretch all the muscles in our body, not just the injured ones. All our body parts work in rhythm. When one muscle is injured, it is weakened, and other muscles work harder to compensate for it. If our triceps are only working at 85% capacity, then the biceps and other surrounding muscles must work at 115% capacity. Our body is in balance when all muscles work at 100%."

Ryan rubs his eyebrow. "Makes sense."

"On the mat," Oshi says. "We are going to start with the toes and work our way up. Put your right foot on your left thigh, pull the toes forward to the ankle, and hold ten seconds. Massage the arch of the foot as you pull on the toes."

An hour later, Ryan is bending his neck to touch an ear to a shoulder.

"On your feet. We are done stretching," Oshi says.

Ryan rolls his shoulder. "That was quite a workout. I feel pretty loose."

"Take a long, hot shower and relax your muscles." Oshi puts her hand on his back. "We will meet you in the kitchen for breakfast."

Forty-five minutes later, Ryan meanders into the kitchen fully expecting some sort of soy and fruit–based breakfast. Jack and Oshi are sitting at the table chatting while eating something green and drinking red juice. Ryan sits down with them.

"You get a newspaper out here?" Ryan asks.

"We do," Jack replies. "But we don't read the paper or watch TV during meals."

Ryan laughs internally, remembering an earlier time in his life.

Oshi fills a large glass with filtered water and sets it in front of Ryan. She and Jack continue their conversation while Ryan looks around curiously, wondering if he needs to ask for some food. Finally, he interrupts their chat. "Is this like a buffet, where everybody serves themselves?"

"No, Ryan, that is your breakfast," Oshi replies.

"A glass of water?" he asks, eyebrows raised.

"Yes. That is all you are going to consume for the next couple days. We need to rid your body of alcohol, tobacco, and other toxins. You will be drinking several gallons a day to flush everything out."

"But I'll starve to death," he replies in a desperate voice.

"Oh, come on now, Ryan, stop your whining," Jack replies, fighting back a smile.

"Mahatma Gandhi once went twenty-one days without eating. You'll be fine."

Ryan scowls at his dad.

Jack pushes the glass closer to Ryan. "Drink up. Oshi has other activities planned for you today."

Ryan drinks until he's swallowed the last drop of water from his glass, then looks at Oshi.

"Now we go for a nice long walk," she says. "We will go up and down all types of terrain. It is important to always maintain a steady pace to keep up the heart rate."

"And be careful not to fall into the stream, son," Jack says with a straight face. "The water's really cold."

"Good to know, Dad."

"Eff you too," Jack replies with a wink. He's loving every minute of Ryan's discontent.

Ryan and Oshi stroll up the trail that Ryan, Sarah, Trey, and Kelci rode horses on many years ago. They walk past Billy's grave.

"Do you think our pets love us?" he asks.

"Of course. Why would you think otherwise?"

"They're animals. How do we really know what they feel?"

"The definition of love is joy in the presence of another, dedicated and devoted . . . Do you think Billy loved you?"

Ryan gets a warm feeling. "Yeah."

After a moment of silence, Oshi asks, "Do you feel stress in your life?"

"Probably no more or less than anyone else."

"We are not talking about anyone else. I am asking you." Oshi maintains a lively pace while breathing steadily and speaking with ease. "When we are stressed, our body releases chemicals that may cause long-term health problems. In severe cases it may even lead to a heart attack or stroke."

Ryan is thinking about what she just said when Oshi disrupts his reverie. "How did you deal with Anne Marie leaving you?"

"I was upset. I drank a lot. People said my patience was short."

Oshi looks at Ryan without breaking stride. "I was told your personality changed. You became more withdrawn. You did not love or trust easily."

"Oh, really?" he says out loud. Then to himself, he says, *I wonder who said that?* He maintains a brisk pace, walking shoulder to shoulder with Oshi. "Time tends to heal. Seeing Jacque and working with the kids at the hospitals brings me happiness. I will admit there may be a void not having Anne Marie in my life."

"Maybe that suppressed love can be shared with your family?" She touches his arm. "You may feel better."

"I suppose so. Keeping busy has made it easier to deal with things." They walk quietly, listening to a cardinal call out to his mate. "I'll try to make a point of reaching out more to people I care about."

"You will find when you are happy with yourself, everyone wants to be happy with you. How are other things in your life?"

Ryan breathes deeply as they maintain their steady pace uphill. The smell of pine is invigorating. "I still have a little bit of anger over the injury and disappointment in how the Angels are dealing with it."

"Do not let things bother you that you have no control over."

"That's not always easy."

"We are going to get you better. I believe in you, and you need to believe in you. Positive energy will help you heal faster." Oshi takes a long look at Ryan. He has a contemplative look on his face. "Tonight, before you go to bed, I will teach you to meditate. It will help rid negative emotions and improve your health. Meditation will also improve your learning ability and help reduce stress and anxiety." She gives Ryan a polite smile. "It may even help you with relationships."

CHAPTER FIFTY-EIGHT

Ryan walks into the kitchen at lunchtime to find Jack and Oshi sitting at the table.

"I feel like I could float away from all the water I've been drinking. It's been three days since I've eaten anything."

Oshi pats the table. "Please sit down and join us for lunch. I believe your body has been sufficiently cleansed. You may start eating again."

"Hallelujah!" Ryan can't decide whether to jump up and down or kiss Oshi. "I'm going into town and order a steak."

Oshi waves her index finger at him. "Not so fast. First off, no red meat. It contains too much fat and is harder to digest than white meat. And no eating at commercial establishments we are not familiar with. We need to know what type of preservatives they put in their food. We only eat food from known sources." The disappointment on his face is evident. "I will fix you a chicken breast with broccoli," she says. "That will give your muscles a good shot of protein. I will also give you pumpkin seeds and almonds to snack on in between meals."

Ryan rubs his belly. "I'm hungry enough to eat an ostrich."

She gives him a strange look. "Why an ostrich?" She opens the pantry door and reaches in to grab a quart jar from the array of containers on the shelf.

"It's the biggest bird I could think of. You know, white meat . . . birds."

"Ah," she politely responds, opening the jar.

"What's in the containers?"

"Herbs. I grow many of them. Some I purchase from reputable suppliers from around the world."

"I saw the aloe plants on the front porch. I heard it's good for sunburn."

"Aloe vera is one of the most underutilized plants in the world. It contains enzymes, anti-inflammatory fatty acids, and wound-healing hormones. You can also drink it to aid in digestion and relieve constipation."

"How do you know all this stuff?"

"Many years of study and experimentation."

Jack joins the conversation. "All right, son, this is a working ranch, no free rides. You can help Joe clean up the barn and tend to the horses after you eat."

Ryan wanders into the barn and spots Joe brushing a horse. "*Hola, amigo,*" he says, shaking Joe's hand. The trusted employee has worked on the ranch for more than ten years.

"*Buenos dias*, Señor Ryan. How are you feeling today?"

"Good enough to shovel some manure," Ryan replies.

"We have a lot of it here." Joe hands him a pitchfork.

Pitchfork in hand, Ryan enters the first stall he comes to. The horse stares at him as he enters his space. "Why such a long face, buddy?" Ryan asks as he rubs the horse's forehead.

Ryan tosses the spent straw from the stall to the middle of the barn. "You know, Joe, it seems that grooming is just a process of transferring dirt from the horse to the person."

"*Si*, that is the way it is. The horses are very finicky. Some of them are worth a million dollars, and they want to be treated like it."

After a couple hours of freshening the horses' hay, filling the water troughs, and making sure they have plenty of oats, Ryan decides it's a good time to stop. The dogs follow close behind him with menacing looks on their faces as he traverses the space between the barn and the house.

Oshi comes out the front door to meet him. "I was just coming to get you." She hands him a large glass of amber liquid. "Please sit down. Enjoy the drink. I'll be right back."

Several minutes later, Oshi is back on the front porch with several large leaves, which are moist and steaming hot. She wraps the leaves around Ryan's arm, from his elbow to his wrist, then sits down next to him.

"Are they too hot?"

Ryan shakes his head. "The heat feels good. What are they?"

"They are noni leaves. They reduce aches and swelling in the joints."

"What was that drink you gave me? It sorta tasted like beer."

"It is a brew of Solomon's seal and yarrow. The local Native Americans use it to strengthen tendons and help bones heal."

"Cool. I should be feeling good in no time."

"These are herbs, not processed medicine, Ryan. It will take a while to get into your system and do the job. Be patient."

Ryan bobs his head. "I'll try."

She reaches into her apron pocket and pulls out a rubber ball. She hands it to Ryan. "Keep this with you all the time. Squeeze it as often as you can."

"Thank you, Oshi."

"You do not have to thank me, Ryan. You are family. I am pleased that you asked for my assistance. I would never have forced my beliefs on you."

Ryan stammers for a second. "Thank you for the arm, but . . . umm, thanks for Dad, also. He was always so angry and hard to talk to. He seems more relaxed and pleasant to be around lately."

Oshi puts her hand on top of his. "Maybe he just seems that way to you because you are more relaxed and understanding of him?"

Ryan shrugs. "We were always different and had our own opinions. We never seemed to agree on a lot of things."

"Although he disagreed with you, did he ever prevent you from being yourself?"

Ryan thinks about it for a few seconds. "I don't think so."

Ryan and Oshi spend the next morning tending to the herbs in her garden. They trim leaves off several plants and bring them into the kitchen. As they sit across the table from each other preparing the herbs, Oshi looks at Ryan and says, "I would like to try acupuncture on you."

Ryan smiles. "I've heard about acupuncture, but I never got the point of it."

"The point of acupuncture is to boost well-being while balancing the flow of energy in your body," she replies, ignoring Ryan's weak attempt at humor. "If the flow of energy is blocked by injury, it can lead to pain and lack of function in affected areas. Acupuncture will release the block, allowing the body's natural healing response to resume."

"Sounds great. When do we get started?"

"As soon as we are finished here."

Ryan sits at the kitchen table with his right arm extended. Oshi sits close to him. She slowly inserts a needle in his forearm, just below the elbow. "Putting a needle in at the P3, LI11, and LI10 spots should release the block."

As she inserts the second needle, Jack wanders into the kitchen. "Watch out. She can be a real prick," he comments as he reaches into the refrigerator for a cold drink.

"She's already starting to get on my nerves," Ryan replies.

Wearing hats with nets to cover their faces and long-sleeve shirts for protection, Oshi and Ryan tend to the beehives. Hundreds of bees swarm around them as they remove the frames containing the honeycomb.

"It's probably a good idea to keep them happy," Ryan says, looking cross-eyed at a couple of bees on his mask.

"The bees are not domesticated. They are free to forage and swarm where they like. Hopefully, they like the home we built for them and return every night."

Recalling a Josh-ism, Ryan asks, "Did you know more people are killed by bees than sharks?"

Oshi maintains her focus on the task at hand. "None of the creatures we share this planet with want to intentionally hurt us. If we do not threaten them, they will leave us alone. Man has killed far more animals than animals have killed man."

Ryan can hear the dogs barking in the distance. He looks over to see a trail of dust rising on the road into the ranch.

An AMC Eagle pulls to a stop in front of the house. Kelci and a man who looks vaguely familiar get out of the car. They pay no attention to the barking dogs. The dogs get flustered from their lack of concern and wander away.

Ryan pulls off his beekeeping hat and strolls over to greet the guests. As soon as he's within ten feet of them, a surge of emotion overcomes him.

"Holy cow! Look who's here. Other than a few gray hairs around your temples, you haven't aged in more than a decade."

CHAPTER FIFTY-NINE

Doc, Ryan's athletic trainer in college and trusted mentor, takes a seat on the couch. Kelci sits next to him. She sets a manila folder filled with documents on the coffee table in front of her. Doc sets the duffel bag he's been holding on the floor.

Ryan gets comfortable in an easy chair across from them, still a little surprised by their appearance at the ranch. "I had no idea you guys knew each other."

"It's not difficult to find a player's representative if you're in the business," Doc says.

"Oh, so this isn't a social call to check on my health," Ryan jokes.

"Hey, Ryan, how's the arm doing?" Kelci asks to appease him.

"Well, now that you asked, it's gotten stronger the past three weeks." He rolls his right shoulder a few times. "My entire body seems more flexible, and my concentration is better."

"That's good news." Doc scoots forward on the couch. "Are you ready to play some baseball?"

"In my mind, I'm always ready to play." Ryan's voice is full of enthusiasm. "I just need to be sure my body is."

"Baseball season starts in a week," Kelci reminds him. "There could be complications if you're not on a roster by then."

Ryan looks back and forth from Kelci to Doc. "I get the feeling you guys are up to something."

"Want to play for the Texas Rangers?" Doc asks.

Ryan scrunches his nose and looks at him kind of funny. "Huh?"

"I work for the Rangers now as team physician. I'm completing my residency in sports medicine. I've talked to the owners about taking a chance on you, and they're interested."

"First off—congratulations," Ryan says. "Are you a real doctor?"

"Pretty soon. I completed all my studies at the University of North Texas."

Ryan looks over at Kelci. "I thought we're under contract with the Angels."

Kelci rubs her chin while maintaining a wicked grin. "I might have convinced the Angels to let you go."

"The Rangers offered a second-round draft pick and cash for you," Doc tells him.

Ryan lets out a hearty laugh. "My value has fallen rapidly. I've gone from league MVP to a second-round draft pick."

"We didn't give the Angels much negotiating room," Kelci says. "Once again, it's all about being patient and playing the waiting game."

"Which you're the best at." Ryan takes a few seconds to fully comprehend the change of direction. "So, I could be a Texas Ranger?"

"If you pass the preliminary examination. That's why I'm here," Doc says.

"Don't tell me. Another trip to the hospital to get poked and stabbed."

"Not necessary," Doc replies. "I have everything I need to make an evaluation right here." He picks up his duffel bag.

Ryan looks over at Kelci. "What are the modifications to my contract?"

"The Rangers have agreed to assume your contract as is, before the injury." She hands Ryan the documents she brought in. "The only exception is if you remain on the physically unable to perform list for more than forty-five days, you're only entitled to the major league minimum salary."

"Fair enough. If I'm a PUP for more than forty-five days, I don't deserve to be paid." He looks at Doc. "Let's get on with the evaluation."

"I just have two tests." He reaches into his bag and pulls out a spring gripping device with a pressure gauge attached.

"I remember you testing me with something like this when I hurt my arm in high school."

"And I vaguely remember what your grip strength was when you were eighteen," Doc replies. He hands the apparatus to Ryan.

"Should I stretch or do some exercises first?"

Kelci gives him a dead stare. "Just squeeze it, knucklehead."

Sitting on the chair, Ryan intertwines his fingers and pushes them outward, cracking his knuckles. He grabs the device and gives it a hard squeeze, shooting the indicator arm around the circular face of the pressure gauge. The highest pressure point of the squeeze remains registered on it. He hands the device back to Doc.

Doc arches his eyebrows and nods as he looks at the gauge.

Ryan gives him an inquisitive look. "So?"

"So, you have excellent grip strength."

Ryan puffs his chest out proudly.

Kelci sits next to Ryan on the arm of his chair. "What's next?"

Doc stands up and grabs his bag. "We need to go outside for the next one."

Doc and Ryan head toward the backside of the barn while Kelci stays inside to chat with Oshi. Doc snaps together two pieces of curved metal to form a ring two feet in diameter, then attaches netting material tightly to the inside. Once it's fully assembled, Doc mounts it on a three-foot-tall tripod. An electrical wire connects the netting to a box on the tripod.

"This device will test your accuracy and your arm strength. Throw as hard as you're comfortable."

Ryan and Doc toss the ball a few times so Ryan can loosen up his arm. Kelci comes out of the house with a couple cold drinks in her hand. She hands one to Doc. Looking at Ryan, she says, "Throw the ball in the net, and you can have a drink."

"Let's get on with it. I'm thirsty."

Doc hits the switch on the box of the tripod and then marches off approximately sixty feet. He tosses the ball to Ryan, who snatches it with his bare hand.

Sixty feet is the distance from home plate to the pitcher's mound. Ryan glares at the net, thinking, *If I don't get it inside the ring, my baseball career could take a turn for the worse.* He lobs his first toss at half speed. The ball clanks off the rim and bounces into the net. He looks at Doc and smiles. "That felt pretty good."

Doc shakes his head. "Not bad for a wimpy throw. Is that all you got?"

Ryan rears back and fires the next ball, nicking the inside of the ring. He and Doc exchange glances. Doc looks at the gauge and shakes his head. "Seventy miles per hour."

Ryan takes a deep breath and throws the next baseball almost as hard as he can. It hits dead center in the netting with a resounding *clonk.*

Doc looks at the box on the tripod and nods. "Eighty-two miles an hour. Better."

Ryan smiles. "I'll take that drink now."

"Not so fast, stud. Let's back up to ninety feet and see what you got." Doc marches off an additional thirty feet.

Ryan clanks his first two throws off the rim of the circle and onto the ground. He follows them up with three consecutive throws into the netting, each more than eighty miles per hour.

"Your mechanics look good. How'd it feel?" Doc asks.

"I might have been able to throw a little harder, but I felt a slight discomfort." He grabs his elbow and rubs it. "I'm still a little nervous about reinjuring it."

Doc walks in front of him. "Stick your arms straight out in front of you." He grabs Ryan's wrists and gives each of them a strong tug forward. "Any pain?"

"None."

Doc looks at Kelci. "Okay, he can have his drink now."

Kelci and Ryan stop to talk on the porch while Doc takes the empty glasses into the kitchen. Oshi is putting a couple small jars into the pantry when he walks in.

"That was a delicious tea," he tells her.

"Thank you. It was sarsaparilla with a little bit of agave for sweetness."

"You seem to know your plants."

"I have used over a hundred different plants for health purposes."

"That's incredible. How do you keep track of them all?"

"I remember most, as I have been studying for years. But just in case, I keep a journal." She smiles.

"You could publish your journal and make a lot of money."

"I do not want to profit from my knowledge. I only wish to help people."

"I think it's fascinating. I'd like to learn more about natural medicine."

"Your friends call you Doc. Are you a medical doctor?"

"I'm in training to be a physician. Doc is a nickname I've had since I was a

trainer." Oshi hands him another glass of tea. "Ever since I was a kid I've had a curiosity for how the body works and achieves peak performance."

"I would like to give you a copy of my studies. It may be of value to you someday."

"Thank you. I like to keep an open mind about medicine."

After dinner that evening, Kelci and Doc sit in the den, discussing the legalities of Ryan's contract. Ryan joins his dad and Oshi in the kitchen to help clean up. At the first opportune moment, Ryan reaches his arm around Oshi's shoulders and pulls her next to him.

"I don't know how I can ever thank you," he says, a soft, focused look in his eyes. "My concentration is as sharp as it has ever been, and my body feels loose and agile. I could have never gotten to this point without you."

Oshi's eyes smile vibrantly. She backs off from Ryan and grabs his hands. "You did it yourself. I was there to show you the way. I am proud of you."

"We're leaving early in the morning," Ryan says. He looks at his dad and Oshi standing next to each other. "Thank you. Thank you both very much." He walks over to his dad and gives him a hug. "I love you, Dad."

"I love you, Ryan."

Oshi looks on with a content face. She holds her hands together and bows her head. "*Na Man Da Bu,*" she says softly.

CHAPTER SIXTY

Ryan and Doc sit in the first-class section of a 747 heading to Pompano Beach, the site of the Rangers' spring training. Doc is browsing through Oshi's journal while Ryan stares out the window.

"May I get you gentlemen a drink?" asks a middle-aged stewardess with hips large enough to take up the entire aisle.

"I'll have a tomato juice," Ryan replies.

"I'll have one also," Doc says, "but put a shot of vodka in mine."

"Do you think you'll find vodka in that journal you're reading?"

Doc shakes his head. "I doubt it. But when I start to read about the perils of drinking, I'll quit reading."

"You know, Doc, I didn't want to say anything in front of everybody at the ranch, but I owe you everything. I wouldn't be where I am today without you. You set me up in Michigan and had people in Montréal looking out for me."

"Don't sell yourself short, Ryan. You're a pretty intelligent and industrious guy. Besides, you were a good kid. I just gave you a little direction."

"Yeah, well, I don't know how I'll ever be able to pay you back."

"You already have. You stuck to your dream, and you're one of the best baseball players in the game. All my efforts to help you paid off. That makes me proud."

Ryan reclines his seat. Happiness glows inside of him.

"Now leave me alone," Doc says as he returns to looking through Oshi's journal. "I want to see if she has a cure for gray hair."

Ryan arrives at the Pompano Beach facility with three days left in spring training. Just enough time for the training and coaching staff to give him a once-over.

Doc sits in the dugout along with Doug Reder, the manager of the Rangers, watching Ryan take batting practice. He sprays line drives to all three fields. None of his hits clear the fence.

Reder pushes his glasses up on his nose. "He looks good."

Doc wears a proud smile as he looks at Ryan. "We need to work a little on his strength and conditioning. He hasn't hit the free weights in a while."

Reder sticks a plug of tobacco in his mouth. "You think we should leave him behind when we break camp?"

"He'd definitely benefit from an extended spring training." Doc glances from Ryan to Reder. "You might also consider a stint in the minor leagues before bringing him up. Let him slowly work up to playing full-time."

"You're in charge when it comes to that. The owners have invested a lot of money in him."

"He'll be worth every penny," Doc assures the manager.

Due to injuries and other considerations, Ryan and a dozen other players remain in Florida when the team breaks camp.

One of Ryan's training partners is a young Venezuelan named Soto. The man possesses incredible talent, but he remains in Florida because he has difficulty maintaining a consistent level of play.

Ryan is in the locker room changing into his street clothes after practice. With no one else around, Soto approaches him. "Want some of these pills, my friend? They help fix the muscles that are hurting."

Ryan looks at the red-and-white capsules in his palm. "My muscles are fine."

"Have some, anyway. I know you have injuries. The pills make you stronger." He pushes his hand closer to Ryan. "Hit the ball farther. Throw harder."

Ryan waves his hand. "I'm good, man. Besides, taking those things is like cheating. Do the Rangers know you're taking this stuff?"

"No, I never tell them." He looks fearful and shakes his head. "They get angry with me."

"Then don't take them."

Soto grabs his lower back. "I get bad pain in my back. It is hard to play with the pain."

"Maybe you just need to rest it for a while." Ryan finishes buttoning his shirt and stands up. "You don't need to be putting that stuff in your body. You don't know what kind of damage it might do."

"I need to play well to make the team."

Ryan grimaces as he thinks about it. "You're struggling to sound reasonable."

After two weeks in Pompano Beach, Ryan joins the Rangers' minor league team in Tulsa. An auto transport company delivers his Maserati. During games, he parks his car in the players' lot next to his teammates' mostly secondhand cars. Many of the players share apartments in the suburbs, while Ryan stays in the penthouse suite at the Hyatt Regency. At thirty-one, he's at least eight years older than many of his teammates, but he gets along well with them despite the difference in age and financial status. The young guys enjoy having a beer with him and hearing about his exploits in Canada and Mexico, which he greatly embellishes.

"I was a real-life Paul Bunyan during my lumberjack days," Ryan says as he sits at the bar drinking a sparkling water with a twist of lime. "With my strength and endurance, all the loggers wanted to work with me. I chopped down more than a thousand trees."

"Yeah, sure. How did you keep track of all those trees?" one of his teammates asks.

"I kept a log."

During the first several games, the coaches use Ryan strictly as a pinch hitter. After a while it's frustrating for him. During a close game, he bats for the pitcher in the bottom of the sixth and pops out to left with a runner on third. He slaps the top of his helmet in frustration. "Rats! That was my only chance to do something this game."

After a week of mostly sitting on the bench and pinch-hitting, the coaches work him into the lineup for half a game. Playing the field and batting two or three times a game helps him to slowly find his groove. Still, the competitor in him still isn't satisfied sitting on the bench, especially during a close game.

The Tulsa players meander off the field after giving up the winning run in the bottom of the ninth inning. Unfortunately, it's a game in which Ryan sat out the last four innings. Grabbing his gear, Ryan starts toward the locker room, then pauses when he notices the coach sitting on the bench writing notes. Feeling a little discontented, he strolls over to have a chat with him.

"Hey, Bob. I need to start playing regularly to find my rhythm." Ryan sits next to him. "This playing half a game ain't cutting it."

The coach appears a little nervous. He's never been confronted by Ryan before. "I'm just doing what I'm told, Ryan. If you go out there and hurt yourself, I could lose my job."

"You've seen me swing. You've seen how I throw and chase down fly balls." Ryan gives him a reassuring pat on the back. "I feel fine. Give me some more playing time?"

Breathing rapidly, the coach looks at Ryan. "I'll see what I can do."

Ryan's feet are propped up, and he's watching SportsCenter in his hotel room when the phone rings. "Good evening."

"Are you threatening your coach?" Doc asks, trying his best to restrain his laughter.

Ryan lets out a hearty chuckle. "Not at all. I was just letting him know that everything is good, and I need to play more to get my timing down."

"He's a nervous wreck," Doc says while laughing. "He's never had to deal with a temperamental superstar before."

"I'll be gentle with him. But I'm ready to play full-time."

"Okay, you know your body better than anyone. I'll talk to him."

Ryan plays nine innings the next seven games. He quickly finds his groove and rocks the minor league pitchers. They all want to challenge him; they consider him a yardstick to measure their skills by. Mostly, they end up providing souvenir balls to the fans in the outfield bleachers.

Many of his young teammates—and sometimes players on the opposing teams—seek him out for hitting advice and to ask questions about life in the big league. Ryan is always willing to accommodate. He remembers the established players who helped him on his way up.

Chatting with kids in the stands, before and after the game, is something he also enjoys doing. When asked about it by one of his younger teammates, Ryan replies, "I love seeing the kids' eyes light up. To be able to bring joy to someone by just taking the time to talk to them gives me a good feeling."

Ryan finally gets the call-up to Texas. The night before he leaves Tulsa, Chet Etzler, sportswriter for *The Dallas Morning News*, asks to meet for an interview. Ryan reluctantly agrees to have dinner with him. "Meet me at the French Hen at 7 PM."

Ryan wanders into the bar at the restaurant around quarter to seven and grabs a seat. An outburst of laughter at the other end of the bar gets his attention. He looks over and notices two young ladies in tight blue jeans and cowboy boots standing close to someone whose face he recognizes but can't put a name to. The gentleman looks back at Ryan, then waves the bartender over. The bartender promptly delivers Ryan a shot of Macallan on the rocks.

Ryan smiles. "J.P.," he says under his breath.

Ryan walks over as J.P. separates himself from his lady friends. "Cheers," he says to Ryan as they touch glasses.

"*À votre santé*," Ryan replies, keeping with the French restaurant theme.

"We watched you at the ballpark today," J.P. comments. "You've come a long way . . . in the wrong direction."

"Sometimes, you need to reflect back on where you came from to appreciate where you are," Ryan replies. "What're you doing in Tulsa?"

"I sold my oil company to Texaco. I'm going to take the money and retire."

Ryan looks surprised. "Retiring a little young, aren't you?"

J.P. dismisses the comment with a quick shrug. "Not if you want to travel the world, climb mountains, race cars, and cruise the Mediterranean on your personal yacht." He pulls one of the women close to him. "I say go for all the gusto while you can. You're a professional baseball player. Surely, you have all the money you need to do as you please."

"Yeah, but right now I'm doing exactly what I please, and I hope to do it for as long as I can."

Ryan looks across the bar and notices Etzler walking in the front door. "Thanks for the drink, J.P. I've got to go. Good luck in your retirement." He leaves a full shot of Scotch on the bar.

The hostess, a cute teenager dressed up to look like an older woman, leads Ryan and Etzler to a table in the back of the dimly lit restaurant. "Would you like a cocktail?" she asks.

"Vodka martini, dry," Etzler responds.

"Ice water with lemon," Ryan replies.

"Relax, Ryan, you're not at the training table."

"I don't need alcohol to relax."

Etzler is in his mid-thirties with a potbelly and receding hairline. His sports experience is limited to being the scorekeeper on his high school baseball team.

Etzler raises his glass. "Welcome to the Texas Rangers. Dallas has some of the greatest fans in all of sports."

"I lived in Texas a good portion of my life." Ryan taps his glass against Etzler's. "Texans are generally known to have a pretty good attitude."

"The paper has been following your progress in Tulsa. You've been tearing apart the pitching down here."

Ryan blows out a deep breath. "I'm a major league player batting against kids."

"You certainly took them to school."

"They learned. They'll be better for it. That's how you get better, playing against good players."

"The Rangers are on a six-game losing streak, 8 – 18 for the year. Think you can turn things around?"

"I've been asked a similar question before." Ryan's jaw tightens. "I can only play my best and hopefully help the team win games."

"Fair enough. You have a home in Los Angeles. Are you planning to move to Dallas?"

Ryan tilts his head and shrugs. "We'll see. I'm a free agent at the end of the year. I'm keeping my options open."

CHAPTER SIXTY-ONE

A throng of fans cheer for Ryan as he enters the terminal at Love Field in Dallas. A woman displays a homemade sign: "Texas ♥ Ryan." He smiles as he waves to the crowd. "Thank you all for coming out. I'm excited to be here."

He makes his way through the crowd to where a grinning Kelci stands off to the side. "Welcome to Dallas," she says.

"Can't think of a place I'd rather be." He gives her a hug and kiss on the cheek, then steps back to look at her baby bump. "When's the big day?"

"Six or seven weeks. I think this will be my last trip for a while. She kicks pretty good to remind me she doesn't like flying." Kelci grabs him by the arm and leads him through the crowd. Several reporters step forward to ask questions. Taking a brief interlude from her normally affable self, she shouts out, "Excuse us. We need to keep moving." She sticks her arm out and brushes people aside. "There will be plenty of time for interviews later." They work their way through the crowd, out the front door of the small airport, and into a waiting limousine.

"Wow. That was quite the welcome," Kelci comments.

"Most airports have slightly better security." Ryan has a proud grin. "It did feel good to be welcomed like that though . . . Where are we headed?"

"To the ballpark."

"Isn't it a little early to head there for a night game? Maybe we could go somewhere and unwind for a bit?"

"Plenty of time for that later." Kelci leans back in the plush seat of the limo and crosses her legs. "Just so you know, I reserved the penthouse suite at The Joule for you."

Ryan leans forward. "Really? What's The Joule?"

"You're going to love it. It's a 1920s neo-Gothic building that sits next to the Dallas Arts District. Your apartment is 2,300 square feet. It has two bedrooms, two and a half baths, and a large balcony that overlooks the Dallas skyline."

Ryan grabs a ginger ale out of the fridge in the back seat. "You have a habit of finding me homes that you love."

"I know what's best for you," she says with a slightly humorous edge. "I also arranged for your car and suitcases to be delivered there. Right now we're heading over to Arlington Park to meet with the manager and general manager. You'll have plenty of time after that to meet your new teammates and loosen up before the game."

Ryan nods in appreciation. "I'd be lost without you."

Kelci smiles and pats him on the thigh. "You've got to be careful if you don't know where you're going, or you might end up someplace else."

Ryan gives her a squint-eyed look.

"You're not the only one who can quote Yogi."

The limo stops outside the players' entrance to the ballpark. Once they're through the outside gate, Kelci points to a ramp. "That leads to the locker room. Right now, we're going to the executive offices." She leads him to an elevator, which they ride up to the fourth floor. Several administrative offices and private suites that overlook the playing field are located on this level. Kelci steers Ryan in the direction of voices that are coming from an office down the hall.

Once they're inside the office, Kelci introduces Ryan to J.D. Graves, the general manager. He's a fiftyish man with a portly build. He's decked out in a seersucker suit and Lucchese cowboy boots. A Stetson Diamante cowboy hat rests on a hat rack behind his desk. Graves rises to his feet to shake Ryan's hand. "Welcome to the Rangers, Ryan."

"Thank you, sir." Ryan looks over at Reder, the manager, and nods. They met in Pompano Beach during spring training.

"Have a seat." Graves points to a pair of brown leather chairs in front of his oversized redwood desk. "Let's talk money."

Kelci smiles while she shakes her head. "No. We already discussed this, J.D. Ryan's in good health, according to Doc. Our agreement is you assume Ryan's contract for the duration of this year."

Graves responds with a big smile of his own. "I would be negligent if I failed to add a few more years to his contract."

"Not an option at this time. We intend to play out this contract and renegotiate at the end of the season."

Graves can sense Kelci is adamant in her reply.

Ryan smiles inside at Kelci's ability to instantly go from a lovable mom and sister-in-law to a merciless businesswoman.

Reder stands up and looks at Ryan. "What do you say we go down to the locker room?"

Ryan looks at Kelci, who winks. "I'll handle this."

"Sounds like a good idea, Coach."

The elevator drops them off on the first floor. Reder leads Ryan into a large rectangular locker room that was designed with players' needs in mind. Each of the wood lockers is over eight feet tall and has inside lighting, a lockbox, drawers, and power outlets, in addition to a controllable ventilation system. Padded chairs sit in front of each unit, televisions hang on the wall, and three black leather couches and end tables are set up in the center of the room.

The equipment manager is in the room, awaiting their arrival.

He approaches Ryan and extends his hand. "Daniel Morales. If you need anything, let me know."

"Thanks," Ryan replies.

Morales leads Ryan to the last cubicle on the far wall. A Rangers home uniform with "Hutson" printed over the number seven hangs in it. "Your agent gave us your measurements. Your equipment sponsors provided us with several pairs of shoes, gloves, bats, and batting gloves to your specifications. I'll grab a couple ball caps for you. What size do you wear?"

"I'm not sure. I'm not in shape yet."

Reder gives him a spirited look. "Reckon your hat size gets bigger the better you play?"

Ryan offers Reder a fake grin. "You're funny."

Assured that Ryan needs nothing else, Morales takes off. Soon afterward, a steady flow of players enter the locker room, most of whom stop and chat briefly with Ryan.

Ryan casually watches ESPN as he changes into his uniform. Mats Wilander is playing Guillermo Vilas in the French Open finals.

Fully dressed in Rangers attire, Ryan heads down the tunnel to the dugout. He drops his gear off in his designated space beside the bench, then jogs onto the field.

Applause from many of the fans already in attendance welcomes him. He waves in appreciation before he sits down in the outfield next to Buddy Bell and Billy Sample. He extends his left leg and grabs his toes, stretching his hamstrings. "It feels good to be back in a big league park again," he tells his teammates.

"I've never seen this many fans before a game," Buddy comments.

"A new superstar is in town," Billy replies in jest.

Ryan scoffs. "I haven't done anything to earn their admiration."

"Just the anticipation of having you here excites them," Buddy says. He turns his back to stretch his hips and lower back. "Can you handle the pressure?"

"I put more pressure and expectations on myself than any fan ever could." Ryan stands up. "Anybody want to throw?"

. . .

Today's game is against the Indians. Both teams are battling for last place in their respective divisions.

Ryan starts the game in left field and in the number three slot in the batting order. There are two outs when he strolls to the plate in the bottom of the first. The fans jump to their feet and give him a standing ovation. Ryan stands outside the batter's box, scanning the cheering fans, then tips his hat.

"Let's go. I want to get this game over before midnight," the umpire moans.

Ryan looks over at the overfed umpire and in a lighthearted voice replies, "You know, Ron, you'd be in pretty good shape if you ran as much as your mouth does."

Ryan slaps a line drive between first and second base. The fans jump to their feet, and the enthusiastic cheering starts all over again.

"That's the most cheering I've ever heard for a base hit of no consequence," Andre Thornton, the Indians' first baseman, tells Ryan.

The next batter goes down swinging.

The game ends up being one of the fastest in major league history. Nine innings are completed in one hour and forty-two minutes. The teams combine for five hits in Texas' 1 – 0 victory.

Ryan goes on a thirty-six-game hitting streak. During the run he feels more flexible than he has in years. His reflexes are quicker and his concentration sharper. He thinks often of how grateful he is to Oshi and her approach of treating the whole person.

He ends the season with a .351 batting average, thirty-nine home runs, and 101 runs batted in, playing in only 121 games. His offensive explosion is meaningless—the Rangers finish in last place. They don't have enough strong pitchers or hitters throughout their lineup to be competitive.

A few days after the final game, Ryan packs what he can into the Maserati and heads north on I-35. When he reaches Oklahoma City, he turns west toward Albuquerque. From there, he drives north into the mountains and to the family ranch.

Oshi and Jack greet him as soon as he steps out of his car.

The dogs circle Ryan, growling softly. Jack shoos them away and gives his son a hug. "Congratulations on a great season. I'm proud of you, son."

Ryan can feel his dad's ribs. He looks a little frail to Ryan when he takes a step back to look at him. *It must come with age*, Ryan figures.

Ryan embraces Oshi. "I had a good season, mentally and physically. Thank you. I couldn't have done it without you."

"You have a good mindset. You can do anything you want."

After two days of relaxing and eating bean sprouts and seaweed, Ryan is back in his Maserati and heading to California.

CHAPTER SIXTY-TWO

Ryan and Lisa finish their meals at The Harbor Restaurant on the Santa Barbara pier. A fluorescent orange sun slowly sinks into the horizon, creating a mirror on the ocean that reflects the red, orange, and yellow from the sky.

"I can't believe you haven't made up your mind about free agency. You must be leaning one way or another," Lisa prods.

Ryan takes a drink of water. "Not really. We're not supposed to entertain any offers until after the World Series."

"Come on, you can tell me," she says excitedly. "Where would you like to go?"

"How old do you think you would be if you didn't know your age?" Ryan asks.

"Twenty-one, but don't change the subject." She gives Ryan a push on the shoulder.

"Seriously, Lisa, I'm not thinking about it. When all the facts are presented, we'll make a decision. Until then, it's not on my mind."

"Okay, we're friends. You'll tell me first?"

Ryan gives her a smile and pat on the hand. "I promise."

"All right, now that that's settled, it's been a long, fun day. I'm ready to call it a night." Lisa looks up at the television behind the bar. "This World Series is about to be history."

Ryan signals the waiter for the check. He looks over at the television and his face beams. "We Are Family" blasts over the speakers at the ballpark; the camera pans to the fans dancing in the aisles and on their seats, then swivels to the playing field. Ryan watches his old teammates hug each other and slap hands. The Pirates win the Series. Ryan looks at Lisa and says, "Man, I wish I were part of that celebration. It doesn't have to be with the Pirates, any team would be fine."

It's been a week since the World Series was completed. Ryan and Josh walk through the front door of the beach house, their hair and clothes covered in dust from a day of four-wheeling at Hungry Valley.

"I'm going to change into my trunks and jump in the ocean. I need to get some of this dust off me," Josh says.

"I'll be out there as soon as I check my messages. Oh, and be careful. Sometimes the sharks disguise themselves as seaweed."

"Good to know."

Kelci's silvery voice echoes from the answering machine after Ryan hits the play button. "The offers are all in. I'll meet you at the condo at noon tomorrow to go over them."

"I really should give her a raise," he tells himself as he hangs up the phone. He takes off his dusty clothes in the laundry room, slips on a pair of shorts, and heads out to the beach.

Ryan stabs a spinach leaf and slice of cucumber with his fork and sticks them in his mouth. Room service delivered a couple of salads with grilled chicken for lunch.

Kelci sits across the dining room table from him, sipping on the hibiscus drink Oshi sent home with Ryan. "Mmm, this is good stuff."

She reaches into a manila folder and pulls out several pieces of paper. "I tabulated the different offers for comparative purposes. There are eight serious players. Three offers are higher than the rest." She slides the chart over to Ryan, who's chomping on a piece of chicken.

He studies the chart for a few minutes. "Angels, Red Sox, and Yankees. Not surprising."

"With everything added in, the Angels' offer is the highest of the three. They included endorsement contracts with their corporate sponsors. Their total package, including equipment sponsors, is 3.2 million dollars per year."

"Is it guaranteed?" Ryan sarcastically replies. "What about the Rangers?"

"They're at 2.4 million a year."

"Any endorsement contracts?"

"None other than your equipment sponsors and your line of men's toiletries, which you have anyway."

"I don't see Montréal on the list."

A look of surprise flashes across Kelci's face. "They offered 1.7 million a year."

"Why didn't you put it on the table?"

"I don't think it's a good move for you."

"My son lives there. Why wouldn't it be a good move?"

"Well, for one thing, there's no telling how long you would stay there. According to a study of economic balance in Major League baseball, it's not likely baseball will survive much longer in Montréal. It's hard to say where they'll relocate the team. You'd have no control over where you'll end up. Trust me. It's not in your best interests."

"Okay," Ryan concedes. "You always have my best interests at heart."

"I love you just like I do my children."

"How's that baby girl doing?"

"Sally is a bundle of joy. It's nice to have a little girl after dealing with those feral boys for years."

As he thinks about the various offers, Ryan's winsome face adopts a deliberate look. "I like how the Rangers stepped up to the plate when the Angels wanted to cut my salary."

"They did."

"Dallas is a pretty relaxed place to live. It doesn't have the hectic feel of L.A., New York, or Boston."

"True."

"But I'll miss the ocean."

"You could always buy a house on a lake."

"It wouldn't be quite the same."

"You can keep the Malibu house as a second home."

"What about this place?"

"The owners of the building informed me that they have gotten several inquiries about the availability of the unit after you were traded to the Rangers. The offers are a half million more than what you paid for it."

"Sounds like you knew which way I might lean?"

She gives him a friendly wink. "I know you. The Rangers and Doc reached out after your injury. I knew that would mean something to you."

"If we go with the Rangers, can we get some incentives thrown in?"

"This proposal is just an offer. I'll fly to Dallas and meet with the owner and general manager. I'll inform them of the deal the Angels presented and see if they want to sweeten their offer."

Ryan spends the night in the condo. Late the next afternoon, he heads to the beach house.

The message light is blinking on his phone when he enters the house. He grabs an orange juice from the fridge and hits the play button.

Kelci's voice fills the room: "We reached an agreement with the Rangers for 2.8 million plus incentives." Ryan pumps his fist in jubilation. He opens the sliding glass doors and wanders onto the patio, where Josh is stretched out on a lounge chair reading a magazine.

"What're you reading, buddy?"

"*Discover* magazine. This article is about the origins and evolution of life in the universe. Scientists are searching for habitable environments in our solar system and on planets around other stars," Josh replies without looking up.

Ryan sits in a chair under a sun umbrella. "Do you think there's alien life out there?"

"Absolutely." Josh sets the magazine down excitedly. "Amino acids just like those that make up the proteins in our bodies have been found in meteorites."

"Really? So any type of creature can evolve from the amino acids?"

"Bacteria, fungi, even cockroaches are all our cousins. We share the same basic molecular machinery."

"Do you think there might be giant cockroaches out there flying spaceships?" Ryan hides his sarcasm behind a serious face.

Josh shrugs. "It's possible cockroaches don't require spaceships for intergalactic travel."

Ryan shakes his head in amazement. "This world is full of protons, neutrons, and morons."

"People like you are the reason aliens won't talk to us," Josh says, then returns to reading the magazine.

Ryan rises and heads for the house, then stops. "By the way, I'm moving to Dallas. You're welcome to stay here as long as you like."

"I've been thinking about going back to Virginia. I have friends and family there." Josh tosses the magazine aside and turns in his seat to get a better look at Ryan. "I saved a few bucks to buy a reliable car to get me across country."

Without hesitation, Ryan tosses him the keys to his car. Josh reaches for them; they bounce off his hands and drop onto the patio. "You can have the Maserati."

Josh bends over and picks up the keys. "I'd rather have the Jeep."

"The Jeep stays with the beach house." Ryan turns his back and walks inside.

CHAPTER SIXTY-THREE

When Ryan gets off the plane in Dallas, he has two immediate tasks: buy a car and find a place to live.

His first stop is Wheeler's Autohaus. Sweat runs down his back as he strolls the lot checking out the Porsches, BMWs, and Mercedes. "Where's the breeze when you want it?" he asks Max Wheeler, the owner of the dealership.

"If you don't like the weather in Texas, wait a day. It'll change."

"Good to know." Ryan places his hand on the roof of a silver Porsche 928. "I'll take this

one."

"Good choice, Mr. Hutson. A very precision-driven automobile, loaded with luxurious features. I'll comp the car if you agree to be our spokesman."

Ryan laughs softly. "No thanks. I don't need any more expectations on my time." He pulls out Kelci's business card and hands it to Max. "My agent will arrange payment for the car, taxes, title, and whatever else."

. . .

The next stop is The Housem Agency, a real estate firm that bills themselves as the company for discerning clients. Ryan spends the rest of the day with Debbie, a slim young lady with flowing blond hair. Debbie has a fetish for driving fast in her Mercedes and talking nonstop.

Their first stop is Highland Park, an older neighborhood of stately mini-mansions situated on boulevards lined with grand pecan trees and large oaks. Ryan is immediately reminded of the Cherry Creek neighborhood in Denver. Only now, he isn't looking to stay in the guesthouse.

Debbie looks over at a grinning Ryan as they get out of the car in the driveway of the first house they stop at. "What's brewing in that brain of yours?"

"Just thinking how far I've traveled."

Debbie leads him to the front door of the house and opens it. "Let's see if you can make the rest of your journey pleasant."

Ryan can tell as soon as he walks through the doorway that the house isn't for him. It's much too formal for his liking. "It's a beautiful neighborhood," he tells Debbie. "But it's really not for me. Everything seems so . . . perfect. I prefer something a little more laid-back. Near some water."

Once they're back in the Mercedes, Debbie spends a minute perusing her multilist catalog. Her eyes widen and she gets a big smile on her face. "I've got just the place!"

Ryan can feel the g-forces against his face as they race out of the city and then across the open plains in her sports coupe. Twenty minutes later, they're sitting in front of a two-story brick colonial with white pillars. The house is surrounded by two acres of land that butts against Lake Ray Hubbard.

"This is a 5,400-square-foot home with five bedrooms and six baths." Debbie gleams with pride. "You're going to love the inside."

The downstairs consists of a great room with a twenty-foot-high ceiling and a formal dining area. A mahogany staircase leads to the second floor and the bedrooms. The master bedroom is equipped with a fireplace and a balcony that overlooks a beautifully landscaped backyard and the blue waters of the lake. Included in the sale is a twenty-foot dock and boathouse. Inside the boathouse are two Yamaha Jet Skis and a thirty-foot ski boat.

"I'll take it."

Shortly after Ryan signs his contract with the Rangers, the team is sold to a group of investors, including Skip, the son of the vice president of the United States. In his meeting with the new owners, Ryan informs them, "It's not a lot of fun for the players or fans to be stuck with a last-place team. You may want to look into increasing the talent level."

Whether they listened to Ryan or it was Skip's ability to misunderestimate, the Rangers add several veteran players. They sign Ramon Paldero, the runner-up to the National League batting title the prior year, and Julian Francis, a perennial .300 hitter and multi-dimensional player. Nolan Ryan, amid a contract dispute with the Astros, also joins the team. At forty years of age, he still throws a hundred-mile-an-hour fastball. Even though he had an off-year the previous season, he quickly returns to form once he gets his curve-ball straightened out. With the new makeup of the team, the Rangers are destined for greatness this year.

On what is going to be his last free weekend before the baseball season, Ryan invites his family to a get-together at his new home. Round-trip airplane tickets and limousine services to and from the airport are included in his invitation.

CHAPTER SIXTY-FOUR

Jacque is the first to arrive in Dallas. His mother insisted that Ryan pick him up at the airport.

Ryan is chatting with young fans in baggage claim when he sees his son riding the escalator down. "Excuse me," he says as he separates himself from the crowd.

Jacque's eyes light up when he sees his dad. He rushes to give him a hug. "This airport is so cool. I got to ride an elevated train to the baggage claim."

"I'm glad you made it without getting lost."

"Get real, Dad. I'm almost nine years old. I told Mom I wanted to take a limo to your place. It would've been really rad to tell my friends. But she said no. She treats me like a kid sometimes."

"That's just the way girls are. They don't want their men to have too much freedom." Ryan steps back and looks at his son. "Growing like a weed."

Jacque has his father's height and eyes. Eyes that could melt a girl's heart. His slim build and dark hair come from his mother's side of the family.

Ryan directs his son toward the baggage belt. "Let's grab your gear and get out of here."

"This is all I brought." Jacque holds up his backpack. "Mom says if I need anything else, you can buy it for me."

Ryan grins. "Okay, we'll get you some Texas clothes. How about a ten-gallon hat and a pair of cowboy boots?"

Jacque's nose scrunches up like he smelled something awful. "No way."

Ryan chuckles at his son's immediate rejection of cowboy attire. "So how's school?" He keeps his hand on his son's back as they walk to the parking lot.

"School is pretty cool." Jacque's eyes get wide. "I'm taking geometry this year. It's kinda neat calculating the size and shape of things."

"Good knowledge for a fourth grader to have," Ryan replies. "How's the music coming along?"

"I'm learning the guitar."

Jacque's response gives Ryan a sudden jolt. "Are you giving up on the piano?"

"No." He shakes his head. "I want to learn to play a bunch of instruments."

"Phew!" Ryan wipes his forehead in jest. "Good, because I purchased a baby grand for the house."

***

Ryan and Jacque sit on the dock behind his house with their feet hanging over the edge. A black limousine cruises up the driveway, disrupting their serenity. Ryan stands up and ruffles Jacque's thick head of hair. "Let's see who it is."

Before they reach the limo, the driver gets out and opens the back door. He offers a hand to Jack, then Oshi as they exit the vehicle.

"It's Grandpa Jack," Ryan says a full second before Jacque takes off in a full gallop toward them.

The young boy is in the midst of a hug with his grandpa when Ryan saunters up. He gives Oshi a hug and a kiss on the cheek.

"You look good, Ryan," she says.

"Thank you." He smiles. "I'm eating much better these days."

Jack and Jacque are rambling on about something to each other in Spanish when Ryan interrupts. "How was your flight, Dad?"

Jack reaches out to put his arm around Ryan's shoulders. "Couldn't have been smoother. An hour-and-a-half from Albuquerque to Love Field without hitting a single air pocket."

Ryan notices the driver standing patiently behind them with their luggage in hand. "Let's go inside. I'll show you to your room."

"Did you meet Jacque at the airport this morning?" Jack asks.

"Nah. I've known him since he was born," Ryan replies.

"Good to know," Jack says.

As they walk toward the house, Oshi holds hands with Jacque. Looking at Ryan, she says, "I thought your brother and his family would be here when we arrived."

"Their flight was delayed," Ryan says. "It won't land until around nine tonight, and it will probably be close to ten by the time they get here. Sarah and Jeanne will be in tomorrow morning."

By noon the next day, everyone has arrived and is enjoying a beautiful day in the backyard. A few clouds slowly drift across the sky, and a light wind blows in off the lake. Tuna steaks and chicken breasts simmer on the upper rack of the grill under the watchful eye of a hired cook. Downwind from the grill, the ladies sit in lawn chairs chatting, the savory aroma arousing their taste buds. Trey and Kelci's daughter, Sally, sits on Oshi's lap. Sam, C.J., and Jacque race around the backyard, behaving as young boys do.

Ryan, Trey, and Jack loiter in the boat, which is tied to the dock. "This baby has twin 250-horsepower engines and a collapsible top to block the sun or rain," Ryan proudly points out.

In the midst of his bragging, a voice sings out from the shore. "Ahoy, me hearties!"

The guys turn to see Sarah approaching the boat.

"Arrgh, yonder comes ye landlubber," Trey responds.

Sarah's face lights up with a radiant smile. "Is this a meeting of scallywags, or may a lady join in?"

"C'mere, me beauty." Jack offers his hand to help her onto the boat.

"Nice boat, Ryan. Actually, your spread on the lake is very nice," Sarah comments. "Must suck to be you right now."

"Ha," Ryan scoffs. "Like having a flat in New York City and a cottage in Paris is a tough life."

Trey looks over at his dad and comments, "I don't think I get enough credit in our family for making my siblings look successful."

Sarah rolls her eyes as she glances at Trey. Shifting her gaze to Ryan, she says, "What's going on in your life? I haven't read about you in the gossip magazines in quite a while."

"Lately, I think the only girl I know who hasn't said 'You're like a brother to me' is you."

"You have all these fancy degrees, what do you do, Sarah?" Jack asks.

"Well . . . in my free time I've taken up rock climbing. I get my exercise when I'm in New York by rowing in the Harlem River, and when I'm in Paris, I jog along the Seine. The exercise keeps me in shape and relaxes my mind."

"I used to climb rocks when I was younger, but I was boulder back then," Trey says.

Not pleased with Sarah's response to his question, Jack tries a different approach. "Okay, if you comedians will shush for a minute, maybe Sarah will tell me what her job entails."

"It's hard to describe in a few words, Dad. But basically, as an international trade specialist, I study the effects of globalization on businesses and develop plans to help companies become successful in overseas ventures."

"Are the markets good in Europe?" Jack asks.

"From the U.S. standpoint there's still a big trade imbalance, but we've reduced it by forty billion dollars the past couple years."

"Forty billion dollars!" Trey's eyes widen. "Wow. It must have been a huge deficit."

"It was 150 billion at one time," Sarah replies.

Meanwhile, in the backyard, the boys stop their running for a breather.

"You want to play catch?" C.J. asks Jacque.

"No. I don't like playing baseball."

"Cowabunga, dude!" Sam's eyes widen. "Your dad is, like, the greatest baseball player in the world, and you don't play?"

Jacque looks at his feet as he kicks the ground. "It's not something I like to do."

C.J. tilts his head. "What *do* you like to do?"

"Sometimes, I play soccer with my friends. But mostly, I like to play music and read."

C.J. and Sam look at each other in disbelief. They've never known a kid that would rather take music lessons than play ball.

Back at the boat, Jack says to Ryan, "I need to stretch. Will you take a walk with me?"

"Sure, Dad."

They meander a quarter mile or so along the lake shore. Jack walks a little more slowly and breathes a bit heavier than Ryan is used to seeing.

"Want to take a break, Dad?"

"No, I'm fine." He puts his arm on Ryan's back as they walk shoulder to shoulder. "I'm proud of you, son. You've done good things with your life."

"Thank you." The compliment gives Ryan a good feeling. "It didn't always seem like you agreed with some of the things I did."

"You had some harebrained ideas when you were younger. But those were your convictions, and throughout the years, you stuck with them."

"Like disagreeing with countries who send their young men off to kill each other to solve political differences?"

"We're having a pleasant conversation. Don't blow it."

Ryan can't help but chuckle. "Yeah, I guess you and I were always different. You never seemed to have any issues with Sarah or Trey, though."

They stop walking and look out upon the lake. A flock of geese honk loudly as they fly overhead. "Your brother and sister take after me. You're more like your mother, God rest her soul. She was a thoughtful and caring person. She loved her animals and always saw the best in other people. My side of the family is pioneer stock—we hunt, fish, and wave Ol' Glory. I was raised to never question the government. You're an independent thinker. If you weren't a professional athlete, I suppose you would have been a writer or a college professor."

"I guess it takes getting older to agree we didn't see eye to eye," Ryan says. "And to learn to appreciate our differences."

"I'm sorry we couldn't do that when you were younger. I hope you don't make the same mistake with your boy."

Ryan's eyes gleam. "Jacque will never be a baseball player, but I'll be proud to see him become a great musician."

Jack's shoulders and arms relax. He feels content and at ease.

"Mom said you drank to hide from some of the ugliness in your life."

"Thankfully, I gave it up before I drank myself to death," Jack replies.

"I hear ya. When Anne Marie left me, I hit the bottle pretty good. Kelci reminds me that I wasn't the most pleasant person to be around. I'm grateful to Oshi for helping me clean up my act."

"She's a good woman. She loves you like you were her own child." They walk a few steps in silence. "I love you, son."

Ryan throws his arm around his dad's shoulders as they turn and head back toward the house. "I love you too, Dad.

. . .

After dinner, everyone piles into the boat for a sunset cruise. The kids sit up front with Ryan next to the controls. Ryan lets them take turns steering. He keeps the throttle low as the boat quietly slices through the water with a minimal wake. When the orange sun nears the horizon and casts a colorful tail across the lake, he cuts the engines. Several small clouds float in front of the sun, creating a masterpiece of flaming pinks and reds. Ryan turns to look at his dad, who's holding hands with Oshi. Trey has his arm around Kelci, and Sarah and Jeanne sit close together. Ryan sits with the kids, wondering what's wrong with this picture.

Oshi gets up and walks over to Ryan. They gaze at the sunset. "This time of day is as magical as it is beautiful," she comments. "It is proof that no matter what happens, every day can end wonderfully."

The adults sit in the living room talking. Sally is asleep in Sarah's arms, and Jacque and C.J. sit on the floor playing checkers. The long day is easing into a peaceful conclusion.

Suddenly, a loud, grating sound comes from the den, destroying the serenity of the evening. Sam shamelessly pounds away on the piano keys, causing several people to tense up.

"Cut that out, Sam," Trey hollers. "You're upsetting your mother. Don't make me call the flying monkeys on you."

"What?" Sarah gives Trey a strange look.

"We watched *The Wizard of Oz* the other night. Sam thought the monkeys were creepy."

Ryan looks over at Jacque and nods toward the piano.

Sam's assault on everyone's eardrums comes to an abrupt halt and is soon replaced with the exquisite sound of Elton John's "Tiny Dancer." All conversation immediately stops as a rich and smooth melody fills the house.

C.J. sits on the piano bench next to Jacque while he plays. When the song is over, he looks at him with great admiration. "That was totally awesome, dude. Know any Eagles?"

CHAPTER SIXTY-FIVE

With a retooled mind and body, compliments of Oshi, Ryan puts up some gaudy numbers in the new baseball season. Unfortunately for the Rangers, the All-Star break comes and goes, and the team struggles to achieve a winning record. With the additional seven million dollars of free agent salary, the team's record is only slightly better than it was at this time the previous year. The few extra wins come at a cost of nearly a million dollars per game.

One of the free agents signed in the offseason is noticeably underperforming in relation to what he's being paid. The fans and media are quick to lose their patience with him. Grumbling and murmuring occur in the stands whenever this player comes to bat. Without naming anyone specifically, Chet Etzler of *The Dallas Morning News* pens an article suggesting some players become complacent when they receive long-term, guaranteed contracts.

Although it's not an elected position, Rangers players and management look to Ryan as the team leader. As such, he feels obligated to pull Ramon, one of the free agents they signed in the offseason, aside after a game in which the slugger was hitless in four at-bats. They sit on opposite ends of the couch in the clubhouse after everyone has moved on.

Ramon takes a swallow of Lone Star beer. "What's on your mind, buddy?"

Ryan rests his arm on the back of the couch and crosses his legs. "You're getting paid almost five thousand dollars every time you bat. Do you think you could be a little more productive?"

"Come on, man. We're halfway through the season—seventeen games out of first place." Ramon throws his shoulders back and glares at Ryan like he's been insulted. "There's no way we're going to catch the A's."

"So you quit putting out maximum effort?" There's a minute of silence as they look at each other. Ramon shrugs, then takes another gulp of beer. "You know," Ryan says, "fans are paying thirty bucks a ticket, four dollars for a beer, and three dollars for a hot dog this year because of the increase in payroll."

"So? You make as much as me."

"Yeah, but I don't take days off. I give it my best every day."

"And we're still next to last in our division." Their eyes lock for a moment. "Ryan, I'm thirty-eight years old. I'm going to retire at the end of my two-year contract, and I'll probably get elected to the Hall of Fame. I got nothing to prove."

Ryan's eyebrows lower, and his eyes narrow. "Not to yourself or the fans?"

Ramon chugs the rest of his beer and stands up. "I hurt my knee earlier this year. I'm not going to jeopardize my long-term health."

"Is it that easy to give up?"

"Ask yourself that question when you're thirty-eight." Ramon grabs his gym bag and heads for the door. "See you tomorrow, Ryan."

Soto, who has been hitting tape-measure home runs for the Rangers' minor league team, is called up to the big leagues in late July. He strikes out frequently, but when he makes contact, his monster home runs send the fans into a frenzy.

The young man is playing in his third game since his call-up to the Rangers. It's a close game in the bottom of the seventh inning when he hits the ball so hard that it ricochets off the facade in the upper deck in center field and bounces back into the middle of the playing field. He's all grins as he high-fives everyone on his return to the dugout. He plops down on the bench next to Ryan. "Man, I love that feeling."

Ryan playfully pushes Soto. "You knocked the crap out of that ball."

"I feel really good lately."

"You've bulked up since spring training."

"I've been hitting the weights."

Ryan nods. "I guess lifting weights makes your voice deeper?"

As the season progresses, Ramon and Soto hang out frequently. As the friendship flourishes, so does Ramon's ability to hit the ball hard and run faster. "See, I can still be productive in my later years," he brags to Ryan.

Ryan stays mum on their steroid use. "They're dealing with the devil behind closed doors, sacrificing their long-term health to play at a level beyond their God-given talent."

Soto's and Ramon's power surges go for naught. In mid-September, the Rangers' dysfunctional season comes to an end. The team *did* move up in the standing—from last place the prior year to next to last this year.

After the baseball season ends, Ryan splits his time between his lake home and his beach house. A typical day for him in Dallas begins with a morning kayak trip. Unless he has somewhere important to go, he might spend the entire day in shorts and a T-shirt. Without

Bobbie Jones supplying a new wardrobe every month, his appearance is more bohemian these days.

Today's afternoon agenda includes a visit to the blood and cancer facility at the Dallas Children's Medical Center.

Ryan sits with a young Hispanic couple next to the bed of their six-year-old boy. "How is Alberto doing?" Ryan asks, rubbing his palm across the soft skin of the child's bald head.

"He is no feeling well lately. He tired all the time, and he bruise easily," his father says. "The chemotherapy is tough on the boy."

"Have you heard anything about a possible bone marrow transplant?" Ryan asks.

The father looks, with sad eyes, at his young wife. "We are not good donors, and our families are in Mexico. We cannot get marrow from them. They are not U.S. citizens."

"There are good hospitals in Mexico City that can test marrow. Contact your relatives and find a good donor. My foundation will make sure Alberto receives it."

The boy's mother covers her face with her hands as she weeps. The father wraps his arm around her shoulders. "*Muchas gracias*, Señor Hutson. But why you help us? We are a poor immigrant family and not baseball fans."

"Every kid deserves a fighting chance."

Ryan leaves Alberto's room and heads down the hallway. A large Black man stands at the nurses' station. Ryan winks and waves at the nurse behind the counter as he walks by. "Have a nice day, Cindy."

"You too, Ryan," the nurse replies.

A deep voice resonates from the Black man. "Hold on one minute."

Ryan stops, slowly turns around, and casually strolls toward the counter. "You talking to me?" At six foot seven and close to 300 pounds, the guy could pass for the Incredible Hulk.

"I am if you're Ryan Hutson."

Ryan nods slowly.

The big man smiles and extends his hand. "I'm Eugene Bennett."

Ryan grabs his hand and eagerly shakes it. "Offensive tackle for the Cowboys?"

"Yep."

"I didn't recognize you without your helmet on."

"Most people don't realize how good-looking I am."

"You may be pretty, but you sure have a mean disposition on the field. I heard they call you 'Doctor Pancake' for all the defensive players you knock on their butts."

"It's 'Father Pancake.' I'm an ordained priest. When I finish my law school correspondence classes, I'll become 'Father-in-Law Pancake.'"

Ryan lets out a polite laugh. "You're one of the nastiest men in football. What are you doing hanging out in a children's hospital?"

"Everyone has stress in their lives. Football is a wonderful way to get rid of aggression without going to jail." He puts his large paw on Ryan's shoulder. "I'm generally a kindhearted, sensitive soul, and extraordinarily creative. I'm the author of a popular collection of children's books. The kids relate to me as the superhero in my stories, so I like to show up to the children's ward every now and then and provide solace." Eugene pauses for a beat as he studies Ryan. "I heard you head up a foundation to help kids in need. I want to help you."

Ryan looks up into his eyes. "I'd be afraid to turn you down."

"You ain't exactly puny for being a baseball player."

"Just because baseball isn't a contact sport like football doesn't mean we're not fit."

"Ha ha," Eugene bellows. "Football ain't a contact sport—it's a collision sport. Kissing is a contact sport." Eugene slaps Ryan on the back, knocking him forward a foot. "I'm going to enjoy working with you," Eugene says as they head toward the elevator. "I can see you're a good man."

"Why thank you, Hugh Gene. I can see you're a man with a keen eye for quality."

CHAPTER SIXTY-SIX

Ryan is roused from a deep sleep by the ringing phone. "Hello."

"It's Kelci. Your accountant called Friday. I guess you were too busy to return his call."

"I've been a little preoccupied. Besides, I figured you would take care of it. So, how is Bill?"

Kelci holds her breath for a moment, then exhales. "It's Bob, and he's received a notice of past due taxes from the British Virgin Islands."

"I thought our offshore account was protected."

"It's not about your bank account. It's the beach bar you have in joint ownership with that Australian guy. The value has escalated significantly, and your partner hasn't paid the additional taxes."

"I'll give him a call."

"Also, your brother has been trying to get ahold of you for the past couple days."

Ryan senses a smidge of exasperation in her voice. He sits on the side of his bed. "You know he's not very good about leaving messages."

"Your dad is going in for open-heart surgery on Wednesday."

Ryan gets to his feet, scratching his head as he paces about the bedroom. "Don't they do that balloon thing before performing surgery?"

"He's already had angioplasty twice."

Ryan scrunches his face. "Why don't I know these things?"

"Maybe because you don't stay in touch. Sarah and Trey call your dad at least once a week to see how he's doing."

"Okay, my bad." He holds his fist up to his lips, letting his breath pass between his fingers. "Heart surgery isn't that big a deal anymore, right? I heard they do it all the time."

Kelci bites her lip, disappointed in what she perceives as lack of concern. "Yes, Ryan, bypass surgery has become more common."

Ryan relaxes from his pacing. "I'm sure he'll be all right."

"We wanted to let you know what's going on." Kelci hangs up the phone, slightly miffed at Ryan's indifference.

Ryan downs a plateful of ham, eggs, and potatoes before he takes the kayak out on the lake. The rhythmic paddling and steady breathing are meditation to him. Observing the mallards and wood ducks on the lake and the occasional deer and red fox along the shore adds another level of serenity.

A flashing light on his answering machine grabs his attention when he returns from his paddle. The message is from Doc, reminding him of his checkup at the University of North Texas Medical Center that afternoon.

Ryan completes his medical exam, then stops by the pediatric ward. Visiting with the kids leaves him feeling uplifted. He's about to walk out the front door of the hospital when he hears someone call his name. He turns to see Doc walking toward him. "Want to grab a bite to eat?"

"Sure. Where would you like to go?"

"How about the Original Mexican Eats?"

Sitting across from Ryan, Doc lifts his glass of beer for a toast. "I reviewed the results of your examination. You're in about as good of shape as I can remember."

Ryan clinks glasses with him. "Other than an occasional beer or glass of wine, I don't drink alcohol—and I tend to eat well, exercise, and maintain peace of mind. My dad said it only makes sense to take care of your body the older you get."

"How is your dad doing? He's starting to get on in years."

"He's going in for bypass surgery."

Doc winces. "I'm sorry to hear that. If there's anything I can do, let me know."

"He'll be all right. I heard that type of surgery is pretty routine these days."

Doc gets a strained look in his eyes. "There's nothing routine about cutting open a man's chest."

They eat their enchiladas and burritos without further word on Jack's pending operation.

Ryan leaves two twenties on the table for a twenty-six-dollar tab. Looking at Doc, he says, "I need to take off. I'm feeling a little out of sorts."

"You are looking a little queasy. Are you okay?"

"I'll be all right."

Ten minutes later, Ryan is in his Porsche, cruising down I-20 toward home. He turns the radio up as "The Living Years" by Mike + The Mechanics comes on the air. The lyrics seem to resonate with him.

Ryan lies in bed that evening, reading *A Confederacy of Dunces*. The book doesn't relieve his tension, and he tosses and turns, unable to fall asleep. A line from "The Living Years" sticks in his mind. *I just wish I could have told him in the living years.*

The next morning, Ryan sits on the back porch in a pair of gym shorts with the cordless phone in his hand. He calls every airline he can think of, searching for a flight into Santa Fe or Albuquerque. Everything is sold out. He's told he can go standby, but there's no guarantee he will get on.

Lying on the chaise lounge with his lips together, he gazes into the heavens and watches a small jet zip overhead. Suddenly he bolts upright. "Of course. Why didn't I think of it." He rapidly flips through the Yellow Pages, searching for charter services. On his fourth call he hits pay dirt.

"We have a jet available, but it won't be cheap at this late notice," the customer service agent informs him. "There also won't be any stewardess or cabin service."

"I'll take it."

The Porsche hums along at eighty-five miles an hour toward Redbird Airport. A small twin-engine Cessna is waiting for him when he arrives at the jet center. It's an older model that's designed strictly for commuter travel. It doesn't have all the amenities that LeClair's customized jet had, but it has a comfortable seat, snacks, and drinks—perfect for an hour trip.

The airplane bounces a few times when the wheels touch the ground. Ryan lifts his head from his slumber. Once it comes to a complete stop, the copilot joins him in the main cabin.

"Welcome to Albuquerque. We hope you enjoyed your flight, Mr. Hutson. Please fly with us again."

"Thanks." Ryan peels a hundred-dollar bill off his money clip and hands it to the pilot for a tip.

"New Mexico Medical Center," Ryan tells the cab driver as he settles in the back seat.

CHAPTER SIXTY-SEVEN

Ryan drums his fingers impatiently on the countertop of the of the hospital's main information desk. "My father, Jack Hutson, is having surgery today. Where can I find him?"

The receptionist, a young lady with a bouncy, feathered haircut similar to Farrah Fawcett's, scans the screen of her IBM 5150. "We have a Carl Jackson Hutson scheduled for open-heart surgery today."

"That's him."

She points to an elevator down the hall. "Take that elevator to the third floor. Someone at the nurses' station will direct you from there."

Ryan enters the room. Jack is lying in bed, Oshi holds his hand, while Kelci, Trey, and Sarah stand alongside the bed.

Oshi releases Jack's hand and walks over to Ryan, wrapping her arms around him.

"Does he really have to go through this?" Ryan asks softly as they embrace.

"The doctors said this is the best thing to do. Your father occasionally gets lightheaded and dizzy, and he has an uncomfortable feeling in his chest. We discussed all the options."

Ryan takes a deep breath and releases it loudly. "What are they going to do?"

"They will remove the piece of coronary artery that has hardened plaque along the wall and graft in a healthy artery. In this case, from the inside of his thigh," Oshi says.

Jack overhears part of their conversation. "I'll be back home in a week and will be feeling like a new man." His eyes are fresh and enthusiastic. "I look forward to playing with my grandkids."

Two orderlies come in the room and raise the side rails on the bed. "We're off to pre-op now. Tell everybody you'll see them later, Jack."

Jack grabs Ryan's hand. "I'm glad you could make it. It means a lot to me that you're here."

"I love you," Ryan says, studying his dad's face. "We'll see you in a bit."

Two hours later, a nurse comes into the waiting room. "The operation is over, and everything went well. Mr. Hutson is being transferred to intensive care for recovery."

Sarah hops to her feet. "Can we visit him?"

"He's still unconscious and will be for a while. His wife may come in, but the rest of you will have to wait until tomorrow. He'll be alert then."

The family gathers in Jack's hospital room the next day. Oshi, who slept in the chair next to the bed overnight, sits on the side of the bed holding his hand. Her clothes are rumpled, and her hair is unkempt. Jack is heavily sedated and seems uncomfortable. He moans and speaks in a strained voice.

A nurse comes in the room to check Jack's vitals. "What's going on?" Trey asks.

"People respond differently to this type of operation," the nurse replies. "His body is still in shock. He'll be all right soon. We'll keep him in the ICU a little longer and continue to monitor his vitals."

Her response pacifies everyone.

The following day, Jack's attending physician makes an appearance when the entire family is present. "Mr. Hutson picked up an infection, and his temperature is very high. We're trying to keep it down while providing antibiotics to fight the infection." He looks around the room tentatively. "At the moment, his body is trying to heal from the surgery and fight the infection. As soon as we get the infection under control, his body can focus on recovering from the surgery. Everything will be fine in a couple days."

Anxiety starts to build in the family over the next couple days. Jack is put into an induced coma. The doctor explains that it's necessary to control the pressure dynamics on the brain. "High pressure can deprive it of oxygen," he says.

On the fifth day after the operation, Ryan walks into his dad's room and finds him hooked up to a pumping apparatus. "Argh!" His lips draw back in a snarl. He walks into the hallway and spots a young man in a lab coat walking toward him. "Are you a doctor?" Ryan asks as they stand outside the door to Jack's room.

"I'm a resident," the young man replies.

"Why is my father on that contraption?"

The resident looks at the equipment hooked up to Jack. "That contraption is a dialysis machine. Your father's kidneys aren't functioning properly. He needs help filtering his blood. Don't worry, he's going to be fine."

"I've heard that before."

The resident ignores Ryan's obvious frustration and continues down the hallway.

A coldness overcomes Ryan, and he starts to shiver. *I need to relax before I go back in there.* He walks down the corridor to a waiting area and collapses in the first chair he comes to.

An elderly lady is the only other person in the room. She's bent over with her head in the palms of her hands. Ryan can hear her sobbing. He moves next to her and gently touches her shoulder. She's a little startled at first but responds by resting her hand on top of his. She continues to softly weep as Ryan sits by her side.

She looks up at Ryan as tears trickle from her red eyes and down a face that's full of character and experience. "My husband is dying," she says meekly. "We've been married for forty-five years. He's the only person I have in this world."

Ryan's heart sinks. "I'm so sorry you have to go through this alone. My name is Ryan. I'm a good listener if you want to talk."

She valiantly fights back her tears. "Bless you, Ryan. I'm Bess. My husband is Grant. I've been with him since I was twenty years old. My Grant was such a dashing young man when he was younger. We married before he shipped off to Germany to fight the Nazis. He was so proud to serve his country. He made the Army his career." She takes a deep breath, her eyes glisten as she looks at Ryan. Our son, Tom, who is probably about your age, joined the Army after he graduated from college." She can't fight the tears any longer. They pour freely down her face as she sobs. "He was killed in Vietnam. He was our only child."

Ryan's stomach tightens. "I'm sure you're very proud of both of them . . . What is Grant in here for?"

"Heart surgery. The doctors told him the only way he was going to live a healthy life was with bypass surgery."

Ryan sits up straight. "What happened?"

"We came in for the surgery last Wednesday. He was fine the first day after the operation. He was sitting up and joking with me like he always does. The next day, he started having pains in his chest and leg. By the end of the day, he lost consciousness." She speaks with short, gasping breaths. "I never got to talk to him again."

Ryan grabs a box of tissues off a nearby table and hands them to Bess. They sit quietly for a few moments before he finally asks, "Why do you think he's going to die?"

"He got an infection. I was told it has spread to several other organs, and they're starting to shut down. They said there's nothing they can do to save him."

CHAPTER SIXTY-EIGHT

Ryan's pulse quickens. "Could I have a way to contact you? I'd like to stay in touch."

Bess gives Ryan her telephone number, then excuses herself, leaving him alone in the waiting room. Ryan leans back, his head resting on top of the chair. He breathes deeply, trying to relax. When he leans forward, he notices a phone in an alcove in the waiting room. He recalls an earlier conversation with Doc and decides to give him a call.

"Hello. This is Dr. Michaels."

"Doc, it's Ryan. I'm in New Mexico with my dad."

"How's he doing?"

"Not well." Ryan informs him of everything that's been going on the past few days.

"It doesn't sound good." Doc's voice softens. "What can I do to help?"

"I'll charter you a plane. Come to Albuquerque and help me understand what's going on. Just for a couple of hours. One day at most." There's desperation in Ryan's voice.

"Ryan, I'm a doctor. I can't just take off."

There's a period of drawn-out silence. Heavy breathing exists on both ends of the line.

"Damn it!" Doc declares forcefully. "Have the charter available to take off at 7 AM tomorrow."

Ryan and Doc walk into Jack's hospital room the next morning to find him hooked up to a respirator. Kelci and Sarah sit at the side of the bed, looking like wilted flowers. Oshi sits next to them with a firm grip on Jack's hand. Trey is at the hotel checking on things in North Carolina.

Kelci looks at Ryan and Doc. "He quit breathing on his own last night."

Ryan pounds his fist on his thigh, visibly upset at his dad's deteriorating condition.

Doc pulls back the sheets to take a close look at the incision on Jack's leg, then the one on his chest. Walking to the foot of the bed, he picks up the chart and studies it. Forcing a composed demeanor, he looks at Ryan and his family. "Excuse me a minute." He walks over to the nurses' station and engages a nurse in a lengthy discussion.

"So?" Ryan asks Doc when he returns to the room.

"He's got a virus they're not familiar with. They're trying different antibiotics, but they don't seem to be working. Some of his organs are starting to shut down."

Oshi covers her face with her hands to hide her tears. Kelci wraps her arms around her.

"It's been a slow, torturous ordeal." Ryan stomps about the room in a walking rage. "That wound on his leg looks miserable."

"It's gangrene," Doc says. "If he survives, the leg will have to be amputated."

Sarah clutches Ryan's arm to stop his pacing. Tears well up in her eyes. "Why aren't the doctors telling us these things?"

"I can't answer that. Maybe because it's happening so fast now."

"Anything else we should know?" Ryan's frustration is turning to fear.

"These are things his doctors should be discussing with you. I would be out of line to second-guess their opinion."

"They keep telling us he's going to be all right. Obviously, he's not." Sarah has a pleading look in her eyes. "We have a right to know what's going on."

Doc tightens his lips while contemplating. "You need to be aware of the potential for brain damage." He pauses for a beat. "If he pulls through this, he may not be able to think for himself."

"You keep saying, 'if he pulls through this.'" Sarah's voice trembles.

"I'm sorry. You need to sit down with his doctor. I have no privileges at this hospital."

Later that evening, the attending physician meets with Jack's family. A private room in the ICU is set aside for meetings of this nature. Doc is back in Dallas.

"I'm not going to lie to you. Mr. Hutson is seriously ill," the doctor says.

"You've been on a roll. Why stop lying to us now?" Trey says.

The doctor ignores the comment. "The virus has done irreparable damage. We'll keep fighting this the best we can, but it's unlikely he'll live a quality life if he survives. We have no idea how damaged his brain might be."

"Where did the virus come from? How did he pick it up?" Kelci asks.

The doctor shakes his head. "We have no idea."

"Likely from the hospital." Ryan's voice is short and abrupt.

"Let's not speak prematurely." The doctor looks at Ryan. "It could have come from multiple places."

Ryan scoffs. "Just a coincidence that two people—Dad and Bess' husband, Mr. Hayes—get infected by the same virus, on the same day, after being operated on in the same room."

Trey finally asks *the* question. "What happens if life support is turned off?"

"Mr. Hutson's body likely could not sustain itself without life support."

Trey, Kelci, Sarah, Ryan, and Oshi sit in silence in the small room after the doctor leaves. A week ago, they could have never imagined themselves in this position.

Trey breaks the silence. "Dad was a proud, self-sufficient man. I don't want to see or have a memory of anyone cleaning up after him and feeding him like a little baby."

"He wouldn't want that," Sarah agrees.

Ryan sits quietly, staring at the floor. He lifts his head and looks around the room with a steady and unwavering gaze. "Don't ever give up. Dad deserves a fighting chance. You never know, he could pull through this." There's intensity in Ryan's face and determination in his voice.

Silence fills the room. No one wants to tell Ryan that it's over.

Oshi stands, then asks everyone to please leave the room. "I want to talk with Ryan privately." They sit on chairs next to each other. She turns her body so she can hold Ryan's hands as she looks him in the face. "The body is a natural and complex system, deserving appreciation and respect. Your father put up the best fight he could, and his body is telling us he cannot fight anymore. It is time to let go and allow him to pass into the next life peacefully." Ryan's bottom lip quivers. "Chemicals and mechanical equipment are not natural. They only keep him alive against his will."

Ryan squeezes his eyes shut as tears roll down his cheeks. Oshi cups the back of his head and pulls his face onto her shoulder.

CHAPTER SIXTY-NINE

Jack lies on his bed, surrounded by his family. The overhead lights are dimmed. Several small lights flicker on the monitors. Blips and spikes in the EKG reflect his heartbeat.

The nurse shuts off the equipment hooked up to Jack, then leaves the room. The family watches with a sense of unreality—this really isn't happening. Oshi holds one of Jack's hands and Sarah grasps the other while Trey, Kelci, and Ryan stand at the foot of the bed. Tears roll down each of their faces. Ryan feels lightheaded.

As the minutes pass by, Jack's breathing gets slower and weaker. After one final deep breath, the blips on the EKG stop and the line goes flat. Ryan's eyes remain intently on his dad as he watches the color fade from his face. He notices a wisp of vapor leave his father's body. He pinches his nose between his eyes to control the tears, but it's no use. Ryan's shoulders heave as he weeps. Sarah releases Jack's hand and comes over to him, wrapping her arms around him and holding him tight. "It hurts," he murmurs in her ear.

Jack is officially pronounced dead. The family staggers out of his hospital room.

"I'm going for a walk with Oshi, then we're going to head back to the hotel," Sarah tells everyone as they plod down the hospital corridor.

"We'll see you later," Kelci replies. "We've got some paperwork to complete here."

"I'll catch up with you," Ryan says. "I'm going to the ICU for a minute."

Trey gives Kelci a worried look. He has reservations about Ryan's intentions but relents anyway. "Sure. We'll meet you at the lounge in the hotel in an hour or so."

"See you in a bit," Ryan says.

Trey looks at Kelci as they amble down the hallway. "He's up to no good."

"Ever since I've known your brother, a barrier has existed between him and your dad. In the past six months, Ryan and your dad have reached out to each other and tried to make up for lost time." Kelci shakes her head sadly. "Now your dad was taken from him . . . and in this manner."

Trey nods. "I'm sure he's also feeling empathy for the woman whose husband died from the same procedure. Right now, he's sad and he's angry." He puts his arm around Kelci's waist as they walk. "Depression is anger without enthusiasm."

Two nurses and an orderly stand at the nurses' station in the ICU chatting. They offer their condolences to Ryan when he walks up to them.

"Thank you. It's been an emotional week," Ryan replies. "I wanted you guys to know my family and I appreciate your kindness and support."

A curtain parts, and the attending physician steps out from a patient's room.

"Mr. Hutson, I thought I recognized your voice. I'm sorry for your loss. I want you to know we did everything we could for your father."

"Cut the crap," Ryan says curtly. "People come to the hospital to get better, not get killed. My dad and Mr. Hayes should both be alive."

"Sometimes things happen that we have no control over, Mr. Hutson."

Ryan opens his mouth but stops before he says what he feels.

Ryan nods at the nurses and orderly. "You guys take care." He leaves the ward without another word.

***

Ryan, Kelci, Sarah, and Trey sit at a table in the dining room at the Hyatt. Oshi wishes to be alone in her room.

A waiter approaches Ryan. "Are you ready to order, sir?"

"Double Scotch on the rocks."

"What brand, sir?"

Still feeling flustered, Ryan blurts out, "I don't know. Give me the best you've got."

"Would you like to order food now?"

Ryan shakes his head. "I'm not hungry."

"Are you sure you want that drink?" Kelci asks after the waiter has left, a concerned look on her face.

Ryan glares at her, steely-eyed. "Get me the best medical malpractice lawyer money can buy."

"As your agent, I'll do whatever you ask. As your sister-in-law, is this really what you want to do?"

"I'm positive!"

"Are you doing it for the right reasons, or are you doing it to make yourself feel better?"

"If they get sued, they might clean their hospital up so things like this don't happen again." Ryan rests his elbows on the table, his fingers interlocked. He leans forward and rests his chin on his hands. "I could've gotten him into the best heart hospital in the country and this wouldn't have happened."

"What happened could have occurred anywhere," Sarah says. "You can't beat yourself up over it. This is where Dad wanted to be. This is the hospital and surgeon he chose."

The waiter returns with Ryan's Scotch. Ryan swirls the glass and then grumbles under his breath, "Any thought about a funeral?"

"We talked about it while we waited on you," Sarah says. "We thought we would have calling hours at a funeral home here in town, then a private service at the ranch. We'll bury him next to Mom." Sarah gazes at Ryan, trying to read a response in his face.

Ryan pushes the Scotch away without taking a drink. "Sounds good."

CHAPTER SEVENTY

Ryan stands at the entrance of the funeral home, welcoming visitors. He's wearing a navy-blue suit, a crisp white shirt, and a maroon paisley tie. An elderly gentleman with thinning gray hair enters the parlor and stops next to him. He offers his hand, and Ryan shakes it.

"Thank you for coming. I'm Ryan, one of Jack's sons."

"I'm John Poindexter. Your father worked with us part-time at Los Alamos. I was devastated to hear about his death. He was a truly remarkable man."

Ryan listens attentively as John recalls fond memories of working with Jack. "Your dad had an analytical mind, but also had a great sense of humor. He once said, 'You can never trust an atom, they make up everything.' Had us all in stitches."

Ryan had no idea his dad worked at the nuclear laboratory in Los Alamos. Nor that he had this great sense of humor John talked about.

John walks away and Ryan scans the room. He notices Sarah indiscreetly beckoning him with a wave of her fingers and nod of the head. She stands close to Jeanne as they talk to a slim woman with blond hair who has her back to Ryan.

Ryan works his way in their direction until he's intercepted by a couple of elderly ladies.

"Look at this young man, Edna. He has got to be Jack's son. He has his eyes and ears."

Ryan touches the side of his head. "His ears?" he says softly. "Yes, ma'am, Jack was my father. My name is Ryan."

"I'm Louise. Are you a movie star or politician? You're so tall and handsome."

"No, ma'am. I'm a Texas Ranger."

"Law enforcement. How wonderful."

Ryan makes no attempt to clarify. "How do you ladies know my dad?"

"Jack would stop in at the mercantile store sometimes while we were buying supplies. He was the nicest man," Edna recalls. "Occasionally, he would join us on the porch for a cup of tea."

"I remember the last time he came into the store," Louise recalls. "It was a hot day, and he was wearing his thongs."

Ryan's eyes bug out and he takes a big gulp of air. "My dad went into the store in a thong?"

"My, yes. All the boys wear them on their feet these days."

Ryan lets out a sigh of relief. "We call them flip-flops where I'm from."

"We were just shocked to read about his death in the newspaper," Louise says. "We skipped our garden club today so we could come to the viewing. At our age, staying alive becomes more of a challenge. Seems like we're always crossing names off in our address book." The ladies look at each other. "Edna and I are at the point in our lives if it doesn't hurt, it probably doesn't work. You ever hurt yourself doing law enforcement work, Ryan?"

Ryan stammers for a second, then looks around the room for an escape route. Lucky for him, he spies Trey walking in his direction. He waves at his brother. "Yo, Trey, come on over. I want you to meet Edna and Louise. You guys have a lot in common."

"Good afternoon, ladies. My name is Trey. Thank you for stopping by to pay your respects."

"Your father was a wonderful man. You look just like him, especially the nose," Edna comments.

"Excuse me, ladies, I have other guests to greet." Ryan pats Trey on the back and makes a quick departure.

Ryan treks across the parlor, stopping to accept condolences every few steps. When he reaches his sister's side, Sarah gestures toward the lady she and Jeanne have been speaking with. "Ryan, this is Mary Elizabeth."

Ryan's breathing accelerates. Mary Elizabeth looks like an angel. She has mesmerizing blue eyes and beautiful soft skin. He offers his hand.

Mary ignores his hand and leans into him for a polite hug. She whispers into his ear, "I'm so very sorry about your father." Ryan holds the hug until Mary pulls back. They stand close, gazing at each other intently.

"Thanks for coming. It's been a tough week."

"I can imagine." She studies him carefully. "You look wonderful."

The corner of Ryan's lips turns up slightly. Her presence leaves him at a loss for words. He's full of questions but holds off on asking any when he notices Doc heading toward him, accompanied by Bobby Valentine and Toby Harrah of the Rangers. He gives her hand a soft squeeze. "I'd like to talk with you, but now isn't the best time."

"I understand." She pulls his suit coat open and slips her business card into his shirt pocket.

After two days of visitation, it's the day of the funeral. Ryan charters a private plane to pick up Jacque. Kelci flies back to North Carolina to pick up her kids.

. . .

Sarah and Jeanne stand behind Oshi, who sits on the stone bench at the head of Meagen's and soon-to-be Jack's graves.

Kelci holds Sally, who has a mournful look on her face. Trey and Kelci's two boys stand tall in front of their father. Jacque stands next to Ryan, his head bowed. The kids all loved Grandpa Jack.

Grief-stricken eyes stare at the casket draped in an American flag. The preacher concludes his sermon: "Jack strived for goodness in all he did. Life is short, but eternity is forever. And as we grieve the loss of Jack's presence here on earth, we must accept he has moved from the physical realm into the spirit realm, where the Lord greeted him, saying, 'Well done!'"

Two members of the U.S. Air Force Honor Guard take the flag off the casket, fold it according to protocol, and present it to Oshi. A lone military bugler plays taps.

In the distance, the mourners can hear, "Ready, aim, fire." A volley of rifle shots follows. Seven riflemen perform the procedure three times.

After several moments of silent remembrance, Jack's casket is lowered into the earth.

Everyone starts to walk away from the grave, except Oshi; she remains seated on the stone bench, a black veil covering her face. Jacque looks at her with sad eyes. He dawdles over to the bench and sits next to her. Oshi wraps her arm around his shoulders and pulls him close. Jacque lays his head on her shoulder. They sit silently as thoughts of Jack fill their heads.

Ryan stands off to the side for five minutes or more, his heart aching, before approaching Jacque from behind. He places his hand on his son's back. "Come on. Let's give Oshi some privacy."

Jacque grasps Ryan's hand as they walk away. "I loved Grandpa Jack. He was fun to be around. He never talked to me like I was a kid."

"He loved you and respected you for who you were."

Jacque has been fighting back tears all day, and he finally breaks down and starts sobbing. Ryan gets down on a knee and wraps his arms around him. "I love you," he says as he looks at his father's grave.

Sam tugs on his dad's sleeve as their family walks away from the cemetery. "Why did those guys shoot guns at Grandpa's funeral?"

Trey shakes his head. "I don't know, son. Why don't you ask them?"

Sam scurries to catch up with the soldiers before they can get in their staff car. When posed with the question, one of the soldiers responds: "It's a way for the U.S. military to honor a great person. It's based on an old battlefield custom that two warring sides cease hostilities to clear their dead from the battlefield. The firing of three volleys meant that the dead had been properly cared for, and the side was ready to resume battle."

CHAPTER SEVENTY-ONE

The day after the funeral, Trey heads back to North Carolina, and Sarah and Jeanne are off to New York City. Ryan and Kelci stay at the ranch with the kids.

"Yesterday was Christmas," Ryan says to Kelci as they sit in Jack's office going through his personal documents. "Seems with everything going on, we let it slip through our minds."

"The kids reminded me. I told them Santa left their gifts at home," Kelci replies. "I don't know if they still believe in Santa, but they still believe in getting presents."

Kelci, acting as Jack's attorney, prepared his will. Knowing that his children are well-off, Jack left all his possessions, money, insurance, and real property to Oshi. Trey, Ryan, and Sarah agreed with his decision.

"I'll file the will as non-contested, and the estate will be turned over to Oshi," Kelci tells Ryan. "The ranch is paid for. It generates a profit of over $150,000 a year after taxes and expenses. If Oshi wants to sell it, it's worth $2.5 million."

"I hope she doesn't. I also hope Joe will stay on to help out."

Kelci stows the documents in a desk drawer. "Oshi is a smart lady. She'll figure it all out when she comes around."

. . .

It's been a week since Jack was laid to rest. The kids are playing in the woods, and Kelci is with Joe tending to horses. Ryan sits at the kitchen table, drinking a cup of green tea and reading the paper.

Oshi comes into the kitchen wearing a pair of jeans, tennis shoes, and a red blouse. "Good morning."

"Good morning," Ryan replies. He's surprised to see her dressed in her usual attire. Since Jack's death she has been wearing dark clothing and keeping mostly to herself.

Oshi fixes herself a cup of tea and sits at the table next to Ryan. She places her hand on top of his and smiles at him.

"Welcome back. We've missed you," Ryan tells her.

"I have allowed myself time for pain and suffering. By meditating toward a state of 'thoughtless awareness,' I have reached deep peace. I have released the painful thoughts that crowded my mind and created stress. I have also unblocked the energy force that flows through my body. Now is the time for the healing process to begin."

Ryan puffs his cheeks and nods.

"I will celebrate Jack's life and the beauty he brought into the world. You, your brother and sister, and the grandkids are the most important part of that beauty."

"He'll live on through his grandkids."

She stands up and grabs his hand. "Come. It is a beautiful day. Let's walk."

They head up the trail along the river Ryan walked many times in the past.

"Your father loves this ranch. He put so much energy and love into making it a home. I have so many positive memories of things he did and said. Once, while we were walking on this trail, he told me how very happy he was. He said, 'My life is good. You are a wonderful wife, and I have three incredible children that I'm very proud of.'"

They walk silently for several minutes before they stop. Ryan looks down at the gurgling creek as it rushes by. His eyes focus on the small colorful rocks beneath the clear water.

"You must unlock your positive energy," Oshi says, recentering his thoughts. "You have lost your natural balance." She pauses, watching him think. "Your compassion and creativity are blocked."

"Huh?"

"I overheard talk of you suing the hospital. The hospital did not intentionally create the virus that killed your father and Mr. Hayes. The doctors tried everything they knew to stop it from spreading."

"It's a hospital," Ryan replies grudgingly. "You expect sanitary conditions."

"Sometimes patients bring in infections they are not aware of or they know nothing about."

"They shouldn't put people with open wounds in rooms that have been contaminated. Surgery rooms should be sterilized. Dad and Mr. Hayes had surgery in the same room."

"You have a lot of anger in your heart, and you need to release it. Let the natural endorphins in your body bring back your positive mood. Think of something that made you happy recently."

Ryan puts his hand on Oshi's shoulder as they walk. "Talking with you makes me happy."

A few days later, Jacque is back in Montréal with his mom, and Kelci has returned to North Carolina with her kids.

Ryan parks the pickup truck in the parking garage next to the hospital. It's the same pickup Ryan gave to his dad years ago when he was a spokesman for Chevrolet. Under Jack's meticulous care, the truck still looks and drives like it just came off the showroom floor.

The administration building is a renovated adobe structure next to the hospital. A small plaque out front informs everyone it was the original hospital built by Spanish priests in 1692.

Ryan is dressed comfortably in a pair of jeans, sneakers, and a pullover sweater.

After passing through the front door of the building, he comes face-to-face with an elderly woman sitting behind a desk. She possesses a very proper and professional demeanor. "May I help you, please?"

"Ryan Hutson to see the administrator."

She nods in casual acceptance. "Please follow me, Mr. Hutson."

She leads him to a room with a door partly closed. She gently knocks on the door and sticks her head in. "Mr. Hutson is here to see you."

"Send him in."

Ryan enters the room. An elderly gentleman sits behind a large maple desk. The entire office is done in maple—bookshelves, tables, and chairs. Everything, from the elderly gentleman's manicured fingernails and perfectly combed gray hair to how precisely all the diplomas and photographs are arranged on his office wall, leads Ryan to believe he's meeting with a very fussy person. A brass nameplate engraved with 'Jeffery Bohan, MD, MBA' is prominently displayed on his desk.

A younger man wearing a silk pinstriped suit sits in a chair in front of the large desk. An empty chair is located close by.

"Have a seat," Bohan says, pointing to the empty chair. Neither man stands up, offers to shake hands, or makes any type of cordial gesture toward Ryan.

"Are you the hospital administrator, Jeffery?"

"You may address me as Dr. Bohan. And yes, I am the administrator. This is Miles Hollenbeck. He's an associate on our legal team."

"Should I have brought my attorney? I thought this was a casual meeting."

"There are no casual meetings when lawsuits are threatened, Mr. Hutson," Miles replies. "The hospital received formal notice of your intent to file a ten-million-dollar malpractice claim."

"I came here today with the intent of resolving this in an amiable manner."

"It's a frivolous claim, Mr. Hutson," Bohan curtly replies. "Looking at you, I hardly think you pose a threat to the state of New Mexico's medical system. Trust me, young man, the hospital has an army of attorneys. Our insurance companies also employ numerous attorneys, and the hospital has many benefactors and donors in prominent positions."

Ryan takes a hard look at the administrator. He reminds himself to channel his positive endorphins, but he can't help but think, *this guy is a pompous ass.* "I came here to do the right thing, Jeffery. But you're starting to piss me off."

"It's Dr. Bohan, and I could not care less if I 'piss you off,' as you so crudely say. You are a mere nuisance. Even if this were to go to court, we could draw a lawsuit out for years until you go broke from legal fees, Mr. Hutson. Frankly, I do not appreciate your attitude."

"My attitude is the result of your behavior. If you change your behavior, I'll change my attitude."

Bohan waves his hand at Ryan like he's shooing away a gnat.

The young attorney coughs to get Bohan's attention. "Sir, you may be underestimating Mr. Hutson."

"Do you really think so, Mr. Hollenbeck? Then why don't you please enlighten me."

"Well, sir, Mr. Hutson is a professional baseball player. Even though he met with us dressed in an impecunious manner, he is very wealthy and could easily follow through on a lengthy lawsuit. Additionally, his legal team is Kutz, Smothers & Berns. One of the top malpractice firms in the country."

"Power doesn't come from just money, Jeffery." Ryan glares at him defiantly. "It also comes from who you know. I'm well connected with *The Dallas Morning News, Los Angeles Times*, and several national magazines. What would your benefactors, board members, and slew of lawyers think if they read your hospital killed my father and Mr. Hayes? Could be a public relations nightmare."

"Regardless of your connections in the media and your personal wealth, the hospital and our insurance companies are not willing to pay ten million dollars for the death of a man in his sixties."

"You need to relax, Jeffery—you're full of hostility. Take a couple seconds and let the positive endorphins take over. I'm not looking to punish the hospital. I just need for you to do the right thing. I've thought it over, and here are my conditions, which are nonnegotiable." Ryan and Bohan lock eyes with hostile stares. "Mrs. Hayes lost her husband's eighteen-hundred-dollar-a-month pension when he died. Your insurance company will establish an annuity that will pay her two thousand dollars a month for the rest of her life. Also, I want to see an environmental and hazardous waste team established for the hospital. There should be specialists on staff to inspect for infectious diseases and prevent them from spreading to other patients."

"We don't have the money in the budget to establish and maintain a department of that nature."

"Find the money, Jeffery. I'm giving you an opportunity to reinvest in your hospital or lose it in a lawsuit. End of discussion."

Hollenbeck looks at Bohan. "I'll report back to the partners at our law firm and recap this meeting. My recommendation would be to accept his offer."

Ryan exhales a long, heavy breath as he slides into the pickup in the parking lot. A wave of calm contentment washes over him. Initially, he wanted to punish the hospital, but now he's satisfied that he forced them to spend money for the well-being of all patients.

CHAPTER SEVENTY-TWO

Ryan pulls the pickup to a stop in front of the main house. The dogs immediately circle him, barking menacingly as he heads for the house. "Shoo," he yells, but that only irritates them more.

Oshi hears the commotion and begins her descent down the hill from where she was meditating.

Ryan strolls into the kitchen, then pours himself a glass of green liquid from a container he finds in the refrigerator. *Mmm, this stuff is good.*

Oshi joins him in the kitchen. "How did your meeting go?"

"I think they're going to come around to my way of thinking."

"Good," Oshi responds. "You are a very thoughtful and logical person when you think properly." She winces when she sees Ryan take another drink of the green liquid. "Did you get that out of the refrigerator?"

"Yeah. It is pretty tasty. What is it?"

"It is a laxative I prepare for the horses. I wouldn't drink too much of it. You will

find it loosens you up."

"Crap," Ryan mumbles.

"Don't worry, I am sure everything will come out okay."

Ryan dumps the contents in the sink and pours himself a large glass of water. He quickly guzzles it then chugs two more. "Is there any antidote for this stuff?"

"Just let it pass through. You will be all right."

"Bleh!" Ryan spits into the sink a couple of times.

Oshi stands patiently, watching Ryan behave like a three-year-old. Eventually, his mouth goes dry from the lack of spit, and he shifts his eyes from the sink to Oshi. She appears very solemn. Sensing something is in the air, he asks, "Is everything okay?"

"I have decided to go back to Japan. I went to your father's grave and informed him of my decision."

"For how long?"

"Right now, I do not foresee myself coming back. I wish to live out my life with my biological family. I came to the United States for a visit to study, but I fell in love with your father and stayed. Now, he is reunited in the afterlife with your mother. It is time for me to move on."

"You're part of our family. This is your home."

"It is not my home without your father. Please, Ryan. I have made up my mind."

"All right. We'll sell the ranch and give you the money."

"Please do not. This house has history with your family. This was Kelci's home before your family bought it. She has fond memories here. Your mother and father put much love into making this place a home, and they are both buried nearby. Please do not sell it."

"I'll give you a million dollars for it."

"No, Ryan. I am very thankful for your concern for me. But I have your father's life insurance and other money we saved. I want to take nothing from here but a few personal items . . . and many memories."

Ryan stands slumped, his hands hang at his sides, unable to focus clearly.

Oshi reaches over and lightly touches the side of his face. She looks into his eyes, aware he's struggling to restore his emotional equilibrium.

Ryan spends most of the evening trying to process the news, while sitting on the toilet.

The next morning, Ryan tracks Sarah down. She's back in Paris.

He holds the phone tightly. "Oshi has decided to return to Japan to live with her family."

"I hope you're kidding. Did you try to talk her out of it? Do I need to come there and talk to her?"

"She'll be gone by the time you get here."

"Oh my God. I love that woman."

"I told her we all do," Ryan replies. "She said our love for her is a most wonderful gift. She loves us equally, and thoughts of us will always be in her mind."

Sarah and Ryan share their despair while rehashing fond memories of Oshi.

"So, now what?" Sarah asks.

"She doesn't want money for the ranch. She'll transfer the title to us and hopes we don't sell it."

"Put the ranch in your and Trey's names," Sarah replies. "I'll come visit, but I want nothing to do with owning a ranch."

"Sarah, the city girl."

"I can put on a pair of cowboy boots every now and then."

"Only if you have a matching purse."

The next phone call is to North Carolina. Trey is on the line in the kitchen, and Kelci is on an extension in the den.

"She doesn't want anyone to see her off. She just wants to leave quietly."

"That's absurd. I'm flying out there tomorrow," Kelci says.

"Hey, babe. It's her wish to leave quietly," Trey says. "You have to respect that. This has been tough on her emotionally."

After several minutes of reminiscing, they move forward on what to do with the ranch.

"There's such a thing as joint tenancy, but you start splitting hairs," Kelci says. "Also, the ranch is a business with employees, so we may have to form a partnership or incorporate it. There's a lot of tax and debt issues associated with joint ownership."

"Okay, so what do you want to do?" Ryan asks.

"You take the ranch," Kelci replies without hesitation.

Ryan's eyes dilate. "Wait a minute, I already own two homes."

"The only possible way it stays in the family is if you take it," Kelci says.

Ryan enters the kitchen the next morning while Oshi is in the midst of packing some items and reorganizing others. "I will leave many of my herbs here. I hope you use them."

"Thank you. I will." He grins. "Hopefully, you've labeled the animal medicine."

"Always know what you are eating before you put it in your mouth," Oshi replies.

"It looks like you've got a lot of packing done already."

"Yes. I do not like to wait until the last minute."

"I talked to Trey and Sarah yesterday. They'd like for me to take ownership of the ranch."

"Excellent. I thought that was the logical solution. I will prepare the paperwork for you."

"Anything I can do to help with your packing?

"No, this is something I prefer to do alone. Every item has a memory that I wish to enjoy."

· · ·

The next morning, Oshi informs Ryan that he should go into town to meet with the county about transferring the title to the ranch. "I have signed the paperwork, and it is notarized." She hands him an envelope. "This is official documentation stating I gift the property to you."

"I'll head out after lunch."

"I would prefer you do it now."

He looks at her with a raised eyebrow. He's confused about the urgency but doesn't want to disagree with her. "All right." He takes the documents from Oshi, then heads out the door to the pickup. Oshi stands on the patio and waves to him as he drives off.

The meeting at the county office goes quickly, at least by government standards. Ryan is in and out in less than two hours.

His stomach grumbles as he strolls back to the truck. "I need some grub." The cuisine of choice ends up being a beer and sandwich at the Buckhorn Saloon. After getting his fill of food and secondhand cigarette smoke, Ryan heads out to the gravel parking lot where his truck is intermingled with twenty other pickups.

After a brief stop at a pet shop, Ryan makes himself comfortable for the long drive home. Bob Marley's "One Love" plays on the radio. The trek home is pretty quiet. The road runs parallel to the mountains, along mostly desert flatlands with low shrubs. Ryan hasn't seen a car for the past ten minutes, other than a Yellow Cab that zipped by from the opposite direction.

The two ill-mannered dogs welcome Ryan back to the ranch. He reaches into a paper bag and pulls out two rawhide bones. The ornery beasts give them a good sniff before Ryan tosses them as far as he can. Both fleabags chase after the bones while snarling at each other.

"You're mine now," Ryan says with a snicker. As soon as he enters the house, Ryan heads for the refrigerator. Oshi left a note under a "Ski Taos" magnet. Ryan's pulse quickens with apprehension. The note is simple and to the point.

I could not handle the sadness in your eyes nor maintain my composure while saying goodbye to you in person. Always remain positive, Ryan. My love to you and your family.
Oshi

Head in his hands, Ryan sits at the table, the silence filled only by the haunting image of her sitting next to him. *"Be strong, Ryan."*

"Yeah," he says, then stands up. While searching the refrigerator for a drink, Ryan finds a container labeled 'orange juice' and pours himself a glass.

Sitting on the steps of the front porch with his juice, Ryan watches the dogs chew on their rawhide bones. Joe walks out of the barn and ambles over.

"Señor Hutson, Señora Oshi told me she is leaving, and the ranch now belongs to you."

"Yep." Ryan nods.

"Will I have a job here?" He takes his hat off and holds it in front of him.

As far back as Ryan can remember, Joe has worked here. He's been a diligent and faithful employee. The man was hired to train and groom the horses, but when Jack became ill he got more involved in the operations of the ranch. Ryan figures now is the time to reward him for his loyalty.

"Joe, you'll always have a job here as long as you want. And so will your family. Have a seat." Ryan points to the step next to him. "Can I get you something to drink?"

Joe sits down next to Ryan. "I do not wish to trouble you for a drink, Señor Ryan."

That's cool with Ryan. He didn't feel like getting up. "I've been thinking, and if it's okay with you, I'm going to have a home built for you and your family. Near where we turn off the main road onto the property. I would like to have you on the property full-time."

"We have a house ten miles from here. We cannot afford another house."

"You can sell or rent the other house. As long as you and your family work on this ranch, the house I build will be yours for free. It will be a nice home with plenty of bedrooms and bathrooms."

"That is a very generous offer, Señor Ryan."

"Not so fast. I expect a lot in return. Your wife and daughter must tend to my house while I'm gone. They must feed the chickens and goats and look after the garden. I want you and your sons and whomever else you need to hire to continue to work with the horses and maintain the barn and property. I'll increase your salary an extra twenty thousand a year, and I'll pay the rest of your family a wage for their work around the house."

"Thank you for your offer, but I am not so good with the books without Señor Jack's help."

"Kelci will get someone to work with you."

CHAPTER SEVENTY-THREE

Ryan and Joy walk into the room Oshi and Jack used for yoga exercises.

"I'd like to put some Nautilus equipment and free weights in here," Ryan says.

"I'll put together an exercise room you'll be proud of," Joy replies.

Joy is a thirty-year-old Hispanic woman with the energy of a six-year-old. Her dark-brown hair is pulled into a ponytail, and her shirt sleeves are rolled up.

Ryan was at the general store checking out the produce when he first met Joy. He had a bunch of grapes in his hand and was looking over other produce when she strolled up and said, "Don't squeeze the grapes too hard —they might wine."

Ryan looked at her with one eye squinted. "I heard from the celery you were stalking me."

She put a hand on Ryan's arm. "Cute. I've never seen you around these parts before. You new or passing through?"

"I've taken over a ranch down the road."

"Jack Hutson's place?"

"Yeah, he was my dad."

"I met him on several occasions. He was a good man. Sorry to hear about his passing. You do anything besides ranching?"

"I play baseball."

"So does my ten-year-old."

"How about you? What do you do?"

"I provide interior design services."

"Let's head over to the den." Ryan motions toward the hallway. Joy follows closely behind, taking notes and asking questions as they walk. "This entire room needs to be updated. My agent, the accountants, the ranch foreman, and I will all be using this as an office. I want functional furnishings and the latest in office equipment: computers, faxes, copiers, whatever you can think of."

"We'll lease the equipment so it can be traded in as technology evolves."

"Excellent idea."

She looks down at her notes. Okay, Mr. Hutson, I'll—"

"It's Ryan."

"Okay, Ryan, I'll put my plans on paper. I think you'll like my ideas for renovating things around the house while maintaining the charm."

He puts his hand on her back. "I like your enthusiasm and energy."

"Thank you." She looks up at him with her dark-brown eyes. "Anything else I can do for you while I'm here?"

"Nope." He shakes his head. "I think we touched on everything. Coordinate things with Joe or his wife when I'm not around."

After seeing Joy off, Ryan goes into the kitchen and pours himself a large glass of milk from a pitcher labeled "goat milk."

With the cordless phone in hand, he heads to the living room.

He sets his milk on a side table, then sits down on the leather recliner. He reaches into his shirt pocket and pulls out Mary's business card. Her home number is scribed on the back. He punches the number into the phone. *I hope she's home.*

She picks up after the third ring.

"Hey, Mary, it's Ryan."

"Hi, Ryan. It's nice to hear from you."

"I tried to call you a couple of times, but needless to say, you don't have an answering machine."

"That's the way I prefer it. Keeps the ball in the caller's court if they want to talk to me."

"Okay. Interesting strategy. It was great to see you. I wish it were under better circumstances." He transfers the phone to his other hand. "But I have to say, you were like a ray of sunshine during a dark storm." He takes a drink of milk, leaving a white mustache on his upper lip.

"Thank you for the compliment. From what Sarah tells me, it was a pretty miserable couple weeks for you guys."

"Looking back on it, I think I was in shock a lot of the time. Sometimes, when you're in that state of mind, you operate on cruise control. Then when it's all over, you wonder where you got all the energy. My dad's wife helped me stay focused."

"I heard she practices holistic medicine."

"She has a pretty cool way of doing things. We're all bummed she decided to go back to Japan."

"That's a shame. What's going to happen to the ranch?"

"It was signed over to me. I'm now the proud owner of a horse ranch."

"Mmm, a baseball player and a rancher. What a manly image," Mary says in a sultry voice.

Ryan laughs. "You make me smile. You know smiling creates endorphins, which makes you a happier and healthier person?"

"Really? Would it make you happy if I tickled you?"

"You make me happy just the way you are. I'd like to see you." He looks at her business card. "I can fly up to Maryland this weekend. We could go out to dinner."

"Ryan, you didn't even think to ask if I'm involved with anyone. Did you think I would just take one look at you and be smitten?"

After a few moments of silent soul-searching, Ryan asks, "Are you?"

"Yes, I am." She mischievously keeps Ryan hanging for several seconds. "I am very smitten with you."

CHAPTER SEVENTY-FOUR

Ryan holds the front door of Haussner's restaurant open as Mary walks through the entrance.

She looks up at the large paintings in ornate brass-colored frames that line the walls of the dining area. "I love the artwork here."

The hostess is a young lady dressed in black slacks, a black blouse, and black horn-rimmed glasses. She sits them next to a large painting entitled *After the Bath*. The artwork depicts nude women sitting alongside a large Roman bath.

Ryan and Mary sit across from each other at a small table covered in a black tablecloth. Within minutes another young lady, clad in a black blouse and black pants with a black apron tied in front of her, stands at the side of their table, ready to take their order.

After their order is taken, Ryan asks, "According to your business card, you're a chief investigator for the Department of Justice. What does that mean?"

"I'm a law enforcement officer. I apprehend the dregs of our society."

"Do you carry a gun?"

"I do. I have handcuffs, also," she replies with a flirty smile.

"Mmm, could be fun. Have you ever been shot at or had to shoot anyone?"

She shakes her head as she takes a sip of wine. "I'm involved in mostly white-collar crimes like embezzlement, fraud, and money laundering. On occasion, I've gone on joint raids with other agencies like the ATF or IRS where I had to wear a bulletproof vest and have my gun drawn. But normally, the only time I take the gun out of the holster is to clean it."

"Why did you decide to go to work for the Feds?" Ryan slides his chair closer to her.

"My father worked his entire career for the federal government. Sometimes, we do what we're familiar with."

"Did you go to college?"

"Umm hmm. I got my undergraduate degree at Tufts, then I went to graduate school at Georgetown."

Ryan takes a sip of wine. "And now you live in Maryland?"

"I have a home in Columbia. I love it there. It's a planned community, and it's laid out beautifully."

After consuming some of the best crab cakes on the planet and finishing off a bottle of malbec, Ryan suggests they go for a walk. "It's a beautiful evening."

Ryan and Mary huddle close, to stay warm, as they venture the streets of Baltimore. The lights of the downtown buildings reflect off the water of the Inner Harbor. After a stroll through Maritime Park, they head back up Thames Street toward The Horse You Came In On pub. A couple of young guys who've had too much to drink stumble out the door, allowing the music to escape into the night air.

"Sounds like George Strait," Ryan says. "Let's go in and catch a couple of songs."

The only seats available are at a small table next to the dance floor. As soon as they're seated, a young waitress with a tattoo of a scorpion on her upper arm and some type of plant extending into her cleavage asks for their drink order.

Mary orders a glass of Chardonnay. Ryan asks for a mug of draft beer.

"It's a lotus," Mary says after the waitress departs.

"Huh?"

"You were looking at the girl's chest."

"Was not!" Ryan replies, shamefaced.

Mary playfully looks down her nose at Ryan. "The lotus is a flower that's used as a symbol of enlightenment."

After playing "Fool Hearted Memory," the band starts in on "I Just Want to Dance with You."

Ryan stands up and offers his hand to Mary. "May I have this dance?"

Mary nuzzles up to Ryan on the dance floor as the music surrounds them. The joyful love song conveys shared happiness and a desire for romantic connection while dancing.

They remain in an embrace on the dance floor after the music ends, looking into each other's eyes.

"We're standing in the last spot Edgar Allan Poe was seen alive," Mary says.

"Maybe we should mysteriously disappear?"

"Do you have any ideas?"

An impish grin spreads across Ryan's face. "I have a hotel room down the street."

"I don't normally sleep with someone on the first date." She tilts her head, and then looks at him with a lopsided grin. "What the heck. You being a famous baseball player and all, I guess it'd be all right."

Within minutes of entering the hotel room, Ryan and Mary are in the shower kissing and caressing each other with soapy hands.

The warm water and soapy foreplay drive their passion to extended heights. They barely dry each other off before diving onto the bed.

Mary wakes up first. She lies next to Ryan studying his face. She softly runs her finger down the bridge of his nose. As if on cue, he opens his eyes and wraps his arms around her. "It feels so wonderful, almost natural, being with you," he says. After a few soft kisses, Mary is straddling him, moving her hips in a slow, rhythmic motion as his hands cup her breasts.

A half hour later, Ryan lies back and takes a deep breath. Mary cuddles him, allowing Ryan to savor the feel of her soft skin against his body. "Let's go to D.C. and take a walk around the Smithsonian."

"Only if I can go home and change my clothes," Mary replies. "I'd like to put on some better walking shoes."

An ominous layer of dark clouds rolls into the nation's capital as Ryan and Mary casually stroll down the tree-lined National Mall. Ryan pulls Mary close. A chilly mist is in the air.

Mary points to the Museum of Natural History. "Would you like to go in there? I heard they have some excellent dinosaur fossils."

"Remains to be seen," Ryan says. "Did you know modern birds are related to dinosaurs?"

"Okay, Mr. Know-It-All, can you name the era in which the dinosaurs lived?"

"You bet Jurassican."

Mary giggles and gives him a push. He immediately bounces back as though attached to her by a giant rubber band.

They walk through the glass door of the National Air and Space

Museum and immediately notice airplanes hanging from the ceiling.

"Look." Mary comments, pointing toward the ceiling. "There's the Spirit of St. Louis, Lindbergh's plane."

"And there's the Red Baron's plane," Ryan says.

Mary looks at him with an impish grin. "How did you know that?"

"Because I saw the Snoopy movie," Ryan replies.

"For your information, the Red Baron was Manfred von Richthofen, a German ace who shot down eighty Allied planes."

"How did you know that?"

"I know things," Mary replies playfully. She leads him away before he notices the museum label next to the exhibit.

They casually mill about the museum, looking at the different memorabilia.

"Some of this stuff is really interesting. I wonder if I could take a picture," Mary thinks out loud.

"I doubt it. They're all bolted to the wall."

"Look, Ryan," Mary says excitedly, "there's the capsule John Glenn orbited the Earth in. He was such a hero."

"Sure, he got all the glory, and Enos got nothing—except maybe a banana," Ryan sarcastically replies.

"Enos?" Mary asks, a bewildered look on her face.

"Yeah, he was the monkey who orbited the Earth before Glenn. He paved the way and made sure it was safe."

"It says here that due to the lack of gravity, his capsule was able to achieve speeds of up to seventeen thousand miles per hour."

"I read a book on zero gravity once," Ryan says. "I couldn't put it down."

Mary gives him a deadpan look. "You are so unpredictable. Sometimes, you say something really intelligent, then you turn around and say the stupidest things."

Ryan pulls her close. He has a problem keeping his hands off her. "Einstein attributed his brilliant mind to having a childlike sense of humor. Several studies have shown the association between humor and intelligence."

"Hmm." Mary thinks for a second, then responds, "Wasn't it Einstein who said the difference between stupidity and genius is that genius has its limits?"

Ryan pulls into the driveway at Mary's house. The rain falls full force as the darkness of night settles in.

"It was fun spending time with you today." Ryan reaches to turn off the car.

Mary puts her hand on top of his, stopping him. "Don't. I have to work tomorrow."

They sit silently in the car looking at each other; the windshield wipers steadily flap back and forth. The corners of Mary's mouth are drawn down. "This is all happening too fast for me."

"It feels good being together."

She lowers her head. "It does. It's almost scary."

Ryan slides his finger under her chin. "There's nothing to be afraid of."

"Falling for someone and then having that someone leave scares me." She forces a grin. "It happened to me before . . . Give me some time to think about this, okay?"

Ryan takes a deep breath, trying to relax. "Okay."

CHAPTER SEVENTY-FIVE

Two days later, Ryan calls Mary from his home in Dallas. "Are you done thinking about it?"

"No, I am not done thinking," she says in an exasperated voice. "I can't stop thinking about you. I'm having a terrible time sleeping and staying focused at work."

He feels a flare of excitement. "I put a spell on you. You can't fight it."

"Damn you, Ryan Hutson! . . . Shame on you. Now you have me cursing."

"Wanna be my girlfriend?"

"I'm going to have to, just so I can think straight again." She sighs, and a moment of silence follows.

"Why do I feel hesitation?" Ryan asks.

"It's not going to be easy, Ryan. My life is in D.C., and you live in Texas. You're a baseball player. You travel all over the country during the summer."

He sits quietly, patiently waiting for her to address her own concerns.

Finally, she replies. "I would rather have you whenever I can than never have you at all."

If Ryan were a dog, his tail would be wagging. "It all started when you stepped in the shower with me."

"Are you complaining?"

"I'll never forget it." His smile spreads so wide his lips hurt.

"Me either. I was really nervous."

"I have to go to spring training in two weeks. Let's go somewhere and celebrate beforehand. How about Paris or Venice?"

"I would rather go somewhere more casual. Somewhere we can talk. Maybe sit in front of a fire, take a walk."

"We could go to New Mexico?"

Mary replies without hesitation. "Sounds perfect. I'd love to see where you live."

"Bring your coat. It's cold up in the mountains."

Ryan pulls the car to a stop in front of the ranch house. Steam comes from the dogs' mouths as they softly grumble and circle him when he gets out of the car. Ryan ignores the beasts as he grabs Mary's luggage and leads her to the house.

Rosa, Joe's wife, holds the door for them as they enter. *"Buenos días, señorita,"* she says to Mary as she helps her remove her coat.

"Gracias," Mary replies.

"Rosa has taken over management of the house," Ryan tells Mary. "She makes sure it's clean and I have plenty of groceries. She even cooks for me sometimes."

A young girl, about fourteen and dressed in a long floral skirt and a white blouse with colorful embroidery around the neck, appears and takes ahold of Mary's bags.

Ryan nods toward the young lady. "This is Alejandra, Rosa's daughter. She helps around the house."

Mary looks at Rosa. *"Es muy hermosa.* She is very beautiful."

Ryan shows Mary around the house and describes some of the changes Joy is making. "Do you see anything that you think needs to be done?"

"Each lady of the house likes to add her own personal touch. I can see little things your mother and Oshi have each contributed toward making this a home."

After finishing off a plate of tacos and enchiladas prepared by Rosa, Mary and Ryan retire to the living room, where a blazing fire welcomes them. A large wool blanket lies across the back of the couch, and an opened bottle of wine and two glasses sit on a table, everything courtesy of Rosa.

Mary cuddles close with Ryan on the couch. Flames flicker as the fire crackles.

"How long will you be at spring training?" Mary asks.

"A little more than a month. We train in Pompano Beach. I was hoping you would spend some weekends with me."

"Won't you be busy?"

"Eh." He shrugs. "We're there to get loose and practice our throwing and hitting. After a week or so, we start playing practice games. It's not going to consume my whole day. Plus, I'll have some time off."

"Aren't you required to stay in some kind of dormitory?"

Ryan shakes his head. "I'll rent a house or condo."

"Did you ever stay in the team hotels?"

Ryan grins. "Oh yeah. I stayed in cheap hotels, rode in ratty buses with no air-conditioning, and lived on a tight budget for a couple years."

"You've come a long way, baby. Now you have people working for you."

"If you mean Kelci, she's my agent. She takes care of everything so I can focus on playing baseball. She's pretty sharp. You met her, right?"

"Sarah introduced her and your brother to me at the funeral."

"Oh really?" Ryan has a surprised look. "You never met Trey before?"

She shakes her head. "What happens after spring training?"

"We have maybe a day or two off for travel before we start the season."

"How much time off do you get during the season?"

"We play 162 games in 183 days. So you figure about twenty days—although some of them are travel days. Then you throw in rain days, which can be kind of boring."

"How often are you in Baltimore?"

"Nine games."

"Not enough time," she deadpans.

"Half my games are in Dallas. There are a lot of unsavory characters in Texas. Maybe the government could see fit to move you there?" He pulls her close.

She rests her head on his shoulder. "Getting ahead of yourself a little bit, aren't you?"

"I'm trying to make up for not being in your past by securing part of your future."

"That's sweet. Can I borrow a kiss from you? I promise to give it back."

Their lips touch as his hand caresses her cheek.

They sit in silence, snuggled together, watching the flames dance in the fireplace.

"What are you thinking?" she asks.

"I think women spend more time thinking about what men are thinking than men spend thinking."

Mary giggles. "If you don't think, then you shouldn't talk."

"I've been told that before." He chuckles at the thought. "I love your laugh. It wrinkles your nose and touches my foolish heart."

"Now, you are being Frank."

Ryan hums a few bars from "Fly Me to the Moon" as gets to his feet and strolls over to the fireplace. He picks up a couple logs and adds them to the fire.

Mary watches as the sparks fly. "Wouldn't it be nice if you had a fireplace in your bedroom?"

Ryan grabs the blanket and a couple pillows off the couch, then tosses them in front of the fire. "Will this do?"

Mary stands up, walks over to Ryan, wraps her arms around

him, and gives him a kiss that makes his toes wiggle. They fall to their knees while holding each other. Ryan unbuttons her blouse as she lowers her head onto the pillows.

CHAPTER SEVENTY-SIX

Mary and Ryan finish off a breakfast of scrambled eggs, ham steak, fried potatoes, and fresh fruit that Rosa had waiting for them when they woke up.

After breakfast, Ryan and Mary cross from the house to the barn, bundled in warm jackets and knit hats. The dogs grumble at Ryan but pay no attention to Mary. Tips of wild grass peek above the snow that fell overnight.

"Good morning, Mr. Ryan, Miss Mary," Joe and Rosa's son, Carlos, says as they enter the barn. He has a couple horses saddled up for a morning ride. They grab the reins and head out the door. Moving from the warmth of the barn to the outside air feels like opening the door of a freezer.

The horses trod along a path that leads downstream from the ranch, the snow crunching with each step they take. They pass tree branches sagging from the weight of the previous night's snowfall. A chilled squirrel hops from tree to tree, carefully scampering along the branches. The melting snow glitters as it reflects the warm rays of the morning sun. Water dripping from the melting snow on the branches adds to the sounds of silence.

"Look!" Mary whispers, pointing toward a pine tree.

A brilliant red cardinal sits on a branch of bluish-green pine needles, a snow-covered branch bowing above him. His chirping echoes through the silent woods. Soon, he is joined by his mate, and they fly away.

As they descend to warmer, lower elevations, Ryan and Mary remove their jackets.

"My butt is getting sore." Mary wiggles in her saddle. "Let's walk for a bit."

With reins in hand, Ryan and Mary walk shoulder to shoulder along the side of the stream, the horses trailing behind them.

Mary says, "I heard they moved Nelson Mandela to another prison because he was uniting the convicts."

"That's crazy. How long has he been in there, about twenty years?"

"Eighteen."

Ryan lets out a snort that makes the horses envious. "For doing nothing but opposing a system of racial segregation established by the privileged whites."

"Well, not quite nothing. He did have ties to the Communist Party, and he conspired to overthrow the country."

"Maybe that was the only way he thought he could bring social justice to his homeland."

"Sounds like a sensitive subject for you."

"Mandela's not a whole lot different than Che, Ho Chi Minh, or Castro. They all wanted what they thought was best for their people."

"You are different than any other man I've known," Mary says, looking intently at Ryan.

"The things that make me different are the things that make me."

Mary kisses him on the cheek as they leisurely stroll down the path.

Ryan puts his arm around her and turns her into him. She parts her lips, accepting his tongue. His free hand travels from her waist to the front of her sweater.

"Don't be getting any ideas," she murmurs as her nipples harden in response to his touch.

"I already have ideas. Now I'm trying to give you ideas."

"I'm not putting my bare butt on that wet ground."

Ryan looks around, grabs his coat off his horse, and then lays it on top of a gathering of pine needles under a tree.

Ryan and Mary hold onto the reins as they amble back to the ranch, the horses trailing behind.

"Oh my gosh! That was so exhilarating. It was like all my senses were alive—the cold air and your warm skin, the blue sky above, birds chirping, and the smell of pine needles."

Ryan smiles at her. "Now, you know tree hugging isn't just for environmentalists."

Mary grabs his hand and holds on. She has a content smile on her face.

"You don't seem to be in the news as much since you moved to Texas."

"I used to have a hectic schedule with all my endorsements. Seems like I was spending all my free time making television commercials, doing magazine shoots, or going to promotional events. I've cut back on my endorsements significantly."

"I miss seeing you on Johnny Carson and in those sexy clothing ads." She bumps her hip against him playfully.

"Not as much as I miss being in the gossip magazines."

She looks at him with inquisitive eyes. "Do you think you get smarter the older you get?"

"Nah, not really. I think you just run out of stupid things to do."

"What do you do with your free time?"

"I'm active with children's hospitals." Ryan looks forward as they walk up the path. "Also, I try to spend as much time as I can with my kid. It's tough sometimes. He's off for the summer when I work, then I'm off in the winter when he's in school."

"Is he like you?"

Ryan thinks a minute. "He's tall like me. He has his mother's dark hair. And he's intelligent and creative like her."

"Don't undersell yourself. You're a pretty sharp guy. Does he excel in sports?"

"He's okay at soccer, but he's more of an artsy kind of guy."

"How do you get along with his mother?" She gazes at him intently as she talks.

"She's a good mother. She's pretty generous with the time she allows Jacque and me to spend together. But she and I talk very little."

Mary gets a curious look on her face. "Why's that?"

"I think she was sad that things didn't work out for us." Ryan looks at the ground and shakes his head. "She couldn't accept my lifestyle. Seems like I was always busy with endorsements and playing baseball. She also might have been disappointed I didn't stay in Montréal and play for the Expos." He pauses for a moment as he contemplates. "She's polite and friendly but definitely likes to minimize the time she has to interact with me." Ryan chuckles softly. "She's French and has this way of giving you the cold shoulder without you realizing it."

Ryan helps Mary onto her horse before he mounts his. They throw their coats on. The cold air returns quickly as they ride up the mountainside.

Rosa greets them at the door of the ranch and helps them out of their coats. "I have hot chocolate for you in the kitchen."

"Mmm, nice," Mary says as she sips on her warm drink.

Ryan sits across from her at the kitchen table. "I can feel the warmth spreading through my body with each sip."

Rosa sets the cordless phone on the table in front of Ryan. "Mrs. Kelci call you. She says it is very important that she speak with you."

Mary looks at him with a mocking smirk. "What's it like being a celebrity?"

Ryan chuckles softly. "It can be intoxicating. I enjoy it sometimes and I hate it other times. To be honest, it all just snuck up on me so fast. I just wanted to play baseball, but I let the fame and money get the best of me in Los Angeles." With a sly grin, he remarks, "Now I'm just a regular guy in Dallas."

"Ha! You will never be a regular guy. A regular guy worries about making the mortgage payment, buying his kids braces, and being able to retire in comfort. You have no worries unless you create them yourself."

"Do you think I'm a different person because of that?"

"You have a good heart and genuinely care about people. That's what attracted me." Mary takes one last sip of her drink, then informs Ryan, "I'm going to soak in the tub for a bit. Make your phone call."

Kelci picks up the phone after nearly a dozen rings.

"Hey, Kelce. You think I'm spoiled?"

"Nah, you've always smelled like that."

"Gee, thanks."

"Good news and bad news, partner. I found you a condo in Pompano Beach near the ocean with a swimming pool."

"And the bad news?"

"There's talk of a players' strike."

CHAPTER SEVENTY-SEVEN

The sun is out in full force, but an easy breeze keeps the morning air mild. Things will warm up as the day moves along. It's March in southern Florida.

The Rangers and Braves are in the bottom of the fourth inning of a scrimmage at the Rangers' facility in Pompano Beach. As the Braves' pitcher starts his windup, Don Ray, the Rangers' union representative, jogs onto the field and throws his hands up in the air, stopping the game. The Braves' rep quickly joins him near home plate. The home plate umpire stands by idly, scratching his butt. The conference between the union reps ends after a few minutes, and the players are waved from the field.

Ryan sits on the bench next to Mike Stanley, one of the younger guys on the team, during the discussion on the field. The young man seems a little confused by the quick change in events.

"Hey, Ryan. What do you think is going on?"

"I believe we are going into a work stoppage unless the union and owners figure things out."

"Oh shit," Stanley responds. "Why now? I was hoping to make it to the big league this year and get paid more than four hundred bucks a week."

"Sorry, buddy. The union is upset that the owners want to block free agency and install a salary cap."

"What're we going to do?"

Ryan presses his lips together. "Chill out and wait."

"I can't afford to chill out and wait. I don't make a million bucks like you."

"It'll pay off in the long run," Ryan calmly replies.

Don Ray lumbers into the dugout and lets out a shrill whistle to get everyone's attention. "As of now, the union requests that we stop all baseball activities. The owners are making a ton of money on escalating ticket prices, television revenues, concessions, and parking. The union doesn't feel we're getting our fair share of the proceeds. We need to stand together and see this through."

"How long is this going to last?" one of the players asks.

"No idea," Ray replies. "The season starts in three weeks. Hopefully, before then."

An eerie silence fills the dugout.

Ryan is sitting back with his legs crossed. He stands up and looks around. "I'll put up a hundred thousand dollars to help the younger guys and the support staff get through the shutdown."

"How about us old guys?" Robbie Harrah, one of the veterans on the team, lightheartedly inquires.

Ryan looks at him and laughs. "Go eff yourself, Robbie. I'm not contributing to your drinking and whoring habits."

Frustrated yet hopeful, the players accept what's happening. Several of them pack their belongings and head home. Since the rent on his condo is paid, Ryan decides to hang around Florida.

A week into the strike, nothing has changed. Ryan sits on the patio of his fourth-floor condo, looking out on the Atlantic Ocean. A flock of pelicans coast above the shoreline in a single line, dipping and curving in the wind like a squadron of fighter planes. He punches Mary's number into the cordless phone.

"Hey, Sunshine. How was your day?"

"I stayed home from work. I was feeling a little nauseated when I woke up this morning."

"I'm sorry. How are you feeling now?"

"I started feeling a little better after I threw up. I've been getting headaches and feeling a little dizzy lately."

"Have you been to the doctor?"

"I went today."

"Did he give you anything?"

She laughs softly. "It's a little too late now."

"Really?" Ryan thinks about it for a few seconds. "I miss you. Come down and see me this weekend?"

"I think that would be a good idea."

The rising sun casts a golden glow across the ocean, welcoming in another day full of new adventures. Ryan dons a pair of linen slacks, leather huarache sandals, and a cotton Cuban guayabera shirt, then begins his stroll into the Pompano Beach business district. He approaches a homeless man in tattered clothes, sitting on the sidewalk. Ryan hands him a five-dollar bill. "Pete, you really need to look for a job."

"It's hard, Ryan, with the gout in my foot and all."

Ryan sticks his hand out to help him up. "Come on. I'll take you to a clinic."

"No, no." He shies away from Ryan's hand. "I'm too tired to go to a clinic. I just want to sit here for now."

"Suit yourself." Ryan enters a small café he discovered his first week in town. The glass front advertises the establishment as a health food restaurant. Several small tables are scattered about the dining area. Ryan takes his usual spot at the juice bar.

"Morning, Mason," Ryan says to the owner, a thirty-year-old beach dude with wavy, long blond hair. Mason has a PhD in aerospace engineering from MIT. He left his job at Cape Canaveral to open a juice shop. Business took off, and the establishment quickly blossomed into a restaurant serving breakfast and lunch.

"Get you some Arabian coffee, Ryan?"

"That'd be great." Ryan scans the menu. "What's the juice of the day?"

"I brewed a mixture of turmeric, ginger, and lemon."

"Give me a tall glass and your omelet special."

"One egg white and veggie omelet coming up."

"Where do you get egg whites . . . from sterile chickens?"

"No, you separate the egg yolks from the whites. Simple process. Not like it's rocket science."

"I guess you would know."

Mason stands behind a grill whipping the egg whites. "So, how long do you think this strike is going to last?"

"It's not really a strike—it's more like a protest. But I have no guess. They'll let me know when they want me to go back to work."

"This little protest is costing Florida businesses millions of dollars. Tourists plan their vacations around spring training—it gives them an opportunity to see the players up close. A lot of them are going elsewhere now." Mason turns to look at Ryan, who's peering out the front window of the café at nothing in particular. "You also have seasonal employees like maids, cooks, and taxi drivers that aren't making money. Most people are too polite to express their anger at the rich owners and players. But the fans are greatly disappointed."

Ryan turns his palms up. "Nothing I can do about it."

"Couldn't have happened at a worst time," Mason comments.

"The only reason for time is so everything doesn't happen at once." Ryan finishes his breakfast, then tells Mason, "Fry up the yolks you took from my eggs and give them to Pete, along with a glass of juice. Put it on my tab."

Ryan takes a brisk walk along the beach, stopping momentarily to toss a Frisbee with a couple young ladies, then heads back to the condo to prepare for his next excursion.

The sun is directly overhead when he hops into the Fiat 124 he rented from Hot Cars of Florida. He lowers the top on the sports coupe, slides a Queen cassette into the stereo, and then heads north on I-95 as the sounds of "Crazy Little Thing Called Love" fill the car.

Forty-five minutes later, he crosses the Lake Worth Lagoon into Palm Beach. He cruises down Worth Avenue until he finds an empty parking space between a Bentley S2 and a Mercedes 450SEL. After guiding the car into the open slot, he casually strolls down the palm tree–lined avenue replete with fountains, balconies overhanging the sidewalk, and interior courtyards with trimmed bushes and ornate sculptures.

Boutiques featuring the ultimate in art, clothing, and home furnishings attract the discriminating buyer to the strip. Ryan pauses in front of Maus & Hoffman Clothier, where he notices a full-length photo of himself in a Bobbi Jones suit in the picture window. A young couple wearing designer clothes exits the store while Ryan is busy admiring himself. Grinning like a Cheshire cat, Ryan points toward the poster and says, "Look at that handsome fella." The gentleman pulls his lady close and looks at Ryan like he's a simpleton. Undeterred, Ryan continues his trek down the avenue. *That picture has to be at least three years old*, he tells himself. *I wonder if they're allowed to use it.* Two blocks later, he reaches his next destination.

"Josef & Allen Jewelers" is etched in large letters across the beveled glass door. Ryan grabs the brass handle and swings it open. As soon as he passes through the doorway, he's welcomed by an attractive young lady. An emerald-and-diamond brooch dangles on a gold chain slightly above her cleavage.

The inside of the store is aglow from chandeliers with hanging glass beads and mirrors that cover the walls. Several glass showcases are strategically arranged throughout the shop.

The young lady offers her hand. "Good day. I'm Stephanie. May I get you a glass of champagne?"

"No thanks. It tickles my nose."

She smiles. "How nice. A sensitive man that isn't gay."

"I'm generally happy most of the time." Ryan takes his eyes off her brooch and gazes about the store. "I'm here to buy an engagement ring."

"You look like the kind of man that would want to create a special ring."

"I may look like that, but I prefer to buy one that I can take with me today."

"Do you have a price range?"

"Nope."

Dollar signs flash in Stephanie's head. She grabs Ryan's hand and leads him to a display case with several black felt trays full of diamond rings. "A man of your character will want a platinum band. You'll want nothing less to put a fine diamond on top of."

"Okay." Now he wishes he did a little homework before coming here.

She smiles. "Let's discuss diamonds. Small diamonds inlaid in the band make a beautiful setting."

She shows him a couple samples. He looks at a few, then scrunches his face and shakes his head. "No."

"That is perfectly understandable. Many people like to focus on the arrangement. It's obvious you're a man with a keen eye. Let me show you several unique arrangements we can offer."

Ryan carefully looks at several trays with various diamond arrangements. "I tend to prefer something like this." He points to a tray containing bands with a single diamond.

"Excellent choice. Now let's discuss the special Cs of diamond buying: cut and clarity. A properly cut diamond unleashes its light. Brightness is the amount of white light that is reflected, and fire is the scattering of white light into colors of the rainbow. A woman likes something bright and colorful. With a lot of sparkle."

Ryan scrutinizes several rings. He points to one. "I'll take this one."

Stephanie grabs Ryan's upper arm and squeezes. "That is a magnificent ring. It's simply breathtaking." She pulls it out of the tray and hands it to him. "This is a three-carat round solitaire. The E color is pure white, and it has VVS clarity. You achieve a high level of fire with this diamond. Will that be cash or credit?"

CHAPTER SEVENTY-EIGHT

Nine AM Saturday, Ryan stands next to a floor-to-ceiling window at the Palm Beach Airport terminal watching a Cessna Citation taxi to the gate. Eight passengers, including Mary, disembark.

She is smartly attired in a pair of jeans, cotton blouse, and navy blazer. Her shoulder-length blond hair is tousled and has the wild look that Ryan finds sexy.

Seconds after entering the terminal, her blue eyes light up as they lock onto Ryan. He hurries over to her, wraps his arms around her, and lifts her off her feet while kissing her. She staggers a bit when he sets her down.

"Did I overwhelm you with that kiss?"

"It's always a little overwhelming kissing you. I just got a little lightheaded."

Ryan grabs Mary's bag with his left hand and puts his right arm around her shoulders as they stroll through the terminal. He leans over to kiss the soft spot between her neck and chin. "It's great to see you."

Her radiant smile is all the response he needs.

Mary puts her sunglasses on and removes her blazer when they exit the air-conditioned terminal and step into the bright Florida sunshine.

Ryan tosses her bag in the trunk of the Fiat, and within minutes, they're cruising along the turnpike. He turns on the car stereo and starts tapping his fingers on the steering wheel to the sounds of Poco's "Crazy Love." He turns to Mary. "Do you have something you want to talk about?"

"When the time is right," she replies. "Where we headed?"

"Somewhere I think you'll find fun."

Forty-five minutes later, Ryan pulls into the gravel parking lot of Blue Springs Livery. The yard surrounding the small wood office is loaded with canoes, aluminum dinghies, and rubber rafts. A spring-fed stream, no more than thirty feet wide, is not far from the building. Several small trees and brush line the bank.

Ryan and Mary walk up the rickety steps to the office and swing open a rusty screen door. A small bell jingles overhead. A couple of young men with long hair, wearing cut-off jeans and T-shirts, greet them.

Ryan explains what he wants. In a matter of minutes, he and Mary are fixed up with a ten-foot aluminum flat-bottom boat with a 1.4-horsepower motor. The two bench seats are covered with cushions, which also serve as flotation devices. One of the young men helps them into their skiff and points upstream. "Head in that direction for a couple miles, then circle back."

"How romantic. A cute little boat ride. Not quite like a gondola in Venice, but hey, carpe diem," Mary says with a hint of levity in her voice.

"Only the best for you." Ryan cranks the small engine with a pull of the rope. They begin their slow troll up the river.

A gentle gust of wind caresses Mary's face, softly blowing loose strands of her hair. She dips her hand into the water, creating a small wake as they lazily motor up the stream.

She marvels at the beauty of the stream. "The water is so clear you can see the bottom and the little fishies swimming around." After several moments of silently gazing into the stream, she shrieks, then frantically slides away from the edge of the boat. She moves with such abandon that the boat almost overturns. "Good Lord, what is that?"

Ryan steadies the boat while attempting to control his laughter. "It's a manatee."

He shuts off the motor and lets the boat drift in a calm pool of water. They look down on the large marine mammal as it slowly meanders along the river bottom. Two more manatees lazily swim into view. Mary sits close to Ryan, holding his arm. "They're so cute!"

They sit in silence, watching the slow, lumbering antics of the sea cows.

"How beautiful and serene is this?" Mary comments. "The weather is perfect, the water is gorgeous, and I am surrounded by funny creatures." She gives Ryan a playful pinch.

Ryan puts his fingers under her chin, lifts her face up, and gently presses his lips against hers. A manatee comes to the surface, gently nudging the boat, disrupting their kiss.

Mary grabs Ryan's hands and looks into his eyes. "I need to tell you something." He meets her gaze without speaking. She seems to be thinking hard about how she wants to say it. "What the hell. I'm pregnant." She nervously awaits his response.

Ryan is initially stunned, but his face quickly beams with happiness. He reaches into his pocket and pulls out the ring box.

When he opens the lid, Mary puts her hand over her mouth and gasps. "It's beautiful."

"Will you marry me?"

"Oh Ryan, I don't want you proposing to me because I'm pregnant."

"Mary, I love you. Besides, I bought the ring before you told me you were pregnant."

She tilts her head and looks at him. "A high school kid could have picked up on the hints I've been giving you."

"I was never good in biology." He gives her the most sincere look he can muster. "There is no one I would rather spend the rest of my life with."

"Of course I'll marry you. I love you with all my heart."

They come together in a full embrace and kiss deeply.

When they pull apart, Ryan takes the ring out of the box. He clasps Mary's left hand in his as he delicately holds the ring between his forefinger and thumb. As he prepares to slide it on Mary's finger, a meandering manatee, who is playfully swimming on its back, slams into the boat, knocking the ring from Ryan's grasp. Ryan and Mary watch as the sparkling diamond slowly flitters to the bottom of the clear stream. The highly reflective diamond attracts the attention of a couple of the curious animals.

"Aww, geez!" Ryan quickly removes his shoes and shirt, takes everything from his pockets, then dives into the chilly water.

He swims to the bottom of the stream and starts pushing and shoving the big beasts away from where he figures the ring must have landed. He stays underwater for as long as he can, battling the manatees, before he surfaces.

His head is above water, and he's gasping for air when he hears a cough. Ryan looks over to the shore and notices a heavyset man in a Smokey Bear hat staring at him. The sun reflects off his mirrored sunglasses and the badge above his left shirt pocket.

Ryan sits at a table across from a U.S. Fish and Wildlife Service investigator and a small-time county sheriff.

Ryan looks at them with wide eyes and an open mouth. "I'm being charged with what?"

"Abuse of a protected species," the investigator calmly replies.

"Those things outweigh me by a thousand pounds. Plus, there were three of them ganging up on me."

"The manatees don't have any arms and legs to protect themselves. You were observed punching and kicking a defenseless animal."

"They were trying to eat a diamond ring."

"Sir, manatees are strictly herbivores."

"Well, they were preventing me from getting to my ring."

The wildlife investigator looks to the heavens and shakes his head.

The sheriff glares at Ryan with contempt. "Hey, tough guy, they're animals, and you're a human being . . . supposedly with a rational mind."

"Holy sea cow. Do I need to call a lawyer?"

Kelci almost drops the phone in disbelief. "You got arrested for what? Hey, Trey, come listen to what your little brother did."

"Aww, geez, Kelci. You don't have to tell everybody," Ryan bemoans.

"Trey wants to know if you kissed the sea cows first."

"Arrgh! I abused them physically, not sexually. And I didn't even do that. I just tried to kick them out of the way."

"Hey, Trey," Kelci says, fighting back tears of laughter. "Ryan says he tried to kick them away, but they kept coming back."

"It must be his animal magnetism," he can hear Trey quip in the background. Kelci and Trey yuk it up for a few moments while Ryan sits patiently. "All right, that's enough," he snaps. "Just get me outta here."

A half hour later, Mary enters the jail to retrieve Ryan.

"You're free to go," the sheriff says, a corner of his lips curled up.

Mary grabs a tense Ryan by the arm and leads him toward the door. Ryan pauses for a second. "Hey, Deputy Dog, other than a $25,000 diamond ring, how much did this little escapade cost me?"

"You've made a donation to the Florida Department of Natural

Resources, Protect the Manatee fund, and the local sheriff's department."

"I'm supporting all kinds of beasts today."

"Have a good day, sir. Oh, and next time, pick on someone who can fight back." The sheriff cracks his knuckles as he glares at Ryan.

Ryan scowls at the sheriff as Mary tugs on his arm.

Ryan gets comfortable behind the wheel of the Fiat while Mary sits next to him. He puts the key into the ignition but doesn't start the car just yet. He lets out a breath of air—"Whew! Pretty special day, huh?"

Mary looks at him with adoring eyes and bobs her head enthusiastically. "Got engaged, found out you're going to be a father again, and got arrested. And all before lunch."

"And lost a diamond ring. Want to go pick out another one?"

She puts her arm around his shoulders and kisses his cheek. "I don't need a diamond to confirm your love. Just a simple gold band when we're married to let everyone know I have someone special in my life."

"That ring had a lot of fire to it."

"So do you."

Ryan starts the car, then guides it from the parking lot of the municipal building onto the main drag. "We have a lot of things to talk about. Such as, when do you want to get married, do you want a big wedding?"

"I'm ten weeks along. I'd like to get married before I start to show."

"Next week?"

Mary smiles. "I love your enthusiasm."

"This work stoppage could end any day, then I'll have to go back to work." He looks at her, then quickly returns his eyes to the road. "I'm not sure when I'll have a couple days off in a row again."

"Hmm, that does make it challenging."

He bounces his eyebrows up and down. "Want to catch a plane to Vegas?"

"That could be fun. It also sounds cheesy. I'd like for my parents to be at the wedding."

Ryan nods. "Are they still in D.C.?"

"They moved to Charlottesville when my dad retired. But I prefer D.C. for a wedding." She pats his thigh. "All my friends are there, and it would be a fairly short drive for my parents."

"Okay with me. My family travels easy, so anywhere is fine. Maybe a small gathering in your backyard—we could decorate the place. Or down by the river. Cherry blossoms will be blooming soon."

"I think it makes more sense to do it at the house. The weather can be unpredictable this time of year."

"Yes, dear," Ryan replies with a smile.

Mary slaps him on the shoulder. "Don't start that patronizing crap," she replies with mock anger. They ride in silence for a minute. "I don't know if my minister will be available on short notice."

Ryan smiles as a wonderfully crazy thought comes to his mind. "Don't worry, I got it covered."

Ryan casually chats with Mary as he keeps his focus on the road. Out of the corner of his eye, he notices Mary lightly rub her cheek. He turns to look at her and notices tears rolling down her face. "Is everything okay?"

She bursts out in laughter as the tears flow more heavily. "I've been in love with you, Ryan, since the first time I saw you."

Ryan grins. "That long, huh?"

"I finally got a minute to catch my breath, and it just set in. I'm marrying the man of my dreams. I am so happy right now." Her eyes sparkle and the corners of her lips turn up as tears of joy stream from her eyes.

Ryan hits the brakes hard and swerves sharply, barely missing another car. The Fiat comes to an abrupt stop on the shoulder of the road. After slamming the gear selector into Park, he reaches over and squeezes Mary. Energy races back and forth between their bodies for several minutes. Ryan pulls back a little and kisses a tear on her cheek. "I'm at a loss for words. I love you so much and . . ." He groans in frustration. "I can't think straight right now to find the right words to tell you how I feel."

"You don't have to say anything. I can see and feel your love."

CHAPTER SEVENTY-NINE

Fortunately, it's a sunny day with little wind in Columbia, Maryland on their wedding day. Planters of peonies, gardenias, and hydrangeas are placed around the beautifully landscaped backyard of Mary's brick ranch. Off to the side of the congregation, a young lady in a flowing gown gently strums a harp.

Jacque stands next to his dad at the altar. A narrow tie resembling a piano keyboard lies beneath his black pinstriped jacket.

Ryan wears a matching pinstriped suit, but a more conservative tie.

Mary stands in front of him, wearing an elegant full-length beige skirt with a matching jacket.

The happy couple holds hands as they stand beneath an archway of jasmine vines covered in white flowers. Twelve rows of white chairs face them. Mary's mother and father sit in the first row along with Sarah, Trey, and Kelci. Trey and Kelci's kids fidget in the chairs next to their parents.

Josh and Jeanne sit in the second row next to several of Mary's friends and co-workers. Josh, looking to get better acquainted with Jeanne, leans over and whispers, "Weddings always make me cry."

Jeanne bolts upright and gives him a stern look. "Please, try to behave like a man," she replies in a staunch French accent. She turns, leaving Josh staring at her back.

As the fragrance of jasmine and the sound of delicate harp music surround Ryan and Mary, Eugene pronounces them man and wife. His massive body faces the congregation as he announces: "Congratulations to the new, happily married Mr. and Mrs. Hutson. Never forget what made you crazy about each other, and try not to drive each other crazy."

Ryan gazes into her blue eyes, his body and breathing relaxed and comfortable. Mary's eyes smile at him. They embrace and share the kiss of peace. The congregation applauds as Ryan holds their hands up triumphantly. Mary leaves Ryan's side to embrace her parents, then to share hugs with her girlfriends.

Juliette, the wedding planner, briefly interrupts the celebration by informing everyone, "Please join us in the house. We have cake, appetizers, and liquid refreshments."

Everyone has a plate of food and a drink in hand when Trey taps the side of his glass with a spoon. "Jacque, you're the best man. Step up and make a toast."

Jacque, who is in deep discussion with the harp player, is caught off guard by the tradition. He mutters something under his breath, then stands and raises his glass of ginger ale. "Here's to Dad, and here's to Mary. May the two of you love each other for eternity." Looking at the chocolate truffle in his other hand, he comments, "Biochemically speaking, love is like eating large amounts of chocolate."

Trey takes a swallow of beer, then looks at Jacque. "Nicely done." He looks across the room and sees Josh pestering one of Mary's girlfriends. "Josh, you're a friend of the groom, why don't you say a few words."

"Excuse me, darling," Josh tells the young lady he's talking to. He stands, scans the room, and then takes a deep breath. "Gosh, what an emotional day. Even the cake is in tiers. I want to congratulate

Jacque on his wonderful toast. I knew he would be hard to follow, and I was right. I couldn't follow a word of it." Turning his palms up, he asks, "What's with this chocolate thing?"

Looking at Ryan with a grin on his face, he says, "Ryan is the best friend I could have ever asked for. Growing up, we lived down the street from each other, so he was actually more convenient than anything else. The fact that he had a hot sister didn't hurt our friendship either." He winks at Sarah.

Josh looks at Trey. "Tell the happy couple what they can expect in married life." He sits down and returns his attention to Mary's friend.

Trey walks to the center of the room; a rousing applause from the gathering accompanies him. Most of them have had a few drinks by now. "Thank you, everybody. In case anyone wants to know, the secret of a happy marriage will remain a secret." Someone tosses a crumpled napkin at him. Trey looks over at Ryan and Mary, raises his glass of beer, and offers this famous quote: "Happiness is the richest thing we will ever own."

"That's sweet," Mary says. "Is it Confucius?"

"Donald Duck," Trey replies.

Mary puts her hands on her hips and glares at Trey in a playful yet condescending manner.

"Get used to it," Kelci says. "You're part of the family now."

The room goes silent when Jacque, who has been sitting next to the harpist for over an hour, scoots behind the harp and starts strumming the Jackson 5's "I'll Be There."

"I had no idea he played the harp," Mary whispers.

"Neither did I," Ryan replies.

With the celebration fading, Ryan and Mary quietly slip away. They each toss a small suitcase into the trunk of her Honda Accord and take off for the private jet terminal at BWI. Tin cans tied to the bumper clang the entire drive to the airport. Upon their arrival, they're led onto a private charter that whisks them off to the British Virgin Islands.

The newlyweds are met by Ryan's business partner as soon as they debark the plane in Tortola. Colin is a forty-year-old Australian bloke with bushy blond hair and a face weathered by the tropical sun. He's clad in a pair of cargo shorts and a freshly ironed white cotton shirt. "G'day, mate," he says as he puts his arm around Ryan's shoulders.

Ryan steps back, giving his friend an appreciative look. "Check you out! Clean shorts and a fresh shirt."

"Always mucking around, ain't ye, mate?" Colin looks at Mary, then wipes his hand on his shorts before extending it. "Crikey, what a beaut ye got, Ryan. G'day, ma'am, I'm Colin."

Mary gives him a pleasant smile as he holds her hand. "Good day, Colin."

Colin grabs their bags and leads them through the small airport to the parking lot. Ryan bursts out laughing when he sees an open-air safari bus with "Colin's #7" painted on the side. The vehicle is a pickup truck with four rows of bench seats attached to the extended bed. A red-and-white-striped canopy above the seats protects the passengers from rain and sun. "We bought this lorry to pick guests up at the airport and shuffle 'em about the island," Colin says. He grabs a rag and rubs a speck of dirt off the hood like a proud dad.

Colin zips through the narrow streets of Road Town with Ryan and Mary sitting in the first row of seats behind him. Mary leans against Ryan, clutching his knee. "No worries, ma'am. We drive on the left side here," Colin says. "If ye see something coming at ya, you know you're in the wrong lane."

After leaving town, Colin guides the safari bus through eight hairpin curves while climbing a steep mountain and ten hairpin curves on the way down. He drives slowly so as not to scare Mary, and to keep a watchful eye for tourists driving on the wrong side of the road.

"We'd be at the bottom now if it were just him and me in the truck," Ryan says with a playful grin.

Mary fakes a sigh of relief. "Thank goodness I inspire common sense in you kids."

Dense tropical foliage lines both sides of the road, except at a turnoff, where they make a quick stop to stretch their legs and take in the view.

"The vegetation was cleared to provide a picturesque view of the ocean and outlying islands," Ryan comments.

Mary stands next to Ryan; the gentle sea breeze caresses her face. She gazes across the lush tropical island and out to the sea. "The turquoise water is incredible."

At the bottom of the mountain, the road bends abruptly then dead-ends at a teardrop-shaped beach that's protected from the open sea. Soft white sand slopes upward from the water to palm trees, flowering frangipani, and hibiscus on the shore.

Ryan helps Mary from the bus. "This is such a beautiful beach," she gushes.

"When I first came here, all Colin had was a little shack that he sold beer and rum out of to the occasional tourist." He spreads his arms wide-open. "Now look at it. 'Colin's #7.' We have a restaurant, bar, and eight bungalows for overnight guests."

Mary gazes about the property, a look of fascination on her face. "And you're part owner of all this?"

Ryan puffs his chest out. "I financed the upgrade and expansion."

Colin grabs their bags. "Stretch yer legs a bit. I'll drop yer bags off in Bungalow 6."

Ryan and Mary hold hands as they stroll to the water's edge. The only sounds are waves gently lapping onto the beach and a few birds chattering in the distance. They stand close, quietly looking at the ocean and the islands in the distance.

"That large island is St. Thomas." Ryan points forward. "It's a pretty sight when the sun sets behind it. The island to the left is St. John. The Rockefellers used to own it."

The 500-square-foot bungalow contains a king bed with luxurious down bedding, a large white ceiling fan, and a seating area with wicker furniture. A doorway in the bedroom opens to a bathroom with a large granite walled shower.

After Ryan and Mary have cleaned up, Colin meets them at the front entrance of the restaurant. "We have an excellent band tonight. Follow me. I've saved you a table near the patio."

The combination restaurant and bar is built in typical Caribbean fashion. The ceiling is made of exposed wood trestles covered in palm leaves. A series of ten-foot-high wood shutters form the ocean-facing wall. They are propped open to welcome the breeze and provide direct access to the patio. The middle of the establishment is home to a large rectangular mahogany bar. Rustic-looking wood tables and chairs line the outer walls.

Colin pulls the chair out from the table for Mary to sit down. "The red snapper was brought in this afternoon by the local fishermen. I highly recommend it pan-fried with fruit."

Ryan tips his head at Colin. "Thank you. You're a wonderful host."

"Bloody oath, mate," Colin replies. He waves over a Black man in a colorful tropical shirt. "Take good care of the boss tonight."

Within the hour, the bar is standing room only. The band Colin referred to is two local musicians. One beats on a steel drum while the other sings and plays a synthesizer.

After finishing off their snapper, Ryan takes his wife's hand and leads her to an open area in front of the band. He puts his hands on her hips and together they gently sway to the intimate vibes of "Turn Your Lights Down Low."

While they're in an embrace on the dance floor, Ryan looks into Mary's eyes and gives her a gentle kiss. "Let's go back to the room, Mrs. Hutson."

They take their flip-flops off and meander along the beach, sand between their toes. Holding hands, they stand on the water's edge as the gentle waves surge around their feet. They pause to gaze at the moonbeam reflecting off the calm waters of the bay. Mary studies Ryan's face as he stares at the full moon.

"Whatcha thinking?"

"My mom would be happy to see us together."

The sun is starting to peek over the top of the mountain. Mary is lying on the bed, her head resting on a couple of down pillows, a relaxed smile on her face. A knock comes on the door, and a woman's voice calls out, "Room service."

Ryan sticks his head out from under the sheets. "Come on in." Looking like a turtle extending his head from a shell, he asks the young lady to leave the cart next to the bed. Mary clutches the sheets near her chest. She smiles at the young lady, her face flush with embarrassment.

"Thank you," Ryan says, then returns his head under the sheets. When he comes up for air, he surveys the breakfast cart. "I wonder what flavor this yogurt is." He reaches over, grabs the cup, and then spills it on Mary's chest. "Oops. Let me clean that up for you." He puts his mouth on her breast and slowly licks the creamy delight. "Mmm, strawberry."

After Ryan expertly removes the yogurt from her body, Mary, still breathing deeply, empties a bowl of cherry jam on his chest. She smears it from his nipples past his belly button. "I love the taste of cherry."

They finish their breakfast, then break out in laughter as they look at the mess they created. Their bodies, hair, and sheets are covered in an array of liquids.

"Other than shower, what else would you like to do today?" Mary asks.

"We could go horseback riding," Ryan says. He uses a finger to rub a spot of jam off her inner thigh.

She closes her eyes and smiles. "Horseback riding brings back wild memories."

Ryan grins. "As will cherry jam."

Mary springs up with anticipation. "I want to go sailing."

Two days later, Ryan is back in Florida for spring training, and Mary is in Maryland packing her belongings for her move to Texas.

CHAPTER EIGHTY

Fast-Forward Four Years

The world championship banners on the facade of Yankee Stadium snap in the chilly September wind.

Ryan kneels in the on-deck circle, studying the relief pitcher like a frog eyeing a fly. Each warm-up pitch pops like a firecracker when it hits the catcher's mitt. He blows into his cupped hands to keep them warm. After watching a few pitches, Ryan turns and looks up into the packed stands, twenty rows above the visitors dugout. Mary sits there with the other wives and girlfriends. Her blond hair dangles from under a Red Sox cap. She looks warm and cozy with the wool blanket wrapped tightly around her. Their gazes lock. She wiggles her fingers at him in that little wave she does.

He nods to her, then returns his attention to the game.

"Let's play ball," bellows the umpire as he lowers his face mask.

. . .

High above home plate, two television commentators sit behind a pair of microphones in a small booth. Curt Gowins, the lead commentator, frowns absently at a speck on his Armani suit as he waits for the broadcast to resume.

Providing color commentary alongside Curt is Buck Buchannon, a country boy who spent more than four decades traveling the back roads scouting baseball talent and coaching in the Minor Leagues.

The red light flashes in the press box, signaling a return to the broadcast from a commercial break.

Curt immediately jumps in: "Welcome back to the game. In case you just joined us, a suspenseful inning-to-inning battle has worked its way into the top of the ninth with the Yankees ahead 2 to 1. The Red Sox have a runner on third and first base with two outs. The Yankees have brought in their young closer to shut the door on the Red Sox rally." He pauses a beat for dramatic effect. "After 162 games, both teams are tied with one hundred victories. The winner of this game will continue to the playoffs."

Curt looks over at his broadcast partner. "Buck, give us your thoughts on the pending batter-pitcher duel."

"You betcha." Buck leans into his microphone. "The next batter is Ryan Hutson, a thirty-nine-year-old veteran who's been in the big leagues for thirteen years. He's a ten-time all-star and led the league in batting six times."

"Impressive," Curt comments with very little emotion attached to his words. "What can you tell us about the new pitcher?"

"Well, Curt, Roy Halverson is a rookie out of the University of Nebraska. The youngster throws a fastball more 'n a hundred miles an hour. He has seventeen saves in his last eighteen attempts." Buck twists his lips, then comments, "His last blown save was two weeks ago when Ryan hit a walk-off two-run homer."

Curt looks down onto the ballfield at Ryan walking toward home plate. "Let's get back to the game."

. . .

Ryan pauses for a moment before stepping into the batter's box. He looks up at the harvest moon hanging over the stadium and touches his hand to his heart. The pitcher looks at Ryan, then spits on the ground. Ryan digs his spikes into the sand and clay mixture of the batter's box. Halverson looks at the catcher, checks the runners, then rears back and hurls a blazing fastball. *Pow!* The ball slams into the catcher's mitt six inches outside of the plate.

Ryan gives the pitcher a curious look, then readies himself for the next pitch. Halverson goes through his pre-pitch ritual, which includes a scratch and spit, then fires another fastball a half foot outside the plate. Ball two.

Ryan steps back from the plate and looks at the pitcher. The gears turn in his head. *They're either going to walk me or make me chase a bad pitch.* As soon as he steps back into the batter's box, Halverson completes his stretch and throws another outside pitch. Ryan's eyes go wide. "Big mistake," he mumbles. "Never throw the same pitch three times in a row." Ryan steps toward the plate, reaches out, and swings at the ball with both arms fully extended. His wrists snap at the precise moment the bat contacts the baseball. The ball shoots off the wooden barrel like a bullet from a gun.

Ryan races toward first base full speed as he watches the ball streak down the right-field line. Yankees fans are paralyzed with fear, and a hush comes over the stadium as the ball crashes into the dirt on the warning track. Ryan rounds first and is on his way to second when he hears, "Foul ball, foul ball!" The umpire dramatically points both hands to foul territory.

A shared sigh of relief bring the New York fans to their feet.

Ryan slaps his hands together as he looks at the first base coach on his way back to home plate. He holds his forefinger and thumb two inches apart. "Dang! Both runners would have scored if it hadn't sliced into foul territory."

The first base coach slaps him on the backside. "Get him next pitch."

Ryan watches Halverson kick at the dirt behind the mound as he picks up his bat. At six foot six and 260 pounds, the pitcher looks like a kid in a gorilla suit. Even though it's less than forty degrees, sweat beads on Halverson's face as he pounds his fist into his glove. "Give me a new ball," he hollers to the umpire.

Ryan digs in the batter's box again and takes a few swings to regain his rhythm. After releasing a deep breath, he hears a loud grunt. He's caught off guard by a quick delivery. The ball is high and tight. He can see the stitching spinning inward. Even though the ball is traveling in excess of a hundred miles per hour, it appears to be moving in slow motion . . . in a direct line to his head. Ryan struggles to get out of the path of the ball. It's his worst nightmare; he can't get his body to respond as quickly as his mind. At the last instant, his perception of the ball returns to normal speed as it crashes into the side of his head.

CHAPTER EIGHTY-ONE

The light in the hospital room is subdued so as not to agitate Ryan should he open his eyes. It's not a concern since he hasn't moved a muscle in four days. Electrical cables connect his body to beeping monitors with blinking lights. The color has faded from his once tanned face, and a bright-purple-and-red bruise stretches from his forehead to his jaw on the left side of his face. The top of his head is encased in a thick bandage resembling a turban. Sarah slouches in a chair next to him, asleep with a book in her lap.

Trey sits across a cluttered desk from Dr. Rolf Stanoski, an esteemed medical practitioner at the Columbia Medical Center in New York City. Dr. Stanoski, at sixty years of age, is a short, heavyset man of East European descent. He resembles Larry from *The Three Stooges*, with poodle-like hair that sticks straight out from his mostly bald head.

The doctor gets to his feet and hobbles over to a VCR. With a thick Slavic accent, he urges Trey to come have a look as he slides a VHS tape into the player.

Trey steps over some magazines, then maneuvers around some boxes lying on the floor to get to where the doctor is standing.

The tape begins as the pitcher releases the ball. Dr. Stanoski presses the slow-motion button. "We were told the ball was traveling in excess of one hundred miles per hour when it struck Mr. Hutson. It hit just under his protective headgear, causing the helmet to fly off his head like a projectile."

Trey's stomach tightens as he watches the traumatic impact in slow motion.

"The ball was diverted just enough by the helmet that it struck him in front of his ear and slightly below his temple." Stanoski touches the side of Trey's head to emphasize the point of impact. "The immense force caused a fracture in his skull, and his brain slammed against the other side of his skull, causing swelling—which puts pressure on his cerebrum."

After he leaves the doctor's office, Trey stops in the lounge area across the hall from the nurses' station to call Kelci. She's at home in North Carolina, taking care of the kids and keeping an eye on their business. "It's a matter of wait and see," Trey tells her. "Until he comes out of it, they don't know what damage was done. Hopefully, there was no bleeding in the brain that could cause permanent damage."

Kelci has a lump in her throat and blinks away tears. "The kids miss you and have Uncle Ryan in their prayers. They said everyone at school is asking about him."

"The kids at school? Really?"

"It's hard to keep your personal affairs private when their uncle is a celebrity."

After a mind-numbing four days, a brief respite from the hospital is beneficial to a grieving wife and young child. Mary and her four-year-old daughter, Allison, take a leisurely stroll through Central

Park. The temperature has warmed up since the fateful night. Joggers and rollerbladers compete with walkers for space on the paved paths. Mary and Allison walk for nearly half an hour before they find an empty park bench. They sit close to each other as Mary tries to explain why Daddy is still sleeping after four days. "Sometimes when you hit your head really hard, you just need a nice long rest to get back to normal."

———

Thirteen days have passed, and Ryan shows no signs of coming out of his slumber.

Mary and Allison enter Ryan's room to find Jacque sitting next to the bed, gently strumming a guitalele. It's pretty common for him to carry the miniature guitar with him to practice chords during idle moments. The boy has grown into a tall and skinny teenager. Long dark hair covers his ears.

"Hi, Jacque," Allison tells her brother as she scampers over to the bed and climbs up next to her dad.

"Anything happening?" Mary asks.

"His eyelids have been fluttering a little bit. The medical guys say it's a sign of brain activity."

Mary studies her husband's face. "That's positive." She gives Ryan a gentle peck on the forehead, then sits in the chair next to Jacque. "How long have you been here?"

"About twenty minutes. I got out of class an hour ago and took a cab over. Trey and Sarah left when I got here."

Mary looks over at Allison. The little girl is rubbing her dad's forehead while talking to him.

"She sure is a chatty one," Jacque comments.

"Kids are at that age . . . How are things at school?"

"I love LaGuardia School of Music and Performing Arts. The education I'm getting here is so much more practical than what I would get at a regular school. Plus, it's a great experience living in New York City."

"Not many thirteen-year-old kids can say that."

Allison has her head on Ryan's chest. "Wake up, Daddy. Please wake up. I love you."

Ryan feels like he's deep within a cave. Darkness surrounds him. He can hear a child's voice calling out to him, but he struggles to figure out where the voice is coming from. "Keep talking so I can find you," he says, but his speech is only in his head.

There's a moment of silence, then he hears it again: "Please, Daddy, we need you."

Ryan's heart races. "She needs my help," he tells himself. "I have to find her." He tries to holler to her, but no words come from his mouth. He keeps moving forward in the darkness; her voice becomes stronger and clearer. He wants to tell her everything will be all right, but no matter how hard he struggles, he can't get a sound to come from his mouth.

The voice stops. Ryan listens intently . . . In the ensuing silence, he feels himself drifting back into the cave. "No, no! I have to find her. She needs me!" he frantically says in his mind. The further he drifts back into the darkness, the more urgent his urge to yell becomes. Finally, his effort to holler becomes so overwhelming that it jolts him from his sleep.

Ryan jerks his head up, startling the little girl. Her sudden shock is quickly replaced with excitement. Ryan opens his eyes and stares at her with a faraway look. He lies motionless, his head raised as his eyes strain to focus on the room. A young man is talking with a woman. He's confused. *I don't know where I am or who these people are.* He touches the side of his head and grimaces. "Oww."

Allison throws her arms around his neck and hugs him. She cries out, "Daddy, Daddy!" Mary looks over, wondering what has gotten her daughter so riled up. "Oh my God, his eyes are open!" She puts her hand on Jacque's shoulder. "Go get somebody!"

Disoriented, Ryan tries to compose himself. He puts his hand on Allison's back as he peers at her. A red ribbon is clipped onto her curly blond hair. "Hi, sweetheart," he says in a hoarse whisper. "What's your name?"

"Oh, Daddy, you know who I am." The young girl giggles. "It's me, Allison."

Mary rushes to Ryan's side. Her body trembles with anxiety. She desperately wants to hug him, but she sees a confused look on his face and quickly hits the brakes. The lights are on, but no one appears to be home.

Ryan stares into Mary's blue eyes. They look familiar.

Mary picks up Allison and holds the child in her arms. Wiping a tear from her eyes, she takes a deep breath, then says, "Hi."

Ryan tries to sit up, but quickly falls back when he feels a sharp pain in his temple. Instinctively, Mary reaches out and touches his arm. She notices the electronic control pad next to the bed and hands it to him.

Ryan looks at it for a second, then presses a button to raise the head of the mattress to an inclined position. He looks silently at Mary and Allison.

"You don't know who we are, do you?" Mary asks, trying to remain calm.

"I heard her call me Daddy," Ryan says, looking at Allison. "She's my daughter." He shifts his attention to Mary's face. "If you're her mother, then you must be my wife. You're a beautiful woman."

She squeezes her eyes shut and sighs heavily. "Thank you. My name's Mary." She gently touches the good side of his face while fighting the urge to hug him. He places his hand on hers. "Do you remember anything about us?" she asks.

Ryan presses his lips together in frustration. "My brain is crammed with thoughts trying to get out. But right now, it's like they're stuck in mud."

Jacque bursts into the room, followed by a young resident and a nurse. Ryan feels a tinge of familiarity as he gazes at the wild-eyed boy, who shakes with anticipation.

The nurse takes a position next to the bed and proceeds to wrap a blood pressure sleeve around Ryan's arm. Mary stands at the foot of the bed with her arms around Jacque and Allison. Ryan notices a nervous twitch in her fingers and looks at her with admiration. It's evident she is being strong for the children.

The resident stands next to Ryan on the opposite side of the bed from the nurse. He's a young man, not much more than thirty years old. His crisply starched bright-white lab coat is buttoned to the top so only the white collar of his shirt and the knot of his silk tie are visible. He lifts Ryan's eyelid and studies his pupil. Taking a small penlight from his coat pocket, he moves it from side to side in front of Ryan's face. Ryan tries to squint, but the resident maintains his hold on the eyelid.

"The light seems to be annoying him," Mary says in Ryan's defense.

Paying no attention to Mary, the resident continues with his examination. "Please bear with me, Mr. Hutson. Follow my finger with your eyes." He moves his finger up, down, and sideways in front of Ryan. "How do you feel?"

"My head hurts, and I'm having trouble concentrating."

"That's understandable. Anything else?"

"My vision is a little out of focus when I look left."

"What's your name?"

Ryan looks down at the paper bracelet around his wrist, then turns his arm so he can get a good look. "Ryan Hutson."

"Good." The resident nods. "When is your birthday?"

After nearly ten seconds of deep concentration, Ryan replies, "December thirty-first." A sharp pain shoots up the side of his face when he touches his temple.

The resident gives him a concerned look. "Are you doing okay?"

"I'm really tired."

"One more question, then I'll leave you alone. Do you know why you're here?"

"No. I just know my head hurts."

"You had a head trauma. You lost consciousness and were brought here."

"What happened? How long have I been here?"

"You're a professional baseball player," the resident says. "You were hit in the head with a baseball."

Ryan recalls a terrifying vision of something flying directly toward his head and being unable to move out of the way.

"You've been unconscious for thirteen days."

Ryan sits quietly. He studies Mary, Allison, and Jacque.

"We can talk about the accident later. You need to get some rest." The resident nods Mary toward the door.

Mary walks over to the bed and kisses Ryan on the forehead. They give each other a longing look as they hold hands for a few seconds. "Come on, Allison, we need to go now. Daddy needs his rest."

"Okay, Daddy, you can go back to sleep, but this time don't sleep so long."

Mary and Allison follow the resident out the door. The nurse stays in the room. Ryan looks over at the boy.

Jacque walks over to the bed. "Hey."

"Were you playing that little guitar while I was sleeping?"

He nods, then softly replies, "Yes, sir."

"I could hear it. It was beautiful and relaxing. You're very good. What's your name?"

"Jacque."

"Are you my boy?" Ryan holds his hand out and Jacque grabs it.

"Yes, sir." Tears stream down Jacque's face. "I've been so scared."

"It's okay now. I'm going to be all right."

Jacque rubs the tears off his cheeks with his shirt sleeve. "Yeah, you will. I know how you are."

"You don't look like your sister at all."

"We're from different mothers."

"Oww." The confusion causes a pain in the back of Ryan's head.

The nurse puts her hand on Jacque's shoulder and tilts her head toward the door. "Come. He needs to get some rest."

"I'll come by and see you after school tomorrow."

Uncomfortable moving his head, Ryan winks at him. "I look forward to it."

The nurse pushes the button to lower the bed back to a horizontal position.

In the hallway, the resident discusses characteristics of head trauma with Mary. "Coming out of a coma can be overwhelming. It's perfectly normal to be tired. After some regular sleep, he should be better. He'll be back in the proper time continuum, and hopefully able to process things more clearly."

"What can we do to help?"

"Ask him simple questions. Talk about things that might stimulate his memory." In a reassuring tone, the doctor informs her, "He hasn't lost his memories. He just needs help finding them."

Allison walks in between her mom and Jacque, holding each of their hands as they make their way toward the elevator. "Can we go out for ice cream?"

"Not now. We need to go back to the hotel and tell your Uncle Trey and Aunt Sarah that Daddy woke up."

CHAPTER EIGHTY-TWO

Ryan sits up in his hospital bed while a Black Hispanic nurse checks his vitals. She's a heavyset woman who refers to herself as Nuyorican. He's feeling much better after a good sleep and eating real food for the first time in two weeks. Removing the catheter and using the toilet on his own increases his self-esteem.

"Just so you know," the nurse tells him, "I rolled your arse over every day for thirteen days so you wouldn't get bedsores."

"Thank you. Me and my butt appreciate you."

"'Twas nothing. I got a few gropes in." She looks at him and grins. "Being from the Bronx and all make me a Yankees fan. I kinda always like you as a ballplayer 'til you decided to play for the Sox. But you know, I still feel bad when you get hit in the head. I remember seeing it on TV. I thought you be dead. Next thing, you here in our E.R."

"Thank you for your sympathy."

"You be a pretty popular man here past couple weeks. Me and the nurses always wonder which celebrity come visit next. The owners of Red Sox and Yankees come by to pay their respects, as do many politicians, TV stars, and other professional athletes. There be Eugene. He say he a preacher, lawyer, football player, and entrepreneur. It don't matter much what he claim to be. Mm-hmm, he quite the specimen of a man. I give him a bear hug. Otherwise, the only regular visitors be the two ladies and man, and the two kids."

There's a knock on the door, followed by Trey and Sarah entering the room.

"Come in. I be leaving now," the nurse tells them. She stops and looks at Ryan. "My name is Lolin. I be looking after you more closely now that you awake."

Trey, being his usual self, breaks any tension in the room by adding his unique brand of levity. He struts in, takes a look around, and then says, "Okay, things are looking good. The blinds are open, the sun is shining in, and Rip Van Winkle is awake. Thank goodness that funky-looking space helmet has been removed from your head."

Sarah hurries over to Ryan and cups his face in her hands. "Oh my God, Ryan, it is so wonderful to see you with your eyes open." She kisses his cheek.

Ryan has a dazed look, feeling a bit overwhelmed. He's not sure how to reply. Her face, and voice are familiar, but there's still a void. She sits next to him on the bed, her hand on his shoulder. Shoulder-length sandy-blond hair frames her heart-shaped face.

"Who is that guy?" Ryan nods toward Trey.

"That's your brother."

"Are you married to him?"

She laughs lightly. "No. I'm your sister."

"Don't tell me. Let me guess." Ryan looks at them in silence for several seconds. Electrical impulses fire in his brain. "Trey and Kelci?"

Trey steps forward. "You got half of it right, baby brother. I'm Trey, but Kelci is my wife. This is Sarah."

Sarah, still on the bed next to Ryan, grabs his hand. "We've been so worried about you, Ryan. It's such a relief to see you awake."

Trey walks over to the other side of the bed and pats him on the shoulder. "It must have been a real eye-opening experience. You know, waking up."

Ryan looks at him and blinks slowly a couple times. "Are we really related?"

Sarah quickly intervenes. "What was it like sleeping for two weeks? Were you totally out to the world?"

"I recall some things happening around me. Like the nurse shaving me and washing my hair. But I couldn't move or say anything. It was like a mental fog." He looks at Sarah. "I remember your voice. You read to me."

Sarah smiles and nods. "I sat here several nights alone with you while I read a book. One night, I decided to sit next to you and start reading aloud, hoping you could hear me and it might help bring you around."

"I don't remember what you read, but the sound of your voice was soothing."

Trey grins. "I tried to talk to you, but you were speechless."

Ryan looks at him with a frown, then says to Sarah, "Is he always like this?"

"He's very, very happy right now. He was miserable the past couple weeks worrying about you. He loves you. We all do."

"What about Mom and Dad?"

Sarah shakes her head sadly. "Dad died about five years ago. Mom about eight years before that."

"Just the three of us?"

"You're married with two kids. Trey has a wife and three children."

"What about you?"

"I'm not married. I do have a special friend named Jeanne."

Ryan waggles his eyebrows. "A French lover?"

"A lady has to have a few secrets," Sarah says with a wry grin.

There's a light knock on the door. A young nurse's aide in a striped apron enters the room, carrying an arrangement of spring flowers.

She takes the card out, hands it to Sarah, then turns to leave.

"Wait a minute," Ryan calls out. "Where are you going with the flowers?"

"Hold on," Sarah tells the nurse's aide. Turning to Ryan, she says, "Years ago, you injured your elbow and had a brief hospital stay. You received a bunch of flowers every day, and you told the nurses to save the cards for you but to give the flowers to patients who didn't have any. You've received enough flowers the past two weeks to fill a double-wide trailer, so we just continued with your earlier wishes."

"You've been sleeping. You didn't need any flowers," Trey says.

"These are colorful. They liven the room up. Why don't we leave them here?"

The nurse's aide sets the flowers on a table and disappears.

Sarah pulls the card from the envelope and reads it.

> We hope you get better soon.
> You came into our lives and made the world a much better place.
> We will never forget you.
> Adam and Ryan

"Do you remember them?" Sarah asks.

Ryan struggles with his thoughts. The strain is evident on his face. "There are so many things floating around in my head. I can't pull everything together."

"Relax," Sarah says. "It'll all come to you." She grasps his hand. "You invest a lot of yourself making sure kids get proper medical treatment."

His eyes brighten up a bit as he thinks about it. "The courage of kids is inspirational."

"You went off the straight and narrow path for a while, but your concern for kids helped reel you in," Sarah says. "Adam, who is probably about seven now, was the first child whose life you touched with your generosity."

Touching his fingertips to his chest, Ryan asks, "I strayed a bit?"

"You weren't exactly Dudley Do-Right," Trey replies. "You used to hit the bottle pretty good and revel in your celebrity."

Ryan looks at Sarah. "Is he making that up?"

She shakes her head. "Unfortunately not. Thankfully, Dad's second wife was a natural healer. She helped to bring you around."

"Is she Japanese?"

"She is," Sarah replies. "You remembered that quite easily."

"She came to me while I was unconscious." The gears turn in his head. "She said something like relax your mind, breathe deep, and allow your body to heal itself."

"Holy shit!" Trey jerks upright. "It's like you tapped into some supernatural connection."

Ryan looks at him with a blank stare. Looking at Sarah, he asks, "What'd you do with the cards?"

Sarah opens the top drawer of the nightstand and pulls out a handful of cards. One drops from her grip and lands next to Ryan on the bed. He opens it and reads it out loud.

Ryan,
Be the strong and confident person I always knew you to be.
You will pull through this.
I am proud of how things turned out for you.
Linda

Sarah looks into Ryan's eyes. They appear to be staring into space. "Do you remember her?"

Ryan shakes his head slowly. "No. But the words along with her name give me a warm feeling inside—like there was a special connection in the past." There's a moment of silence in the room. "Is there an address with the card?"

"No," Sarah replies.

CHAPTER EIGHTY-THREE

The door to the hospital room opens; Mary and Allison enter cautiously, not knowing what to expect. There's a moment of silence as everyone looks at each other.

"Hey, there's my two favorite girls," Ryan chirps. "Come here and give me a hug."

Allison races over and climbs up onto the bed. She kisses her dad and gives him the biggest hug a little girl could muster.

"Mmm, that feels good," Ryan says.

Mary walks over and sits on the bed next to Ryan. Her hand gently rubs the side of his face. "Hey, handsome, how you doing today?" She kisses him on the lips.

"Much better, seeing you two."

"Like getting a dose of positive endorphins?" Mary asks.

Ryan's gaze is distant as he tries to catch a thought that's just beyond his grasp. "Yeah, something like that."

Trey and Sarah retreat to the two chairs in the room as Allison and Mary surround Ryan on the bed.

Ryan laughs at Allison as she crawls all over him. "You're just like a little monkey. Is your name Cheetah?"

"My name is Mary Allison, not Cheetah," she says while crossing her arms with a pout. "You like to call me Emma."

Ryan's eyebrows rise in mock disbelief. "Do I really?"

"Momma's name is Mary Elizabeth. You used to call her Emmie when she was a girl."

Ryan gazes at Mary, his mind scans her face, processing this new information. "Emmie, from next door," he softly murmurs. His face lights up as they share the look of love.

Mary's eyes water. "It's Mary Elizabeth. Nicknames are for little girls. I'm all grown up now."

A positive energy flows between them as they clutch each other's hands. Ryan lets go and wraps his arms around his wife. "I love you, Sunshine."

Mary squeezes him back as tears pour from her eyes. "Oh, Ryan, it has been such a long two weeks. I missed you. I needed you."

"I'm back, and I won't ever leave you." A lopsided smirk crosses his face. "I remember the night I got home from my high school football game all beat-up and pissed off. You snuck into the—"

"Shhh." Mary quickly puts her hand over Ryan's mouth. "There are other people in the room," she says, looking around red-faced.

"Heard it before. I was your best friend, you told me everything," Sarah reminds her.

"I haven't heard the story," Trey quips.

Sarah gives him a "behave yourself" look.

"There are little ears in the room," Mary reminds everyone.

Sarah looks at Allison, then hops to her feet. "Come on, honey. Let's go get some ice cream." She grabs Allison's hand and leads her to the door. Stopping at the door, she looks at Trey, who is still seated. "Would you like to get some ice cream also, Trey?"

He hesitates. Sarah points toward the door. Trey reluctantly rises from his seat and follows them out.

Mary lies across Ryan as they share an impassioned embrace and deep kiss.

Ryan grins. "That night you snuck into the shower certainly changed my thoughts about you."

"It took a lot of nerve for me to do that." Mary lies quietly while looking at him with adoring eyes. "It's sad to say, but we may not have reconnected if your dad hadn't passed."

Memories of his dad fill his mind. "I remember a practical, no-nonsense kind of guy." His thoughts return to the present, and he cuddles Mary, softly caressing her body. His fingers linger in certain spots.

Mary enjoys it for a few moments, then pulls back. Laughing softly, she says, "It seems the concussion didn't affect your libido."

Ryan pulls her back into him. "You arouse *all* my senses."

Mary kisses him, pulls away again, then informs him with flushed cheeks, "Somebody can walk in here at any minute."

"Lock the door."

"I already checked. It doesn't lock."

"Put a 'do not disturb' sign on the outside of the door."

"Maybe later tonight. When it's less crowded around here."

Ryan pulls his hand from under her blouse, sulking. He feels like he was caught raiding the cookie jar. Taking a deep breath, he sits up and puts his arm around her shoulders. "Nurse Lolin says I play for the Red Sox? The last memory I have is with the Rangers."

"The Rangers traded you to the Red Sox in August. Your dream has always been to play in a World Series. It wasn't going to happen in Texas. Boston had a good shot to make the playoffs and gave up several young players to get you on their team for the stretch run."

Mary watches intently as Ryan rubs his forehead. She looks at him lovingly and brushes his hair away from his face. The action brings fond memories of his mother.

"Do we live in Boston?" he asks when he breaks from his trance.

"We sublet a flat in Beacon Hill, not too far from Fenway."

"Do we have a house in Texas?"

"Sold it." She pats his arm as she talks. "We own a beach house in California and a ranch in New Mexico."

Ryan taps his lips lightly with his fingertips. "Mom and Dad are buried at the ranch. For some reason, the name Billy comes to mind."

"Billy was your dog when you were a kid. He's buried there also."

Ryan bites his lower lip as he looks down. "A big yellow dog. I remember him. He was special." After a moment, he adds, "There are a lot of things I don't remember in between getting married and waking up in here."

Mary gets a buzz of energy. She's excited to help him regain his memory. "We had our daughter. You finished your college degree, like you promised your mom. We spent several months in Scandinavia visiting my relatives. You loved Norway and all the people. The Rangers never won more than half their games while you were on the team. Needless to say, you were excited to get traded to a playoff contender."

Before she can continue, there's a light knock on the door. After a moment's pause, Sarah sticks her head in the room. "Is it safe to come in?"

Mary smooths out the front of her blouse and runs her fingers through her hair. "Of course, come on in. It's not like we can't control our urges," she quips.

"What urges are you talking about, Mommy?" Allison asks as she waltzes into the room. "Do you have to use the potty?"

"No, I don't, dear."

Jacque strolls in behind Sarah and Allison. "Look who's here, Ryan," Mary says, looking to change the subject.

"Come on over here, boy, and give your old man a hug. Did you bring your little guitar with you?"

"No, sir," Jacque replies. "But I brought my ocarina." He whips a potato flute out of his backpack and plays a few bars of the *Cheers* theme song.

"How's your mom doing?"

"She's doing well. She asks about you all the time. Well, I mean since you got bonked on the head."

"Where does she live?"

Jacque rubs his eye, a look of bewilderment on his face. "In Montréal."

"You met her when you played ball in Montréal," Sarah tells him. "You left Montréal to pursue your career in Los Angeles."

"She didn't come with me?"

Sarah pinches her lips together as she shakes her head. "She had her own dreams. Besides, you guys never married."

Ryan frowns. "Best to leave that discussion for another day." He gives Jacque a supportive nod. "Your mom did a good job raising you. You seem like a good kid."

The next morning, Sarah walks into Ryan's hospital room. The bed is empty. She looks around; an overweight middle-aged man with a salt-and-pepper flattop is the only person in the room. He looks at home sitting in a chair with his feet propped up on a side table. He's writing in a paper tablet and pays no attention to Sarah.

"Excuse me, do I have the right room? I'm looking for Ryan Hutson."

"Yup, you got the right room, honey," he says without looking up.

Sarah stands in silence for a few seconds, watching him scribble in his notebook.

"Could I trouble you to tell me where he is?"

"He had a brain aneurysm and was rushed into emergency surgery," he replies, still focused on his writing.

Sarah's knees go weak, and she struggles with her breathing. "Oh my God! When did this happen?" She grabs the door handle to steady herself.

CHAPTER EIGHTY-FOUR

The man casually looks up at her for a second or two, showing no emotion. "Relax. I was just kidding. He's out stretching his legs. He'll be back in a few."

Sarah takes a step toward him, her fists clenched at her sides. She has a sudden urge to slap the shit out of him. "On what level do you find that to be even remotely funny? And who the hell are you and what are you doing in here?"

Before he can reply, the door opens and Ryan enters the room accompanied by Nurse Lolin. He's wearing hospital scrubs and a pair of tennis shoes.

Sarah lets out a sigh of relief while looking at Ryan, who appears energetic and alert. "Do you know this . . . this grub?" she asks. Her neck and shoulders are tense as she points a finger at the seated man.

Ryan studies him for a few seconds. "Nope."

"Seriously? You don't remember me? You really got it bad. Roland Snedley. Sportswriter, *New York Press*."

Ryan looks at Sarah. "Is there a problem?"

"This, whatever you want to call him, told me you blew a blood vessel in your brain and were in emergency surgery."

"Aww, geez!" Ryan's jaw clenches. "What's the matter with you? Get the hell out of here." He looks over at Nurse Lolin. "Call security."

"Don't be so hasty, Ryan," Snedley replies as he stands up. "Lest you forget, I have national syndication and twenty million readers."

"And that entitles you to what?"

"You're a popular player, and there's a story to be told. Give me the exclusive. I'll make you a hero."

"And if I don't, will you make me look like a villain?"

Snedley locks eyes with Ryan. Neither one says a word. The silence is broken when a large Black man in a blue uniform walks in. An Acme Security Services patch is on the shoulder of his sleeve, and the name Tony is sewn above his breast pocket.

"What's up, Ryan?"

"This gentleman is lost, Tony." Ryan nods toward Snedley. "Could you show him the way out?"

Tony reaches for Snedley's arm, but the louse quickly pulls it away. "Don't touch me!"

The guard grabs the door and holds it open. "Let's go, sir."

"Be nice to him, Tony. He works for the *New York Press*. He can make you a hero."

Ryan walks over to Sarah as Tony escorts Snedley out of the room. "Sorry to get you caught up in this kind of crap. The guy must have been neglected as a child."

"Probably the kind of kid who pulled the wings off flies," Sarah replies. She sighs a big breath of relief and wraps her arms around Ryan. "You look great. There's lots of color in your face."

"Nurse Lolin and I walk the corridors often. We went outside for a bit today. She's a big baseball fan, and it helps my memory to talk with her." Ryan sits down on the side of the bed. "I've been stretching and getting massages to limber up my muscles."

There's a gentle knock on the door, and Mary enters the room with Allison. The little girl immediately charges over to her dad, who scoops her up in his arms. Mary sets the small suitcase she's carrying down and snuggles into Ryan's free arm. They exchange a peck on the lips. "Hey, babe," Ryan says.

"I brought you some clothes. The nurses said you might be released tomorrow."

"I'm ready to get out of here."

"We rode over in a cab with Kelci. She's meeting with a doctor right now. She should be here in a minute."

"He's looking much better, isn't he?" Sarah comments to Mary.

Mary looks into Ryan's eyes and nods. "You can see it in his eyes and mannerisms."

"There are a few things I still struggle with," Ryan says. "But the doctor thinks once I get back into familiar surroundings things will come back more easily."

"Speaking of familiar surroundings, now that you're getting better, I'm going to fly to Paris tomorrow," Sarah says. "I've been neglecting work for nearly a month."

Mary grabs Sarah's hands. "We appreciate you being here. You've been a pillar of strength."

A tall woman with long, wavy dark hair enters the room. A middle-aged gentleman in a white dress shirt and tweed jacket follows closely behind. Gray hair adorns his temples.

The room is momentarily quiet. Everyone looks at Ryan to see if he recognizes the newcomer.

"Hey, Kelci," Ryan says without hesitation.

They meet in the middle of the room for a hug. "Hello, Ryan. Your memory doesn't seem to be as bad as everyone says."

Ryan gives her a teasing glance. "Mary mentioned that Kelci was on her way up."

Ryan looks closely at the gentleman she came in with and offers his hand. "Sorry. I have no memory of who you are."

"We've never met. I'm Dr. Ojos, a physician for the Red Sox. I've been asked to take a quick look at you."

"Isn't it a little premature?" Ryan asks. "I've only been moving around a few days."

"I have to meet with the Red Sox to discuss your contract," Kelci interjects. "You have two years left."

Ryan nods. "I think I've got at least two more good years left in me." Lightheartedly, he asks, "Do you think the Sox will want me back?"

Kelci huffs a laugh. "If you return to form, who wouldn't want you? You batted at least .330 the past four years, in addition to hitting forty or more home runs each year. The Sox just took the Mets to seven games in the World Series. They probably would have won if you'd played."

Ryan feels a small surge of adrenaline. "Sounds like unfinished business."

"I hope so, but there are still a few things I'd like to evaluate," Ojos says.

Ryan rubs his hands together. "Sure, Doc. You want to do it now?"

"That's what I'm here for."

CHAPTER EIGHTY-FIVE

Allison squirms, wanting to get off her mother's lap. "I think Allison and I are going to take a walk to the cafeteria." Mary grabs her daughter's hand.

"I'm going to join them, then go home and pack," Sarah tells Ryan. "Don't blow a blood vessel while I'm gone."

"I only do that when irritating people are around."

Sarah and Ryan hug and kiss. "Love you," she says.

"Love you too. Thank you for being here." He feels the warmth of her love in their hug. The two ladies and little girl walk out the door together.

"What was that all about, 'blowing a blood vessel?'" Kelci asks.

"Some idiot reporter from the *New York Press* made a stupid comment to her."

"Was it Snedley? I saw him going out the main door when I came in."

"It was. He wants to write my memoirs." Ryan chuckles. "Like that'll ever happen."

"Somebody should," Kelci says.

"Okay, let's go ahead with the evaluation," Ojos interrupts. The doctor stands in front of Ryan. "I want you to keep looking forward, but don't turn your head. I'm going to move my finger to the right. Tell me when you can't see it anymore." He moves his finger a little more than three feet to the right of Ryan's face before Ryan says, "Gone." Ojos repeats the same procedure moving his finger to Ryan's left. After about two feet, Ryan says he's lost sight of the doctor's finger. "Now, keep your eyes on my finger. How do you feel when I move it away from you on the left side?"

"I feel a little twinge near my temple, and my vision gets a little blurry."

Ojos nods in contemplation. "Let's try something else." He whispers something in Kelci's ear. She moves to the far side of the room, fifteen feet from Ryan.

Ojos stands a couple feet in front of him. He holds up his hand. "How many fingers?"

"Two," Ryan replies.

He drops his hand abruptly. "How many fingers is Kelci showing?"

It takes Ryan a second or two to focus. "Three." He shrugs. "So . . . what gives?"

"Let's look at one other thing," Ojos says. "Stand on one foot." Ryan wavers for a second. "Now grab your ankle and pull your leg back." Ryan loses his balance momentarily, then stabilizes himself.

There's a brief pause before Ojos speaks. "I've seen enough."

"Enough of what?" Ryan asks.

"I've seen enough to know that your depth perception, peripheral vision, and balance are off. For a normal person, it's probably nothing to be concerned about."

"What? I'm not a normal person?"

"No." Ojos shakes his head. "You're a professional athlete." He looks at Ryan for a few seconds without speaking. "I'm going to recommend that you go to an eye center for more in-depth testing."

Ryan looks at Kelci. She's leaning against the bed, her arms crossed, seemingly lost in thought.

"Sure," Ryan says. "I don't think they'll find anything wrong with me."

The door swings open and Mary walks into the room. "Am I interrupting?"

Ryan smiles at her. "Never. Where's Allison?"

"We ran into Jacque. He took her to get ice cream."

"The little girl is just like Snedley, always looking for a scoop," Ryan says.

"She's going to be the cream of her class in sundae school," Mary quips. She takes a seat in the chair next to the bed. "Everybody looks so serious. What's going on?"

Kelci sticks her hands in her pockets, trying to appear calm. "The doctor thinks there could be damage to Ryan's eye."

Mary is startled by the news. She looks over at Ryan, who doesn't seem concerned. "Do you think it will affect his baseball skills?"

Ojos shrugs. "It could be more difficult for him to play at the level he's used to."

Kelci walks over and stands next to Ryan. "Do you think rehab can help?"

Ojos turns his palms up. "Maybe. But if there is permanent damage to the nerves, I don't think he will ever recover a hundred percent."

"Enough with the doom and gloom," Ryan breaks in. "Spring training doesn't start for four months. I'll be fine by then. Right now lot of the doctor's saying is speculation?"

Ojos looks at Kelci. "I'm going to leave. I'll be back in touch after we get the results of the eye examination."

After Ojos leaves the room, Mary lets out a deep breath. "Looks like you've got some things to think about," she says to Ryan.

"I've been thinking baseball for thirty years."

Mary puts her arms around Ryan. They stand inches apart, breathing the same air. "Maybe it's time to start thinking about giving it up."

Ryan takes an immediate step back. "Hold on. This conversation is moving too fast—in the wrong direction! I'm trying to remember my past, and you guys are planning for my future. Let's just relax and be a little more supportive. We can talk about it after I get the eye examination."

"Good idea," Kelci says. "But remember, you're almost thirty-nine years old. You're not a young man anymore." She looks at him with a closed-mouth grin.

Ryan's mind flashes back to a conversation he had with a free agent on the Rangers. The player was taking steroids at thirty-eight to stay competitive. "See how you feel when you reach my age," Ramon said. The words echo in Ryan's mind. He quickly shakes the thought of steroid use from his brain. "No way," he tells himself. "I'll be all right." He looks at the ladies. "Excuse me for a second, I need to grab something from the bathroom."

Kelci looks at Mary and in a hushed tone says, "He won't give up. He's too strong-willed."

CHAPTER EIGHTY-SIX

The elevator door opens on the first floor of the Columbia Medical Center. Nurse Lolin pushes Ryan forward in his wheelchair. Mary, Allison, and Jacque follow close behind.

"Best wishes to you, Ryan," Nurse Lolin tells him. "It has been a pleasure to know you and your beautiful family."

"Thank you," Ryan stands up and gives her a hug and kiss on the cheek.

She pats him on the butt.

Mary squeezes her hands. "We appreciate you."

They head across the main lobby toward the revolving-door exit. Mary spots a familiar face approaching. A T-shirt with the inscription "Growing Old Is Mandatory, Growing Up Is Optional" is stretched across a large potbelly. The overhead fluorescent lights reflect off a bald spot on the top of his head. What hair he has is long and stringy and hangs over his ears and the collar of his shirt.

Jacque notices him at the same time as Mary. She puts her hand on his shoulder and whispers, "Take your sister to the gift shop before she sees him."

"Okay," Jacque replies. "Come on, Allie, let's check out the gifts for sick people."

"Errgh, I don't like being called Allie."

Ryan looks down at Allison. "Did she just growl?"

The man approaches Ryan. "Hey, buddy. I drove up from Philly as soon as I heard you were awake. You're looking good, man."

Ryan studies him long and hard, then replies, "Thanks."

They stare at each other for several seconds.

"You don't know who I am?"

"I have no idea," Ryan replies.

"This is the second time you failed to recognize me. Good to know."

Ryan's response starts off as a low chuckle and ends up a boisterous laugh that bounces off the walls of the lobby. "If you have crazy friends, you have everything you need." He reaches out and gives Josh a hug. "Sorry, buddy. It's not how I remember you looking."

Josh steps back and rubs his Buddha belly. "I've put on a bit of weight since I became a computer nerd. I sit in front of a computer all day drinking chocolate milk."

"The cows must be working overtime to feed you. What are you doing on a computer all day?"

"I design computer games for a living. You know, shooting flying snakes with laser guns."

"A flying snake is like a dragon," Ryan says.

"Yeah, but everyone knows dragons don't exist."

"Flying snakes do?"

"Maybe. They're staying underground while they plot their attack."

"Ahhh, good to know. We're going to grab a bite to eat. I've had enough hospital food. Care to join us?"

"Sure. I enjoy a good meal."

"Yeah, I can see that."

Allison's eyes light up as she sees Josh standing with her parents. She rushes forward, clutching a purple unicorn she bought in the gift store.

Josh gets down on a knee to pick her up. "How's my favorite girl?" He looks at Jacque and nods. "Maestro."

Hand in hand, Ryan and Mary exit the hospital, followed by Josh, who carries Allison on his back. Jacque maintains a lively stride alongside them.

It's been two months since Ryan was discharged from the hospital. He and Mary sit on the deck of the ranch wearing heavy sweaters and sipping cocoa. Allison is in the yard in front of them, chasing after a brood of squawking chickens. Two yapping dogs romp behind her.

"Them dogs aren't that playful with me," Ryan says.

"They don't care much for you," Mary replies. "They would probably bite you if you were ever mean to that little girl."

"Somebody needs to remind them who buys the dog food around here."

Mary winks. "I think Rosa does."

A Ford Taurus pulls in front of the house, and Kelci steps from the car. "Greetings," she calls out.

Ryan and Mary both stand and give her a polite hug. Ryan slides a rocking chair over for her to sit on while Mary goes inside to grab another cup of cocoa.

After everyone is seated with cocoa in hand, Ryan asks, "How did your meeting with the Red Sox go?"

"The neuro-ophthalmologist at the University of New Mexico Hospital sent the results of your eye examination to them."

Ryan sits solemnly, looking at his feet. "I know the results weren't what we were hoping for." He looks up at Mary, then Kelci, fire in his eyes. "But it's still early. We got two months until spring training."

"The Red Sox released you," Kelci says.

"Then we'll just sign with another team. I feel myself getting better every day. I've been playing catch with Joe's son to stay loose."

"And?" Kelci asks.

"When I face him, I see the ball fine, for the most part. But when I stand sideways, the ball is a little out of focus when he first releases it. It'll get better."

Kelci bites her bottom lip before speaking. "The report said your head injury caused damage to the muscle and nerves around your eye. It appears to be blocking the normal flow of blood to the eye's internal structures."

Ryan throws his hand in the air. "We can hire a vision therapist. Even if I don't make it back by April, mid-season will be fine."

Mary and Kelci look at each other. "Maybe it's time to give it a break," Mary says. "You have your communications degree. You can broadcast games. You would be a great coach if you wanted. You don't have to give up baseball completely."

"For your information, you have plenty of money," Kelci interjects. "You don't need to work. Your investment portfolio has gone up a hundredfold, and you have a steady stream of money from endorsements and business investments. It's time to relax, enjoy yourself. You've earned it. You have a wife, a young daughter, and a son. You should spend more time with them."

Ryan studies the two ladies, clearly frustrated at their lack of understanding. "Are you suggesting I retire? It's just a little setback. I can still play."

Kelci sets her mug on the table. "Trey told me Mickey Mantle was your favorite player when you were growing up."

Ryan's face lights up. "He was my idol. I modeled my game after his."

"You did a good job. Mickey won a Triple Crown and the league MVP a few times. He also finished his career with a .300 batting average and averaged more than thirty home runs and a hundred RBIs per year." Kelci watches Ryan lean forward, a gleam in his eyes. "Did you know he has the highest stolen base percentage and lowest percentage of hitting into double plays of anyone with more than six thousand at bats?"

Ryan smiles proudly. "Yeah, I knew all that."

"You probably also know the last year he played his knees were so bad they had to put him at first base. He batted .237 that year with eighteen home runs."

Ryan frowns, rubbing his brow. "Yeah."

"Probably not the last memory you wanted to have of him, was it?" Kelci asks.

Ryan closes his eyes, deep in thought, as he moves his head side to side slowly.

Mary gets to her feet and dawdles over to Ryan. She lowers herself onto his lap and lays her head on his shoulder. "You fulfilled your boyhood dream. You have nothing more to prove." She has a wry look on her face. "If you miss the game, you can play on a church league softball team."

Ryan chuckles. "You've been trying to get me to go to church with you for years. What about you, Kelci? What would you do if I retire?"

She relaxes her body, then breaks into a slow smile. "Probably take it easy. It's been a lot of work looking after you all these years. I've enjoyed it, and it has been a challenge, but I need a break also."

"Let's be honest, Ryan." Mary looks at him with watery eyes. "You'd be frustrated not playing at the level you expect from yourself."

Ryan puffs his cheeks out, then releases a deep breath. "I'm just not ready to quit. I want to play in the World Series." He leans his head back and sighs while watching a cloud float across the sky. *It looks like an elephant on a surf board.* "I've fought through injuries before."

Kelci dips her chin slightly. "You have an unbreakable spirit in pursuing a goal."

"Can you find another team that would sign me?"

"Maybe Doc and Texas will have an interest."

"Meh. They'll never make it to the World Series."

"It may be your only option to stay in the game."

Ryan offers a faint smile accompanied by a dismissive shoulder movement. "Guess it could be worse."

CHAPTER EIGHTY-SEVEN

Ryan stands at the entrance to The Room on Main, greeting his guests. The six-thousand- square-foot ballroom is a historic venue with hardwood floors and large ornate chandeliers hanging from the thirty-foot-high ceiling. They are dimmed for the special occasion. Forty-two tables, each covered in a white table-cloth and topped with a vase of freshly cut flowers, are equally spaced throughout the room. The faint sound of Frank Sinatra singing "My Way" flows from speakers set up on the stage.

Several guests, with cocktails in hand, converse while looking out the fifteen-foot-tall windows. The nighttime views of down-town Dallas are stunning from the sixth floor; however, the most popular spot in the banquet room is next to the two bars.

Kelci coordinates with the servers as they load heated trays of lobster, prime rib, and roasted chicken onto a buffet table that's as long as a basketball court.

During an animated discussion with one of his guests, Ryan notices the vice president of the United States enter the room. "Wel-come, Herb." Ryan shakes his hand, then tilts his head toward the gentleman he's talking with. "This is my golfing buddy, Huey."

The vice president's eyes dart about the room, then rest on Huey. "I recognize him. Are you a baseball fan?"

"I love my Giants." Huey gives Ryan an apologetic look, as if to say, "Sorry, partner." Looking toward the stage, he says, "Excuse me, gents, I should help the boys set up."

As Herb and Ryan discuss the latest in world dynamics, a trim blond-haired woman in a sleek cocktail dress makes her entrance. Ryan kisses her on the cheek while they share a hug.

"This is Lisa Bower," Ryan informs the vice president.

Herb clasps her hand as a crooked smile crosses his face. "Pleasure to meet you."

"Lisa is a correspondent with the *Associated Press*." Ryan puts his arm around her waist. "She's going to write my memoirs. We go back many years."

Lisa gives him a playful look. "Many is more years than I can remember."

"Thanks for explaining 'many,'" Ryan says. "It means a lot."

Herb snorts a playful chuckle. "Excuse me, it's an election year. I should mingle with the voters." He takes a quick look at the banquet table. "I hope they're not serving broccoli tonight."

"Good evening, Mr. Vice President," Mary says as they pass each other. She pauses next to Ryan. "Should I be jealous of this scene?" she asks, looking at Ryan's arm around Lisa's waist.

"A little jealousy can be a good thing. It reminds you to appreciate what you have," Ryan teases.

Mary and Lisa give each other an air-kiss on the cheek.

"Glad you could make it, Lisa." Mary places her hand on Ryan's shoulder. "You should circulate among your guests."

"Yes, dear," Ryan replies, bowing his head.

She playfully slaps his arm. "Stop that." She turns to Lisa. "He's always trying to make me look like a nag."

Ryan smiles at Lisa. "I'll talk with you later."

Ryan and Mary's first stop is at a buffet table, where Josh is loading up a plate.

"You keep eating like that, you're never going to get in shape," Ryan comments. "Oh, that's right. I forgot round is a shape."

Josh looks down his nose at him, then smiles at Mary. "Hi, Mary. Nice to see *you*."

Kelci ventures up and touches Ryan's arm. "Nice turnout."

"Must be the free booze and food," Ryan replies.

"Ha," Kelci chaffs. "A crew from the local television station is out front. They want to know if they can come in."

Ryan thinks for a second. "I suppose, as long as they stay at the back of the room. They don't need to walk around sticking their cameras or microphones in anyone's face."

"I'll let them know."

The first table Ryan and Mary walk up to is occupied by Red, Eugene, and two stunning young ladies in tight-fitting and low-cut dresses.

"Well, isn't this a motley crew," Ryan comments. "I see you both brought dates."

"These are my ladies," Eugene replies, tight-lipped. "This maggot and some fat bald guy"—he eyes Josh, who's still standing by the buffet—"keep trying to horn in on them."

Paying no attention to Eugene, Red sits at the table, mumbling as he struggles to bust open a lobster claw.

Ryan walks behind him and puts his hand on his shoulder. "Be careful not to hurt yourself."

"Yeow!" Red shrieks, chafing his knuckles on the lobster.

Red glares up at him. Ryan squints and glares back in jest.

A tapping sound comes from the speakers. "Test."

A hush falls over the room. Everyone looks up to the front, where Kelci and Doc stand on the stage, a microphone in front of them.

"Good evening, everyone." Kelci has her hand on the microphone as she scans the crowd. Over 150 people are in attendance. Most of them are sitting at their tables by now. "Thank you all for coming. There's plenty of food at the buffet, so don't be shy. As you all know, we put together this little party to welcome Ryan back to

Texas." She continues to scan the crowd, looking for him. "Let's bring up the guest of honor."

Ryan strolls onto the stage, waving to the crowd, amidst polite applause and a few friendly taunts. He clasps Kelci's hands and gives her a kiss on the cheek. He and Doc hug briefly. Doc steps up to the microphone with a glass of wine in his hand. "I've known Ryan since he was in high school. I have been his medical advisor, shrink, and confidant for more than twenty years. It's been a wild ride." He laughs softly. "Throughout it all, Ryan has been someone that I'm proud to call my friend. He has touched many people's lives in a positive way. The true measure of a man is shown in the lives he's enriched and the legacy of kindness he leaves." Doc raises his glass of wine. "You've done well, Ryan."

Most everyone in the gathering raises a glass. "Cheers."

Ryan approaches the microphone, then adjusts it to his height. "Thank you. I'm humbled. Umm, I'm not sure how to start."

"How about at the beginning," someone shouts.

Ryan points toward the heckler. "Just because you said that, I'm going to start at the end. I was thrilled the Rangers signed me after I was released by the Red Sox. Texas is the team I want to retire with. There are wonderful people in this town and within the organization." He hesitates for a beat as he notices a man in a wheelchair entering the room with three other men. It's too dark for him to make out who they are. He returns his attention to the people seated at the tables. "For those of you thinking this is a welcome home party, it's not. I've gathered you here to announce my retirement from baseball." Murmurs fill the room as Ryan gazes upon the crowd. "Most of you have touched my life in some way and were part of my journey. Thank you for supporting me. Playing professional baseball has been a dream of mine since I was a kid. I used to tag along with my older brother to play ball with him and his friends."

"My mom made me take him with me," Trey jeers from his front row table.

Ryan grins. "That's my brother, Trey. We don't know if he's ignorant or apathetic. Of course, he doesn't know, nor does he care."

A couple flashbulbs go off, and Ryan blinks. "Reminds me of my modeling days." He playfully raises his chin in a confident pose. "I have been lucky and blessed throughout my career. My success as a ballplayer was a team effort. There are so many people to thank." He makes eye contact with Doc and Kelci and a few other people in the crowd. "You know who you are . . . thank you." He lets out a deep breath. "Wow. Umm, I'm not one to talk about myself, so let's get back to the party. The band should be starting soon."

CHAPTER EIGHTY-EIGHT

Ryan turns and starts to walk off the stage when a reporter from the back of the room hollers, "Whoa, you aren't getting off that easy. You took a fastball to the head and were laid up for a month. How much of an impact did that have on you?"

Ryan looks to the back of the room and notices the red light glowing on top of a TV camera. "How much of an impact did it have?" Ryan twists his lips as he stares up at the ceiling, thinking. "Probably a couple thousand psi to the side of my head." He relaxes his face. "Being hit in the head is a mind-shattering experience. You learn to appreciate your health. I love baseball, but I also love my wife and kids." He gives a look toward Mary, who is sitting at the table with Trey. Mary has her hands in front of her face, half smiling and half looking like she might cry. "It took a hit to the head to make me realize it's time to slow down and spend more time with my family."

"I have a question," another reporter asks. Ryan looks into the bright lights coming from the TV camera. He holds his hand above his eyebrows to reduce the glare. "You led the league in batting several times and won the Triple Crown once. You also played in ten All-Star Games. What do you feel is your greatest accomplishment?"

"That's an easy one." Ryan stands erect, his hands in his pockets. "The 7 Foundation is the thing I'm most proud of. Through this organization, we've helped thousands of kids get proper medical attention and lead normal lives. Playing baseball was my dream. By living out my dream, I was able to help others live their dream of having a healthy life."

From the middle of the room, a man stands up from his table and hollers, "Hey, Ryan, Chet Etzler, *Dallas Morning News.*"

"I know who you are," Ryan deadpans.

"Well, maybe not everybody else here does," Etzler replies, his face flushed. He's still a little put off Ryan chose Lisa to write his memoirs. "You had a great career, broke a lot of records. Some people might say you are one of the best to ever play the game. Your baseball career was delayed several years while you lived in Canada. Do you think you could have broken more records if you had played those years . . . ? And what kind of message do you think being a draft evader sends to young kids?"

"Aww, geez, Etzler. It's 'conscientious objector.' Who invited you anyway? We were having a good time here," he jokingly replies. There's polite laughter in the crowd. "I don't know how many more records I would have broken because I don't keep track of records. I just play the game. I let guys like you keep the stats." He bites his lip and looks into the crowd. "As far as Vietnam goes, I was one of more than 100,000 American men who chose not to fight in a war they didn't believe in. I hope our country learned something from Vietnam and we won't ever have to draft our young men to fight again. I made the choice that was right for me. I would tell kids to listen to their heart and do as their intuition tells them. You'll find the right path." He quietly scans the crowd. Everyone is hanging on his words. "Don't ever let anyone force you to be something you're not."

Tired of answering questions, Ryan turns to face Huey and signals for the band to start playing. He and Doc walk from the stage side by side. Ryan leans his head toward Doc. "Did you see those guys that came in while I was talking?"

"Yeah, I saw them." Doc puts his hand on Ryan's shoulder as they walk along the wall, past their seated guests. "Let's go talk with them."

As they venture toward the back of the room, guests periodically stop Ryan to congratulate him. During one of the pauses, Mary catches up with him and slips her arm through his. "You looked so handsome up there," she says. "You're my hero."

Love shines brightly in his eyes. "I'm so incredibly thankful to have you in my life."

Mary moves her eyes from Ryan and toward the band. "Look up on the stage."

Ryan turns and gapes as Huey Lewis and the News perform "The Heart of Rock & Roll." In the middle of the band, hopping around like a crazy kid and delivering a lively performance on the saxophone, is Jacque. Ryan busts with pride. He gives Doc a nudge on the shoulder and points to the stage. "That's my boy."

When the song ends, Ryan and Mary resume their walk to the back of the room. Doc leads them up to the elderly gentleman, who is sitting in the wheelchair next to a table. A familiar face sits on each side of the gentleman. "Oh my . . ." Ryan freezes momentarily. He looks at all three men in amazement and immediately goes to one knee to talk to the man in the wheelchair. He feels it's disrespectful to look down on him while talking. Ryan grabs his hand. "Mr. Michelli. I'm honored you're here."

"When Doc told us you were retiring, we wouldn't have missed it." Michelli grabs Ryan's hand. "You did well, son. You didn't let us down."

Ryan looks up at Doc, an uncertain look on his face. "I don't understand the connection here."

"This is my Uncle Tony. My dad changed our name from Michelli to Michaels when we immigrated to the States."

An ocean of thoughts rushes through Ryan's mind as he thinks back on his journey. Speaking to Mr. Michelli, he says in a hushed tone, "Everything fell in place and went so smoothly for me when I left Texas. You made sure of that."

"I asked my best guys to keep an eye on you."

"Thank you, sir." Ryan gets to his feet and shakes Dr. Colletto's hand, then Matt LeClair's. LeClair pulls him into a hug. "I'm proud of you, Ryan."

Ryan draws a little circle with his index finger between Doc, Michelli, Colletto, and LeClair. "You all knew each other when I was a scared and lost kid?" he asks in disbelief.

"Matt and I kept an eye on you until you found yourself," Colletto says.

"Nobody wanted to get Uncle Tony upset," Ryan recalls hearing several times during his journey. He had no idea who they were talking about.

Mary stands behind Ryan with her hands on his shoulders. Ryan guides her to his side. "Mr. Michelli, this is my wife, Mary."

The old man's eyes light up as he looks at Mary. "I remember you. You're the girl that lived next door. You got Ryan all upset one day and nearly ruined my golf outing."

"He's always spoken so highly of you, sir," Mary replies. "Thank you for keeping him safe for me."

Doc chuckles. "It wasn't always easy."

Michelli's dark eyes bore into Ryan. "You're a good man, Ryan. When we saw the good things you were doing with the 7 Foundation, the Family donated two million dollars to support your cause."

Before Ryan can reply, Smash appears out of the shadows and hands LeClair a Scotch on the rocks. He has a mug of beer in his other hand.

Ryan jerks his head back in surprise. "I'll be buggered. If it isn't the big buster himself." They slap each other on the back while embracing—half of Smash's beer spills down Ryan's backside. "Aren't you a little out of class, hanging with this crowd?" Ryan jokes.

"Not at all." Smash stands tall with his shoulders thrown back and gives Ryan a withering look. "Tobias retired a few years back.

Got himself a place on a beach in Costa Rica. I took over as Mr. LeClair's assistant."

Mary, Ryan, and Doc grab a seat at the table with Michelli and his troupe. They laugh and joke as everyone revels in Ryan's adventures and misadventures in Michigan, Thunder Bay, Montréal, and Mexico.

CHAPTER EIGHTY-NINE

The lights and calypso music from Colin's #7 spill onto the beach. Ryan and Mary lie stretched on a hammock connected between two palm trees. Mary snuggles close, her head resting on his chest. Jacque and Allison sit on the beach as gentle waves roll up on their toes. Releasing a deep sigh of satisfaction, Ryan gazes at the stars and the flickering of lights of St. Thomas in the distance. A full moon hanging over St. John descends slowly behind a mountain—signaling the end of a long journey.

9 798234 010261